# BORDERLANDS

To Nadine

With thanks for your
encouragement

Fran March

# BORDERLANDS

## FRAN MARCH

This is a work of fiction. Names, characters, places, and incidents either are the product of the author's imagination or are used fictitiously. Any resemblance to actual persons, living or dead, events, or locales is entirely coincidental.

Copyright © 2024 by Fran March

All rights reserved. No part of this book may be reproduced or used in any manner without written permission of the copyright owner except for the use of quotations in a book review. For more information, contact: FranMarchAuthor@gmail.com

First paperback edition 2024

*Book design by Publishing Push*

ISBNs:
Hardback: 978-1-80541-623-4
Paperback: 978-1-80541-611-1
eBook: 978-1-80541-610-4

*For my sister, with love*

# Contents

Acknowledgements ix
Introduction xi

**Chapter One** The Ambassador 1
**Chapter Two** The Blācencynn 11
**Chapter Three** Handfuls of Grain 27
**Chapter Four** Strange Meetings 31
**Chapter Five** Grimsdene 51
**Chapter Six** The Seelie Court 65
**Chapter Seven** A King Deposed 87
**Chapter Eight** Bringing in the May 95
**Chapter Nine** The Hare 113
**Chapter Ten** The Lord and the Bowman 123
**Chapter Eleven** Black Chore Hugh 133
**Chapter Twelve** Luc-Nan-Har 145
**Chapter Thirteen** Business 155
**Chapter Fourteen** The Forest 183
**Chapter Fifteen** Roads Between 205

| | | |
|---|---|---|
| **Chapter Sixteen** | The North Gate | 221 |
| **Chapter Seventeen** | The Messenger | 239 |
| **Chapter Eighteen** | Hired Hands | 257 |
| **Chapter Nineteen** | Harper's Barn | 273 |
| **Chapter Twenty** | Strangers | 289 |
| **Chapter Twenty-One** | Sudden News | 297 |
| **Chapter Twenty-Two** | A Convenient Truce | 313 |
| **Chapter Twenty-Three** | The Mereburg | 333 |
| **Chapter Twenty-Four** | The Oarsman | 369 |
| **Chapter Twenty-Five** | Waiting | 385 |
| **Chapter Twenty-Six** | Wyrtræd | 397 |
| **Chapter Twenty-Seven** | The Nine Stones | 409 |
| **Chapter Twenty-Eight** | Farewell, Fair Blācencynn | 417 |
| Epilogue | | 437 |
| Glossary, Notes, Sources & Bibliography | | 441 |

# Acknowledgements

With thanks to Kristina, Project Manager, and the editorial team at Publishing Push, for their expert guidance, help and patience.

I must also thank the following people:

Anthony Clarke: (the OE Poem *Exodus*) and Roy Kirk, retired University of Leicester Librarian: (copyright advice).

Very special thanks to Jane Brown for believing in the manuscript, and especially to my family for bearing with me.

# Introduction

This is a fantasy tale, inspired and shaped by Scottish Borders legends of William de Soulis, Lord of Liddesdale, and Thomas the Rhymer. Their characters, as written here, grew from these seeds.

With affection and deep respect and, I hope, keeping their context and appeal, I have run with these wonderful legends, with deference embellishing and remodelling them.

The narrative does not include Thomas the Rhymer's prophecies.

Descriptions of religious and magical practices are imaginary or reinterpreted.

The Author's Notes give more information about these legends, and the sources used, together with other traditions and mythical motifs that both inspired and influenced this story.

The Glossary, while not essential, may give an insight into pronouncing certain phrases, words and names.

*F.M.*

A maiden sat sewing damasked linen in the chequered spring shade, and an older woman seated beside her smiled.

'Læren, you've excelled yourself,' she said. 'It's the finest stitching in all Faerie and the weft is subtle.'

'It's taken an age, Raldis,' said Læren, inspecting the garment. 'This shirt is long as my gown.' She glanced at the folded clothing in a basket beside her. 'Who are these for, anyway?'

'Mortal men.'

Læren giggled. 'But mortal men only exist in tales.'

## Chapter One

# The Ambassador

A solitary raven surveyed the snow-covered hills and moors from a high granite peak: the scattered farmsteads, the frosty ploughed fields, and Hermitage Castle standing in grim isolation amongst the naked trees.

The bitter March wind snatched at sombre banners fluttering above the battlements, guards patrolled the ramparts, and firelight flickered through the hall windows. Rich, gilded furnishings within should have made the room opulent. Instead, it smelt fusty; was dark, despite the many burning candles; cold, despite the large, blazing fire. William de Soulis, Lord of Liddesdale, sat alone, still smarting at his jousting defeat, at how an unknown stripling had left him sprawling in the dirt.

Soulis had returned to Hermitage humiliated. He petitioned the King, demanded compensation, made threats, and instructed his guards to allow any messenger in, night or day, no questions asked; but after months of insulting silence, he invoked another authority. No one answered him. Now, he stared at the fire, fists clenched, planning his next move, unaware of the falling dusk.

A slight movement distracted him. He stood up and, his soft voice unpleasant as the twilight, spoke to the two figures standing in the doorway.

'We do not welcome the uninvited.'

A tall, fair-faced young man with dark tousled hair, wearing fine grey clothing, bowed, and ignoring the contemptuous tone, answered, 'We would not presume to visit unsolicited. Perhaps my lord forgets sending for us?' Without permission, he sat at the table. He gestured to Soulis to join him, and with one long hand on his chin, regarded the middle-aged face, dull, dark eyes and powerful build; the shaggy, grey-tinted dark hair and beard, the sneering mouth and the heavy, squirrel fur-trimmed robes.

The visitor spoke, his tone velvet smooth. 'My lord, William de Soulis, your peers scorn you, admiring only strength and power. Have both, my lord, then threats become redundant.'

Soulis almost snarled, 'I demand their respect.'

The stranger remained calm. 'You cannot deny using spells to achieve this, but to no avail, these being but trifling country charms.'

## The Ambassador

Soulis could not deny it, having cleared his chapel and altar of iconography: the cross, the statue of the Virgin, every vestige of the faith already gone. 'We do not play childish games,' he said. 'Nor is it in our guest's interest to pass judgement on practices he does not understand.'

The man placed Soulis' petition to the King on the table. At ease, he sat back, speaking in a quiet, almost patronising tone. 'We serve one who commands a vast realm, who has taken an interest in thee of late, recognising and admiring your strength, Lord Soulis, and wishes to discuss an alliance.'

'We do not make "alliances", my friend, without knowing his demands and terms.'

'He demands nothing,' said the ambassador, looking left and right, his voice almost inaudible, 'but will accept anything offered. For example, what is your honour worth?'

Soulis stood up, leaning forward to intimidate. 'I would give *blood* to see these petty, so-called earls grovelling before me, even if it takes all eternity.'

The man did not blink. 'Only immortals can afford eternity, my lord.'

Soulis sat down. 'What are the terms, Master Ambassador?'

'My master believes that, with support, you shall have honour, second only to the King.' He fixed his gaze on Soulis, noting every facial reaction. 'If my lord Soulis wants respect, he shall have it; greater wealth, if so desired. Perhaps my lord Soulis yearns for troops strong as stone, who do not sicken, or tire, and obey without question; maybe he craves lands, a mightier fortress, and an "eternity" to enjoy them.' He looked around the chamber; everything was arranged by someone with an almost pathological need for order. 'If my lord finds the proposition unappealing, I suppose this hall is adequate for a man of little consequence.'

Soulis considered this proposition: what it might give him at no personal cost. The wall hangings now seemed shabby, their gold thread brassy in the candlelight; a silver jewelled flagon and goblet on the table, mere pewter. He spoke, his moderate tone oily.

'A generous offer indeed, my friend. Your attention flatters us.' He leaned forward again, his eyes lustful. 'We agree on these terms, expecting a rewarding alliance.'

The ambassador rested his hands, palms uppermost, on the chair's arms. 'My master does not employ untested men. You will aid him in reclaiming land a clan exiled him from; and you will recover a valuable weapon and war horn they stole.'

Soulis frowned in sudden doubt. 'He should not need aid if he has the strength you imply.'

Aloof, the man examined his fingernails. 'It's but a test of your loyalty.'

'And if I am found wanting?'

'We renegotiate terms.' His shadowy companion placed a large Bible, which Soulis had forgotten he owned, on the table, together with a heavy candle and a wide, shallow stone bowl, and the envoy, his eyes conveying nothing, gestured to them. 'This requires your absolute commitment,' he said. 'If my lord has parchment, quill and ink, we will draw up the deed.'

'A quill you may have,' said Soulis, taking a pen from a shelf, 'but a contract is worth only the ink it's written with. Ink may fade, but blood is indelible.'

The man lit the candle, which gave an unpleasant, overpowering, sweet smell, and placing a thin-bladed knife on the Bible, gave an enigmatic smile. 'Then my lord shall use his blood, already pledged, and he shall seal the document with this candle wax.'

Soulis snatched up the knife, tore out a page from the Bible at random, and scraped off the illuminated script, saying, 'You cannot cheat me, my dispensable ambassador, and shall record only what I say.' He made the smallest cut in one forefinger, but the blood came fast, half-filling the bowl. Undaunted, he paced the chamber, speaking aloud, offering surplus grain as payment, the ambassador writing the contract as dictated. Soulis signed, sealed and proffered it. 'We thank thy master for his interest in us,' he said. 'We await his acknowledgement, and rewards, forthwith, my friend, and you shall deliver our invitation.'

The man smiled. 'If my lord forgives me, did I not explain? Impatience brings no reward; nor is anything given without payment. I cannot touch a signed agreement between you and my master. You must call him.'

Soulis replied, his tone loaded with spite. 'Answer me this, *ambassador*. How, when you refuse to deliver the invitation?'

The man shrugged. 'I am both your tutor and intermediary, but you need someone else to help you. Perhaps your most trusted servant?'

Soulis fell silent. He despised his attendants as unwashed, ignorant, but necessary irritants; suspected them of constant plotting; all but one. As though summoning a dog, he whistled; a stooped, scruffy, timid old man shuffled in from an adjoining room and stood the required seven feet and four-fifths of an inch away. Soulis pointed at the flagon and goblets.

'You may serve our guest.'

The servant bowed in silence; gave a sudden, hollow gasp, and fell dead. Soulis stared at him, noting the interesting pattern the oozing blood made through the clothes, and at the ambassador, now standing, holding the bloodied knife.

'My master may not make demands,' he said, 'but you will pay me anything I desire for our every consultation.'

Furious, Soulis held the parchment over the candle flame. 'Then we withdraw.'

The response was a disdainful laugh. 'I wrote, and you signed this contract with your lifeblood, my lord Soulis. Destroy it, you will die.' He wiped and sheathed the knife. 'My first instruction is in the candle-making your loyal servant gave his life for; for the more you make, Lord Soulis, the greater your reward. We will meet again two nights hence at moonrise, and every night thereafter, until you master this art.'

Soulis sneered. 'You will come when sent for. If the King wants "payment", he must collect it.'

'I do not serve the King.' Fear came on Soulis too late, and the ambassador, giving an unpleasant laugh, placed a large hood on the table. 'I serve Robin Redcap, Lord of Dark Faerie. My second instruction: you will report to him every seventh day; will answer his every summons, wearing this hood each time, if you wish to keep your soul. Fail, you will lose everything, and your… brave… man here would have died in vain.' He stood up and leaned forward, almost touching Soulis. 'You have until the equinox.'

Soulis lifted his upper lip, but his voice tremored. 'You stand too close, Master Ambassador; you forget your place.'

'Oh, I will come much closer than this… *sire,*' said the ambassador, giving a disdainful smile. 'Remember: it wasn't I who signed the contract, and it's not just servants who are "dispensable".' He bowed. 'We thank my lord Soulis for his commitment.'

\*

Ten burning candles, positioned an exact hand span apart around a blood-filled shallow stone bowl on the altar, gave an unpleasant smell; weird, animated shadows danced around the chapel, and faint daylight came through a small window. Soulis placed a key and the contract on the altar, stared at a grotesque carving on the wall behind it, and drank. He pulled on the hood down to his twisted mouth and, his arms outspread in supplication, taking slow, deep breaths despite the noxious smoke, uttered a distorted prayer.

'Lord Redcap: I burn these candles and drink this blood in thy honour, giving thee my treasury key. I pledge to find the weapon and horn, the aid to thy reclaiming thy ancient homeland. None shalt withstand thee.' He paused, listening to deep surrounding murmurs before speaking again, in the same velvet reverence. 'I am Soulis, immortal, worthy of command. Redcap, I summon thee; thou shalt answer.'

The ground trembled, shaking the altar. Looming darkness and many crowding presences came on him, then a sudden, silent stillness, and he removed his hood.

All the candles had blown out, the key and contract had gone and the ambassador, watching from the silent shadows, nodded, giving a malicious smile.

## Chapter Two

# The Blācencynn

Penda Blācencynn, hungry, thirsty, longing for company after a month of isolation, lay waiting, staring at the crannied roof, watching shadows from a burning candle fluttering around the small, cold, draughty cave.

Someone opened the heavy door, and Penda stood up, facing the nameless, middle-aged Priest who stood there, holding a staff and torch in either hand. He wore an outlandish costume: grey fleece trews, a long blue cloak fastened with a cord, but no shirt, and a gleaming helmet, without a visor, over his long, fair hair. Many feared him, believing he summoned spirits from the barrows, and few dared visit him in his temple. He swept a brief, summing glance over Penda: the coarse tunic fraying at the knee, slender build, and handsome, boyish face; the long, black hair and the neat beard, now neglected; and the kind, dark eyes that belied a certain determination to pursue personal goals, sometimes to the detriment of his own affairs or more important matters.

The Priest spoke, his voice a detached monotone. 'The Lord of the Higher Hall summons you, Lyblæca: do you answer?'

Penda glanced at a shelf piled with scrolls he could learn no more from, met the icy stare with steady eyes, and replied, his voice deep for a youth approaching twenty. 'After ten years' training, I am ready.'

He followed the Priest through labyrinthine caverns: gutters and culverts channelled chuckling surface water into reservoirs, graffiti on the walls masked more sinister images carved in the remote past, and strange forms peered from the shadows.

Two robed older men, one carrying a spear, the other a plain wooden cup, met them at a dark porch, and the Priest faced Penda. 'You are the youngest to undertake this rite, Lyblæca,' he said. 'Beware the Hall. It can overturn your mind if you are unprepared or have doubts.'

Penda did not flinch. 'I have no doubts.'

A tall, bearded young man, whose charisma commanded any space he walked into, stepped from the shadows. His thick red hair reached shoulders that implied a toned physique, his pleasant, steady, shining grey eyes, a rare shrewdness, a shy, empathic nature and a dry wit. He wore a strange metal amulet on a short leather cord around his neck and plain, though good quality clothing, only the silver buckle fastening his tooled leather belt hinting at his rank. The Priest spoke with scant deference, considering his former pupil as little more than equal.

'My lord Rædwulf, you need not stay for his initiation.'

Rædwulf seldom did anything without first dissecting every pro and con; he thought the Priest obdurate, dismissive of anything beyond his field, yet valued his advice and replied with guarded respect, his deep, measured tone one that men listened to, that women trusted. 'As his mentor, I will; as his brother, I must.'

No woman had entered the Higher Hall where inscribed runes gleamed on the floor and carved intertwining beasts leapt around the glittering walls in a perpetual dance; a plain, thirty-foot-tall stone central column, the Lord of the Higher Hall, stood beneath a sky-shaft. Aimed at the North Star, it radiated a primitive power, and all worlds turned around it.

One priest laid the spear on an altar, the other hung the torch on a wall bracket behind it, and the High Priest poured something that had an unpleasant herbal smell into the cup. 'This Black Mead,' he said, proffering it to

Penda, 'gives either sight or blindness. It's your choice, Lyblǣca.'

Penda, a down-draught blowing through his hair, doubting himself for the first time, glanced at a ladder leading to a platform suspended from the sky-shaft rim. '*My choice,*' he whispered, took the cup, repeated aloud, 'My choice,' and drank the creamy, bitter Mead which might kill or cure; full of tiny seeds, it coated his mouth and throat, making him nauseous. The greybeards removed his shoes and stripped him down to his loincloth, and the High Priest led him to the ladder.

'You will confront your greatest fears on the platform, Lyblǣca,' he said, 'by reliving vivid childhood nightmares, or humiliation from forgotten misdeeds, and will die if you run from them.'

Penda understood, sighed, and began scaling the ladder, stopping halfway up, sweating, giddy and seized by sudden cramp. He glanced down at Rædwulf and the priests, who marked his every move; looked through the opening above and saw a thousand stars glittering in a clear midnight sky.

He overcame his faintness, climbed to the platform and, cold, trembling, cautious, lay down on it, very aware of the empty forty feet between himself and the chamber floor.

Rædwulf turned to the High Priest. 'What will happen to him up there?'

The man shifted his hold on his staff. 'This test is the first of three. He will have neither food nor drink, nor comfort, for two nights and days; if he doesn't forget all he knows, he will take the Black Mead again before facing his next trial; he will visit the Flame.'

The Flame: all Blācencynn believed it had formidable power, but men avoided it, regarding it as the province of women.

Rædwulf, staring into the Priest's dispassionate eyes, whispered, 'Ordinary men cannot approach it.'

The Priest shrugged. 'Lord Penda is not ordinary, but much depends on his strength of will. Say nothing to anyone yet, lord, but if he passes his second test, if confronting the Flame doesn't send him mad, you will oversee perhaps his most dangerous challenge: you will guide him, unarmed and unescorted, to Grimsdene.'

Rædwulf flinched at his surfacing memories he believed long since buried; he frowned, his eyes glittering. 'You never explained this. I'm no priest and cannot subject him to such an ordeal, nor will the Council sanction it.'

The Priest gave him a supercilious look. 'Neither the Council nor you would deny Lord Penda something he has spent years training for; as his mentor, you have no choice, and you've visited Grimsdene before.'

'And I vowed I'd never go back.'

The Priest stepped forward and whispered, 'Only very few may enter Grimsdene, sire. You know more about herbs than most and may prepare the cordials; but hold your own power in abeyance, and on no account aid him, even if he seems on the point of death. Above all, do not allow Wyrtræd to interfere—if you should meet him.'

Rædwulf baulked as though fearing the name but said nothing. Filled with sudden, clawing misgivings, meeting the blue eyes with a stare that could cut through steel, he marched away, pausing only to glance back at the platform.

\*

Wretched, cold, paralysed, believing himself lying on his back in bed, Penda opened his eyes. A diffuse, unearthly light filled the room. He checked a cry when he saw a grey-clad veiled woman winding a thin luminous thread from his navel onto a spindle she held in one aged hand; in the other she held shears, poised, ready. He watched, transfixed, defenceless against those deadly blades; closed his eyes, fending off panic, then opened them; felt the precarious platform beneath him swaying in a soft breeze coming through the sky-shaft and saw the stars above fading in the dawn.

\*

Days after his ordeal, Penda stood watching an underground river sliding past a wharf, the water shimmering in the torchlight; he shivered, as though troubled, and glanced at Rædwulf standing beside him.

'I know it's daunting visiting the Flame,' said Rædwulf, 'but the Priest advised it.'

Penda stared at the water. 'It's not this. Since I came down from that platform, Rædwulf, I've had nightmares of shadows coming from nowhere, roaming the Caves. I feel sounds I can never hear, and the very air quakes.' Rædwulf met the troubled gaze with searching eyes. Penda returned the look. 'And all the stone,' he whispered, 'in all the caverns, is afire.'

Rædwulf frowned. 'Have you told anyone about this?'

Penda shook his head. 'Just you.' He paused, watching a torch burning on the quayside, and added, 'I've heard that the Flame sends dreams; will I find answers there?

Rædwulf gave a slight, inimitable shrug. 'I don't know. Maybe.'

A small boat, lamps at prow and stern, approached from the dark. Penda flinched when he saw the oarswoman, but she wore white robes, not grey, her hands and stooped posture implying late middle age. She stayed the boat alongside them.

'I am the High Priestess Lybbestre,' she said. 'The Flame has burned since the Old Ones came from beyond the icy seas and can grant visions to the chosen. You are not here to learn its mysteries, Lyblæca, but to seek its counsel, maybe from the Goddess herself. You may come with us, my lord Rædwulf, for the Flame is restless, but you must keep the sacred silence.'

Penda and Rædwulf sat huddled in the boat, shivering in the cool breeze. Infrequent musical drips of water echoed like secretive whispers in the dark, and distorted faces, leering from the rock and flickering reflections, vanished the moment Rædwulf glimpsed them. Lybbestre guided the boat into the largest cavern, where a deep lake reflected the cavern roof to infinity and the walls shimmered with enchanting rainbow hues. She tied the boat at a mooring; they disembarked and climbed seven wide steps to a dais where the Flame, flaring and shrinking at random, burned in an altar. Penda took an exquisite shimmering crystal ring from his hand, hesitated, and dropped it into the Flame, which shrank. He kneeled, eyes closed, waiting until the visions came: a tall, unknown hooded man standing in a cave, as though waiting; bloodied, weary men fighting against grotesque creatures swarming through a wide gate, an expansive wilderness beyond; he heard battle cries, saw weapons. A kindled arrow pierced the hand he raised in defence; crying out in pain, he came to his senses, opened his burning right hand and found the crystal ring in his blistered palm. Confused, he stood up and faced the now flaring Flame.

'I gave this ring to honour thee. *Why do you scorn me?*'

Again, the Flame shrank, fading echoes the only sound. Penda could do no more; he replaced the ring on his finger and looked at Rædwulf, whose sliding glance towards the boat meant 'go'. The Flame now burning high behind them, they left as they had come.

Lybbestre tied the boat at the wharf and taking the lamp from the prow, led Rædwulf and Penda up a long flight of steps to a small porch. She faced them, the burning wall torches painting her robes red and gold.

'You now have a power, Lyblæca,' she said, 'that will not leave you until either it has fulfilled its purpose or passed to another mind on your death. It might defend you, but it will not protect the weak.' She walked away, taking the lamp with her, her whispering footfall fading to silence.

Penda sat down, staring at the opposite wall. 'I never asked for this, Rædwulf. I don't want it. Why has this happened?'

'I doubt even the woman knows,' said Rædwulf, examining the burns, 'but this injury needs treatment.'

\*

It was late when Rædwulf returned to his unpretentious living quarters, rooms that smelt of sweet herbs, with plain, woven mats on the floor. Leather-bound medical texts he had collated for years, together with a manuscript and a small box containing a keepsake lock of hair, were on a desk. Earthenware jars of herbs stood on a shelf above his clothes chest, a jug and plain cups on a side table; understated gold leaf on the modest wooden chairs glimmered in the torchlight, and his sword hung on the wall beside his curtained sleeping area.

'Harald,' said Rædwulf, handing his shoes and belt to his servant, 'I want you to pack some dried food and blankets.'

Harald, a thin man in his early thirties, his long hair already grey, hairline already receding, placed the belt on the clothes chest. 'You're going *away?*'

'In a few days,' said Rædwulf, giving a pleasant smile, 'with Penda, but we'll return in a fortnight. Don't bother with my sword; I won't need it.'

Harald gaped. 'A *fortnight?* Without your *sword?*'

'Yes, and you're staying here.'

'But, sire, who will attend to you?'

'I'm not incapable.'

'But I've served you since you were a child, sire.'

'Then long enough to trust me,' said Rædwulf, taking his tunic off.

Harald subsided. 'Yes, sire.'

The door guard challenged someone outside, and Harald, understanding the commanding look Rædwulf gave him, investigated, returning a second later.

'Lord,' he said, 'someone's here to see you.'

Rædwulf, awake since before dawn and needing sleep, frowned, both surprised and irritated. 'It's a bit late for visiting. What do they want?'

'Best ask her,' said Harald, beckoning a woman in.

Rædwulf cast a flickering, summing gaze over her: strong, he thought, judging from her sturdy frame; handsome rather than pretty, with blue eyes, loose long brown hair and a distinctive chevron tattoo on her neck. As a healer, he had assumed she wanted medicinal treatment. His mistake: she approached, and he, watching her flowing, almost transparent shift rippling over her curves, wondered why she bothered wearing it. He raised an eyebrow, threw his tunic onto a chair and, without looking at his servant, said, 'Trot off, Harald.'

Harald obeyed, smirking.

Almost within touching distance of Rædwulf, she curtseyed, amused at the sight of a barefoot lord clad almost as a servant. 'Forgive this intrusion, sire,' she said, 'but perhaps my lord might enjoy some company this evening.'

His soft grey gaze glimmering like water in moonlight, he bit off a smile. 'You've no need displaying your wares, lady; I know what you're offering.'

'I've heard,' she said, envying his long eyelashes, 'that you can charm a woman with a mere glance, or a single word.'

His voice bedroom pitch, he said, 'You shouldn't believe hearsay,' gave her a slow, come-on wink, and drew the bedchamber curtain aside in silent invitation.

\*

Rædwulf stood alone in the Council Chamber, studying a twelve-foot-diameter shining spiral—an ancient symbol suggesting a kind of stasis no-one understood—carved on the wall behind his chair. 'My lord,' said a guard from the opposite doorway, 'the lady Priestess is here.'

Rædwulf did not move. 'Very well.'

Lybbestre came forward, noting the sword at his hip, his hair, and the understated silver braiding on his tunic gleaming like the spiral. He belonged. 'My lord,' she said, 'you sent for me?'

He did not turn. 'Yes.'

'Sire, I sensed your uncertainty yesterday; why the doubts, my lord?'

He turned, taking a moment to reply. 'I'm told I must take Lyblæca to Grimsdene, but I'm in two minds whether I should.'

'You must, lord,' she said, 'both as his mentor and guide. The Lord of the Higher Hall keeps the North Gate closed against darkness, but his priests are ageing. Even the High Priest is older than you'd think. This initiation ensures fresh blood.'

'And the Flame? Penda fears its power.'

'With good reason, sire,' she said, glancing at the amulet. 'It can cause delusions in those craving or possessing it; can open the Gate at will; but it also exposes truth: cold, hard, naked truth. Have you met with your guardians?'

He hesitated, shutters closing behind his eyes. 'Not for a while.'

'Perhaps you should,' said she. Without waiting for dismissal, she curtseyed and withdrew.

\*

High, sheer walls formed a perfect circle, the cavern open to the sky after a roof collapse; jagged rocks littered the floor, and twittering birds flitted across the space to their roosts; ferns, self-sown stunted trees and thin smoke drifting from a fire burning on a ledge gleamed in the slanting evening sunlight.

Rædwulf held a broad, sharp knife he seldom used over the flames, examining the strange pictograms on the blackening blade, steeling himself against something he had spent days preparing for. He rolled his sleeve back and pressed the searing blade into his outstretched left arm, adding to the scars already constellated there; watched the blood, drop by slow drop, trickle into the flames. Woozy from the fragrant herbal smoke, he lay down, watching unfolding visions and half-dreams, meeting with his guardians until the images faded at dawn.

He extinguished the fire, drank something to cure his headache, made his way to a deep, torch-lit, silent crypt and stood beside the newest of several long, low tombs, his fingertips tracing the runes inscribed on it.

'I miss you, Ælfwynn,' he whispered. 'They call me a healer, yet I could not save you.'

Reluctant to leave, he stood silent, gathering himself for something; felt, rather than heard, his resonant heartbeat. He climbed the steps, stopping to look back at images of a sword suspended over a flame embroidered on a huge black banner almost covering the far wall. No draught disturbed the burning torches, yet the banner wafted and the air murmured.

He met Penda and the High Priest in a small cave; the Priest gestured to food and drink on a table.

'Take your fill now,' he said. 'I will come back in an hour.'

Pale, weary, apprehensive, silent, Penda ate nothing but drank. Rædwulf, picking at some bread, looked at him.

'Penda, are you sure about this?'

'I've trained for this since boyhood, Rædwulf. They'll think me a coward if I refuse, and I am no coward.'

Rædwulf did not reply.

The Priest took them to a wide cave mouth and turned to Penda. 'You have learned the ways of the living spirit, Lyblæca, but you must also understand those of the dead.' He pointed his staff towards the open countryside beyond and turned his detached gaze on Rædwulf. 'You go on foot, with rations for two days; after that, you must forage or hunt.'

'I do this under protest, my lord Priest,' said Rædwulf, glancing at Penda, 'but I leave you in charge.'

Without a word, the Priest nodded, turned, and entered the cavern.

## Chapter Three

# Handfuls of Grain

*Milk for the dairymaid, honey for the Queen, ale for the labourers living in between. An ox for the ploughman, for pulling the plough, a goat for the goatherd; for the housewife, a sow. Grain for the farmer, for the shepherd, a sheep; portions for the castle lord, living in the keep.*

Lord Soulis demanded more, and more again, from his tenants, turning surplus to famine; had insidiously dispensed with his guards and attendants, no longer needing them. Now, he sat in a dark, austere room, new armed retainers lurking in the corners, unobtrusive but there. Farmers and labourers stood facing him across neat piles of documents on a table, and he turned to someone behind him.

'Remind us of the issue.'

The delegation neither saw the man's face nor heard his reply, but Soulis sat back, waving one languid hand, speaking in a voice soft as his velvet robes.

'Forgive me, I didn't catch your name.'

The spokesman moistened his lips and swallowed. 'Moris Cope, my lord.'

Soulis looked at him with disdain: the close-cropped hair, tanned, weathered face, clothing of moderate quality and grubby hands. 'And how can we help today, Moris Cope?'

Moris, glancing at his fellows, swallowed again. 'Sire, we beg relief from our tithes until the next harvest.'

'We all pay our taxes, yeoman,' said Soulis. 'You pay your lord, as I pay mine. Was last year not a good yield?'

'Good enough, sire; but we've little left to feed ourselves, let alone our livestock, and with due respect, there will be no harvest if we starve.'

Soulis leaned forward, his eyes glinting. 'Have you brought transport?'

Moris nodded. 'Aye, my lord, we have a wagon.'

Soulis stood up, giving a weird smile. 'Then must spare what we can. I will oversee the distribution myself.'

A strong wheat smell filled the granaries, and mouldy straw on the floor fell through gaps between the boards. Soulis gestured to the sacks of grain piled to the rafters.

'You may take as much as you can carry,' he said. '*In your hands*.' Drawing his knife, he slashed a sack open.

## Handfuls of Grain

Dismayed, the men kneeled, scrabbling at the precious grain pouring onto the floor, trying to gather what they could before it disappeared into the void beneath. Soulis watched with cold eyes before strolling away, accompanied by his Spriggan guards, their constant, shadowy presence irritating but useful: already a new stone tower cast a vast shadow across the courtyard in the late afternoon sunlight.

The ambassador, arriving at dusk, stood before Soulis in the hall, wanting answers. 'My lord Redcap appreciates my lord's oath,' he said, 'but is disappointed the weapon and war horn remain outstanding. For all his strength, he needs their protection from hostile forces.'

Soulis sat back in his chair. 'We cannot give him something we do not have.'

'If I may give advice,' said the ambassador, 'it would be in your best interest to find them before he loses patience. He has methods, sire, certain powers of persuasion, which you would rather avoid.'

Soulis leaned forward, gripping the chair's arms. 'We do not respond to threats, *Ambassador.*'

The response was a humourless smile. 'These are facts, not threats, my lord. Consider, sire, that he who fulfils his pledge wants for nothing. Now, if my lord allows, I will take the first payment.'

Soulis led him to the courtyard and the ambassador, watching Spriggans already loading a cart, missed nothing. 'There's less here than agreed.'

Soulis almost snarled, 'We have no more, sir.'

'Regrettable.' The ambassador faced him. 'I suggest my lord Soulis widens his catchment.' He climbed aboard, took the reins, and fixed his hypnotic eyes on Soulis. 'You will receive instruction to move at a moment's notice, so prepare. I'll let you know if I have news of the weapon and horn.'

The cart moved off, somehow fading into the night before reaching the gate.

## Chapter Four

# Strange Meetings

New leaves and wildflowers speckled the fields and hedgerows, and birdsong filled the warm, scented air, but snow lay on the distant northern hills, the nights remained cold, and dusk came early. Thomas Learmont, riding home later than intended, his cloak clasp and the bridle mounts glinting in the afternoon sunlight, followed a track he knew well along a ridge, then into an ancient oak forest.

He had ridden at a walk for half a mile, through utter silence and mist curling between the trees, when his horse shied from something flitting across the narrow path ahead. Thomas dismounted, giving a sharp command, 'Stand! Stand, sir,' but the startled horse bolted, knocking him off his feet. Disheartened, he picked himself up, looking around, but saw nothing, the lower branches now hidden in the mist. Alone, cold, miles from anywhere, slipping on leaf mould, stumbling over tree roots, pushing through thorny undergrowth in the dark, he followed a winding path and stopped at a stream at the foot of an incline.

Hazy moonlight broke through the mist, revealing a woman, bent double under the heavy basket of kindling on her back, pacing back and forth along the near bank, as though choosing the best place to cross. A red shawl on her head overshadowed her face, her brown skirts hid her feet, and she, having stopped her pacing, now stood just beyond his arm's reach, facing the stream. His voice jarred his ears.

'Shall I carry you across, Old Mother?'

Without looking at him, she answered, her voice a winter gale through leafless branches. 'Why would I need help, colt? Why are *you* here? You are in no position to offer aid, Thomas Learmont.'

Unnerved, he said, 'You know my name?'

'We know much in Faerie,' said she. 'You are wilful, you have courage, and an eye for a pretty lass, but would you dare kiss *me*?'

Surprised, a smile tugging at his mouth, he shrugged. 'If you like. It makes no odds to me whether I kiss you or any obliging lady I meet on the road.'

'Then be true to your mortal word, kiss my mouth, or stand here, cold as stone, forever a way marker for the lost.'

She took the shawl from her head, revealing sparse silver hair and her pale, wizened, moon-like face. Her inscrutable gaze from fathomless pits transfixed him: it stripped his soul bare, took in his athletic six-foot bearing. Aghast, he stepped back, looking for escape, but saw only darkness and impenetrable thorns behind him. Trapped, fearing he must meet her demand or die, he swallowed his disgust and did as asked.

Her demeanour unchanged, she placed one withered, claw-like hand against his chest.

'Strength and Courage are but fickle servants, Thomas Learmont,' she said. 'They might desert you when you most need them, but Pride is a vengeful mistress few men would lie with if they knew her price. Do not hasten to bear a burden you may never rid yourself of.' She withdrew her hand. 'Where are you going, Lord Ercildoun? Why do you follow the Faerie path?'

He frowned, staring at her. 'Home, but my horse bolted, and I've lost the way.'

She gave a disquieting laugh. 'Your way lies beyond the stream, Learmont. Can you swim?' Surprised, he scanned the knee-deep stream, flowing blood red in the peculiar moonlight. 'Wade, if you can, Learmont,' she said, retreating into the shadows, 'and meet your fortune.'

Fleeting shadows dissolved into the darkness, wolves howled in the distance, and furtive night beasts rustled the undergrowth. He waded across the stream, but the path beyond faded and he stopped, disoriented, listening to invisible, trickling rills and distant owl calls; the moonlight transformed trees into bizarre, twisted forms and the wolves howled, closer than before.

Hungry, thirsty, weary, groping through snagging twigs, he entered a deserted moonlit glade after midnight; knelt amongst brambles, a barbed stem whipping across his face. Uneasy, nursing his injury with one hand, he surveyed the empty clearing until he fell asleep. He awoke an hour later. Every leaf glowed in a soft, golden light; he smelt wood smoke and roasting meat, and peered through the thorny mesh again.

Smoke drifting across the glade half-obscured a grazing horse, tethered on the far side, and a man, wearing heavy pelts and an antlered crown, seated beside the vigorous, central fire. His knife glinted in the light as he carved meat from bone, his hounds waiting at his feet, watching for any morsel. He spoke in an earthy tone.

'Come, Thomas Learmont; I'll share meat with you.'

Suspicious, Thomas approached, staring at him across the fire. 'Drink this,' said the stranger, proffering a bottle; waited in vain for a reply, then made an insistent gesture, repeating, 'Drink. Don't be afraid of it.'

His eyes fixed on the man, Thomas took a mouthful of pungent wine and, suppressing a sneeze, returned the flask. 'Who are you?'

The man, ignoring the abrupt tone, indicated the meat. 'I will say once you've eaten something.'

Thomas sat beside him, accepting food and drink, only the dogs, gnawing at bones, breaking the silence.

'Let me see you,' whispered the stranger, and turning Thomas' head towards him by the chin, studied the long, tawny hair framing the young, bearded face; the straight, bold brows shading piercing green eyes. 'So,' he remarked, lowering his hand, 'Thomas Learmont has entered Faerie.'

'Faerie?' said Thomas, looking at the surrounding trees.

'You dared kiss the Elder Witch,' said the man, as though explaining everything.

Thomas masked a shudder, then had a sudden idea. 'Were you looking for me?'

'Yes.'

'Why?'

The man gave a quiet laugh. 'Do you not know me? Long ago, men sought my favour, honouring me; yet now they say I am a devil that carries away unchristian folk, and unbaptised children, naming me the Hunter of Souls. Do you not know me, Thomas Learmont? I am Cernunnos, Lord of the Animals.'

A vague foreboding settling on him, and watching the firelight flickering around the glade, Thomas said, 'Am I for the Wild Hunt?'

Cernunnos gave a slow, grim nod. 'Ah, so you know the tales. No. I'm offering you something.'

Thomas gave a curt laugh. 'Advice?'

'You don't need advice.'

Thomas stretched his legs out, giving his strange companion a sharp look. 'I'm listening.'

'What price do you put on fame?'

'Whose?'

'Yours.'

Again, Thomas fell silent. At length, he said, 'I don't court fame.'

'Ah. Then what price would you pay for going home?'

Rattled, Thomas stared at him. 'What do you mean?'

'Your path homeward will be long and perilous, Thomas Learmont, with many diversions, if you accept the challenge of Faerie.'

'And if I refuse?'

'You will not go home at all.'

Thomas now saw a cold, gleaming, impenetrable lattice around the glade. Alarm flashing across his face, he stared at his companion, then bowed his head to his knees. 'What should I do?'

'Do you know of the Blācencynn, Thomas?'

'No.'

'They are mortals, with strange creeds, who for generations have guarded the North Gate, defending the Mortal realm against evil.' Cernunnos paused, put more wood onto the fire, then sat back, staring at it. 'They forged a sword, ages ago, to destroy anything from Dark Færie; it's said that they see the future in a flame and guard an ungovernable power men desire but cannot understand; men like Lord Soulis of Liddesdale, if you've heard of him.'

'I've heard he's in league with the Dev–' Thomas glanced at Cernunnos. 'You know what I mean.'

Cernunnos leaned forward. 'He has entered a pact with Robin Redcap, Lord of Dark Færie, an alliance that has given him immortality. Redcap seeks the flame's power and thus dominion over both the Færie and Mortal realms.' He paused, studying Thomas' pallid face, then stood up, his antlers glinting in the firelight, and taking a horn from a satchel hanging from his belt, spoke, his voice muffled.

'This belongs to the elves who guard the South Gate at the Mereburg; like the Sword, the Blācencynn made it to defeat Faerie evil.'

Surprised, Thomas stood up, glancing from Horn to man. 'So, why don't you return it?'

Cernunnos ignored Thomas' barbed, suspicious tone. 'The Bright Elves hid it long ago, knowing Redcap wants it destroyed. None knows where he is, but it's rumoured he is moving down from his hills with his brethren, with Soulis as his lieutenant; we cannot approach the Mereburg, nor must the Horn go anywhere near it, if he is already there.'

Thomas frowned. 'And the Sword?'

'Lost. A long time ago. The Blācencynn cannot defend themselves without it.' He shook his head. 'I doubt they number more than a hundred, and only a few mortals remember them.'

Thomas scratched his nose, thinking. 'You haven't warned them?'

'The North Gate closed long ago, and it's hard speaking to people through a locked door. This is your challenge, Thomas Learmont: to return the Horn to

Adan, lord of the Mereburg, and to aid the Blācencynn; the gates must not open.'

Thomas sighed. 'What choice do I have?'

'None,' said Cernunnos, laying the Horn across Thomas' stiff hands.

Thomas examined it. It was long as his forearm, six inches wide at the mouth, wrought of a silvery metal he did not recognise, the designs engraved along its length hard to see in the dying firelight. 'How will I know the Blācencynn?'

'They have an outlandish look,' said Cernunnos. 'You will know them, Learmont. You won't doubt it.'

Perplexed, Thomas stared at the trees. 'Where do I go? I can't just sit here.'

Cernunnos handed him the satchel, then walked to his horse, saying, 'You know you can't go back, Thomas Learmont, so you must go forward.'

A sudden rushing darkness blew through the glade, the lattice and fire disappeared without a trace, and a cold, sinister fog unfurled between the trees again. Left alone, Thomas put the Horn in the satchel, slung it across his shoulder, then followed a tangled moonlit path to a hillcrest on the forest eaves where he had an open view of the wilderness; ahead, the steep path descended into a fog-bound gully, then climbed a higher hill beyond. The moon cast faint shadows and a slight breeze whispered through the forest. Thomas walked crab-like downhill, clutching at small shrubs and tussocks; he stopped at the fog halfway down, and the wolves howled again, louder, closer, from beyond the hill behind him. He slipped, sliding a short distance into the gully where he stood up; turning around at a loss, he glimpsed something, or someone, walking on ahead, who melted into the wafting fog. Shivering, teeth clenched, blind, he followed, his every step testing the ground for hazards, the further hill looming like a fortress wall in the night, hiding the moon.

Thomas climbed the slope, pushing past gorse and stunted hawthorn, until he emerged from the fog as though from a door and halted. Peering through the dark, he followed a winding narrow path to the summit and walked through a gap in some earthworks into a wide enclosure. Weary, cold, his hair dripping, he crept forward and halted again. There was silence, no breath of wind, yet he sensed a watchfulness, saw wolves patrolling the rampart at a creeping, predatory trot, their eyes glinting in the moonlight. He sought refuge in a small, ramshackle hut nearby, the door hanging askew.

'No, my fine gentlemen,' he said, stepping inside, securing the door as best he could. 'No, you won't have me for supper tonight.'

The hut smelt of apples and stale grain; moonlight coming through holes in the roof showed hay littering the floor; he heard mice running about the place but, dropping the satchel on the threshold, he lay down on a smelly, uncomfortable sack pile and slept. Awaking at dawn, he found a tub of apples; he choked when he tried eating one and gasping, went outside. He knelt on the wet grass, unaware of two men approaching, one fair-haired, the other dark. The fairer of them lay Thomas back, saw the apple in his hand, understood, and spoke to his companion.

'Dagan, fetch some honey, and be quick. He could die.'

Dagan soon returned. 'Here, Cynwæd.'

Cynwæd sat Thomas up, and setting a small jar to his lips, said, 'Take this, stranger; all of it.'

Thomas obeyed, then, light-headed, confused, stood up and leaned on the hut wall, asking a barrage of questions.

'What happened? Who are you? What is this place?'

'Cynwæd,' said Dagan, 'inform the High Lady: a mortal man is here.' He turned to Thomas. 'Don't speak, stranger. We know what you've eaten. It won't kill you, not now, but you must explain your purpose here to the High Lady.'

Thomas could not hide his suspicion. 'And where is "here"?'

'The Seelie Court.'

'*Where?*'

'The Seelie Court,' repeated Dagan, nodding towards the foggy space beyond the hut. 'And here is your escort.'

Thomas watched Cynwæd approaching with a guard, and turning in sudden alarm to Dagan, pointed to the satchel on the hut threshold. 'Take it.'

Confused, Dagan did not respond.

'Take it,' insisted Thomas, giving him a brief, earnest glare. '*Hide it.*'

Dagan obeyed, secreting it under his cloak. The guard marched to within arm's reach of Thomas and began circling him, looking at him with contempt.

'*This?*' he said, flicking pieces of straw from Thomas' tunic. 'I'm taking *this* to the High Lady?' He forced Thomas around, bound his hands behind his back, forced him around again, and spoke as though to a child. 'I am Finnian, the Court Champion, my Lady's Captain of the Guard. *You* will show me respect, Master… *Scarecrow.*'

Strange Meetings

Thomas glared. 'Only when you've earned it.'

Finnian shoved him forward, sniggering when Thomas stumbled. 'You will *walk*, Master Scarecrow—unless you prefer crawling? Follow!' he barked at Dagan and Cynwæd. 'The crow must not escape.'

He marched Thomas to an open space before a large timber hall, up a short flight of wooden steps, past guards standing on either side of the open door, and pushed him into the building. Ankle deep in fresh rushes and herbs, Thomas looked around.

Benches stood alongside long tables set with white burning candles; painted carved beasts, birds and flowers, both mythical and real, covered the pillars and high beams; bright tapestries covered the walls and an enormous cauldron hung from a long chain over the fire burning in the wide central hearth. The place smelt of wood smoke and fragrant herbs—and timber.

Finnian, gripping Thomas' left shoulder until it hurt, pushed him across the hall towards a beautiful, tall lady standing beside a large white chair on a low dais opposite the door. Thomas gave her a guarded look.

She wore a flowing, bluebell-coloured gown, the thin silver circlet on her head glittering in the candlelight, her unbound black hair falling like twilight shadows to her knees. He glared at her with undisguised suspicion while she appraised him with soft, summer midnight eyes he could lose himself in.

Finnian, pushing Thomas to the floor, resting one threatening foot on his neck, spoke as though to a dog. 'You will kneel before the High Lady of Faerie.' He bowed low. 'My Lady,' he said, 'this intruder is a mortal, and mortals always bring bad news.'

She said nothing but continued studying Thomas, who, shrugging himself from under Finnian's foot, spoke in an abrupt, heated tone he could not control. 'My mother taught me not to *stare* at people.'

Finnian grabbed Thomas' neck, but she spoke without malice. 'We thank you for your vigilance, Finnian, but return to your post now and keep watch.'

Finnian hesitated, as though about to protest, but changed his mind, bowed, and withdrew.

'Cynwæd,' she said, 'help him up.' Stepping down from the dais, she walked around Thomas, taking in every detail: his muddied, now shabby clothing, his handsome face, a superficial scratch below his right eye, the straw in his beard and tangled hair, while he stared ahead. At length, she stepped onto the dais again.

## Strange Meetings

'Why do you visit Faerie?'

He glared at her. 'I didn't know I was. I was on my way home until I was Pixie-led here.'

Cynwæd stepped forward, holding out the half-eaten apple. 'My Lady, he has eaten this.'

Her calm demeanour changed to that of one dishonoured. 'You steal from us. You steal from the Elves.'

'I don't consider it stealing,' he snapped, 'taking something that doesn't seem to *belong* to anybody.'

In silence, she lowered her gaze, considering, then spoke in a softer tone. 'This apple is bitter, and hard to swallow, but confers prophecy and a tongue that cannot lie on any who dares taste it.'

Nonplussed, he said, 'I'm no seer.'

She ignored this. 'Cut his bonds, Cynwæd. He poses no threat; find him a bed and give him what food and drink he needs.' She met Thomas' defiant glare. 'We will discuss these events together once you have rested.' His sullen gaze lingering on her, he followed Cynwæd from the Hall.

Dagan held out the satchel. 'My Lady, he brought this with him.'

'Open it, Dagan,' she replied. 'Maybe this stranger has thought to bring his Lady a gift.'

'He told me to hide it,' he said, holding the Horn out to her.

She stared at it in silence for a moment. 'The Blācencynn forged this to defend Faerie,' she said. 'It belongs to the Mereburg and has a companion. Dagan, set a watch upon our borders, for other strangers may seek refuge here, and do as he asked: hide it.'

'But where?'

'Do your best, Dagan,' she said. 'I will speak with our guest tomorrow evening.'

He bowed and withdrew, and she looked towards the door, speaking to herself. 'With the Mereburg Horn surrendered, the Blācencynn cannot be far behind.'

The mist had not lifted. Cynwæd led Thomas to a small, cold, musty house, furnished only with a table, stool and bed. There was no fire. Cynwæd lit a lantern, hung it from a peg on a low cross beam, and closed the shutter.

'Rest here,' he said, casting a disapproving eye over Thomas' clothing. 'We've no garments for you—yet. Make yourself comfortable; sleep if you need to, but don't leave this building until my Lady summons you. I'll bring you some food and something to drink.'

Thomas lay on the bed and at once fell asleep, awaking hours later, and lay calculating the spider population lurking in thick cobwebs festooned from the thatch. The now burning fire smelt of oak; daylight slanted through the closed shutter, and he saw bread, dried meat, fruit and ale on the table. He ate and drank with appetite until there was nothing left and lay on the bed again, listening to sounds outside: passing footsteps and chatter; dogs and livestock; hens; and slept again.

The summons came at dusk. Thomas followed Cynwæd along wattle paths, through the soft, scented twilight; glimpsed homely, lamp-lit tableaux within buildings he had somehow missed before. Cynwæd stopped outside a round house, motioned that Thomas should wait, went in, and returned, giving a beckoning nod.

Scented candles burned on every surface, bright tapestries hung on the walls and sweet smells came from herbs scattered on mats covering the floor. There was a rug draped over a couch beside the central hearth, and the fire smelt of apple wood.

The Lady, seated alone on a dark wood chair facing the door, wore a loose, soft, dusk-coloured woollen shift, with a wide leather belt around her waist. Cynwæd bowed, leading Thomas further in.

She stood up, smiling. 'Welcome, guest,' she said. 'Now you've rested and eaten, perhaps you feel less hostile towards us.'

Cynwæd withdrew, closing the door behind him.

'Will you not drink with me, Thomas Learmont?' she said, pouring wine into two silver cups. 'I trust you have forgiven Finnian: his loyalty is beyond question, but he distrusts outsiders.'

He took the proffered cup, speaking in a suspicious tone. 'How do you know who I am?'

She did not acknowledge this, saying, 'We need to discuss things, you and I, that I cannot share yet, even with my household.'

He took a draught, then sat on the couch. 'Such as?'

'What did Cernunnos say?' She met his sharp look. 'I know you spoke with him because you brought the Horn here.'

Reminded of events, he barked, 'Where is it?'

'We have hidden it, as you instructed.' She drank, then repeated, 'What did Cernunnos tell you?'

Thomas, rolling the cup between his palms, repeated the discussion to her, almost verbatim.

She walked to the chair, then faced him. 'What are your intentions?'

'I *want* to go home.'

'That is your choice.'

It was a loaded statement. She approached him, the firelight behind her revealing her shapely form beneath her gown, and he missed nothing. He drank, put his cup down, stared at his clasped hands, and sighed.

'It wasn't a chance meeting, was it? Nor a coincidence that I'm here.'

She sat beside him. 'You don't trust me, do you?'

'Not entirely, no,' he said, staring at the fire.

'Why?'

He met her gaze. 'Elves are tricky to deal with, saying yea when they mean nay.'

'Sometimes,' she whispered, searching his face, 'but not here, not now. I have watched you for many weeks, Thomas. All winter I've watched you from afar.'

He leaned towards her. 'Don't do this, Lady; don't make me want you. You don't know me.'

'I know you're impatient,' she said, stroking his beard, 'hot-tempered… uncouth….' She kissed him. 'Ungentle…' Again, she kissed him. 'But not unkind.'

He smiled, shaking his head. 'Lady, you needed only to knock on my door if you wanted me to make love to you.' He touched her hair, ran his fingertips down her neck, and began untying her gown. 'Say no, Lady, and I'll leave… Just say no to me, and I'll leave you alone.'

Chapter Five

# Grimsdene

Granite lay scattered across the hillside, and after two days of almost constant walking, Penda immersed his head in a fast stream to ease his fatigue. Rædwulf lay watching a raven circling overhead, following its flight towards a deep, forested glen all Blācencynn feared, its dense woodland undisturbed by any wind on earth.

He recalled fragmented memories of his previous visit there, aged fifteen: his drinking unsavoury broth and bitter cordials the High Priest gave him; spending days and nights on end trapped in a tiny shelter, huge night creatures prowling outside, pushing their terrifying weight against the walls, thrusting their snouts and snarling jaws beneath the door, their paws scrabbling on the flimsy roof, never quite breaking through; and his going home, only to learn of his father's sudden death. As Lord Blācencynn in his own right, Rædwulf had grown up fast; the advisors soon learned this was one youth no one could manipulate, he being always two thoughts ahead of them.

He surfaced from this daydream and surveyed the valley again. Drawing a long breath, he murmured, 'Grimsdene: where the Dead walk,' and beckoned Penda.

It was a long two hours before they reached arable land on the woodland margins. Penda stopped and pointed towards a plough team a hundred yards ahead.

'I see people,' he said. Rædwulf watched them: one man leading the oxen, another guiding the primitive plough, a woman following, broadcasting seed, their conversation muted as though coming from far away. He heard the scratch and strake of the plough as they toiled back and forth across the field; he clearly saw, despite the distance, their muddy shoes, every thread and weave of their coarse clothing, the flies on the animals' sweaty flanks, but the image was odd, two-dimensional; shifting like a tapestry in the breeze, it melted into the land, and Penda stared at the deserted field. 'Where did they go?'

Rædwulf sighed. 'They are but shadows, Penda, mere echoes.'

Penda sat down. 'The Priest said you've already been here. Can you tell me what happened?'

Rædwulf, staring into space, spoke as though entranced. 'I remember burning strange herbs mixed with blood drawn from self-inflicted wounds on my inner thighs and arms, the smoke almost choking me. I had nightmares and frightening visions… I met Wyrtræd and my guardians here… here, I met the Goddess.' He blinked, meeting Penda's astonished look. 'If you understand me.'

Penda stared at the trees. 'What's it like in there?' There was no reply. 'Rædwulf?'

Rædwulf took a breath. 'Hazardous, and not for the faint-hearted. The light is no broader than dusk, the paths, treacherous and misleading, but like it or not, Penda, you must confront it, or fail. Follow me.'

Half-seen trails, winding through thick undergrowth and dark glades, bypassing mires and stagnant pools, brought them to the seething river.

Rædwulf flinched at another memory of the High Priest forcing him to dive, hands tied, into those deep, turbid waters to retrieve something valuable he now wore around his neck. He shivered.

'I'm not crossing that. We might camp, if we can find somewhere in this pathless tangle.'

They retraced their steps, often losing their way in the deepening twilight until, pushing through thick evergreens, flowering nightshade, foxgloves and hemlock, they entered a timeless, moonlit glade, the full moon hanging overhead like a huge primitive skull. Penda slept while Rædwulf kept watch through endless silence until dawn, when a subtle, though threatening, sound brought him to his feet and awakened Penda; but it soon stopped.

'Rædwulf, what was that?' Penda whispered.

'Disquiet,' said Rædwulf, running one hand through his wiry hair. 'Time we moved, I think.'

Another distinct, though not unpleasant, sound broke the velvet quiet, stopping soon as they heard it. Penda threw Rædwulf a quizzical look.

'Did you hear something?'

'Singing?'

Penda nodded. 'Very faint.'

'It sounded like a woman.' Rædwulf paused, thinking. 'Alright, we'll find somewhere to build your shelter, perhaps on higher ground.'

Sounds of flowing water led them to a sunny space, the first sunshine they had seen since entering Grimsdene. Ferns, stunted trees, moss and small flowering plants clung to crevices in high rocks; a waterfall plunged into a deep pool feeding a stream that was soon lost amongst the primal green. The place smelt of cool air, damp earth and water.

Penda took his shoes off, waded into the cold shallows to bathe his aching feet, and stopped, sensing an ancient, surrounding presence; he swallowed, coughed, and looked back at Rædwulf.

A low, melodious voice, with a hint of warning, came from the pool. 'Who disturbs my quiet home?'

Rædwulf dropped his jaw, and Penda, looking at the pool again, saw a beautiful girl watching them from the middle of it. Her large, clear eyes matched the shimmering water, and her golden hair flowed around her pale, naked shoulders. He recognised her as an elf, breathed the word *'Asrai'* and cleared his throat.

'We are Blācencynn,' he said; 'we don't intend–'

Without a splash, she submerged, then stood from the water close to him; her long hair, decorated with a flower and tiny translucent gems, could not hide her ethereal nakedness.

'A kiss for the Sword, *Lyblæca*,' she said, proffering something.

He took it, glancing at her breasts, but thinking she would melt if he touched her, did not otherwise move. She kissed him, murmured, 'Keep it well,' and vanished.

He waded ashore and sat, staring at the sodden leather he held. 'What's going on?' he said. 'What sword?'

'Let me see,' said Rædwulf. He took it, unwrapped it, and drew the weapon from its scabbard. A convex rock crystal on the guard flashed like liquid sunlight, and he read the runes engraved on the glinting, unblemished blade.

*'I am the Flame, I am fire.'*

He sheathed the Sword, wrapped it again, and setting it aside, lay back, eyes closed, recounting Blācencynn legends to himself: As a reward for exiling Spriggans already dwelling there, the Bright Elves had granted the Blācencynn the Caves to live in, providing they guarded the Mortal realm against Dark Faerie.

'This defends the North Gate,' said Rædwulf, thinking aloud, 'and we made a horn for the Mereburg Elves to defend the South.' He fell silent for a long time, thinking, then looked at Penda. 'But for unknown reasons, we lost contact with Bright Faerie, and the Sword disappeared generations ago.'

Penda met the steady grey eyes. 'I thought the Higher Hall pillar protects us.'

Rædwulf sat up. 'In a way, it does,' he said, giving a slight shrug. 'It keeps the Gate closed, gives our warriors their strength and the will to fight without fear, but who knows what the Flame, or rather, its power, can do? I wonder if even the Priestesses know its true nature.'

'And now we've found the Sword.'

Rædwulf stroked his beard. 'Mmm.'

'Coincidence?'

'I don't believe in coincidences. If something threatens the Blācencynn, we should go home. Keep the Sword, Penda; for a while, at least.'

Everything he had trained for collapsing, his hopes dissolving, Penda sat forward. 'I haven't finished here, Rædwulf; I can't go back without shame. In case you've forgotten, your duty as my mentor is to help me.'

Rædwulf threw him a glittering glare. 'My *duty*, as Lord Blācencynn, is to defend the Caves and our kin. You can finish this another time, Penda; don't argue.'

Sullenly, Penda glanced at him. 'We might at least eat something first.'

Rædwulf regarded the shimmering pool with suspicion; he knew many tales of elves, none reassuring. 'Alright,' he said, 'though I don't want to disturb *her* more than necessary.'

He allowed only half an hour before moving, but the path soon dwindled to nothing. Dusk became a timeless night, moonlight silvering every leaf and bough, and every sound seemed muffled. Penda, looking everywhere, stopped.

'This place is dangerous, Rædwulf,' he whispered. 'The wind holds its breath, and the sky seems hostile.' He peered through the thick, silent murk beneath the trees, saw nothing, but felt a faint, resonating throb, marking slow time, coming from the ground beneath his feet. He gave Rædwulf a sharp look.

'Hear it?'

'That pulse? Yes, and I don't like it.'

'It's louder now,' whispered Penda. 'It's coming in waves.'

Harsh shrieks shattered the silence; the pulsing ground shook, shadows loomed beneath the dark trees, and Penda yelled, 'Spriggans are here! They're here! Run!' But Rædwulf stood rigid, mesmerised, watching nightmarish creatures he had never imagined swarming forward. Penda yelled again, pulling him away, and they fled, through blind dark; through barbed branches and trailing brambles, across folded ground, treacherous with exposed, snaking roots. An inner compass guiding them, with the Spriggans almost on their heels, they climbed and scrambled up the valley side for what seemed like hours until they reached high open moorland, the waning moon beyond Grimsdene giving just enough light to see by.

A barrow fifty yards ahead stood black against the night, and they ran towards it, Penda snatching the Sword from his belt, the pursuing Spriggans giving wild, triumphant shrieks. The gusting wind blowing his hair into his eyes, Penda faced Rædwulf and gestured towards the open land. 'Keep going! Don't stop unless you drop dead. They won't have both of us.'

Rædwulf, pulling Penda by the arm, yelled against the wind, 'I'm not leaving you here!'

Penda shook his head. 'The hill has great magic. I can use it.'

'You can't use evil magic.'

'I'll judge that! Move! Before they catch us!' Uncertain, Rædwulf hesitated; Penda, afraid and glancing at the closing shadows, now less than twenty yards away, shoved him. 'Go! I'll make the Sword work for me!'

'You're mad!' yelled Rædwulf. 'You're insane!'

*'Run, Coppertop!'*

Rædwulf glanced at the encroaching, shrieking shadows, turned and, expecting death with every stride, leapt and ran, leapt and ran, across shaking ground riddled with sudden ridges and hidden hollows, the rising gale blowing clouds across the moon.

He tripped on the tangled heather, fell headlong, twisting an ankle, and ignoring the pain, scrambled to his feet, fell again, staggered to his feet, fell. Sweat-drenched, breathless, dizzy, he stood up and limped on for a few yards before coming to an abrupt halt as dense, billowing fog enveloped him. For a breathing space, everything was still, the ground quiet; then a chilling cry came across the land and he envisioned Penda lying dead, those palpable shadows dismembering him like ants he had once seen pulling a spider apart.

He ran. Unable to see his outstretched hand, he stepped into space and giving a brief cry, fell into an icy river swollen with melt water, its unrelenting current sweeping him away. He surfaced, sank, tumbling, whirlpools swallowing, then disgorging him, now his hands, then his feet scraping the riverbed; surfaced again, battled across the torrent, colliding with punishing rocks and branches winter storms had snatched from the riverside. Pinned against the opposite bank, his strength almost gone, he crawled ashore, sodden, bruised, coughing up water; took two paces forward, the fog closing like a curtain behind him, and fell, almost unconscious; heard benevolent voices murmuring, and someone leaned over him.

'Where is Raven-hair?'

Almost asleep, Rædwulf answered, 'He's making the Sword work for him.'

\*

Penda ran to the mound top and watched the surging shadows. A sudden gale blowing his hair and cloak about, his thumping pulse at one with the throbbing ground and the Spriggans' marching feet, he wrenched the Sword from its scabbard. Grasping the hilt with both hands, he lifted the weapon, aiming it at the sky, and stood, a shadow against the fitful, glimmering starlight. Blue-white light in the crystal shot along the blade, lighting the sky like a beacon. Power and pain overwhelmed him, and he gave a maniacal, eldritch cry that split the shadows asunder.

*'I am the Flame, I am fire!'*

A sound of splintering stone echoed across the moor.

The wind dropped, and light and sound shut off. Lowering the Sword in one slow movement, Penda fell to his knees, and the thick fog closed over him.

Borderlands

\*

Sounds of heavy footsteps awoke Lybbestre at dawn, but she saw nothing. The sounds continued, of someone pacing the adjoining chamber; she approached a curtain hung across the entrance and pulled the drapery aside. The sounds ceased, leaving a brooding quiet. Someone sighed. She saw, vague at first, becoming more defined in the half-light from the sky-shaft, a tall man, a voluminous cowl overshadowing his face, his shoulders boasting some physical strength. A diffuse cloud, rising from the hearth beside him, hovered a foot above it, and his voice came from the surrounding rock.

*'Look at the visions in the mist.'*

She heard a faint, sinister incantation and a war horn; saw a dark vault, grotesque images carved on the beams, unpleasant herbs spread on the floor. A rancid smell came from candles burning around a blood-filled bowl on an altar; she saw a sword lying in deep, clear water; an enclosure, a large, blue banner billowing above the high palisade, and a man swimming for his life across a wide lake. Then the visions dissolved.

As though casting off a fragmenting shell, the apparition transformed into a short, grotesque creature clad in a thick animal hide, a crimson cap covering the thick, plaited, white hair. It stared at her with cold, leering eyes, its long fangs dripping venom; the same voice resonated around the cavern.

*'Look well on it, Lybbestre. See what is coming.'*

## Chapter Six

# The Seelie Court

Rædwulf awoke from a nightmare and realised he was in a comfortable bed, the soft blankets against his skin giving him the cosy reassurance he remembered from childhood. Sunlight leaking through the closed shutter and door revealed a small, dusty, unfamiliar room, fragrant with wood smoke from the fire and the fresh rushes on the floor. He could name at a glance every herb hanging in bunches from the beams; saw with relief Penda snoring in an adjacent bed and the Blācencynn Sword propped between them against the wall. Hens and passers-by chattered outside, and he heard flurrying footsteps. Someone flung the door wide open, and Rædwulf shielded his eyes from the sudden glare. A tall, dark-haired youth in the doorway gave a smile and a slight bow.

'Welcome to the Seelie Court, Lord Blācencynn.'

Too weary for surprise, Rædwulf lay back on the pillow, closing his eyes. 'I don't know,' he said, 'whether

I feel hungry or sick, I've an almighty headache, and I ache all over.'

'I would suggest,' said the elf, rummaging in a heavy wooden chest, 'that you are hungry. You've slept for some time, and I suspect you remember but little of events.'

Rædwulf flinched. 'Nothing after I crossed the river. I'm assuming you have a name?'

'Dagan,' said the youth, glancing at Penda.

'He'd sleep for a week,' said Rædwulf, throwing off his covers, 'if allowed to.'

'I'm listening to everything you're saying,' said Penda without opening his eyes.

Dagan smiled again. 'You seem rather groggy, my lord Penda.'

'I feel I've travelled ten years in as many miles.'

Dagan laughed and placed a bundle on each bed. 'We've new clothes for you, as yours were… damaged somewhat; and the High Lady has granted you both leave to explore.'

He showed them the Hall, the residential buildings, the smithy, workshops, and animal pens. People hurried about the enclosure, beginning their working day, and guards patrolled a high walkway on the surrounding palisade.

Rædwulf stopped, pointing to a huge, shimmering blue flag billowing on a pole above the open gate. 'Dagan, what's that?'

'The Faerie banner, my lord,' said Dagan. 'It stands, so do we.' Girlish laughter floated from beyond a high wattle fence. 'The weaving houses and bakeries,' he said, pointing towards several roofs peeking above it, 'where our womenfolk live and work—and men cannot go.' He glanced at the white, feathered clouds blowing across the blue sky on a gentle breeze and added, 'If my lords might excuse me, I have to be elsewhere now, but you may go where you wish.'

They returned to the shady workshops and watched the wood turner for a while until Penda wandered off; Rædwulf turned to explore elsewhere, but Finnian blocked his way, sneering.

'What's this? A mortal man, dressed in our finest elfin garb? How did you worm your way into my Lady's favour, I wonder?'

More than surprised, saying nothing and detecting a cold, stony smell, Rædwulf gazed at him, noting every detail in an instant. Rædwulf was tall, but Finnian, his dark hair tousled, clad in garments trimmed with silver braid, and armed with a sword and a knife, was taller.

He circled Rædwulf, looking at him with pale blue eyes that exuded contempt for almost all they surveyed.

'I'm watching you, *Blācencynn*,' he said. 'I shall know your every move.' Turning on his heel, he walked towards half a dozen elf guards who stood to immediate attention; Rædwulf scrutinised them from behind a nearby hay cart piled with hawthorn.

Most stood in the bright sunshine, their long shadows stretching across the ground, while Finnian kept to the shade. He moved from his position, and Rædwulf thought he saw, only for a second, a distinct, short, distorted shadow, unlike the others; stopping a passer-by, he nodded towards the group.

'Who is he, the tall one over there, dressed in grey?'

'Finnian, the Court Champion,' said the elf. 'He's odd, if you ask me—he doesn't seem to like the sun.' He leaned in, whispering so no one an arm's length away could overhear. 'Of late, he's been following a Court maiden, everywhere, all the time, although she doesn't even *know*.'

Rædwulf held his informant's gaze with steady eyes. 'What maiden?'

'Læren… pretty little thing.'

'And no one objects?'

The elf could not hide his resentment. 'He's the Court *Champion*, sire. *No-one* dare gainsay him.'

His informant gone, Rædwulf watched Finnian walk towards the open entrance and, wary of the peculiar bearing and furtive gait, followed at a distance; losing sight of him where the path divided into three, he paused, considering the choice, and followed the right-hand path.

It led him up a steep flight of smooth, narrow, treacherous stone steps that wound through an open woodland, all wildflowers, bird song, and patches of green shade. He came to a scented garden, three sides hedged with blossoming hawthorn, the fourth with the woodland behind him. A lawn ahead sloped down towards a dell forty feet away, and he heard two hidden women talking.

'All bright elves can do this,' said one with absolute authority. 'I'll show you again. One thread for each of the nine worlds, each half as long again as the next; lay three across your palm, three across them, another three to tie them.'

'You make it seem easy, Raldis,' said her young companion, 'but it's *so* complicated.'

'It will come, given practice.'

He stopped on the brink of the dell, his shadow stretching before him, and the chattering stopped. A graceful, statuesque woman, wearing a green gown and aged about sixty, walked up the slope a moment later, her elegant poise and faded beauty showing him she would have been a remarkable lady in her youth. She wore her dark-grey hair styled into four long braids over each shoulder; a set of keys and a large bag hung from her leather belt. She stopped ten feet away, appraising him with clear, amber-coloured eyes.

'I am Raldis,' she said, her tone commanding immediate respect. 'I'm in charge of all the Court maidens and can gauge your character in a heartbeat.'

His grey eyes sparkled. 'Can you, now?'

Her tone did not change. 'For example, I *see* you are two yards and a hand span tall; I *sense* you hide something few know about, that fewer still have seen.' She swept her gaze over him again. 'How long have you been here?'

He shrugged. 'I'm not sure; a couple of days or so.'

'Our guests must give all names folk know them by. You must declare yourself, sire.'

'Rædwulf… Blācencynn.'

'Men cannot enter this garden, Rædwulf Blācencynn.'

'Forgive me, lady; I'm rather lost, I think, but the path led me here.'

A small, pretty maiden, aged about eighteen, he thought, ran towards them from the dell. Her gleaming yellow hair curled over her plain cream linen dress, and a spindle and large bag, stuffed with fleece, hung from her grey linen belt. Radiant, untainted, she personified wildflowers in sunny, ripening cornfields. Without noticing him, she stopped beside Raldis.

'I've done it!' she said. 'Look, Raldis—I've done it!' Looking up, she met his gaze; her eyes, sparkling like sunlit water, widened when she realised what he was, and he, looking away, could not suppress a gentle, wry smile that could make any maiden's heart flutter.

'Oh!' she said in surprise. 'Good day to you! Raldis, who's this?'

'That's not your concern, Læren,' she said, without taking her eyes from him. 'I'll meet you in the dell in a few moments.'

Læren left without a curtsey; Raldis gave Rædwulf another sweeping, appraising glance, missing nothing: his long, wild hair, strong shoulders, shining grey eyes; the strange, weighty metal amulet at his neck; the Sword, and the hilt crystal glinting in the sunlight.

'Pray forgive her, my lord,' she said, 'but she is a novice and has not yet learned our protocols. You will neither approach nor speak to her.'

His smile gone, he spoke, his tone low, measured. 'Perhaps you should have saved that speech for her. Good day to you, Raldis. Maybe we shall meet again at some point.' He walked away, stopped after a few paces, and faced her. 'Out of interest, what *were* you teaching her?'

'Elves tie a pretty knot,' she said, 'making things seem other than they are.'

He half turned, but again faced her. 'What do you know of Finnian?'

She disguised a flinch. 'I'm not responsible for the guards.'

He pondered this for a moment, and nodding an acknowledgement, gave a reassuring smile. 'Good day, lady.' Raldis, watching him walk towards the steps, did not move.

Rædwulf was not halfway down the flight when he glimpsed Finnian, often stopping, looking behind for anyone following, beginning to climb the steps. Crouching behind boulders, Rædwulf watched him through a narrow gap; he glanced back towards the hillcrest, considering his options. Despite his misgivings, he knew he could not confront Finnian on a mere hunch, that Finnian would see him if he moved, and, somehow, that he should not find the women. Finnian turned at a dog's leg in the path, and Rædwulf threw a branch over the hilltop; no reply came. Finnian was coming closer and Rædwulf, with no other idea, removed his amulet, tied it to a piece of granite big as his fist, and hurled it towards the garden, hoping Raldis would understand; he crouched again.

Raldis saw the missile fall, picked it up, recognised the warning, pocketed the amulet amongst her skirts, and hoping Rædwulf was nearby, sang, her voice soft but loud enough for him to hear her.

*Blācencynn, Blācencynn,*
*Sends a sign to Faerie-kin.*
*Faerie-kin, Faerie-kin,*
*Sends a sign to Blācencynn.*

Finnian heard her, paused, then retreated, Rædwulf following him at a distance, watching every move he made.

Læren, determined to repeat her success, sat practising her new skill and did not look up when Raldis approached.

'I thought I heard you singing, Raldis, but I couldn't make it out.'

'It was nothing, just doggerel.'

'Who *is* that man? Why is he here?'

'A stranger,' said Raldis. 'Ignore him. Let me see how you're doing… Oh, yes, this is excellent. We'll go back to the weaving house now. I have another project there for you.'

Raldis stopped within sight of the enclosure, sent Læren ahead, and examined the amulet, whispering, 'You are brave, Rædwulf Blācencynn, and you are strong, but are these enough?'

Rædwulf, halting at the gate, saw that Finnian was nowhere in sight.

'I think you may have dropped this, Lord Rædwulf,' said Raldis from behind him, pressing his amulet into his right hand. 'Be careful you do not lose it again.'

He looked around; he was alone.

\*

Bright sunlight coming through the open weaving house door shone onto the looms within. Læren stood at one, bolts of white linen and green wool in a large basket at her feet, but her two maiden companions, rather than working, stood gossiping about Rædwulf.

'You've *seen* him, Læren?' said one. 'What's he like? Is he handsome?'

Læren felt her face burning but shrugged. 'I don't know. He's just a man.' She paused, shuttle in hand. 'He has red hair and a beard and wears a strange amulet around his neck.'

'*I* heard he fought Spriggans,' said the third maiden, 'then swam the river Colmarch at night, high though it was.'

'And *I* heard he has a companion,' said the second, 'who fought a whole troop of Spriggans, single-handed, at Dark Barrow.'

Raldis spoke from the doorway. 'There's too much chattering in here. More chat, less work.'

'Oh, Raldis,' said the second girl, 'it's just harmless gossip.'

Raldis ignored her and, pointing to the basket, said, 'Læren, take that to the sewing house, please.' When Læren had gone, Raldis faced the maidens. 'Harmless gossip?' she said. 'There is no such thing.' Gazing towards the enclosure beyond the fence, she whispered, 'It's told that Læren will lose her heart once, and forever, to a mortal man. I want to spare her this fate.'

## Borderlands

\*

Penda glimpsed greenery and flowers festooned on the rafters and pillars in the Hall and paused in the doorway. 'What's happening in there?'

'It's May Eve,' called a passer-by, carrying more greenery, 'when we welcome the May King. He shall choose his queen from the maidens; then we will dance in the woods, celebrating their union.'

Penda smiled. 'I hope I might attend such a merry evening. Is the May King a forest wight?'

The elf could not hide his disapproval. 'No. We've always chosen him from the courtiers, but now it's more… self-appointed. It's always Finnian, the Court Champion.'

'Why?'

'No-one speaks against him, sire.'

Penda, glancing at the Hall again, strolled off and called to Rædwulf, standing on the palisade walkway.

'What are you doing up there?'

'Looking at the view. Come up.'

Penda climbed the steps and stood beside him, surveying the countryside, inhaling the mingled smells of resinous warm timber, wild thyme, hawthorn and spicy gorse. He glanced at Rædwulf. 'Something's on your mind.'

'Mmm.'

Rædwulf, ignoring the river meandering in the middle distance, continued staring at the wide expanse: undulating land and woodlands to his left; to his right, the nearby hillside hiding the garden beyond, and the higher hills on the skyline.

'Have you met Finnian yet?'

'No, though I'm told they will crown him as the self-appointed May King tonight, and that he will take a court maiden as his queen.'

'If elves are strange, Penda, he is the strangest, and I'm convinced he holds everyone here in thrall.'

'I know that tone. You're planning something.'

'I just think it's high time someone called his bluff.'

'*Why?*'

Already walking away, Rædwulf faced him. 'Because, Penda, if I'm right, we could be in real trouble.'

Penda pursued him down the steps. 'Rædwulf, you're not in charge here; you can't start upsetting people the moment you walk in.'

'*I* don't intend to.'

'What if you're wrong?'

'I'll swallow humble pie, Penda, much as I dislike it.'

'We should at least tell the Lady.'

'I doubt she'll listen.'

Dagan approached them and giving a slight bow, said, 'My lords, the Lady wishes to speak with you.'

They followed him through a small gate, along a broad green lane between steep grassy banks, trees and blossoming hawthorn, and across a hay meadow full of flowers, bees and butterflies flitting from one bloom to another. A hill, half-seen through the trees, overlooked an apple orchard; spiralling petals settled on the grass, scents of hawthorn and apple blossom drifted on the breeze, and Dagan stopped, pointing towards gnarled trees surrounding a dovecote.

'There.'

With flowers in her hair, her primrose-coloured skirts arranged around her feet, the Lady sat in its shade, her women in attendance and guards standing nearby; neither Raldis nor Læren was there—nor Finnian. Penda raised an eyebrow.

'Does my lady always hold court under fruit trees?'

'No,' said Dagan, 'today is different. Follow me.'

She stood up, greeting them with a warm smile, her kind, though deep, eyes noting the scattered petals on their hair, but Rædwulf and Penda saw no beauty; this was a bent old woman with silvered knee-length hair, a thin, drawn mouth, and fragile, papery skin, yet she seemed the embodiment of the land: every glen, forest, stream and hill; every moorland and standing stone; every history. Rædwulf and Penda felt insignificant by comparison, and, oh, so mortal.

'Bright Faerie welcomes you, my lords Blācencynn,' she said, 'although we lost contact with you many years ago. Declare your intentions here.'

Rædwulf gave a brief, self-conscious bow. 'We never meant crossing your borders, my lady, but events overtook us somewhat and, to be blunt, we were not so much directed here as brought. Perhaps my lady can explain how we came here.'

'We will discuss this later,' she said, 'for another mortal is here.'

'Another?'

'Yes,' she said, 'you will meet him soon, but first,' she signalled to her women, 'have breakfast with us at your leisure.'

Borderlands

\*

Confined in his lodging since returning from her bower, and not wanting to become some exhibit in a freak show, Thomas kept the house door and shutters closed. Cynwæd, bringing food and drink just after dawn, had exchanged a few words but had not returned since. Now edgy, impatient, bored, Thomas paced from wall to wall, then began carving a design into the tabletop with his knife. Cynwæd interrupted this vandalism by marching in, leaving the door wide open.

Thomas shielded his eyes. 'Good God, Cynwæd, are you trying to blind me?'

The elf smiled. 'Not at all, sire. The Lady summons you.'

Thomas flicked a contemptuous finger at his shabby clothes. 'Like *this*?'

Cynwæd handed him a bundle, laughed, and closed the door. 'That won't do, sire. We've better clothes for you.'

Thomas examined them as he dressed: the linen shirt, damasked with a subtle pattern seen only in oblique light; the fine woollen trews, knee-length tunic, long, dark green cloak with large cowl attached to it, and long leather boots. He wore his own belt.

'There,' said Cynwæd, brushing residual fluff from the cloak, 'dressed in green, as an elf guard should be.'

Thomas pulled up the hood. 'What's the occasion?'

'We have guests.' Cynwæd lowered his voice. 'The Blācencynn are here.'

Thomas raised his brows. *'Here?'*

Cynwæd nodded. 'Yes, lord.' He grasped the door latch, changed his mind, and faced Thomas again. 'Sire, I must caution you: keep your temper. Finnian is on the prowl.'

'Is he indeed?'

'Sire, please, don't provoke him, or you may not be… here for long.'

Thomas responded with typical sarcasm. 'Is that so? Well, let me tell you something: your precious little champion would never better me in a fair fight, and he knows it.'

Cynwæd, knowing better than to argue, took him to the dovecote. Thomas, his hood drawn almost to his eyes, bowed to the Lady and sat in an empty chair. Penda recognised him from the vision he had had at the Flame but said nothing. The Lady motioned to her guards and women to withdraw beyond earshot and sat, listening with utmost attention, to everything Rædwulf and Penda said. Thomas reiterated what Cernunnos had told him.

Penda frowned. 'Where is the Horn now?'

The Lady whispered, 'In a safe place.'

Rædwulf, studying Thomas in silence, said, 'Is Soulis dangerous?'

'His alliance with Redcap answers that,' said Thomas. 'I've never met him, but it's said he's the Devil's spawn.'

Rædwulf stroked his beard. 'The Sword and Horn defend us against Dark Faerie; I'd guess Redcap intends to destroy them and use Soulis to find them.'

'And if he does?' said Thomas.

'Redcap could open both Gates,' said the Lady.

'Why were the Sword and Horn hidden?' said Rædwulf.

She did not answer at once but sat thinking. 'We hid the Horn for its own protection,' she said at last. 'Perhaps the Blācencynn concealed the Sword for the same reason.'

Still stroking his beard, and staring at his feet, Rædwulf said, 'We must go home, warn our people, and prepare our defences.'

'It took you but little time reaching us, Rædwulf Blācencynn,' she said, 'but your journey home will take longer. Distances through Faerie can be deceptive, and time in Grimsdene certainly so. You may have spent longer there than you think, and if Redcap threatens the Caves, then the Mereburg also lies exposed.'

Penda stared into space. 'Have they sent word?'

The Lady regarded him. 'No, nor replied to messages, and the wind gives no news. I would have advised that you take the Horn there now, if Cernunnos hadn't forbidden it, yet any delay may prove costly. I have already sent scouts; what happens next, my lords Blācencynn, will depend on their findings, but Thomas will aid you.'

With sharp doubt in his eyes, Rædwulf said, 'What help could you offer us, Thomas Learmont?'

The reply hinted wounded pride. 'I can use my fists and wield a blade if I need to.'

'You'll need to.' Silent for a moment, Rædwulf nodded. 'We accept any aid, Learmont, that you can give, with thanks.'

The Lady smiled. 'That is for another day; in the meantime, some merriment may not go amiss, and I ask that you all attend the feast tonight. Thomas, I wish to speak with the Blācencynn alone; you may wander at will, but don't leave the enclosure.'

He bowed and withdrew, and she turned to Rædwulf.

'What do you understand of the Flame, lord?'

'If you mean its power, very little. I believe it opens the Gates at will, conferring absolute command of the Mortal and hidden realms. But the Blācencynn believe the stone pillar prevents this.'

'Your stone pillar has no influence,' she said, 'and legends often distort the truth. To defend ourselves from mortal ills, and to protect mortal lands from Faerie evil, we, the Bright Elves, used that power to close both Gates and then confined it in the Flame, so severing our contact with the Blācencynn. It is an uncontrollable force men crave, yet it gives no dominion; the Sword and Horn attract it, and the right hand will unleash it.' She looked at Penda. 'It protects both itself and its instruments but makes no distinction between friend and foe, and might prove destructive if misused. Its transference is itself a warning, Penda Blācencynn; ensure it does not turn against you.'

*

Thomas wandered around the enclosure as he wished, watching elves bustling about, preparing for the evening.

He saw the now empty cart outside the hall and heard a stifled squeal and something heavy clattering to earth within.

Intrigued, he stepped inside. A blossom garland lay on the floor, a fallen heavy ladder was leaning against a long table, and he saw Læren clinging onto a roof beam fifteen feet from the ground, her feet flailing.

He swallowed a laugh, playful mischief igniting his eyes. 'Need any help? I mean, I wouldn't want you falling and damaging the floorboards.'

Almost losing hold of the beam, she squeaked again, and he propped the ladder against it. Somehow, she clambered down, sliding the last few feet, and landed in a heap. In one glance, he noted her grimy, flushed, pretty face, her grubby cream gown, and the small spider on an exploratory excursion through the garland debris in her hair. Shaken, she sat on the floor, brushing over her gown. 'Oh! I'm covered in dust and cobwebs, and I'm sure I've splinters in my fingers.'

His grin broadening, he ignored her distress. 'Though you look very fetching, I must admit. What were you doing up there?'

'Only helping decorate the Hall for tonight's feast,' she said, dusting herself off again.

'If you had fallen, lass, I'd have caught you.'

'Thank you, sir, but I'd rather break the floor.' Glancing at him, she blurted out, 'I made those clothes!' and cast a brief, critical look over them. 'I hope they fit you.'

He gave an engaging open grin, designed to flatter. 'Thank you, they fit very well,' he said and clicking her a wink, walked away.

Chapter Seven

# A King Deposed

Everyone gathered outside the Hall, the maidens on one side of the space, talking amongst themselves. The Lady and her women stood on the steps, Thomas some distance away, awaiting the May King.

One maiden nodded towards Rædwulf standing near the Hall. 'Is that the man you met?' she whispered to Læren. 'Red hair... beard?'

Læren shrugged. 'I suppose so.'

'He's... *beautiful.*'

'He's mortal,' said Raldis from behind them, hinting he was best avoided. 'Keep your counsel, ladies.' An expectant silence rippled through the crowd.

Finnian, bedecked with flowers, strode into the space and stood in the shade before the Lady; he turned, his arms outspread, and giving everyone a sweeping, imperious glance, declared, 'Behold the May King, here to choose his Queen!' He walked around, always keeping to the shade, making a slow inspection of the crowd. Rædwulf never took his eyes from him.

'Who shall be my Queen?' said Finnian, strutting before the maidens. They exchanged discomfited glances with one another. 'Here's a pretty one,' he said, reaching out to Læren, but she drew back, and Raldis placed one steadying hand on her shoulder. 'You need not fear me,' he said, giving a peculiar smile. 'For a sweet maiden shall have all she desires as my Queen.'

*'Stand with me in the sunlight, Finnian.'*

Finnian stopped his posturing, turned towards the powerful voice, and sneered, 'Who dares challenge me?'

Rædwulf took several slow paces forward, his left thumb hooked into his belt, his right hand hidden in his long cloak. 'I dare.'

Finnian looked him over in pure disgust. '*You?* I am not in the habit of taking challenges from, from *vermin!* Don't delude yourself, mortal, that you can stand against me.'

Rædwulf, unflinching, glanced towards a patch of sunny ground behind him. 'The afternoon sun casts long shadows, Finnian, and shadows reveal a thing's true nature,' he said quietly.

## A King Deposed

Finnian recognised the subtle threat and, speaking with savage loathing, approached him. 'How dare you even think of contesting with me? I know who you are, *Blācencynn.*' He turned to the Lady who was glancing in disbelief from elf to man. 'Did I not warn you, my Lady, that mortals never bring good news? This man looks to usurp your Court Champion for his own nefarious aims.' Again, he faced Rædwulf, who had not moved. 'Is that not your intention, *Blācencynn?*'

By now, they were circling each other, Rædwulf speaking through clenched teeth, his cold eyes staring Finnian down. 'I wouldn't want it, even if offered it on a silver platter.'

Unsure whether to intervene, the guards stepped forward, but Finnian rebuffed them. 'Return to your posts. I need no help against a mere... *man.*'

Someone called, 'Watch out for his sword, mortal!'

Finnian lunged, but his sword splintered against the Blācencynn blade and he stepped back, looking in consternation at the hilt in his hand. No Blācencynn warrior would use a weapon against an unarmed opponent; Rædwulf, tossing the Sword to Penda, pulled Finnian towards him and growled, 'Let us see you in the light, Court Champion.' He pushed him with force into the sunshine, throwing him to the ground and scattering flowers everywhere, but Finnian proved an agile adversary. In less than one heartbeat he grabbed Rædwulf around the knees, flooring him, and they rolled, wrestling, across the dusty ground, each grunting and giving powerful blows. Rædwulf scrambled away, but Finnian fell on him before he could stand, one hand closing around his throat, fingers digging in like claws, a long knife in the other, ready to stab. Rædwulf grasped Finnian's wrist, trying with all his strength to push the blade away, thinking that for once, he had perhaps miscalculated, misjudged his strength and fighting prowess. He assumed that no-one could, or would, help him, fearing reprisals should Finnian win; but not everyone there thought like that.

Læren rushed forward. 'Stop! Stop it!'

Penda, arms folded, leaning against the hay cart, spoke, his quiet, reassuring voice stopping her in her tracks. 'Hold your step, lady maiden. Never approach fighting men whose bloods are up, because they just won't see you.'

She did not turn. 'You scold me,' she said.

'Not at all. I'm warning you.' He signalled to Raldis, who led Læren away without a word.

## A King Deposed

Finnian snarled, revealing long, sharp fangs; startled, Rædwulf gave a brutal kick, forcing Finnian to drop the knife. Then it was Rædwulf kneeling on Finnian, he who held the knife to the exposed throat, he who had the stranglehold, and he leaned low, snarling under his breath.

'You're not the only one who can keep watch here. I know what you are, and what you pretend to be, you slimy little piece of shit. You so much as squeak, and I'll cut your lying head off.' He tightened his grip. 'Why won't you stand in the sunlight? Could it be you fear it?' He wrenched Finnian to the Hall steps where the sunshine was brightest, and pressing the blade through the grey clothing, piercing the skin beneath, forced him to face the Lady.

White-faced, she spoke, her gaze and tone enough to freeze molten iron. 'I did not expect our honoured guest to show my loyal captain such contempt, Lord Blācencynn. Explain your insolence, your turning our sacred festival into a tavern brawl.'

Other men might have quailed; not Rædwulf. 'I beg no pardon, Lady, for your so-called *champion* is a disguised Spriggan, deceiving you. *I've seen his shadow.*'

The low sun cast two shadows across the ground: one long and robust, the other short, distorted, vague. Without warning, Finnian squirmed free; knocked aside, Rædwulf fell onto the Hall steps, flinging the knife from his hand; Thomas, on impulse and unmarked, picked it up.

The guards rushed forward, but Finnian, moving like quicksilver, ran towards the closed gate, leapt over it before the guards could intercept him, and ran screeching into the wilderness.

Clutching his bruised right side and muttering, 'That was close,' Rædwulf disregarded a young woman on the steps, smiling at him.

Penda helped him up and handing him the Sword, whispered, 'Rædwulf, he knows who we are, where we're from.'

Rædwulf ran a slow eye over the weapon. 'And that we have this.' Mounted guards rode through the now open gate at speed. Rædwulf watched them go and turned to the Lady.

'I very much doubt they will find him, madam,' he said. 'He'll secrete himself in the very landscape, free to plot his mischief.'

She smiled, beckoning to Thomas. 'We can also hide, and defend ourselves, my lord Blācencynn. Come to the Hall this evening when the sun rests on the western hills; you shall all sit in honour at my table, and we will welcome in the May tonight, King or no King.'

Thomas watched Rædwulf and Penda walk away. 'I cannot think,' he said, 'that I deserve such attention.'

Only he heard her reply. 'You helped Læren.'

'Did I?'

'False modesty, Thomas Learmont,' she said, 'does not become you.'

## Chapter Eight

# Bringing in the May

Appetising smells wafted from broth brimming in the cauldron, and the Hall glowed in the candle- and firelight. Læren and Raldis stood with other servants in the shadows; guests sat at the long tables, and Rædwulf, seated on the dais between Penda and the Lady, read every nuanced glance she and Thomas exchanged. A practised musician, Thomas borrowed a lute and played a few tunes, some merry, others lilting, but left the singing to others.

Læren, inexperienced and awkward, slopped ale while attending those seated at the high table, and somehow stumbling against Rædwulf, almost sat in his lap; some male elves applauded her, calling for entertainment. With a knowing twinkle in his eye, giving her a quiet half-smile and a teasing wink, Rædwulf said in a deep-toned whisper, 'Steady there, sweetness. Let's not rush things.' Mortified, she retreated.

Raldis and the maidens withdrew at midnight, while many elves went to the woods for further merriment; the Lady took Thomas to her bower, and Rædwulf and Penda retired to their own lodging. Shaken awake in the small hours, Rædwulf saw a servant leaning over him.

'Sire,' said the elf, 'follow me.'

'Now?' muttered Rædwulf, half asleep.

'Yes.'

Dressed only in his shirt and trousers, he followed the servant to an isolated building. 'In here if you please, sire,' said the elf, and walked away.

Bewildered, Rædwulf entered the house; it had a primitive, earthy smell mingled with perfume and the scent of beeswax from one wall-mounted candle. The woman who had smiled at him earlier lay on thick pelts covering a deep bed half the width of the house.

'Close the door if you're staying,' she whispered. 'There's an awful draught.'

He understood and closed the door, his slow gaze assessing her olive skin glowing in the flickering light, her long dark hair, the soft, revealing folds of her umber-coloured gown. Læren had evoked cornfields; this lady, dusk-bound pine forests and heather moorland. He took two paces to the bedside, the candlelight shining in his eyes, starlight of a thousand years in hers. She, now kneeling on the mattress, fingered the glittering amulet resting against his collarbone.

'A strange ornament,' she said. 'Does it mean anything?'

His modest, wry smile would have seemed sly on anyone else. 'You might call it a… clan emblem, something hard-earned, that I'll never part with; it owns me, much as I own it.'

Close enough to feel his body heat, she touched his beard. 'I haven't kissed a mortal man before.'

He brushed one gentle thumb across her mouth. 'And I've never kissed an elf woman.'

She surrendered—to his kiss, to his searching hands unfastening her robe—and they fell, clinched, skin against skin, rolling across the bed, wrapped in those luxuriant furs, his touch, his warmth, his strength enchanting her; and he knew it.

\*

Nothing disturbed the silent crypt or burning torches in the passageways, banners hung inert in the sleeping, night-bound Caves, and the Flame burned small. A subtle, snickering breeze crept along the tunnels, into every nook and crevice, into the Higher Hall; the crypt banner wafted in the draught, and the Flame wavered. Dogs began howling; horses, snorting, pulled at their halters.

A faint, resonating pulse thudded, stopped for a long time, then started again, and the breeze returned, stronger, gusting through the Caves; the banner in the crypt billowed, igniting in the closest torch, and the now constant wind fanned flames along every tunnel. Faint whispers became loud, wild laughter that shook the air; the pulse, now closer, more sustained, resonated throughout the caverns, and the ground trembled.

*

Rædwulf, watching the woman lying alongside him, tracing her face with one drowsy hand, whispered, 'Why, lady? Why allow me this?'

She, propping herself on one elbow, looked into his eyes and spoke, her voice soft as the dying candlelight. 'A reward for a noble deed, given with my Lady's blessing. For you revealed Finnian as an enemy, delivering us from his deceit, not to mention helping the maidens.'

He closed his eyes. 'I never even considered them.'

'You're weary,' she said, and kissed him. 'Sleep now, fair Blācencynn.'

With his arms wrapped around her, holding her close, he drifted to sleep.

\*

Stone fell from every wall. The High Priest ran to the shaking Higher Hall, where the platform lay smashed on the floor and the elder priests, reciting incantations, drew arcane sigils on the ground with the spear. He snatched it from them, faced the pillar, and called out, invoking its latent power to repel the assault coming from every quarter. The juddering column, fracturing six feet above its base, toppled onto the elder priests, killing them.

\*

Cold, the bed covers having fallen onto the floor, Rædwulf awoke at dawn, the sleeping woman lying nestled against him. He gave a quiet sigh, got out of bed, dressed, then, being Rædwulf, placed the pelts over her, kissed her forehead, and left without disturbing her. He crept into his lodging.

'I won't ask where you've been,' said Penda, his mischievous eyes glinting in the half-light.

Rædwulf glared at him. 'Shut up.'

Penda smiled his close-lipped smile, turned over, and fell asleep, but his dreams became troubling, fractured, and he awoke as the early light filtered into the house. Rædwulf lay snoring, and a cockerel crowed. The crystal ring cast shimmering hues across the room that melted away.

Penda saw it all: the burning crypt banner; fire running through the Caves; warriors fighting shadows, and dying; terrified people trying to escape. He saw the dumbstruck High Priest staring at the dead priests; he saw the churning lake, and he felt the ground shaking.

\*

First a trickle, then in torrents of screeching shadow, stone-hard beings came crawling from every crevice, invading, violating every space, both secular and sacred, taking survivors to deep dungeons from which no-one could escape.

They defaced the spiral; ransacked Rædwulf's chamber, burning his books and manuscript; smashed his treasure box and the jars; overpowered the Priest, taking his helmet. Lybbestre, standing alone before the Flame, did not move as they swarmed forward, shrieking, overcoming her, but she had her own blade hidden in her robes, and plunging it into herself, fell to the bottom step. Penda saw the blood that came; what they did to her afterwards; heard them chanting Soulis' name; and the Flame burned high. He tried calling, could make no sound, and tried again.

'*Rædwulf!*'

\*

It was all over. Bitter draughts blew ash along the tunnels. Light from the sky shafts revealed a devastated culture. Soulis toured the Caves, inspecting everything with sneering satisfaction: the shattered column in the Higher Hall, the obliterated wall frieze and floor runes; the river to the Flame choked with rubble, and the shattered crypt roof fallen on the gaping tombs. The Spriggans had burned every scroll, destroying wisdom garnered for generations; and still, the Flame burned high.

Nightmarish statues now stood sentinel around the council chamber, the walls almost covered with drab banners, all sized to some yards and an important four-fifths of an inch; thick furs and bear skins swathed a new, ostentatious chair. Enthroned, Soulis studied the Priest standing chained before him and spoke, his tone soft, unpleasant.

'How dilatory, to cower in a corner, allowing the destruction of your kin?' He gave a quiet, derisory laugh. 'I call you neither lord nor equal. Forgive my taking your title. Kneel, serf, for I am Lord Blācencynn, am I not?' The Priest making no reply, Soulis leaned forward, and lowering his voice further, repeated, *'Am I not?'*

Whipped, bleeding, held fast by Spriggans, yet still unbowed, the Priest spat at him.

Soulis did not retaliate for now; he stood up and circling him, looking him over, spoke again, his tone unchanged. 'Surrender the stolen weapon and horn, and I will spare you the fate awaiting your kindred.'

The Priest, struggling against his captors and chains, said nothing. Soulis signalled to the guards. 'Feed dog meat to the prisoners,' he said. 'If they refuse, offer them other meat. Should they find that unappetising, perform the ritual. The children first. As for this,' he added, sneering at the Priest, 'he shall hold a higher position than before. We shall take him to the temple. Follow me.'

The Spriggans dragged the Priest to the Higher Hall; the pillar base, converted into a huge vat, now stood over a burning furnace.

Soulis picked up the Spear, gazed at it for some moments, and faced the Priest. 'So, this is what you tried hiding from me, but what of the Horn? This is nigh useless without it, so legend says.'

The Priest snarled but otherwise said nothing. Soulis spat at him. 'The Earth lord who once dwelt here shall dwell here again, despite your silence.' He signed to his guards. 'You shall see what awaits those who defy me, and you will not close your eyes to it.'

The guards pushed the Priest to the floor, sewed his eyelids open, and shackled him high on the wall beside the entrance; they fixed an iron bar across his throat almost to strangulation point, yet still, the Priest remained silent.

Soulis swept from the Hall, saying, 'Keep it alive.'

\*

White-faced, the ruin of his kindred, as Penda had described it, unfolding before his mind's eye, Rædwulf stood stunned on the walkway by the flagpole, his fists clenched; his amulet gleamed in the sunlight, his hair and cloak blowing around him, the flag flapping back and forth in the breeze. Drawing the Sword and giving a long, anguished yell, he dealt the mast a violent blow, dislodging a small splinter; the pole barely shook.

He came to his senses, sheathed the Sword, walked to a bench, and sat, his hands clasped between his knees, his head bowed, ignoring people bustling past. Glimpsing a movement, he glanced up, saw Læren standing a few feet away, regarded her with utter hopelessness in his eyes, then hung his head again.

'Can I bring you anything, lord?' she asked. 'Something to eat or to drink?'

In silence, staring at his hands, he shook his head. She hesitated, wondering what else to say, until Penda approached, meeting her gaze with heavy eyes.

'Thank you, lady maiden, you may leave us,' he said and sat beside Rædwulf, who made no move. 'This isn't your fault, Rædwulf.'

Rædwulf sighed. 'There were signs, Penda, but I didn't see them.'

'Did anyone?'

Rædwulf replied with a bitter fury. 'How could this have happened, Penda? Happen, when I was—' He bit off the rest. 'How could it happen so fast? An ancient culture snuffed out in a single *night*? We should have stayed.'

'They would have killed us with everyone else, Rædwulf; the power would have passed to another.' Penda grasped Rædwulf's forearm. Lowering his voice, he said, 'Think who that might have been. We wouldn't have found the Sword if we'd stayed. We still stand, Rædwulf, still breathe, and can still fight, fight to avenge our kindred.'

Rædwulf stared at the ground. 'How? The elves won't fight for us.'

'Force won't defeat this,' said Penda, 'but the Flame and Sword can.' He paused, glanced at the ground, then met the heavy grey eyes again. 'You know I'm right.'

Rædwulf, looking at his feet, rubbed his forehead. 'We need to talk; not just you and I, but with the Lady and Thomas Learmont.'

Penda nodded. 'They're waiting for us in the Hall.'

'Alright.'

Dagan met them on the steps and led them into the Hall where Thomas stood, leaning against a table; the Lady, standing alone on the dais, gave a muted greeting.

'Circumstances have changed, my lords, and your plans must change with them.'

Penda sat down, but Rædwulf remained standing, arms folded. 'It's clear who Finnian is working for,' he said, 'and he'll tell Redcap everything.'

'It's no coincidence that the North Gate opened when the power was no longer there,' she said. 'Dark Faerie hides from we who dwell in the light, and we cannot know their intentions until Redcap makes his move.'

Penda stood up, walked to the wall, then back to his chair. 'He's already shown his hand.'

Rædwulf sat down. 'With respect, madam,' he said, 'and with all gratitude for your hospitality and kindness, we cannot stay here.'

'I agree,' she said. 'Neither can we wait for news; tomorrow, you must take the Sword and Horn somewhere neither Redcap nor Soulis knows of: Luc-Nan-Har.'

Rædwulf snorted. 'Finnian must know it, even if they don't.'

'Yes,' she said, 'but he cannot reach it. Faerie roads never lead to the same place twice.'

Dagan protested. 'Earth Wardens haunt Luc-Nan-Har, my Lady. No-one can enter it.'

'Not without good cause,' she said, 'but it offers sanctuary from evil. The Wardens will guard these men until Lord Mereburg claims the Horn. It's time we returned it.' Nodding towards Raldis and Læren now standing in the doorway, she beckoned them forward.

Læren hesitated at the dais, faced Rædwulf, and taking the bag from her belt, declared, 'Raldis says I must give you this.' Sharing an incredulous glance with Penda and Thomas, he stood up; Læren, glancing at Raldis, cut the bag open, revealing the Horn nested in the fleece. 'I'm *so* sorry,' she said, 'but I didn't even know you wanted it.'

He picked it up. 'We forged this and the Sword in the Flame,' he said and met her clear eyes. 'You have our thanks, lady maiden.'

'Will they come and kill us all?' she said, staring at the floor. 'Spriggans, I mean,' she added, turning to Raldis. 'What shall we do if they come?'

Thomas folded his arms. 'Well, I'd suggest you pick up your skirts, lady maiden, and run to the hills—as fast as you can go.'

'They don't scare me,' she said, 'and I won't run.'

This convinced nobody, and Thomas, his wink making her flush to her hair roots, smiled to himself as Raldis led her away.

'*Raldis.*'

Surprised, and telling Læren to leave, she turned. Rædwulf, holding the Horn, approached her.

'Finnian knew she had this, didn't he?' he said, his heated tone becoming more demanding with each word. 'That's why he followed her everywhere, isn't it? *Isn't it?*'

She met the steel glare, glanced at the Horn, and sighed. He took a breath to berate her, but Penda, now standing behind him, intervened.

'Dagan hid it, Rædwulf, as asked. The dame is not at fault, nor the maid.'

Rædwulf glimpsed Læren speaking to someone outside, her glimmering hair and radiance holding his softened gaze. She gave a merry, girlish laugh, and he turned back to Raldis, his eyes again of steel. 'Courage and inexperience make a potent mix, Raldis, that might lead the unwary into trouble.' Almost thrusting the Horn at Penda, he marched outside.

'You've bruised his pride, Raldis,' said Penda. 'Forgive his outburst.'

Raldis nodded, said, 'Sire,' curtseyed and walked away.

He faced the Lady. 'If Rædwulf has faults, it's a tendency to hold grudges; he can sulk for days, and it's hard reasoning with him when he's in this mood.'

Thomas hesitated, then said, 'I'll talk to him.'

He found Rædwulf standing on the walkway by the flagpole, stood beside him, and leaned his forearms on the parapet. 'Are you sure Penda didn't dream it all?'

Rædwulf, glowering at the hills, did not move. 'The power in him shows truth, Learmont. Have you disturbed me only to ask meaningless questions?'

Thomas glared at him. 'I'm here to support you.'

Rædwulf looked at him. 'Why?'

Thomas studied his hands. 'I've no choice if I'm to go home, but that's beside the point now. You need to avenge your kinfolk, and I need to help mine if Soulis has Ercildoun in his sights.' He leaned against the parapet again, this time watching the bustling elves in the enclosure, and said, his tone soft, measured, 'I don't wish these good people harm.'

Rædwulf faced him. 'Elves are devious, capricious, and self-serving.'

Thomas, watching Læren laughing and dancing with the maidens, shook his head. 'Not all of them, Rædwulf.'

Rædwulf, following his gaze, remained unconvinced. 'Don't let a pretty face cloud your judgement, Thomas. They are quite content to let others fight their battles while they sit here, oblivious to what could come on them, until it's breaking down the gate. The Lady believes this place secure, but Finnian will watch it, and us, sure as day. I warn you, Thomas: this task may test us beyond our endurance.'

Thomas fixed his unwavering gaze on him. 'I need no nursemaid, Rædwulf. Whatever perils you face, I will face too. If you fight, I'll fight with you. If you sleep under the stars, so will I. I'll ride all night… swim rivers if I must.'

Rædwulf raised an eyebrow. 'Bold claims, Thomas Learmont.' Studying, gauging him, he said, 'Are you afraid?'

Thomas glanced at the hills, met the steady gaze again, mumbled, 'It makes no difference,' and walked away.

*No*, thought Rædwulf, watching him walk down the steps. *No, it doesn't.*

\*

Despite torture, the Priest told Soulis nothing, but less brave captives told what little they knew of the power burning in the deepest cavern: conflicting, scant information Soulis thought he understood, and he demanded his Spriggans search the Caves for the Horn.

Faint, sustained murmurs surrounding him, he stood staring at the Flame, at the new flight of stairs leading to a new ledge and tunnel, twenty feet above the flint-black, unreflecting lake. He lifted the spear, his loud cry dying almost as he uttered it.

'I am Lord Blācencynn! Surrender the power none can withstand.'

The faint echoes faded, and the Flame burned small. He faced the lake, taking slow, deep breaths, sensing a subtle change in the air: a vague sensation of the cavern breathing. He raised the spear again, calling out, 'It is mine,' then returned to the Higher Hall and approached the altar, the candles burning around the stone basin full of Blācencynn blood. He turned towards the Priest with contempt.

'I find your allegiance to your kin touching and shall reward your loyalty.' He made to throw the spear but instead lowered it, the Priest's involuntary flinch amusing him. 'You shall watch me make my candles.'

Spriggans carried Harald in on a metal frame, positioning it over the sizzling vat. Naked, broken, dying, he could not even moan.

\*

## Borderlands

The first waxing crescent moon hung low in a starry sky, soft lamplight glimmered from every building in the silent, night-bound enclosure, and Rædwulf, his guilt and grief-ridden fury now an implacable ruthlessness, stood scanning the darkness beyond the palisade, the banner fluttering above him.

Raldis, holding a lantern, approached him, her voice softer than the night. 'What do you see out there?'

'Blackness,' he said. 'Do you know the Blācencynn call the full moon the Night Watchman? I wonder where I might be when He next keeps watch.'

'My lord, think of today, for it governs tomorrow.'

He sighed. 'You offer me comfort, Raldis, and I thank you, but I will find none until I have avenged my kindred.'

She retreated into the shadows, and he spoke to the night, his quiet voice cold as the night breeze that carried sounds of sheep and cattle from the hillside pastures. 'I am Rædwulf. I am Blācencynn. This curse I send upon the wind: I will find you, Soulis. I will find you. *And I will kill you.*'

## Chapter Nine

# The Hare

The Lady, standing with Raldis, Læren, Cynwæd and Dagan on the dais, looked in turn at Thomas, Rædwulf and Penda.

'My lords,' she said as though uncertain, 'you now leave for Luc-Nan-Har. We will loan you horses for the journey and Dagan will guide you, but neither he nor the horses may stay with you. Lord Rædwulf will carry the Sword; Thomas Learmont, you will carry the Horn and stand guard against pretenders. My lords Blācencynn, you shall sleep spellbound at Luc-Nan-Har until someone lifts, or sounds, the Horn, and you will either aid Lord Mereburg or drive out anyone who has not first lifted the blade.' Giving Thomas and Penda each a plain sword and scabbard, she said, 'These, made to defend you, may fail if used for another purpose or pitched against a force stronger than your courage or will. Remember this.'

Thomas glanced at Læren; she stood looking at the floor, fingering her silver enamelled cloak clasp, which bore a motif he had seen before, somewhere, and he frowned. The Lady led Dagan and the men outside where clouds and the cool breeze threatened rain. Her voice soft as the chilly velvet dawn, she said, 'Farewell, my lords. Go with Faerie blessings upon thee,' and returned to the Hall before they could acknowledge her.

They rode slowly in the whispering rain, passing red-eared faery livestock grazing the pastures; entered the forest where Thomas had met Cernunnos, following dim pathways between mossy trees and dripping leaves, the deep leaf mould silencing the horses' hoofs. There was no birdsong, no movement; no sign of anything watching in this green, moist twilight where earth and air smelt of damp. A steep, narrow animal track led them uphill to a wide glade; here, they dismounted and approached a narrow opening in a sheer rock face not twenty feet ahead. The forbidding, yet fascinating, darkness within gave Thomas a sudden longing for home, for the Court, for the wilderness—anything that might excuse him from the task ahead. Pride alone kept his mouth shut. 'Understand, gentleman,' said Rædwulf, inspecting the cave mouth, 'we'll either leave here alive with Lord Mereburg… or not at all.'

Dagan portioned out a few rations, saying, 'We should break our fast now,' but he allowed them only an hour. He lit two torches, gave one to Rædwulf, and led them into the cavern. The torchlight cast huge, sinister shadows, and whispering underground water echoed everywhere.

Sensing a trap, Penda whispered, 'There's menace here.'

Thomas nodded. 'Yes, it's everywhere.'

Dagan followed a low, narrow, winding tunnel, often stopping, choosing a way through hazardous rubble, until he came to a wide, unobstructed space; a steep, slippery stair beyond climbed into darkness.

Rædwulf hesitated and looked back. 'My skin crawls,' he said. 'Who knows what awaits us here?' He stepped forward to follow his companions and giving an involuntary cry, fell into a sudden fissure opening under him. Somehow, he grasped a rock with one outstretched hand but found no foothold. The burning torch dropped onto a ledge not a yard below him; tinder and debris piled there ignited, feeding high, eager flames. Nothing scared him more; he felt the heat through his shoes, smelt his cloak singeing; his fingers slipped on the rock, and he cried out again. Penda pulled him out by the wrists, and he scrambled away.

'The Earth Wardens keep watch at Luc-Nan-Har,' said Dagan.

'Then perhaps,' retorted Rædwulf, 'you should remind them they should guard, not kill, us.'

A steep incline beyond the stairs led into a huge cavern, ringed with pillars, a low plinth at its centre. Dagan led them a short distance along a side tunnel, stopping at a wall.

'This hidden door,' he said, 'opens either at midnight or by command.' He knocked seven times.

Bright daylight streamed in through a sudden gap, water from a nearby spring trickled across a narrow path winding down the hillside, and Thomas smiled, recognising the countryside beyond.

'Luc-Nan-Har,' he said. 'It's the Lucken Hare, the Eildon Hills—I'm home.'

They returned to the cave and stood around the plinth in silence, Penda often glancing over his shoulder, sensing unseen, hostile, watching eyes. Dagan wedged the torches in the walls, and with some reluctance, Rædwulf and Thomas laid the Sword and Horn on the plinth. Dagan held his hands over them.

'Lord Ercildoun shall guard thee and the secret gate,' he said. 'Thus I tell the Earth Wardens.' Then, commanding Rædwulf and Penda to sit against the wall, he touched them with his either hand, chanting, *'Here you will lie until called to slay, drive away, or obey.'*

They fell into an immediate deep sleep, Thomas looking at them in concern, and Dagan, proffering him a small, though weighty, bag, smiled.

'These Faerie gold coins, Thomas, give blessing, or curse, depending on the intentions of those you give them to, and also on yours, so have a care.'

Not unafraid, Thomas took the bag, glanced at Rædwulf and Penda, and nodded. 'I understand.'

'The Earth Wardens will guide, even control you,' said Dagan, 'although you won't see them. Walk abroad only by night, challenging anyone you meet to see the wonders of Luc-Nan-Har, but on no account cross the hill stream, for it protects you from Dark Faerie.'

Thomas saw, now clear in the torchlight, the acorns engraved on the Horn: the same pattern damasked in his shirt; the same design as Læren's cloak clasp. 'If Finnian has followed us,' he said, 'he'll tell Redcap; Spriggans will wait for us, won't they? They'll attack us the moment we leave.'

'My best advice,' said Dagan, placing one reassuring hand on Thomas' shoulder, 'is that you should follow Lord Adan and at first keep to the Faerie paths this side of the stream. Now, I must leave you, hoping for the best. Shall I give my Lady a message?'

'No.'

Dagan bowed and walked away, leaving Thomas watching the shadows dancing around the silent cavern, his gaunt face pale in the torchlight. The gate closed.

\*

Læren, a small, evidential bundle of spare clothes and food at her feet, stood between guards in the Hall, with Raldis on her right. The Lady, standing on the dais with her women, spoke.

'The guards found you outside the palisade after dark, Læren,' she said. 'Explain why you tried leaving Court during curfew.'

'To help those men,' said Læren.

'They left two days ago,' said the Lady. 'Leaving my Court now, Læren, risks not just yourself but them as well, and all Bright Faerie. You will return to the women's lodging and remain there under house arrest.'

## The Hare

Læren protested. 'House arrest? My Lady, Raldis, please: those men are just mortals; they don't know about Spriggans and might die if we don't help them!' but the guards led her away.

'Rædwulf Blācencynn hinted she might try this,' said Raldis. 'I fear neither vigilance nor lock will restrain her.'

\*

The lightweight helmet fitted Soulis, bestowing on him a certain cachet, but also unbounded hubris. Redcap answered his every summons, giving him all he wished for. Almost all, for although his Spriggans explored the Caves, searching every niche, they could not find the Horn; and the ambassador, his visits now almost routine, always arrived at dusk. Today, Soulis greeted him in the Higher Hall with contempt.

'Again, you honour us with your presence, Master Ambassador. Pray, tell us why you devote *such* attention to us.'

The ambassador gave an ambiguous smile. 'I am here to collect my payment.'

Soulis clenched his fists. 'We have no more grain, sir.'

'Then I suggest you pay with livestock; I must also remind my lord of his promise to deliver the weapon and horn.'

Almost smiling, Soulis presented the spear. 'We have a surprise for you, my estimable guest. You may take this mighty, though cumbersome, weapon to your master while we search for the Horn.'

The ambassador scorned him. 'This spear is mere ash wood, sire, unfit for lordship. No one suggested you would find either token here. You must find a sword.' He turned towards the tortured, half-conscious Priest. 'Does my lord imagine that Lord Blācencynn hangs here? Nay, Lord Soulis, I bring news: he escaped you with his brother and, with Thomas of Ercildoun, guards both Horn and Sword in a place only very few may enter.'

Soulis returned the disdain. 'One wonders how a simple servant knows this.'

'Bright Elves are creatures of habit,' said the ambassador, simpering. 'Know their practices, sire, and you will know their minds. My lord might retrieve the Sword and Horn, but only by mastering certain arts—unless he finds the task too daunting?'

Soulis shouted, exposing fear. 'We will do *nothing* unless you give your name, if you have one.'

The ambassador almost sneered. 'I am Finnian,' he said and came closer. 'Dealing with mortal scorn is one thing, enduring that of Dark Faerie quite another. Invading an undefended fortress is child's play. My lord risks losing everything if he breaks oath. You *will* obey.' He stepped back, beckoning with both hands. 'Come, lord, come.'

Like a reluctant dog pulled on a leash, Soulis followed.

## Chapter Ten

# The Lord and the Bowman

Soulis stood, spear in hand, mocking the tormented Priest hanging half alive on the cavern wall.

'You both amuse and disgust me, my little pet. Do not think I am witless. I need not waste my time, nor sully my hands, in searching for the Horn and Sword.' His mouth twisted. 'No, my friend, I have other plans, for weak-minded men are easy bought, men who will find them for me; and these pathetic Blācencynn, this Thomas Learmont, will fuel my candles.'

He stepped closer, this time speaking as though in conversation. 'I could kill you and cast this spear aside, but that would spoil my game. No, I shall keep my toy.'

He placed it beside the altar, lit the candles, drank from the bowl, pulled the hood over his eyes, and began the incantation:

'I keep my oath, Lord Redcap. I summon thee. My prisoner sacrifices his left eye, and you shall see with his sight.'

## Borderlands

Agonised screams reverberated around the caverns, a Spriggan placed the eye on the altar, and a low, distant throb became louder; the Caves trembled, shadows crept from the walls, the darkness lifted, the throbbing stopped, and Soulis took off his hood. The eye had gone.

\*

Mist drifting across the lake hid a remote, wooded island; secret paths led to concealed oak groves where the forest elves would dance, singing in the seasons. Basalt pillars—the Steps—formed natural towering battlements on the high summit, guarding a large, round Hall in a deep, green dell: the Mereburg.

A wide bay on the northern side of the island faced the nearest landfall almost a mile away. Many boats, little better than canoes, lay berthed there, and two elves patrolled the jetty, drowsy after the night watch. The tallest stretched and yawned.

'Time to change the watch,' he said. 'Stay here, Hirnac, until the relief arrives.'

Hirnac, shifting his weight from right foot to left, and leaning on his bow, scanned the surrounding woods.

'I'm uneasy, Gar. There hasn't been a breath of wind for days, and I'll swear I heard a horn.'

Gar unmoored a boat and faced him, rope in hand. 'That was hours ago. It didn't answer our challenge, nor come any nearer. I say it was swans.'

'I'm not convinced.'

Gar leaned on the oars. 'Report it then, if you're so concerned.'

'Would they listen?'

Gar gave a dismissive shrug, and Hirnac, watching him rowing away into the mist, listened to the whistling waterfowl hidden in the reeds. The dawn became a strange twilight, the ground juddered, all the waterfowl around the lake took flight, abandoning their nests, and glinting weapons approached from the deep forest shadows.

He leapt into a boat, threw the mooring rope aside, and rowed fast to a secret inlet on the far side of the island, a weird, smothering pulse keeping time with his every stroke. Already hearing battle cries, he jumped ashore, climbed between pillars and buttresses to the island summit, and walked into chaos.

Hirnac leapt forward through shadows rushing upon him from all sides, fighting things he could not see until, with elves dying around him, his every arrow shot, he retreated to the Hall and found everything within overturned. Gar lay dead near the door, and battle sounds filtered through the walls. Adan, Lord Mereburg, his sword drawn, stood with his few guards by stairs leading underground; gesturing towards Gar, he shouted to Hirnac, 'Take his arrows, Bowman, and stand with me.'

Hirnac flinched but obeyed, and facing the open door, watched the looming shadows. Adan pushed his unruly black hair from his face. 'Where are they coming from?'

'Everywhere, sire,' said Hirnac. 'From the forest, the rocks around the dell; from the very ground.'

Burning arrows set the roof alight; Adan leapt forward through falling, burning thatch and smoke, yelling, 'Defend the Gate! Defend the Gate!'

Hirnac followed, arrow nocked; the incessant pulse shook the ground, tearing the Hall apart. Burning timbers trapped the guards by the stairwell, and Adan dragged Hirnac outside; elves lay headless or dismembered, the light from the blazing Hall showing everything in awful detail. Darkness came from opening voids in the shaking ground, formless shadows came from everywhere, and everywhere smelt of death. Adan stood, sword raised, battle-ready, his foes ephemeral as smoke.

'It's hopeless, sire,' said Hirnac. 'We're the only ones left and must escape before it's too late.'

'Where to, Bowman?' said Adan. 'I will not abandon the Gate. I will avenge my people or die in the attempt.'

'Sire, we've lost the Mereburg. Please, my lord, we can take refuge at the Seelie Court.'

They fled, slipping on gore, trampling over corpses, evading long arms reaching for them from the dark, and climbed to the dell rim. Half-blinded with leaf litter whipped up in a sudden gale, almost deafened by piercing shrieks and the thudding pulse, the Steps falling around them, they scrambled down to the boat in almost total darkness.

Adan sat rigid in the stern, staring at an immense red plume rising above the burning Mereburg, while Hirnac rowed hard across the roiling lake, through floating rafts of reeds; reaching the mainland, he beached the boat near the jetty.

They groped their way through unrelieved darkness for two days, but the familiar paths had gone. At last, lost and exhausted, they rested in a small hollow, not daring to light a fire or sleep. Burdened with grief, Adan scanned the silent forest stretching for miles ahead of him; the Mereburg, miles behind, lay hidden behind a ridge in the cloudy dawn. Hirnac shook his head.

'What did we do wrong?'

Adan sighed. 'We did nothing wrong.'

'Sire, if the Gate opens…'

'Then Bright Faerie will fall.' Adan frowned. 'I thought I knew this forest—every leaf and grass blade—but I don't trust the paths anymore. They may lead us back to the lake, or into traps, but neither can we stay here. You're right; we should go to the Seelie Court.'

A slow, cool breeze brought hints of daylight, smells of blossom and greenery, and Hirnac glimpsed a subtle movement amongst the trees, a mere impression amongst the leafy undergrowth of someone stepping from the shadows, a figure resolving into a short, sturdy man, clothed in green, leaning on a longbow. His briary beard and hair almost hid his weathered, oak-brown face, and deep creases showed around his bright hazel eyes. He studied Adan and Hirnac, moving his slow gaze from one to the other: Adan, small for a grown male elf, but strong, with wild, shoulder-length black hair and darting eyes dark as twilight; Hirnac, tall, lithe, bright-haired, with sky-blue eyes.

## The Lord and the Bowman

Adan and Hirnac stood up and bowed. 'My lord Forest Father,' said Adan.

'A good morning, my lord Adan and Hirnac Strawfax,' the man replied, giving a slight nod. 'I bring news, though we cannot speak here. Come.'

He led them along a shady green path to a small hut, pulled aside a green curtain hanging across the doorway, and ushered them inside where a steaming bowl hung over the burning oak fire. There were four stools beside it and a heavy oak chest against one wall. Daylight coming through the opposite window hinted at leaves, sunshine, and green shade. The man gestured at the bowl.

'Break your fast with me, my friends,' he said, and beckoned when they hesitated. 'Come, you're safe here—for now.'

He handed them bowls of broth, and they ate with him. 'You said you have news,' said Adan.

The Father held out a parchment scroll. 'Indeed. Seek Thomas Learmont, and wind the Mereburg Horn at Luc-Nan-Har.'

Adan, glancing at Hirnac, took the letter, noted the Seelie Court seal, opened it and read it twice to himself:

*'Adan, Lord Mereburg. The High Lady sends greetings. Soulis of Hermitage Castle and Robin Redcap*

*have taken the Blācencynn Caves and now move against you. Meet Lord Thomas Learmont of Ercildoun at Luc-Nan-Har, raise the Sword, and wind the Horn before Soulis and Redcap lay to waste the Mortal and Faerie Realms, but beware: raise the Sword first.'*

'Who delivered this?' he said, glaring at the Forest Father, who replied without rancour.

'A Seelie Court messenger named Cynwæd. He couldn't wait, fearing an attack there.'

Adan passed the letter to Hirnac, stood up, walked across the room, and stood facing the wall.

'Why were we never warned?' He turned his angry gaze on the man. 'Why did no one tell us?'

'Messages can go astray,' he said. 'I received this two evenings since, when it was already too late to send you a warning, and hid the forest paths, hoping to protect the Mereburg.'

'The Blācencynn,' said Hirnac, staring at the document, 'It's said they forged the Sword and Horn in the Flame, imbuing both with unparalleled power.'

'The Horn is a weapon,' said the Forest Father, 'that only Lord Mereburg may wield, but anyone can claim that rank.'

Adan, frowning, returned to the hearth and stared at him. 'What do you know of Soulis?'

'I perceive his mind,' said the Father. 'He can conjure every horror you can imagine, and Redcap controls him. It was Redcap, not Soulis, who attacked you.' He sat, arms folded, eyes closed. 'I saw them, cloaked in darkness: Spriggans and elementals, nightmares that haunt living things, bringing you confusion and despair.'

Adan frowned. 'Who is Thomas Learmont? Do you also see into his mind?'

'I know he is a mortal man, and I sense turmoil he is yet unaware of.'

Adan considered this. 'We know little of mortals,' he said, 'though it's said they are vain and unreliable. What do you think he'll do next?'

'Learmont?'

Adan nodded.

'That's up to you. Like it or not, you must cross the divide to the Mortal realm.'

'Luc-Nan-Har,' said Hirnac. 'I've heard it's the safest place in all Bright Faerie.'

Adan sighed, took the parchment from Hirnac, and stared at it. 'There are no direct roads from here,' he said, 'hidden or otherwise; seems we have a long walk ahead.'

The Father stood up and went to the chest. 'You are a Wayfinder, Lord Adan,' he said, opening it. 'I have rations for you, and better weapons and horses. Burn the letter in the fire before you leave.'

He gave them supplies and re-armed them: Hirnac with bow and arrows, Adan with both blade and bow. He led them outside, watched them mount their waiting horses, and pointed towards a tortuous path winding downhill between brambles and fireweed.

'Soulis will move soon,' he said. 'Remember: if you reach Luc-Nan-Har, you must raise the Sword first, or die. Afterwards, seek further help and instruction from my agent in the forest, then… you must trust your own judgement. I know you're weary, but you must go fast, in secret, and beware all you see. Redcap reads the wind, they say.'

They bowed and rode away, scattering dew and petals behind them.

## Chapter Eleven

# Black Chore Hugh

Flies and sweaty, mucky odours filled the crowded marketplace; the ground was trampled to a quagmire, and people jostled, arguing amongst themselves, most disputes coming from a horse fair separated from the market by straw bales. A young, weedy individual, desperate to sell his only horse before business closed, ran the creature up and down until it showed signs of collapse; a middle-aged farmer called out, unimpressed, 'Hoy, Hugh. Give the donkey a rest before you kill it.'

Red-faced and irritable, his thick, dark hair falling across his freckled face, and making furious, futile attempts to ward off the flies, Hugh turned on the laughing crowd.

'There's none better at the fair. Fine lords would pay a handsome price for it.'

'If only for the stews,' said the farmer, giving a sarcastic grin. 'What did you pay for him, Black Chore?'

'I had nae coin, so traded a pony.'

The man laughed again. 'Duped by your own trick, were you?'

Angry, dishevelled, the horse butting at his shoulder, Hugh shouted at the dispersing crowd. 'You know what's coming if you belittle me. One day, you'll find all your livestock and treasures gone and your hay barns all on fire. You won't laugh so easy then.' He lashed out at the still-butting horse. 'Leave it out, can't ye?'

Left alone, he led it to his lodging, meeting the hefty, peevish landlord in the yard.

'You haven't paid your bill, sir.'

Hugh steadied himself. 'I told ye I'd pay once I had coin—or you can take the horse instead.'

The landlord, folding his arms, spat into the mud. 'Now you insult me. If I'm not paid by nightfall, I'll haul you before the Sheriff.'

'And I'm sure he'd like to know about all the stolen goods you've handled.' His voice became snickering breath. 'Go ahead, bring me before the Sheriff—*I dare ye.*'

An old man, steadying himself on a heavy staff, approached them and spoke in an affable, modulated tone. 'Gentlemen, please don't bicker. God knows there's enough anger in the world, and I've seen what it leads to. I'm happy sharing what little I have. If you agree, I will pay for your lodging, sir, if you've nowhere else to stay, and a meal, and buy the horse for three silver pennies. What do you say?'

Hugh, knowing this far exceeded the horse's worth, and wondering what else he could con the old man out of, gave an eager nod. 'A fair price, sir.'

The old man fixed his enquiring gaze on the landlord. 'And you?'

The man spat again. 'I don't care, as long as I'm paid.'

Hugh pocketed the coins and followed the ragged old man into the smoky ale room. He sat opposite him in an isolated corner, thumped the table, calling, 'Landlord, some ale!' and studied his companion: the long, white, tangled hair and thin, pale, lined face; the dull, dark, hypnotic eyes. 'You've not been here before, I'll wager,' said Hugh, leaning in. 'I warn ye, don't trust anyone here. They'll steal your coin purse and the clothes from your back, however ragged they may be.' He drank, wiped his mouth, and spoke as though sharing secrets. 'Who are you?'

The old man drank and placed his mug on the table with meticulous care. 'Forgive me, I should have said: my name is Robert. I suspect you've had little or no luck today.'

Hugh paused, the tankard halfway to his mouth. 'Nah. They humiliate me, saying I sell sick horses.'

Robert sat stone-still for a while, thinking. 'I've three sturdy horses I might have sold today, had I arrived in time; I understand there's a horse fair some miles north of here, but I cannot travel that far. Could you sell them?' He saw the doubt and leaned forward. 'There's no outlay. All I ask in return is a share in the profit.'

'Aye, I can do that. Where is this horse fair?'

'Near the Eildon Hills, and you may meet someone there who stole my only property, leaving me destitute.'

'What property?'

'A horn and sword, heirlooms of my noble house.' Robert sat back, shaking his head. 'I am frail, unable to challenge him, unable to reclaim them.'

Hugh, seeing he could turn this opportunity to his advantage, replied, his tone again secretive. 'Maybe I can help you? I'm strong and can overpower him, whoever he is.'

Robert stared at his long hands. 'Lord Ercildoun,' he said, and sighed. 'Or so he calls himself. He guards them with his life. Return these things to me and earn reward beyond price, enough to avenge your tormentors.'

## Black Chore Hugh

Hugh stared at him over his mug. 'Eh?'

'You are a struggling horse thief, selling horses at inflated prices to those you first stole them from. Is this not so?'

Alarmed, Hugh whispered, 'Keep your voice down.'

Again, Robert leaned forward, whispering. 'This is your chance, friend, to become Lord of Eildon.'

Hugh stared, open-mouthed, then said, 'You'd give *me* that chance?'

'It's yours for the taking. What do you say?'

'Landlord!' shouted Hugh. 'More ale! And some for my friend here.' He lifted his full mug, toasting Robert's good health. 'I'd burn them all out, the farmers and tenants who laugh at me, who think I'm too dull and daft to remember my own name.'

Robert, his cold, flat eyes looking left and right, whispered again. 'Secrecy is paramount, friend. Others may challenge you should they hear of this. You need to start soon.'

'Half an hour? Dusk comes late, and I can travel a good way before nightfall.' Hugh frowned. 'Ah, but I'll need rations, and fodder.'

'Oh, I will supply them, a little bonus, part of the bargain. In half an hour, then.'

Robert kept his word. 'Where shall I meet you, friend?' said Hugh, tying the provisions onto a horse.

'Here, and I will help you avenge your humiliation.'

The contract sealed with a handshake, Hugh led the horses through the town gates into the evening sunshine. Robert watched him go, stepped into the shadows, and whispered to the two figures hiding there.

'Watch his every move; bring Learmont, the Blācencynn, and this… *boy*, to me alive; and you may dispose of the decrepit beastie he sold me.'

One figure bowed. 'Yes, Lord Soulis.'

\*

Hugh halted at dusk. Clouds threatened rain, the breeze whistled through heather and scrub, the horses dozed, and owls gave sombre calls. He did not sleep well, so he set off before dawn, riding north, following a narrow, meandering track. When he approached a hillside croft, he left the horses at a trough full of water rippling in the rain and scanned the cottage. It seemed deserted, but smoke seeped through the thatch; there was firewood stacked near the door, and someone called from within before he touched the latch.

'Come in, and shelter from the rain.'

Hesitant, unnerved, he entered a small, bare room; stew bubbled in a pot suspended over the burning fire. An old woman, wearing a coarse linen gown, her grey hair plaited over each shoulder, sat by the hearth, eyes closed, rocking herself back and forth with each slow breath. She held an open book in her lap, the pages covered with strange symbols and ciphers, and without opening her eyes, she pointed to the pot.

'Help yourself if you're hungry.' Then, sensing his hesitation, she took a long, deliberate breath. *'You're afraid.'* It was a slow, penetrating statement. 'Watchers hide in the shadows,' she said. 'You interest them.' She stopped rocking. 'You smell of horses. Work with them, do you?'

'Yes,' he said, licking gravy from his fingers.

'Dealer, yes?'

He sat down, staring at her, believing she could sense more blind than he could see with open eyes. 'How do you know?'

She did not explain this. 'You are far from the nearest horse fair. This road leads only to the Eildon Hills.'

'I, I didn't know.'

'Yes, you did.'

Hugh finished his meal in silence and, looking around for anything worth stealing, snaffled a metal spoon hanging from the trivet.

Her insidious words crawled into the very fibre of his soul. 'I see a tall man guarding great treasures. These things fill your mind.'

Trembling, putting down his plate, he tried to sound scornful but could not hide his tension. 'I don't care about such things.'

She gave a sharp, sensing intake of breath. 'You do because you desire all they might give, yet the guardian stands in your way. Would you kill him? Would you dare?' She opened her amber eyes, her penetrating, indefinable glance shredding his nerves. '*We gave him voice when he was mute,*' she chanted, '*sight, when he was blind, life when he was dead.*' Falling silent, she began rocking again.

He stood up, knocking his chair against implements stacked behind it, fumbled for the latch, and ran outside, her voice at his heels.

'The shadows have eyes, Black Chore Hugh, and the night is sentinel. Beware Luc-Nan-Har.'

\*

Hirnac looked towards the Eildon Hills standing like huge sentinels challenging the very sky, their dark shadows stretching across the land.

'Well, sire, there they are,' he said.

Adan, shading his eyes against the sunset, stared at them, knowing that, somewhere within, Thomas Learmont guarded the Sword and Horn. 'We've done well, Hirnac, but our rations are almost gone. Is anything watching us?'

Hirnac looked around. 'I see nothing, lord, but my skin creeps. Maybe it's the Hills.'

Adan nodded. 'Shall we rest here for a while?'

'As you like, sire.'

For two hours they watched in shifts, surveying the silent meadows, hearing only occasional owl calls, and broke camp at moonrise. The track led them away from the Hills, across land hazardous with deep, swampy folds, impossible to navigate at night, and branching paths led nowhere. The horses snorted, sensing menace in the wind, and Adan halted at a road leading to a market town a mile away.

'We're weary,' he said, 'but can't rest here. If we're careful, we might bypass that place unnoticed, camp somewhere, and find another path come daylight.'

## Borderlands

They rode in slow silence, staying on the grassy verge and keeping a watchful eye on the torches burning on the town walls; surprised that the gate stood open after dark, they glimpsed deep, unnerving shadows along the cobbled streets beyond.

Men, shouting, scuffling, carrying torches, surrounded them and wrenched them to the ground. Adan lay winded, disoriented, and a man leaned over him, holding his torch almost close enough to singe. He yelled to his comrades.

'Look! The old man was right! An elf! Elves are plotting treason. Disarm and bind them.'

The men obeyed, and tying them with tough leather thongs, drove them like cattle through the streets to the town jail.

'They can stay in here,' said the leader, producing a bunch of keys, 'until the Sheriff sees them next week.'

He pushed Adan and Hirnac into a small room, all flagstones and draughts, marched them down steep stone steps and along a foul-smelling corridor, unlocked a tiny door to a cramped, windowless cell, and shoved them to the floor. He untied them, crouched over Adan, spat at him, placed his knife against him, and snarled.

'No elf tricks, see? The King himself will see you once he learns of your treason. We reinforced this door with iron—everyone knows elves fear it—and shouting won't help, my treacherous little friend, because no one will hear you. There's no way out.' He withdrew, locking the door, leaving Adan and Hirnac in absolute darkness; they heard his voice receding along the corridor.

'It's well I kept watch, though I expected them sooner. We'll send for the Sheriff first thing in the morning.'

Adan pushed the door, but recoiled, clutching his scorched hand, and sat bemused on the filthy floor. 'What now, Hirnac?'

'We can't blame these folk, sire,' said Hirnac.

Adan spoke through his teeth. 'No; someone's misled them, and I'd wager it was Soulis, but that doesn't help us. How can we escape?'

Hirnac tried optimism. 'We may have some light, come dawn.'

'Much good it will do us, Hirnac. Fever must be rife in this cesspit.'

Hirnac's voice came, a hissing whisper. 'Listen, sire.'

A faint, insistent pulsing underpinned all sounds in the dungeons, and Adan spoke in despair. 'They're coming, Hirnac, they're coming, and we can only watch.'

CHAPTER TWELVE

# Luc-Nan-Har

Hugh had seen the Eildon Hills a thousand times before, scornful of local tales of hollow hills and Faerie rades, but now he stood in awe, gazing at them a mile away, their gigantic shadows stretching towards him. Weary, dispirited, with chin on chest, he was hurrying to reach shelter before dark. He led the horses across a stream and sensed ever-wakeful, malicious, watching eyes, but he saw nothing through the cold, damp mist, its ghostly shreds wafting over the land in the fast-fading light.

'Who approaches Luc-Nan-Har?'

A tall, cowled, shadowy figure, taking slow, deliberate steps, advanced from the dark, then stood, as though watching. 'I am the guardian of Luc-Nan-Har. State your purpose.'

Hugh, his bravado evaporating, stopped, swallowed hard, and gabbled, 'Hae ye nae mind tae buy my horses?'

Thomas looked them over. 'Fair enough,' he said. 'I'll take these,' and gave him four gold coins. Plenty, thought Hugh, to last him several indolent lifetimes, yet he lusted for more.

'These beasts are worth more than pennies,' he said, pocketing the coins anyway.

Thomas gave a soft, unnerving laugh. 'If this isn't enough, then come; you will see things worth more than gold.' Without waiting for a response, he led the horses away.

Hugh gave an unpleasant smile. He envisioned mounds of precious gems; dismissed the cottage witch as a passing childish night-terror. Excited, legs shaking, heart racing, he followed Thomas uphill.

Thomas stopped at the cave mouth and faced him. 'Who follows you?'

Hugh, glimpsing the beard and glinting eyes beneath the cowl, stuttered, 'No one has followed me.'

'Yet I sense things waiting in the night shadows.'

In alarm, Hugh glanced back, saw only mist and moonlight, and repeated, 'No one has followed me, master guardian, I swear.'

Thomas said nothing for half a minute, his silence instilling fear. Then he entered the cave and, leaving the horses aside, led Hugh into the heart of Luc-Nan-Har. There were no gems, gold or silver. Torchlight painted unearthly hues on the walls; creeping shadows flitted between gaps and across the empty cave.

'What's this trickery?' said Hugh. 'You said there was treasure here.'

'I said no such thing,' said Thomas. He stood behind the plinth and threw back his hood; fixing a slow, threatening stare on Hugh, he gestured at the Horn and Sword with either hand. 'Choose well.'

Hugh stared at them: the Sword, to his eyes, plain, uninspiring, the Horn gleaming, gem-encrusted silver. At last recognising who this guardian was, he sniggered.

'Guardian of Luc-Nan-Har? You guard nothing, Lord Ercildoun, for I take your earldom.' He picked up the Horn, but before he could wind it, a sudden, still silence enveloped everything.

Hugh felt a blade placed against his shoulder, and Thomas made no move; then Hugh turned around. Rædwulf and Penda stood watching him with cold eyes, Penda with his sword levelled, Rædwulf needing no weapon to intimidate. Hugh dropped the Horn, fumbled for the Sword, and tried dealing Penda a blow but cried out in pain, his right arm bleeding. Rædwulf wrenched the weapon from him and, holding it slack in one hand, glowered.

'The blade you had no right touching wounds you.'

A dull rumble from the already closing gate echoed through the cave, and Thomas spoke, his voice menacing. 'You cannot cheat Faerie.'

Dumbfounded, terrified, Hugh fled, the gate closing almost on his heels. He ran to the foot of Luc-Nan-Har, where he stopped, breathless in the dark. Something snaked around his legs, and swarming chimeric forms his worst nightmares could not have conjured grabbed him. With Luc-Nan-Har closed to them, and finding only pebbles and withered leaves in his coin purse, they hauled him away, his frantic struggling no match for their strength, his stifled cries of terror unheard.

*

Seated by the cell door, Hirnac sighed, shaking his head. 'We can't just sit here, my lord... Perhaps we could send the Seelie Court a message.'

Adan buried his face in his hands. 'How? We've neither means nor time.'

Hirnac fumbled for a bowl of water. 'Drink this, sire.'

Adan sipped, spat, and coughed. 'It's foul.'

A profound silence crept through the prison. 'It's so quiet,' Hirnac whispered. 'I can't hear anything at all outside.'

Soft, slight footfalls stopped outside the door, and a distorted voice, quiet as a breeze, said, 'Is Adan there?'

Surprised, he crawled to Hirnac's side. 'Yes.'

Hirnac struggled to hear the reply. 'Listen, my lord, Soulis has caused much mischief, disguising himself as an old man, and might have already taken the Horn and Sword were it not for Thomas Learmont. Now you must find them, Lord Adan. Make haste, but take care, for Luc-Nan-Har has taken its first victim; ensure you are not the next.'

Adan whispered through the lock. 'Who are you?'

'Perhaps you will find out another time. All the guards are asleep, but they'll wake soon. You will find your weapons here, outside the door, and your horses tethered behind the jail.'

Slow and silent, the door swung open. Adan and Hirnac crept into the deserted passage, the torchlight almost dazzling them; they found their weapons and ran.

They rode through the open gate at speed, following the road until moonset when Adan drew rein, stood up in his stirrups, surveying the night, and pointed to a pale, branching track.

'There's a path,' he said, 'beyond that stream. I've almost forgotten what fresh water tastes like.'

Hirnac glanced at him. 'We'll have time enough for drinking, sire, once we've found the Horn.'

Adan nodded, giving a self-effacing smile. 'Point taken, but I hope this Thomas Learmont, this Lord Ercildoun, or whatever he calls himself, can offer us some food, or we might as well give up now; but we could eat the heather, I suppose.'

They crossed the little stream and followed a faint path through tussocks, shrubs and a surrounding, implacable silence. A sudden breeze whistled through the heather, and a tall, cloaked, hooded man approached from the dark.

'Who rides by the hill of Luc-Nan-Har?'

Adan and Hirnac drew rein. *So*, thought Adan, *this is Thomas Learmont.* Undaunted, unmoved, he dismounted.

'I am Adan, Lord Mereburg, and I believe you keep something for me.'

Thomas beckoned him. 'Come with me; but your servant must stay here.'

Adan hesitated, then nodded. 'Very well.'

Thomas stopped at the cave mouth and faced Adan. 'You may still refuse.'

Adan bristled. 'It's taken me days finding you, Lord Ercildoun, and not without misfortune; I've no intention of leaving now.'

Thomas nodded, then led him to the inner chamber. Macabre, watchful shadows shivered across the cavern walls, and Adan, glimpsing the tethered horses and the sleeping Blācencynn, studied Thomas, who stood behind the plinth, his hood drawn back: the long tawny hair, pale, bearded face, straight brows and piercing eyes.

'I've heard,' said Adan, 'that Luc-Nan-Har has claimed its first victim—y*our* victim?'

A brief, vivid vision of the luckless horse thief flashing before him, Thomas said, 'He wasn't here by mere coincidence. Someone sent him, and had I allowed him his chance, we would now be dead.' He gestured to the plinth. 'The Horn and Sword: choose, Lord Mereburg.'

Adan, glancing from Rædwulf and Penda to Thomas, who continued staring into space, lifted the blade, its crystal glimmering with an inner fire. Then, picking up the Horn, he blew a resounding call, the echoes lasting many minutes before fading. He turned towards a slight sound behind him and saw Rædwulf and Penda, standing as only warriors can, Penda presenting him his sword hilt. Rædwulf, his wild hair gleaming in the torchlight, stepped forward.

'We are Blācencynn, my lord,' he said, 'and have much to avenge.'

Adan, turning the Horn over in his hands, studying the engravings, sighed. 'We have everything to avenge. If you are indeed Blācencynn, then I could not hope for better allies. Soulis and Redcap have overthrown the Caves… the Mereburg… and now set their sights on the Seelie Court. How can we stop them?'

'We have more hope than you think,' said Rædwulf. 'Their victory may be brief.'

The Sword and Horn glimmering in his hands, Adan said, 'These aren't iron?'

Rædwulf shook his head. 'No, the Blācencynn call it *Eversteel.* Indestructible once made, it's a forging process long forgotten.'

'Then it seems fitting,' said Adan, 'that you wield the Sword.'

'We must decide our next move,' said Penda, sheathing his blade. 'Come, my friends, we shall leave Luc-Nan-Har to her shadows.'

# Luc-Nan-Har

\*

Hallucinations haunted Soulis, almost to paranoia: shadowy, slinking beasts followed him everywhere. Once, he awoke to find an immense grey wolf with fiery eyes crouching over him. He sat up, giving a terrified yell, and it disappeared.

Comfortable at first, the helmet gave him headaches and became difficult to remove; he tried destroying it, but it proved impervious to either hammer or fire. Unable to bear the agony any longer, he threw it into the lake, and its effects ceased.

He now felt invincible; he had gold and gems, young women to satisfy his lusts, the finest food, and prisoners, but resenting his constant supplications to Redcap, he now stood bare-headed, spear in hand, the burning altar candles casting his vast shadow onto the wall and floor behind him. His powerful voice resonated throughout the caverns.

'I command the greatest power on this earth. I no longer need thee, Robin Redcap. I dismiss thee.'

## Chapter Thirteen

# Business

A cockerel crowed from a hidden yard, and the smell of peat smoke lay heavy in the mid-morning air. Thomas led the three horses along the muddy cobbled street, strewn with straw and detritus. He weaved between passing carts, chattering crowds and market stalls, avoiding beggars and playful children, and stopped at a saddlery near the town centre. Having tethered the horses outside, he drew his hood back and leaned against the doorjamb, looking in.

Wood shavings, sawdust and off cuts covered the floor, heady scents of wood, leather and oil filled the workshop, a youth sat leather working at the back, and a small man, surrounded by various tools, sat at a workbench sanding a piece of linden wood. He glanced towards the door, paused, looking Thomas over in astonishment, and stood up, gawping.

'Well, look what the cat dragged in! If it isn't Thomas Learmont.'

Thomas studied the curly fair hair, grey eyes, freckled face and wispy beard, folded his arms, and smiled. 'And a good morning to you, Matthew McMartin.'

'What the devil are you doing here?'

'I need saddles and bridles for three horses.'

'*Three?*'

Thomas nodded. 'By nightfall today.'

'By *when?*'

'Nightfall,' repeated Thomas, unruffled. 'One for myself, one for a man about my height and weight, and one for another less tall, of more slender build.'

Matthew scuttled around the bench. 'Are you mad? I can't just conjure them from thin air.'

'Well, you'll have to conjure them from somewhere.'

'It's not that simple, Learmont; any saddle needs to fit the horse. Making *one* takes days—be reasonable.'

Thomas nodded towards two saddles stacked, ready for collection. 'What about those?'

'You can't take *them*,' said Matthew, wiping his hands on his apron. 'They're for the bailiff and his official—for collection in a few days, and before you ask, they're not in town now.'

Thomas glanced at him. 'My need is greater than theirs.'

Business

Matthew mopped his forehead. 'I've only one more, but it's for a woman and won't serve you. I'm happy to make any saddle you need, given time.'

Thomas raised his brows. 'I don't *have* time.'

Matthew shook his head. 'Your patience hasn't improved, Learmont.'

Thomas glanced towards the apprentice. 'Is he any good?'

Matthew, folding his arms, drew himself up to his full five feet four. '"He,"' he said, 'is my son, and he's coming on very well.'

'I didn't recognise him. Alright, he can make the bridles. While you're about it, I need rations: food and blankets for five men and fodder for five horses, to last about a week.'

Matthew snorted. 'You don't want a lot, do you? I can't imagine what the bailiff will do when he finds his commission missing—throw me in the lockup, like as not, and we can't manage without income.'

Thomas remained unmoved. 'I'll pay you well. If you need me, I'll be either at the inn or somewhere else in town.'

Matthew could not disguise his disapproval. 'I can guess what for. I'd bet everyone already knows you're here, beard or no beard; there's no one in the town taller. You've some nerve coming here, with everything going on. Stay away from the inn.'

Thomas glared at him. 'Good God, Matthew, you sound like my mother.' He leaned on the doorjamb again, watching the street, and swallowed his annoyance. 'So,' he said, 'what *is* going on?'

Matthew glanced at his son, making sure he could not overhear. 'An old man visited the town a fortnight ago.' He looked at the floor, shaking his head. 'He was a bad one, if I'm any judge; people have been looking for you ever since, and I doubt they mean well.'

Thomas faced him. 'What people?'

'The town jailer and his cronies.'

Thomas snorted. 'Tell me his mother didn't mate with a gargoyle.'

Matthew sighed. 'Look, I know there's no love lost between you two, but even you can't fight them single-handed.'

'That… *cur*,' said Thomas, pointing towards the door, 'might have disinherited me by forging my father's signature on a false deed.'

'Still rankles, eh?'

Business

Thomas glared at him. 'Nothing would give me greater pleasure, my dear Matthew, than to clamp that *charlatan* in his own stocks, or watch him rot in his own cell.'

Matthew tried reasoning with him. 'Listen, you'll just draw unwelcome attention if you go anywhere near the inn, let alone anywhere else in this town; I've heard the jailer locked up two nefarious-looking men, but they escaped.'

Thomas drew him aside, speaking into his ear. 'It may surprise you, McMartin, that I know those so-called "nefarious-looking men", and that I'm both big and ugly enough to defend myself.'

Matthew shook his head. 'How on earth did we become friends?'

'Because I stopped a snivelling low-life from robbing your wife when you were bedridden with fever, if you remember.'

Matthew glanced at him. 'We're not ungrateful.'

Thomas persisted, entreating him. 'So now I'm calling in the debt. Come on, McMartin, you owe me. Have I ever lied to you?'

'I've known you to spare details, that's for sure.'

'Only when it suits my purpose, and today it suits my purpose. Three saddles, three bridles, to be ready by nightfall. You'll know where I am if you need me.'

\*

Fire and candle smoke filled the dark, squalid inn that smelt of the sawdust on the floor, yesterday's food and old ale. Thomas, his hood hiding his features, sat near the door, watching the few customers gambling at rickety tables; listening to a half-dozen women gossiping in the shadows. The innkeeper, a woman in her fifties, approached him, folded her hefty arms, and gave him a sweeping, mistrustful glance.

'What're you wanting?'

Thomas leaned back against the wall. 'What would anyone want at an inn?' Waiting in vain for a response, he became impatient. 'A meal, and ale.'

She snorted, disappeared into the gloom, then returned, plonking stale bread, a bowl of tepid, unappetising slop, and a mug of sour ale on the table.

Thomas continued watching the clientele from the privacy of his hood, glancing from one to another as he ate and drank, relieved no one had any interest in him.

## Business

He was almost on the point of leaving when a robust, very young, attractive girl perched herself on his table. He noted her light brown plaited hair and grey woollen dress, the leather cord tied at her waist; but her awkward, fidgety demeanour and pale eyes conveyed a simpleton, and alerted, he leaned back, one ankle across his knee.

'Well, lass, can I help you?'

'That depends, sir,' she said, tripping over the words.

He became impish. 'What did you have in mind?'

'Whatever you want,' she mumbled.

He leaned forward, folding his arms on the table. 'Alright, what's your fee?'

'Fee?'

He had heard enough. 'You'd better come with me,' he said and led her across the rear courtyard to a small, gloomy room he knew of. A bed, a high-backed chair and an oak chest were crammed within. It was malodorous with stale perfume, musty male sweat and damp straw scattered on the floor. He walked to the chair, turned, drew his hood back, and glared at the girl lingering on the threshold.

'What are you playing at?'

'I don't know what you mean, sir.'

'Yes, you do. Your voice says one thing, but your eyes tell me something very different. I may have accepted your kind offer had I thought, even for a moment, you meant it. I'm not a fool, lass; what's your game?'

'Sir, might I sit down?'

He gestured into the room. 'Be my guest.' Then, irritated, 'Not on the floor, you silly girl.'

She sat on the wooden chest. 'I was told to wait for you.'

'But you don't know who I am, since we've never met.'

She glanced at him again. 'I know just who you are. You're Thomas Learmont. "A tall, impatient man," he said, "with proud bearing and a swagger."'

'Thank you, lass, I know my faults.'

She glanced everywhere, anywhere but his eyes, then took a small bottle from her pocket. 'I was to give you this,' she said.

He glanced at it. 'And what is "this"?'

'I don't know. I was told it would drop an ox.'

'Oh, would it indeed? And who told you that?' She hesitated, looking at the floor. 'I don't have limitless patience,' he said. 'Tell me.'

She bit at her lip. 'The town jailer.'

## Business

'*That* weasel?'

Startled, she met his eyes at last. 'Aren't you afraid of him?'

Thomas leaned his forearms on the chair back. 'I'm strong enough not to be.' He gestured at the bottle. 'So, what would happen to said "dropped ox", may I ask?'

She looked at the bottle and met his steady gaze again. 'He said there's a price on your head. He said I must tell him you're here.'

Thomas approached her, stopping halfway. 'Any more vipers in this nest?'

She hung her head. 'I don't understand, sir.'

Exasperation showed in his eyes. 'Never mind. Is anyone else "looking" for me?'

She sounded plaintive, almost pleading. 'I don't know, sir; honest, I don't.'

Despite himself, he began pitying her, began, also, planning what he might do with the jailer once he had hold of him, and crouching at her feet, looked at her with kind, steady eyes. 'If you could just do one thing for me, lass, then please trust me.'

She glanced at him. 'I'm not sure... he said you're a traitor.'

His eyes twinkled. 'Do I look like one?'

Hunched, staring at her lap, she said, 'No, you look kind.' She paused, then blurted, 'I didn't want to do it. It seemed wrong.'

'Then why did you try?'

'He said bad things would happen if I didn't.'

'What sort of things?'

'He didn't say. Just bad things.'

'Alright.' He held out one hand, giving a reassuring smile. 'I'll take that bottle, you will go home, and leave the jailer to me.'

Still doubtful, she laid the bottle in his palm.

\*

Occasional rock falls echoed through the caverns, and light and shadow moved across the Hall with the day. The Priest, infection oozing from the eye socket, remained pinned to the wall, his frantic, feeble, unanswered calls echoing through the cold, dark voids. He almost longed for Spriggans to appear from the stony gaps, to hear Soulis coming and going, his daily incantations, but there was nothing.

Then he heard the faint pulse, murmurs, footsteps, saw approaching glimmering torchlight, and Soulis

## Business

strode into the Hall with his guards. He hung the torch behind the altar, filled the bowl with blood from a jug, lit the candles, picked up the Spear, and approached the Priest.

'Well, my friend, I have now met my neighbours, who supplied the Blācencynn with food and fodder, in return for what? Protection? There is no protection from me, for I gave them a fair choice: supply me, as they did the Blācencynn before, or face ruin.' He sighed, shaking his head in mock sympathy. 'Woe to them, for they chose ruin. We have taken their grain, their children, their women, hung their menfolk from the trees, and the same fate awaits any settlement that defies me.' He looked up at his prisoner. 'I see you long for death.' He gave a long, vindictive laugh. 'No, my friend, you shall live, for my game is not yet over.'

\*

His hopes for anonymity dashed, Thomas pulled his hood forward and, keeping a covert watch for any threat, made his discreet way to the jail. Stopping at a junction, and surprised the iron gate stood open, he surveyed it from the afternoon shadows, weighing risks, unaware of soft, approaching footsteps. He sensed someone behind him, spun around, grasping his knife hilt, then stared, dumbfounded, at the slender young woman standing there, at her waist-length dark hair, her tight, faded blue gown and the red linen girdle tied at the waist. She smiled, as one greeting a friend.

'Why, Thomas Learmont, I believe I startled you.'

He relaxed. 'Greetings to you, Mistress Deakin.'

She approached him. 'Where *did* you find those *archaic* clothes?'

Impishness glinted in his eyes. 'They cover me, don't they? Or perhaps you would rather I walk through town stark naked? Now, *that* would feed the gossipmongers.' He winked. 'Eh, Mistress Deakin?'

'Tell me,' she said, ignoring the comment, scanning him with enticing eyes, 'What brings the handsomest Borders man here today?'

'Stop flirting with me. Now is not the time.'

'You'll give in, Thomas,' she said, running her fingertips along his tunic collar and giving the toggle fastening a playful tug. 'You always do in the end.'

He gave a brief glare. 'Not *now*. I'm on an errand that won't wait.'

## Business

'What *are* you doing here?' she said. 'Why do you hide?'

'I've unfinished business with the jailer,' he said, nodding towards the prison.

She stared in disbelief. 'You can't go in *there.* He'll throw you in a cell and throw the key away.'

'I'm hoping to avoid that. Do you know a young maid with brown hair and pale grey eyes? Timid? Nervous?'

'Yes, I do. Alice Bowyer. She's harmless, but so gullible she'd do anything asked of her, good or bad, and not know the difference.'

'And fears her own shadow.'

'Her mother's a cripple,' whispered Agnes, 'her brothers idle, and her father a drunkard. I've heard he beats them for the slightest mistake, he's paying the jailer mounting gambling debts, and they'll lose everything if he defaults on the repayment. I think Alice should be a nun before she becomes either a thief or a—'

'Whore?'

'Thomas, you haven't said how you met her, or where, or anything.'

'I don't need to. It may surprise you that our "illustrious" jailer almost bribed her into killing me.'

She stared at him. 'Thomas, you must jest.'

He ignored this remark. 'Where would he be now?'

'He's more than likely doing his rounds with his… jolly company.'

'I need to meet him alone,' he said, scrutinising the jail again, 'but I'm not sure how to separate him from his comrades.'

'Thomas, have you ever thought I could help?'

'No, in all honesty.'

'How typical of a man!' she snorted. Tapping her forehead, she added, 'Whores have minds too, you know,' and stood thinking for a moment. 'You said he's looking for you… What if I tell him I've seen you, that you're at unawares?'

He gave this brief consideration. 'That might work. Where have you seen me?'

'I think… the inn.'

Thomas gave a slow, deep smile. 'I think so, too.'

Sounds of marching feet, voices and jangling keys came from beyond the crossroads, and Thomas, pulling Agnes into the shadows, watched the jailer, one of his three companions carrying a flagon, escorting a scruffy, inebriated man into the jail.

Business

'Alright, Mistress Deakin,' said Thomas, 'go: tell them you've seen me at the inn, that I'm in a fighting mood… tell them *anything*, but make sure the turnkey stays in there, alone. He'll think twice before involving me in his corrupt little schemes.'

Giving him a flirtatious smile, Agnes sauntered to the jail, while he watched from the corner.

Whatever she said to them was effective. The three guards appeared and marched along the road towards the town gate. She soon returned.

'The jailer's taking the prisoner to a cell,' she said. 'But you must be quick. They'll soon come back.'

He gave her his most charming smile, and a sudden kiss, saying, 'You've a heart of gold.'

'So, have you,' she said. 'Be careful.'

He winked at her, smiled, and making sure no one saw him, approached the jail and entered the small, smelly damp room. He found the flagon, full of ale, on a small table and emptied the bottle into it. Hearing jangling keys and footsteps fast approaching from the cell stairs, he hid behind the door, watching.

The jailer, a middle-aged little man with thick, short black hair and watery eyes, sat at the table and drank the ale in one draught. Thomas, his hood pulled low, slammed the door shut. His tone was almost submissive.

'I heard you were looking for me.'

The jailer, gazing at this apparition in brief amazement, approached him, sneering as he came. 'Well, Thomas Learmont has entered my lair. Are you tired of running, Learmont, tired of keeping up the pretence as a fighting man?' Taking the keys from his belt, he jangled them under Thomas' nose. 'I've prepared a special cell for you, Learmont, small, dark, no larger than a kennel, and I have the key to it.' Thomas, glancing at the keys, said nothing. 'Lost your tongue?' mocked the jailer, grabbing Thomas' arm. 'What's happened to the famous sarcasm?' He turned him towards the stairs. 'Tomorrow, I will tie you to the whipping post in the town square, and when I've done whipping, I'll lock you in chains, keeping you as a lesson to my infant son, for he shall view you every day, learning what traitors are. You won't look so clever hanging from the gibbet.'

He pushed Thomas along a short corridor, down narrow, winding stairs, dark despite the torches burning on the damp walls, and stopped at an iron-bound door, which he unlocked and opened. Thomas stood in silence, watching, waiting, until the jailer had almost pushed him into the cell.

Thomas wheeled, twisting the man's arms, and shoved him hard against the damp wall. Holding his knife to the jailer's neck, he spoke, his tone threatening as his blade.

'Who was the old man? Here, two weeks ago. Who was he? Where was he from?'

The jailer, his grazed face pressed hard against the wall, his arms held halfway up his back, wheezed. 'There was no old man.'

Thomas slammed him against the wall again. 'Don't dare lie to me. Who was he?'

'Michael,' uttered the jailer between gasps. 'He said his name was Michael.'

Thomas tightened his hold. 'Oh, and I suppose I'm the Archangel Gabriel? Where was he from?'

The whimpering man made no reply.

Thomas glared, twisting the arms again. 'Where was he from?'

Grimacing, the man cried out, 'He was a messenger!'

'Where *from*, Master Turnkey?'

'The Blācencynn.'

'Don't *lie* to me.'

'From the Blācencynn, the Blācencynn.'

Rattled, Thomas hissed, 'The Blācencynn send no messengers.' He wrenched him around, grasping the tunic, his knife drawing blood. 'You would have sold us, wouldn't you? Me and the little maiden.' Then, watching the trickling blood, 'Seems you bleed like a man, but can you fight like one?'

He released his hold, waiting for an attack, but the jailer, trying to lunge forward, staggered and fell to the floor. Thomas sheathed his knife, giving a quiet, intimidating laugh.

'Better to check the ale is good before you drink it down.'

He hauled him into the cell and held him against the wall, gagging him with one firm hand, almost throttling him with the other, and speaking in a quiet, threatening tone.

'You're dealing with me now, Master Turnkey, not some simple-minded wench. You will swear this oath, on your infant son's life, that you will cause neither harm nor mischief to anyone in this town and allow me and my companions to go wherever we wish, unhindered, unwatched. Should you even *think* of breaking your word, be sure the Seelie Court will know, and so will

I.' He leaned further forward, watching sweat trickling on the jailer's face, grasped the tunic again, and shook him. 'I lay this curse upon you: Should you break your word, the elves shall steal your infant son away to Faerie and leave you with a changeling. Don't think I won't do it.'

The jailer nodded, mumbling. Thomas took his hand from the man's mouth, allowing him to gasp, 'I give my word.'

'Again, Master Turnkey.'

'My word.' The jailer slumped unconscious to the floor. Thomas, staring at him, snorted.

'Drop an ox, would it? Ha! Some ox.' He locked him in the cell, pocketed the keys, and walked fast towards the workshop, ignoring everyone, until a soft, familiar voice hailed him from close by.

'Good afternoon, Thomas Learmont.'

He stopped in his tracks, almost rolling his eyes, and faced Agnes, who stood outside a humble dwelling, holding the door ajar. 'Greetings to you again, Mistress Deakin.'

'Why the hurry?' she said, then more salaciously, added, 'Have you been in a fight?'

'I wouldn't quite say that.'

She smiled, opening the door further. 'Then what would you say? If you would give me but an hour of your time, sir, perhaps you would tell me about it?'

He leaned forward, his beard touching her face. 'You are nothing if not persistent, Mistress Deakin, I have to say.'

'Please, sir, call me Agnes.'

He remembered the room, the shabby rug spread on the floor, the coarse, patched blankets covering the lumpy straw mattress on the small bed in a corner, the iron kettle hanging from a trivet over the smouldering fire, and the stool beside it. A pine wood box, where she kept her only other dress, was against one wall and, stacked on a shelf, one or two cups, earthenware bowls and her one treasure, a chipped, green glazed jug. He liked the mingled dusky smells of her perfume and lingering peat smoke and flung his cloak onto a bodge-worked table.

Agnes closed the door, retrieved a red cloth from the window, closed it, faced him, and giving him an impish smile, began unfastening his tunic.

'What makes you think I'm not in the jailer's pay?'

His smile matched hers. 'Because you like me too well.'

She fingered his shirt. 'What gives you that idea?'

Business

He shrugged, his smile now that roguish, flattering grin. 'Oh, the flush in your cheeks, the gleam in your eyes, the smile you can't wipe from your face whenever we meet; but if you're going to kill me, Mistress Deakin, at least wait until I'm lying sprawled, spent and naked across your bed.'

\*

Hirnac lay relaxed beside the fire, hands behind his head, but Penda sat tense, arms around his knees, fists clenched, staring at the flames in silence. Adan paced to the eaves of the copse where they had camped.

'It's well past mid-day,' he said, looking towards a smoky haze rising behind a ridge. 'He only needed three saddles and bridles.'

Rædwulf approached him. 'And rations. Give him time, Adan; trust him. It may not be that simple.'

'How long does he need? He said he knew the townsfolk but was maybe overconfident. We should have gone with him.'

'He'll draw enough attention to himself without having us in tow. I've no reason to doubt him, Adan; nor have you.'

'If he met that jailer…?'

Rædwulf sighed. 'Then I'm sure he can defend himself.'

Adan leaned on his bow, looking at Thomas' sword propped against a tree. 'He has courage, I'll admit.'

'Yes, he has, and he's no fool. So, *trust* him, Adan. He said he'd return by nightfall, at the latest.'

'And if he doesn't?'

Rædwulf raised an eyebrow. 'Then we've a problem.'

\*

Thomas spared Agnes more than an hour and now, dozing, enjoying her fingertips running through his moderate chest hair, gave a deep, contented sigh.

'You promised you wouldn't fall in love with me.'

Indignant, she sat up. 'You flatter yourself, sir.'

'I don't. I speak the truth.'

She got up. 'I thought you said you're on an urgent errand,' she said, pulling on her shift.

His eyes remained closed. 'I did. I am.'

'Well, you can't snooze here all afternoon, can you?'

## Business

Thomas gave her a fond, sidelong look. 'You don't stand nonsense, do you, Agnes? I like that.' He got up, dressed, and kneeled, helping her tie her garters. Sudden doubt showed in her eyes.

'Thomas, if the jailer knows I helped you, he might whip me, throw me in the lockup, accuse me of witchcraft, lock me in the Scold's Bridle—anything.'

'He wouldn't dare.'

This surprised her into meeting his eyes. 'What makes you so sure?'

His gaze hardened. 'Because I know how to make my curses stick.'

She took a long breath. 'Remind me to never anger you.' She stared aghast at the six gold coins he pressed into her palm, thinking them a king's ransom. 'What's this for?'

'Take Alice Bowyer to a nunnery,' he said, donning his cloak. 'Give half the gold to the Sisters there. Keep the rest to buy or rent yourself some land, raise sheep, sell the fleece, and become a Goodwife. If you use this for another purpose, you will have nothing. And nothing will save the girl.' He kissed her cheek. 'Thank you for your time, Mistress Deakin.'

\*

Matthew, covered with sawdust and wood shavings, oiling a saddle at his workbench, glanced up at Thomas leaning on the doorjamb, then resumed his task.

'There's three bridles ready. I've altered those two saddles and made this one from scratch.'

Thomas approached him. 'I need it *now*, McMartin.'

Matthew pushed his hair from his dusty, sweaty face. 'The stirrup and girth straps still need attaching.'

'I'll take it as it is, then.'

Matthew wiped his forehead. 'Then I can't guarantee it's safe.'

Thomas glared. 'Then I'll have to chance it, won't I?'

Matthew secured the straps as best he could. 'You avoided the jailer?'

'Not exactly.'

Matthew stared, open-mouthed. 'You haven't killed him, have you?'

Thomas laughed. 'I only gave him some of his own… potion, and left him sleeping it off. They'll find him, given time.'

## Business

Matthew sighed, lifted the saddle from the bench, told his son to bring the bridles, and led Thomas to the stables. His son dumped his burden on the floor.

'Are you sure about this, Learmont?' said Matthew, shaking his head as he eyed the piled saddles.

Thomas lifted one. 'As certain as I can be. I'll saddle them, you bridle them.'

Matthew gestured to some bundles stacked by the door. 'Here's the rations and blankets you asked for, Learmont. You'll have to use your horses as pack animals.'

Thomas smiled, handing him a handful of gold coins. 'Here is your payment, enough to keep you and your family comfortable for a twelvemonth, but I warn you: squander this, you shall be destitute.'

Matthew met his gaze. 'You're a generous man, Learmont, that I'll grant you.'

'The payment is fair,' said Thomas, throwing him the keys. 'Give these to the bailiff once he's back.' The sun sank behind the nearby hills as he led the horses towards the gate.

\*

The sombre torchlight in the council chamber could not reach its furthest recesses. A new long, foot-high plinth, a deep line carved across its width, stood against one wall, and Soulis, seated in his immense chair, regarded Finnian with contempt; he wanted rid of him, but as the Spriggans were unruly and unpredictable without him, he needed to keep him close.

'Well, now, Master Ambassador,' he said, his tone enough to shrivel leather, 'we have a problem: my retainers seem to forget their loyalties—or perhaps you forget?'

Finnian gave a perfunctory bow. 'I have not forgotten, sire, but as you have not reported to my master for some days, he has become anxious that perhaps you have forgotten your commitment, although remains grateful that you still allow my humble service.'

'Humble indeed,' said Soulis, twisting his mouth, 'and wearisome.'

The reply was oily. 'Perhaps my lord should consider his situation: I am duty-bound to remind him of his agreement to find the Horn and Sword. Robin Redcap does not forgive those who break their oath.'

'Then let him do his worst, my friend,' spat Soulis. 'We neither fear mere imps, nor need your meddling guidance. Yet, you have other uses: you will remind

## Business

your errant brothers of their allegiances, my humble, *dispensable* servant, and will leave us again only at our bidding.'

Finnian lifted his upper lip. 'Redcap will assume treason if I don't return and can destroy the contract in the blink of an eye.'

Soulis slammed one fist on the chair arm. 'We do not honour a fraudulent agreement, sir.'

Finnian, his smile enough to freeze the very rock, spoke in a tone mocking as his bow. 'My lord must earn trust; the longer he takes to honour the contract, the higher the toll. Payment is now overdue.'

Soulis growled. 'Payment! You have had all the livestock available. These peasants have nothing left worth taking. Perhaps you, my reverent ambassador, look to relieve us of our gains?'

Finnian shook his head. 'I don't want gold; nor caves suitable only for wild beasts. Consider, my lord, what these so-called peasants value above all, and that only my master's goodwill stands between you and oblivion.'

## Chapter Fourteen

# The Forest

His sword drawn, Penda stepped between giant oaks surrounding a misty clearing and froze, horrified. Lybbestre, a spear in her left hand, a cup in her right, stood between the two elder priests, the lifting mist revealing their inscrutable faces and her bloodied robes. He could not ignore her beckoning him; the priests seized and disarmed him, forcing him to his knees before he could stop them. She proffered the goblet, her voice hollow, distant.

'Lyblæca, drain this cup of mead your forefathers made, and hear the old ones speak.'

Bathed in sweat, he stared at the dark liquor he knew he should not touch, and in sudden panic, said, 'This is not for me. No, not for me.'

'Give the ancestors voice, Lyblæca,' she said, forcing the rim between his lips. 'Let them speak.'

Alarmed, he freed himself, grasped her wrist, and forcing the cup away, lunged onto her. He plummeted into darkness, giving a terrified yell, and awoke, shaking and sweating.

Nothing moved through the silent copse, and unable to settle again, he took watch until dawn when Rædwulf approached him.

'Have you watched all night?'

Penda yawned. 'Most of it. I couldn't sleep, so I relieved Adan. Thomas offered to watch, a few hours ago, but I told him to rest.'

'Are you alright?'

'Yes. Don't worry about me.'

Unconvinced, Rædwulf, sighed. 'We'll break camp after breakfast.'

Adan led them along deserted narrow trails, through heather and gorse, between rocks and grazing livestock, until late afternoon on the third day when they climbed a high, isolated hill and dismounted. White clouds raced across the sky, the breeze carrying sounds of crows, sheep and hunting eagles and smoky smells from distant wood and peat fires. Bow in hand, Adan surveyed the wide, empty grassland and pointed towards the forested horizon.

'There,' he said. 'That's where we're going.'

Thomas folded his arms. 'A broad and treacherous river cuts through that woodland, Adan, and the trails are broken or non-existent. We should take the road and use the bridge.'

Adan adjusted his hold on his bow. 'The road is unsafe, Learmont, and will take us miles from our way. If you know the forest, Thomas, then I know it better. We'll take Faerie paths men don't know about, paths we can follow, unseen, unheard, and cross the river at a Faerie wade I know of.' He walked away, adding, 'If that's too daunting for you, Learmont, perhaps you should have stayed behind.'

'He's right to avoid the road, Learmont,' said Rædwulf. 'People have watched for us since he and Hirnac escaped from the jail. I'm as concerned about the forest as you are, but we've little choice.'

\*

Alone, shadowed against the cloudy sky, Soulis stood on bare rock; the only sounds of life were harsh calls from a distant rookery, carried on the biting wind. He turned, raising the Spear high at each compass point, and called across the hills.

'The Flame obeys me; I govern all. I am Soulis… I am… *might*.'

\*

Adan stood with his companions on the steep, overgrown riverbank, watching surface eddies implying sinister depths, and Thomas scowled at the opposite bank over fifty yards away.

'Well, Adan? Shall we fly?'

Adan pointed to a ford on their right. 'The Forest Father advised us to meet his agent here, so we must cross there.' He mounted, gathered his reins, and looked at Rædwulf. 'I'll go first, Hirnac next, but if there's trouble, find another way.'

Hirnac, Rædwulf and Penda followed him down the slippery bank. Thomas waited until they had reached the other side before he began the crossing, keeping a wary eye on the causeway, forgetting that Faerie paths could move.

The path, only a narrow pale ribbon inches beneath the water, vanished, reappearing yards away to the left; the horse plunged into the depths, Thomas hit the water hard, and something wrenched at his left leg. Penda, hearing his brief cry of alarm, looked back and blanched.

His foot trapped in the stirrup, his cloak, sword and the undertow dragging him down, Thomas fought to gain

## The Forest

the surface. Matthew's doubts had been well-founded: the saddle slid onto the horse's flank, taking Thomas deeper. Trapped upside down, trying to avoid the kicking hoofs, pivoting, fumbling for his knife with one hand, he somehow righted himself; his free hand grabbing the stirrup strap, he slashed it through. He surfaced, gasping, swam, and coughing, disoriented, crawled ashore, Rædwulf hauling him up the slope. Hirnac pulled the horse from the river and led it into the forest.

Ignoring the pain in his left leg and refusing any help, Thomas walked to a tree stump, sat down, and launched into a furious tirade at Adan.

'"Follow the road," I said. "No," you said. "The road's unsafe," you said. Well—*so are fucking Faerie paths!*'

Dusk came fast, a soft, wafting twilight beneath the brooding trees. Hirnac, who could make anything burn, lit a fire in a nearby clearing, and Rædwulf crouched beside Thomas.

'You're wet through, Learmont–take your clothes off; they'll dry soon enough by the fire.' With some reluctance, Thomas took his cloak and tunic off, and Rædwulf smiled.

'I hope she was worth it, Learmont. You've your shirt on inside-out.'

Thomas gave a broad grin. 'You don't miss a thing, do you?'

Rædwulf shrugged, giving his wry, unassuming smile. 'Well, I like to think I'm fairly observant.' He handed Thomas the stirrup, strap and all. 'You'd better keep this. It needs mending, and so do you, but you need to take your trousers off, if I'm to treat you.'

'Shame Wyrtræd isn't here,' said Penda, watching Rædwulf examine the injury.

Hirnac, unsaddling a horse, glanced at him. 'Who's he?'

'A wandering Blācencynn healer,' said Penda. 'I've heard he's the best doctor in the North.'

Rædwulf, preparing a dressing, scowled, as though affronted. 'I wonder if he deserves such a lofty reputation, but some men attract… fables.'

Thomas winced under his touch. 'You know him?'

'I've met him,' said Rædwulf, raising an eyebrow and wrapping the bandage around Thomas' thigh, 'although it's been a while since I've spoken with him. I believe he was away when…' He paused. 'When the end came.' He tied the dressing in place. 'There, you'll do for now. I suggest you keep your weight off it for a couple of days, if you can.'

## The Forest

'I hope we meet with this forest agent soon,' said Penda, upending an empty bottle over his palm. 'Maybe he'll give us provisions.' He shivered, scanning the dense undergrowth around the glade. 'This place glowers at us,' he said, 'and I feel eyes on my back. I don't understand it.' He looked at Adan. 'Time to draw lots for the watch, I think.'

Hirnac drew the short straw and sat by the fire, watching the darkness, the silent bank of brambles and the looming trees until Thomas, wrapped in a blanket, limped across to him.

'I can't sleep, Hirnac,' he said. 'I'll take the watch.'

In pain, naked beneath his blanket, shivering, having never been more uncomfortable, he sat listening to distant owl calls, howling wolves and furtive night creatures rustling through the undergrowth. Vulnerable and afraid, but not daring to admit it, even to himself, he knew he could neither run nor fight if anything assailed them now. He looked at his clothes, hanging by the fire, hoping they would dry by dawn. Penda stirred, murmuring in his sleep, 'Cerin.'

A robin started singing close by, and night began lifting to dawn; a distant, though distinct, girlish laugh, gentle but unnerving, froze Thomas to the spot, but he saw nothing. His trousers and shirt now dry, he dressed and awoke his companions.

Again, Adan followed the Faerie paths, fallen trees and dense undergrowth often blocking the way. Thomas, riding with Penda at the rear, reined in.

'Penda, what does Cerin mean?'

Confused, Penda drew rein too, looking at him. 'I don't know. It's a strange word. Why do you ask?'

'You talked in your sleep last night. I wondered.'

Penda peered into the green twilight on either side where sunlight seldom came. 'I sense eyes on us again,' he said, 'and something ahead—trouble, perhaps. Who knows what lurks in this forest?'

Daylight faded under heavy cloud, thunder echoed through the trees, rain dripped from leaves and undergrowth, and Thomas, in his shirt sleeves, shivered; but the squall was brief. Sunshine penetrated the forest canopy here and there, revealing secret glades, hidden streams and fallen, stark, mossy logs lying some distance from the path; every leaf was still. The horses often stopped before picking their way through brambles and ferns, and the men listened for any call, however innocuous, but there was only a strange, dense, blanketing silence.

## The Forest

Uncertain, they rode at a cautious walk, looking everywhere for any threat, until entering a pretty glade where bees and butterflies settled on the wildflowers entwined in the long, lush grass. The men dismounted; Thomas eased himself onto a flat stone and sat massaging his cramped thigh. The horses began grazing; a thrush sang nearby; a clear, pleasant laugh rang around the clearing, and Penda whispered, 'Listen, something's behind us.'

Another laugh from above them made them look up towards a tree where a maiden sat on a bough, watching them, her eyes blue and deep as a clear midnight, her hair cascading below her perch. She giggled, vanished behind the tree, reappeared beneath it, and stood watching these unkempt newcomers, who smelt of sweat and horses. Weary but aware, they saw a small, pretty maiden, with nut-brown skin and cherry blossom speckling her hair, dark as forest shadows. Her baggy, blackberry-coloured gown, unfastened at the neck in her innocence, and with a green woven girdle tied at her waist, hinted at the charms beneath.

Embarrassed, Thomas was blunt. 'Who are you?'

She seemed surprised. 'I'm Cerin. Welcome to my garden.'

'Cerin?' said Penda.

'Yes,' she said.

He saw a vague flicker in her eyes and looked away, fighting off a knowing smile, but said nothing while she bowed, her hair disguising her blushes. Thomas came to the point.

'Have you been spying on us since last evening?'

She looked from him to Rædwulf. 'I wouldn't presume to spy on anyone,' she said and looked at Adan. 'You're Adan, aren't you? I believe the Forest Father told you to meet his agent here.'

Adan glanced at his bow. 'Him? Yes, he said that–' He broke off in sudden comprehension. 'You.'

'I am his daughter.' She glanced from Hirnac to Rædwulf, to Penda, then at Adan again. 'It's said Lord Soulis is now poised to overrun the Mortal realm, that no sword can kill him, and Redcap is preparing to move against the Seelie Court. You may seek help from yonder tower,' she pointed to a path behind her, 'but you can rest here tonight in safety.'

She led them to a shady, hidden glade surrounded by oak trees, ferns, tangled flowering honeysuckle and tree stumps. Wisps of sweet-scented wood smoke from a fire drifted through the trees, and flowering brambles formed a low arch over a path to one side of a forest stream flowing over mossy rocks. Butterflies skittered about on shaded wings, violets speckled the lush, cool grass, birds sang from every branch, and woodpeckers drummed their tattoos amongst the trees. She served food and drink in wooden platters and cups, Thomas keeping his innate teasing in check, Penda smiling to himself again whenever she caught his eye.

Thomas laid out his damp cloak and tunic by the fire and sat beside it with the others while Cerin skipped about the glade on her own business. She soon showed a puckish trait; her high-spirited, playful teasing bordering on the flirtatious, she sprinkled petals over Penda's hair, tucked a honeysuckle flower in Adan's cloak clasp and bluebells behind Rædwulf's right ear, for good measure tying a knot in his hair, which took him an hour to disentangle. Hirnac found the reins tied into a cat's cradle, and Thomas had to ask her to retrieve his stirrup from a high tree branch, but they took these pranks with good humour, each man charmed in different ways.

Penda, taking watch on a fallen tree some yards from the camp, and out of sight, began whetting his knife and glimpsed her approaching.

'Well, Cerin? What can I do for you?'

'May I speak with you?'

He concentrated on his task. 'If you like.'

She kneeled at his feet, leaning forward. 'Your injured friend seems fierce.'

Penda, giving a slight smile, stopped his movements. 'He's alright.'

She leaned further forward, and he, glimpsing the shadowed breasts, looked away; but he could not resist another, surreptitious, glance. 'Well,' she said, 'he seems it to me.'

He smiled, winking at her. 'He's but a sheep in wolf's clothing.'

'Some sheep.'

Amused, he continued whetting his knife, his ring radiating colours in the sunlight, and she gasped.

'What's that?'

He tested the blade's edge with his thumb. 'What?'

She came nearer, almost touching him, breathing on his hands, while he caught a clearer view.

'A ring,' she said. 'How strange it is! Look, it shows all the colours of the rainbow.'

'It shows more,' he said, 'in the right light.'

'What kind of light?'

Aware of the sagging gown, he returned her gaze and shrugged. 'Moonlight.' He frowned, pulling at his lower lip. 'Cerin, do you know nothing of men?'

She sat back on her heels, at last veiling her body from him. 'Not much. I heard some are fools, some, cowards, and—' she glanced towards the camp, lowering her voice to a whisper, 'some are dangerous.'

'Well then, if I were you, I'd make sure to tie my clothing... just here.' He brushed her neck with his fingertips, a gentle touch that somehow reached her soul. He stood up, sheathed his knife, smiled at her, and walked away.

Thomas, sitting beneath a large oak tree, trying to repair the stirrup strap with a needle and thread he had in his purse, saw her approach and kneel a few feet away.

'Can I help?' she said.

He gave her a sharp glance. 'I can manage, thank you.'

She hesitated, then said, 'Are you in pain?'

Defiance flashed from beneath his brows. 'It'll pass.'

She paused, thinking. 'Are you weary?'

'I didn't sleep last night.'

'Not at all?'

'No,' he said, stabbed his finger with the needle, and stifled a curse.

'You know,' she said, in genuine concern, 'I can mend that for you, if only you'd let me try.'

He hesitated. 'Alright then.'

She held up the needle. 'The tip's bent—did you know? No wonder it wouldn't go through.' Inspecting the strap, she said in surprise, 'How did this happen?'

He leaned back against the tree trunk and closed his eyes. 'I fell from my horse when crossing the river. I could either drown, or let a panicking horse kick me to death, or cut myself free and swim.'

Awed, she said, 'That sounds very brave.' She paused, then added, 'I'm not very brave. I just tend my Faerie glades and hide from bad things.'

He gave her a brief glare. 'Bravery had nothing to do with it, given the options I had.'

'Is that how you hurt your leg?'

He closed his eyes again. 'Yes.'

She re-examined the strap, thinking. 'You know, Penda told me you're a sheep in wolf's clothing.'

He raised his brows and looked at her. 'Oh, he did, did he? And what did you say to that?'

She glanced at him, then admitted, 'Some sheep.'

The Forest

There was the briefest pause before Thomas gave a warm, genuine, self-effacing laugh that became a quiet chuckle. 'I think I see your point.'

'You know,' she said, 'you should smile more. It makes you seem friendly.'

His tone matched his kind eyes. 'I'm not an ogre, Cerin, even if I look like one.'

He fell asleep while she mended his stirrup strap, working in silence until, glancing up, she stared at him. Dappled sunlight through a low, leafy branch had given her a fleeting illusion that he wore a crown of oak leaves. She left the repaired strap beside him.

The moon was high before they prepared to sleep, Cerin retreating beyond the bramble arch, Rædwulf taking the watch. Thomas, his face pale in the flickering firelight, sat in his shirtsleeves for a while, breaking off sections from a long grass stem he held, throwing them, one by one, into the flames.

Cerin lay restless, thinking of Penda, of the ring that gave such enchanting colours. After an hour, wrapped in her cloak, she crept to the camp, stood listening to the men's breathing as they slept, saw Penda lying on his side, and knelt behind him. He spoke without even opening his eyes.

'I'm not asleep. What do you want, Cerin?'

She gasped. 'How did you know it was me?'

'Rædwulf is on watch,' came the prosaic reply. 'I would not have heard Hirnac, I can hear Adan snoring, and Thomas couldn't be stealthy if his life depended on it.' He turned over. 'Well?'

'Will you come with me, Penda? Please?'

For a moment he wondered whether to humour her, then threw off his blanket. She led him by the hand, under the flowering bramble arch and along a path to an immense yew tree in the middle of a glade hedged with ferns, blossoming brambles and honeysuckle. A nightingale was singing somewhere close by, and fireflies were everywhere. She stopped at a narrow gap in the tree trunk.

'This is my retreat,' she said, leading him in.

Light from the small central fire, fireflies and many rushlights shone onto the dark, burnished walls; a woollen blanket covered a deep fern bed, stars glimmered through the latticed branches, and dappled moonlight fell onto the floor strewn with wildflowers.

'The moon is shining, Penda,' she said, 'and you said the ring shows unusual colours in moonlight. Would you show me? Please?'

## The Forest

Half doubtful, he raised his right hand to waist level, the ring glittering with pure light, and Cerin gazed, entranced, at the shapes the glimmering pastel hues threw onto the dark walls.

'They're seen better from here,' she said, sitting on the bed. 'See that one? It looks like an eagle on the wing.'

They sat for a while, talking in whispers, playing the game of naming the dancing shadows, then stared at one another in sudden silence, held in each other's spell. Penda leaned towards her, his gentle fingers pulling at the cloak.

'By your leave, Cerin.'

It fell, the soft light revealing her glowing nakedness. He expected her to protest, to draw away; instead, nestling against him, she offered him her mouth, and they coupled on the ferny bed, the fireflies dancing above them.

\*

Torn between remorse and an obscure sense of achievement, Penda lay with his right arm stretched over her, watching her sleeping until, mindful he should return to the camp, he dressed and kneeled beside her. She awoke and looked into his eyes.

'Are you leaving today, Penda?'

'Yes.'

'I wish you could stay.'

He held her. 'I know, but I can't. I'm sorry. Don't regret tonight, Cerin, if I've had your maidenhead. You wanted me, as much as I wanted you.' He kissed her forehead. 'Stay in the forest, pretty lady, and tend your Faerie glades.'

He returned to his bed-place beside Rædwulf and lay down.

'I won't ask where you've been,' hissed Rædwulf, his accusing eyes glittering in the firelight.

Penda returned the stare, said, 'Shut up,' turned over, and slept until shaken awake. He grunted, opened one eye, and saw Adan propped on his bow, kneeling beside him.

'Your watch, Lord Blācencynn.'

Half asleep, he took the watch, listening to the dawn chorus; thought he heard Rædwulf say something, but on checking, saw him asleep and snoring beside the fire, and stayed on watch until Rædwulf marched towards him at dawn. He met that drilling, steel gaze, expecting an argument.

## The Forest

'I'm in no mood for lectures, Rædwulf, so save your breath.'

Rædwulf sat beside him. 'What's the point? The trails in the grass led to the flowered archway, and I read the signs. She saw a kind young man she'd do anything for, and you grabbed the opportunity.'

Penda bristled. 'So what if I had some fun?'

Rædwulf replied, his whisper intense as his eyes. 'I couldn't care *less*; s*he's* not my concern.' He paused, surveying the sunlight slanting through the boughs. 'No, my concern is her father. Did it never occur to you he placed her under our protection? Your lying with her doesn't bother me, but he might consider it a betrayal.'

Penda glared. 'He doesn't need to know.'

Rædwulf stood up and faced him. 'The forest holds open and hidden dangers; he *is* the forest, Penda. Of course he knows. Think about it.' He marched off.

Cerin watched the sunlight filtering through the yew branches above her, but the magic had gone, the shadows inanimate in the growing dawn. She dressed, made her way to the glade, and glimpsed a circlet of violets, made by clumsy, unpractised hands, hanging from a lower branch near the bramble arch; flattered, she took it down.

She found the men already breaking camp: Hirnac, rolling blankets up; Thomas, now wearing his tunic and cloak, saddling his horse; Penda, Adan and Rædwulf standing together talking.

'The path leads almost straight to the Laird's tower,' she said, 'but will you not break your fast with me before you go? I wouldn't want you to leave here hungry.'

Adan smiled. 'Thank you, lady. We'd appreciate that.'

Heavy-hearted, they spoke in whispers, Penda saying nothing throughout the meal until it was time to take their leave. Thomas, not trusting his stirrup strap, scrambled onto his horse. Cerin, standing close by, looked up at him.

'Have a care with that strap, lord,' she said. 'It may break again, but maybe the Laird can replace it.'

He smiled, and giving her a brief wink, said, 'My thanks, pretty lady.' Seeing the violets in her hair, he whispered, 'Those blue flowers suit you very well, Cerin.'

The compliment surprised her. 'Oh, yes,' she said, 'I like violets.'

'They're violets?'

'Yes, but they're purple, not blue.'

## The Forest

He gave a sudden, very pleasant smile. 'I know nothing about flowers.'

She smiled, not at him, but at something else. 'Whoever made it,' she said, 'is very kind.'

He leaned low from his horse. 'I made it, Cerin.'

Penda approached her, kissed her hand, whispered, 'Remember what I said, lady,' mounted his horse and rode away with his comrades.

## Chapter Fifteen

# Roads Between

Early summer: the hungry gap; the tenant farmers of Liddesdale sent their older children foraging through the countryside for roots, wild herbs or early berries, but they did not return. Anxious, frantic, calling them, everyone searched outhouses and haylofts, combing each field and copse until dusk, to no avail.

Now afraid, families placed herbs in the swaddling clothes and bedding to protect the younger children and babes; hung charms over the cribs, beds and doors; but the following morning brought despair. Their bairns had gone, snatched in the quiet night, replaced with wooden effigies, with Soulis' distinctive crest disfiguring each face.

\*

A vigorous wind drove clouds across the sky, the hills half-obscuring the tower which rose like a giant's fist from the ground. Rædwulf and his companions approached it, and a challenge came from the parapet above the closed gate.

'Declare yourselves, and your purpose.'

Rædwulf, glancing at the many heraldic flags flapping on the high battlements, made a disarming gesture. 'We wish to meet with your master,' he said, 'believing he expects us.'

'Wait there.'

With his injured leg hurting, Thomas dismounted and waited with his fidgeting companions for fifteen minutes before the same voice hailed them and the gate opened.

'You may enter, my lords.'

In silence, they dismounted in the courtyard, the gates clanging shut behind them—a vague echo of Luc-Nan-Har. A stocky, red-haired guard, armed with an axe, hurried forward, giving the visitors an appraising glance and a brief bow.

'My master has granted you an audience in the Hall. Follow me.'

A groom led the horses away, the small crowd of whispering onlookers dispersed, and Rædwulf, saying nothing, feeling somehow hemmed in, followed their guide up a wooden staircase to a door. The wardens on either side gave him a brief, summing look. At eye level with the top of the gate, he stared out at the forest eaves a mile away and hazy hills beyond, then followed his companions into a long, lofty hall, closing the door behind him. Shields, weapons and stags' heads were mounted on every wall, and a tapestry hanging behind a large wooden chair gleamed in dusty sunlight coming through high, unglazed windows and the opening above the central hearth. Inert flags hung from the rafters and rushes covered the floor. Rædwulf coughed.

A richly attired, overweight, middle-aged man with sparse gingery hair entered from a side door. Giving a broad, welcoming smile, he came forward, servant in tow.

'We've been expecting you, my lords,' he said. 'Come, come, sit beside me, and tell me of events.'

He gestured to the servant to serve wine, sat back in his immense chair, goblet in hand, and began musing.

'Four days since, an old man came here, begging us to meet him, saying that one Thomas Learmont, Lord Ercildoun, might well seek my help in the coming days; but he also said that Thomas Learmont was a traitor, plotting against the King, and I should imprison or kill him and his companions. I would have more land as my reward, he said, more wealth, more influence.' Alarmed,

Thomas sat forward, only Penda's sharp glare stopping his protest. The Laird stared into his goblet, swirled its contents, and drained it. 'He would not give his name, nor say where he was from… yet I felt I knew him from somewhere, that he was false.'

Rædwulf drank, then rested his cup on the arm of his chair. 'We know him, my lord. He is Soulis, of Hermitage Castle, and if he accuses Lord Ercildoun of treason, he might look at himself. He seeks power, my lord, by any means.'

The Laird nodded, meeting the grey eyes. 'Soulis, eh? Ah, now things make sense, for he'll do anything to line his pockets; and he wasn't alone. A young man stood behind him like a servant, but it takes no genius to know who the puppet-master was.' He sat back, studying Adan. 'So much for Soulis, but I've other news: two nights since, an outlandish-looking messenger knocked on our gates, begging for an audience, saying she came from Faerie but again, gave no name.'

'*She?*' blurted Thomas, astonished. 'From *Faerie?*'

Rædwulf leaned forward, suspicious. 'Can you describe her?'

The Laird shook his head. 'I wish I could, but she would not lift the veil from her face.'

'Was she very tall?'

Again, the Laird shook his head. 'I wouldn't say tall.' He sat back, looking at Rædwulf. 'She said Soulis seeks domination of any who stand against him, that I should aid the men sent from Faerie. So I'm told that Thomas Learmont plots treason, but I've also heard otherwise: it would be dangerous ignoring either. Rumours run rife that Soulis is destroying settlements hither and yon, and from what you've said, I know I'm in his sights; but it's well not to offend Faerie folk, so I choose to believe the latter.' He held out his cup in mute command, speaking as the servant filled the goblet. 'I must protect my own and cannot spare you any of my men, but I will supply anything else you might need. You've only to say.'

Adan drank, then ran his forefinger around the cup rim. 'Our purpose is to defeat Soulis, and we have few needs, asking my lord only for a few days' rations.'

The Laird smiled. 'I would also suggest a knife for your friend, as he appears not to have one.'

'I lost it,' said Thomas, glancing towards Adan, 'in a river.'

The man's smile broadened. 'I'll make sure it's replaced.'

Goblet in hand, ankle across his knee, Thomas gave an acknowledging nod. 'If I might ask another favour, I need a stirrup strap and saddle girth replacing. I've risked my neck with them once already and don't intend on doing so again.'

The Laird stood up. 'Leave it with me, but it will take time. You have this hall at your disposal until then, and we'll feed you. Maybe you haven't seen meat for a while.'

\*

The small, feeble Flame burned behind Soulis, who stood alone, looking around the darkened, torch-lit cavern and at the jet-black lake surface. He raised the Spear high, shouting, his voice fading in the gloom.

'I am Soulis; none dare assail me.' He lowered the Spear, climbed the narrow steps, strolled to the Higher Hall, gave the High Priest a mocking bow, and raised the Spear.

'My friend,' he said, 'the Flame now obeys me, burning high, or low, as I wish. No longer do I need this… *toy.*' He threw the Spear aside. It fell against the vat now full of foul, solid lard, and he swept from the Hall, ignoring the Priest's anguished cry.

*

With two servants in attendance, the Laird approached Rædwulf and his companions waiting in the deserted courtyard in the late afternoon, nodded to the groom standing nearby, then smiled at his guests.

'We have rations for you,' he said, 'and have replaced your stirrup and girth straps, Lord Ercildoun, and we also have this.' He gave him a broad-bladed knife in a stout leather sheath.

Thomas bowed. 'My thanks, lord.'

The Laird faced Adan. 'We would have invited you all to stay here overnight had your errand not been urgent. It's dangerous travelling after dark.'

Adan glanced around the courtyard and bowed. 'We appreciate your help, lord, but warn you to remain vigilant, for threats may come in any guise.'

'Then we wish you Godspeed,' said the Laird. 'But beware: if Soulis has tried bribing us, then he will try the same with others less staunch. Don't use the road.'

Adan gave a brief bow, implying agreement, and rode away with his companions. They travelled across country for miles until stopping in the lee of a low ridge. A slight breeze snickered through the heather; no beast moved or called, and the coppery sun touched the western hills.

'I'm uneasy,' said Adan. 'Perhaps we should have stayed with the Laird after all. It might rain later, and there's no cover here, from either weather or foe.'

'We can't go back,' said Rædwulf.

'We might find shelter in a village I know of,' said Thomas, 'just beyond this ridge, and if we move now, we'll reach it before dark.'

'Somehow, I never doubted *you'd* want for a bed,' muttered Rædwulf.

They surveyed the country beyond the ridge crest, shading their eyes from the bright sunset ahead, watching crows circling above woodland beyond buildings clustered by a stream a mile away.

'They've found something,' said Hirnac.

'Yes,' said Penda. 'Carrion.'

They found the settlement deserted, every building burned, every cart, plough and weaving loom lying broken in the street. Smoke hung in the air and crows perched in the treetops, their harsh calls breaking the thick silence. Hirnac drew rein at the woodland eaves, appalled at the half-eaten bodies hanging from the branches.

His companions dismounted and followed Thomas, who, stopping at a beech tree, saluted a corpse suspended from the lowest branch. The eyes had gone, but he recognised the friend he had spent many convivial hours with from the peculiar bulbous nose and striped hose he always wore; whose spirited young daughter Thomas recalled teasing, knowing she admired him, his impish playfulness making her blush and giggle.

'Good day to you, Gilbert Raith. Is your daughter still pretty?' This throwaway remark punched him, bringing savage reality home, and he could only whisper, 'I knew this village, Rædwulf. These folk harmed no one.' He walked away.

Rædwulf stroked his beard, scrutinising the woodland. 'These people hanging here, Adan,' he said. 'Have you noticed they're all men?'

Adan glanced towards the beech tree, saying, 'This is Redcap's work, Rædwulf; we should make for the Mereburg.'

'No,' said Rædwulf, 'I don't agree. Soulis has stamped his name all over this. We continue to the Caves.'

Adan stared at him. 'Rædwulf, are you mad? It's Redcap we need to confront, not his lackey.'

Rædwulf met his gaze with steel eyes. 'I will not rest, Adan, until I've avenged my kindred.'

'Nor will I. I shall not forget the cries of my people dying in the darkness.'

Rædwulf pointed to the trees and village behind him. 'Look at it, Adan. Look at this place. Remember the Laird telling us that Soulis is razing settlements? Which village do you think might be next?' Adan glanced towards Thomas, who now stood talking to Hirnac, and Rædwulf nodded. 'There must be no more raids.'

'If I've understood all you've told me,' said Adan, looking at Penda, 'nothing withstands the Flame's power. Use it, Penda; kill Soulis with it.'

Penda shook his head. 'Until it decides otherwise, it will only defend us, but at least it keeps the Spriggans at bay.'

'We'll leave now,' said Rædwulf. 'We've miles to go.'

\*

Alder and birch trees stood amongst tussocks and shrubs half-seen in drifting mist, and ephemeral, glimmering lights, enticing and deadly, danced above stretches of sullen water. Sinister green moss and nodding cotton grass grew either side of a wattle path laid between leaning wooden stakes.

Adan drew rein. 'We've had little rest since yesterday,' he said, 'and we'll have scant more until we've crossed this.'

Thomas shuddered. 'Adan, it's a death-trap. One false step, no one will find us. Rædwulf, you must know this place.'

'Yes,' whispered Rædwulf. 'We bury our executed outlaws here.'

Adan looked towards the sunlit hills rising beyond the mile-wide wetland. 'We'll use the path,' he said. 'Yes, it's narrow, and difficult to see, but it's our only way across. We'll lead the horses in single file, two horse lengths apart, but don't lose sight of the man in front. Follow me.'

Rotten in places, the swaying wattle path yielded almost six inches underfoot, making the way treacherous, and the horses often stopped, disliking the unstable ground. Hirnac chanted something that calmed them, and they walked on, their footfalls the only sound in the flat quiet. Something slithering across the path ahead of Adan sploshed into a dark pool. It took them two hours to cross the mires; two more before reaching the ridge crest, stunted trees punctuating the steep slopes. A path led down the further slope to a wide glen scented with heather, thyme and gorse; an otherworldly silence conveyed anything but peace, and already the sun hung low.

Penda, gazing at a line of high hills beyond the glen, murmured, 'So, Soulis waits, and the Flame gives visions.'

Rædwulf took a slow breath. 'I can't believe things have changed so fast.'

'The very earth seems afraid,' said Adan. 'We'll need to stand guard tonight.'

'Alright,' said Penda, pointing to a stand of oaks and hazel in the glen, 'we'll camp in that thicket.'

'There's a mist rising,' said Adan. 'It won't lift until well after daybreak and will hide us.'

Penda nodded. 'Then we'll start at dawn.'

Thomas' tone bordered on sarcasm. 'Where is the entrance, Penda?'

'There's a secret way we can use, which I doubt they've found yet. We'll leave the horses in the trees and foot it from there.'

They reached the thicket at twilight; Penda lit a fire, Hirnac prepared a meal, and Thomas took first watch beside a nearby stream flowing between gorse and granite. A shadow flitted from one rock to another, and squinting through the gloom, he beheld an old woman crouching on the opposite bank, washing clothes, laying the garments on the surrounding rocks to dry. Oblivious, she began wailing, as though grieving, her eldritch screech fading into sudden silence. He stood rigid, unable to move or call, his heart thumping in his ears, and looked across the stream again, but she had vanished with the sound, and with the feeble light he had seen her by.

Adan, now standing beside him, whispered. 'I saw her too, Thomas, the old washerwoman of the wilderness. From now on, we'll watch in pairs.'

\*

Penda climbed the steps to the altar, the Flame a mere glow. A tall, beautiful woman he did not know stood beside it, her hair and robes white as frost, her eyes icy blue, her voice cold and hard as stone.

*'All the Blācencynn lie dead, Lyblǣca. Why return home when the Blācencynn all lie dead?'*

'To close the Gate,' he said.

*'Only I may close it, if the power returns,'* she said, *'and if the power returns, he who now rules the Caves shall do so forever.'* She extended her right hand. *'I control thee, Lyblǣca. I am fire, and I burn.'*

Hungry flames erupted around him, trapping him in searing agony; he screamed, awoke, and could not sleep again.

\*

Since leaving the forest, bright, multi-coloured geometric patterns, or fleeting shadows, had disturbed his vision. Sometimes, when things were quiet, or as he fell asleep, unknown voices disturbed him, speaking words he could not catch, giving him little peace. Twice he thought they called his name. Now, unable to ignore them, almost tormented, he paced back and forth, keeping everyone awake, until Rædwulf took him aside, beyond his companions' earshot.

'What's wrong, Penda?'

'I'm alright, Rædwulf; don't concern yourself.'

'No, you're not. You're tense; that's not like you.'

Penda sat down, clasping his hands between his knees. 'They're talking.'

Alarmed, Rædwulf said, 'They?'

Penda rested his chin on his clenched fists. 'They're talking. Voices in a closed room, but I can't hear what they're saying, and, and my eyes hurt.'

Rædwulf sighed. 'Come back to the camp, Penda. The company will do you good, but I will say this: whatever we may confront in the Caves, remember we are Blācencynn.'

CHAPTER SIXTEEN

# The North Gate

A pearly sun hung low as Penda led the way towards looming crags, the rough trail becoming a broad, shallow, almost level gully. Thomas looked back towards the glen many feet below, hidden beneath the mist.

Penda, sensing an ancient, seeping power, stopped at a low cave mouth, and afraid, hearts pounding, they crouched, peering at the darkness within.

'Anyone brought a torch?' said Adan.

Penda whispered, 'I have, and keep your voice down. If they hear us, we're dead. And take care; the tunnel's narrow, and only about four feet high.'

He lit the torch, and they crawled forward in single file, feeling for hazards, but the floor proved smooth, level and unobstructed. Water trickled down the walls, the flickering torchlight throwing huge, macabre shadows against the wet rock; cold draughts wafted along the tunnel, and a faint pulse, the slow heartbeat of a sleeping beast, came from everywhere. They reached another corridor, wide enough for them to walk abreast; Rædwulf leaned against the glistening wall.

'The entire place reeks of death,' he said. 'They must have murdered everyone.'

Hirnac pointed towards a faint, flickering light ahead. 'Look there,' he said. 'That's torchlight.'

'So,' said Adan, 'they have found it and won't be far away.'

Rædwulf led his companions towards it and recoiled at the tunnel entrance in horror; he recognised the faint tattoo on the flayed female human skin hanging on the opposite wall. Penda stifled a cry; Thomas glanced from them to Adan, and Hirnac turned away.

Rædwulf snarled, 'I will show no mercy, Soulis; no mercy.'

'Spriggans,' said Adan, 'are like dogs: coming when called, but impossible to dismiss.'

Hirnac looked around the cave. 'They must be watching us,' he said. 'Why don't they attack?'

'Because they're waiting,' said Adan, 'hiding in every nook and crevice.'

'And will find us, given time,' said Penda. Torch in hand, expecting an attack, he followed winding passages and stairways, leading everyone through caverns he knew so well; but all his boyhood playgrounds, all his secret adolescent trysting places, lay damaged, scorched; all silent, but for the slow, unnerving pulse, and he stopped outside the Higher Hall.

'Guard the entrance, gentlemen,' said Rædwulf, turning to Adan. 'Only the Blācencynn may enter this temple.'

Penda handed his torch to Hirnac and followed Rædwulf in. A sour stench filled the Hall; the gleaming floor runes had gone, and they gazed aghast at the foul, unlit candles, hood and empty stained bowl on the altar. Rædwulf, recognising the fatty mass within the vat standing amidst it all, picked up the Spear.

'I'll teach you how I make my candles.'

Rædwulf and Penda, turning towards the feeble, reedy voice, stared horrified at the emaciated Priest hanging on the wall; at his mottled skin, bleeding from many wounds; at his infected eye socket, the remaining eye almost blind; and at the foul stain on the wall below him. He spoke again.

'Not tallow… the candles… are not tallow. I know you, Rædwulf. I'll show you how I make my candles.' Dumbstruck, Rædwulf stared at the candles again. 'They are not tallow, Rædwulf… not tallow… watch how I make my candles…'

Before Penda could stop him, Rædwulf hefted the Spear and threw it, killing the Priest outright. He approached the altar, examined the hood, pocketed it, and drawing the Sword, smashed everything to dust in one violent sweep. Penda stared, first at Rædwulf, then at the Priest.

'Rædwulf, what have you done? *What have you done?* You're a healer; you could, *should,* have saved him, but instead you murdered him.'

Rædwulf faced him. 'Do you think I wanted to? I can't work miracles, Penda. He was beyond aid, even if we broke his shackles. Sometimes death is the only cure.'

Penda could not believe his callousness. 'What would you have done if I'd been hanging there?'

Already in the archway, Rædwulf faced him again. 'The same,' he said and walked away, but the deed forever haunted him. Penda stared at the Priest for perhaps a minute before following.

Resolute, silent, Rædwulf led everyone to a well-lit tunnel lined with regimented, wall-mounted, burning torches. Fallen rock littered the floor, faint echoes whispered from every cranny, and voices approached from ahead.

The torch Hirnac held burned out. 'Listen,' he said.

## The North Gate

Rædwulf ushered his companions into a narrow side passage. Here, hidden, weapons drawn, they watched five Spriggans, helmeted, stone-armoured, carrying vicious blades, march around a corner ten yards away with Soulis amongst them, his demeanour one of pure evil.

Rædwulf, giving a silent snarl, turned to Thomas and whispered, 'This passage leads to the upper chambers. Stay here; let no one pass you.' Locking eyes with Penda, he said, 'It's time; wind the Horn, Adan.'

The thundering call hammered the pulse into silence and stopped Soulis and his attendants in their tracks. Rædwulf roared, '*Blācencynn!*' and led a sudden attack, killing two Spriggans within seconds. Their comrades, their weapons no match for the Sword, closed ranks, pushing Soulis towards the side tunnel. Rædwulf followed, selecting his target, but his prey struck first. Experienced and crafty, the Spriggan leapt forward, and with unlimited ammunition to hand, now used a more primitive weapon: a slingshot. Rædwulf retreated, dodging missiles; Penda beheaded the Spriggan, and Soulis fled, Rædwulf, for once reckless, pursuing him.

Another guard leapt into the passageway, Thomas meeting it with fierce sword blows. Adan and Hirnac engaged with the fifth, but it leapt from floor to walls, to floor again, avoiding their arrows and blows, until it stood before Hirnac, poised to kill; Penda had a split second to intervene.

'Kill me, if you can reach me, *stone-wraith*.'

It faced him, slavering, leaping and dancing like a weasel before its prey; Adan and Hirnac came behind it, ready to strike.

Fighting hard, with little space to manoeuvre, Thomas heard marching feet approaching. 'They're behind me!' he yelled. 'Adan!' Adan and Hirnac ran to him, killed the guard and, shooting arrows, forced the advancing shadows into retreat.

With a blue light in his eyes, sword raised, and staring the Spriggan down, Penda spoke, his voice hollow, as though coming from elsewhere. 'Kill me, and destroy yourself, for you are mere stone.'

A sudden rock fall distracted him, breaking his concentration, and in that brief moment, the Spriggan struck him. The power blew it apart. Penda, with a wound to his collar bone, cried out, staggered, almost fell to his knees; recovered, and despite his pain, ran after Rædwulf.

\*

Soulis opened the long plinth and looked down the narrow flight of stairs descending into a torch-lit void, while behind him, slow, silent, ignoring the echoing shrieks of Spriggans already approaching, Rædwulf entered the council chamber.

Soulis turned, and Rædwulf, facing his enemy alone, with piercing hate in his eyes, levelled the Sword. 'Why do you not draw your weapon, *Lord Foulguest*? Are you a man? Can you not fight?'

Soulis drew his sword. 'What of you?' he said, lifting his top lip, a sneer reminding Rædwulf of Finnian. 'Are *you* a man, or are you nothing but a half-trained cub? Nothing can kill me.'

'I have destroyed your altar, Foulguest,' said Rædwulf, his gleaming eyes deadly as his blade. 'You can no longer summon Redcap to your aid.'

Soulis raised his left hand. 'I need no altar, for Robin Redcap, all Spriggans and the Flame obey me. Do you think you can reclaim your home, aided by ragged men? There is nothing left of it, Blācencynn, nothing left of you. The Rock Sprites will come upon you, binding you forever to the walls of Caves you once called home.'

Penda entered the chamber and stood beside Rædwulf, who gave a low, threatening growl. 'You command nothing, Foulguest.' They attacked Soulis, dealing unremitting savage blows, but to no effect, as though he wore invisible armour. He stepped back, his derisory laugh echoing beyond the cavern.

'You can't kill me!'

Penda, calling, 'Foulguest! You have no shield!' raised his right hand; the ring issued blinding light, and the Sword came down. His right arm wounded, Soulis leapt down the stairway; the trapdoor closed before Rædwulf could reach it and would not open again. Penda, straining to lift the cover, and having seen Rædwulf destroy the altar, said, 'Use the Sword to open it, Rædwulf.'

Rædwulf glanced at the ugly statues and carvings around the chamber. 'I can't,' he said; 'not without risking bringing everything down on us.' He faced Penda; saw his ashen face, the seeping blood, and touched the now sopping clothing in alarm, knowing he had neither time nor means to treat the injury. Penda, his eyes steady as rock, read his thought. He whispered, 'I can still fight. We must close the Gate, and there's only one place to do it.'

Rædwulf stared at him. 'The Flame? Penda, there's only one way there; that river's half a mile long if it's a yard, and I doubt we can swim so far in darkness. Can we not do it from here?'

Resolute, Penda whispered, 'We've no alternative, Rædwulf. The Caves feel different now, do you not sense it? Their very fabric has changed. I know what I'm doing, so leave me alone.'

Rædwulf recognised the truth, nodded, took him back to Adan and the others, and led everyone through tunnels, up stairways, and across a narrow, rickety bridge. Footfalls, quiet as moving air, came from behind them and Adan glanced back.

'I hear them coming,' he said, 'and there's no room for a sword fight here.'

Penda led them along a narrow passage at a run, snatching a torch from the wall as he went, and came to a sudden halt at a jagged opening in the wall. He looked in.

A new, wide tunnel, the floor unobstructed, sloped downward, straight towards a faint light only a hundred yards ahead. Turning to his companions, he said, 'Follow me,' and they ran forward.

Without warning, over twenty Spriggans blocked the way. Men and elves came to a sliding halt, stood motionless for one breath, then charged, Penda passing through the troop before they knew he was there. Adan and Hirnac fought for ground, Thomas and Rædwulf battled against the three strongest Spriggans, Rædwulf felling them with the merest blow of the Sword, and the Spriggans retreated, fearful of such a weapon. Penda attacked them from behind, beheading two; Thomas, one dead Spriggan at his feet, did not see another, waiting behind him, and Rædwulf yelled, 'Thomas!'

Thomas wheeled and killed it, but another leapt at him. Adan, coming at it from behind, struck its neck, and Thomas, caught in a foul deluge, reeled, giving a cry of disgust. Cowed and screeching, the remaining Spriggans fled, the torchlight revealing five weary men, their dead foes transformed into stone.

'Don't wait!' said Penda, waving them forward. 'This way.' They entered the cave and stood on the ledge, breathless and weary. His wound throbbing, and with blood trickling to his groin, Penda looked in disbelief around the bleached, silent, torch-lit space: at the rough steps leading down to the dais and at the black, sinister lake twenty feet below, and more than twice as deep again. The Flame hissed, shrank, and flared.

Spriggans leapt from the tunnel, yelling as they came, pressing Thomas against the wall and surrounding

Rædwulf, no longer fearing his blade. His strength ebbing, fighting off blows, he fell to his knees; Hirnac and Adan fought, keeping their way of retreat open. Penda ran to the stairway; he never reached it.

Howling Spriggans swarmed towards him, blocking his way, and weakened, he stood on the brink, facing them. His left arm useless, he dropped the torch, drew his sword, and only half aware, spoke to them, his low, distorted voice somehow penetrating.

'Come to me.'

They ran at him, dealing him a violent blow; he reeled and plummeted into the lake, Rædwulf screaming his name.

Everything stopped for seconds; then the men fought on, Rædwulf leading a reckless, fruitless defence. Sudden, searing blue-white light filled the cavern, and they crouched, shielding their eyes, while around them, the blinded Spriggans, stumbling in every direction, fell from the ledge and drowned in the depths. The light went out, leaving a residual glow. Rædwulf and his companions looked down at Penda standing on the dais, small, distant, vulnerable, his wet hair clinging to his face and shoulders. He lowered his right hand and stood rigid, watching the Flame, wondering what had brought him here; how it had come to this. His exhaustion, his pain, his draining life blood no longer mattered. The power poured from him; the Flame flared and shrank: it was all. Lightning flashed across the cavern, distant thunder echoed through the tunnels, and the rock trembled. His fists clenched, he chanted, his whispered words becoming a loud cry:

*'The North Gate shall close.'*

Again, Rædwulf yelled, 'Penda!'

Thunder shook the Caves, and lightning struck the stair, sending splintered stone cascading into the lake. Rocks falling from the roof fell close to Adan on the ledge, and Thomas fell, stunned by a glancing blow. Rædwulf, staring at the Flame, spoke through gritted teeth.

'He'll kill us all.'

Lightning struck the walls; the cavern shook, rocks fell into the churning lake, and Penda continued chanting, turning about on the heaving dais. Then came a sudden calm, and in overwhelming pain, he kneeled, weeping.

'It's over,' he whispered. 'All the Blācencynn are dead. The Flame has no power. It need not burn at all.'

The echoes repeated: *'The Blācencynn are dead.'*

He staggered to his feet, calling again, his voice more frantic. 'The Blācencynn are dead. *We are all dead!*' Again, he raised his right hand, giving a devastating cry. *'The North Gate shall close!'*

The ground heaved, throwing him off his feet; the roof fell before he could stand, destroying the altar and dais, and his despairing scream of terror echoed into dark, ghastly silence. Rædwulf crawled forward until his groping hands met space, and he lay teetering in the blind darkness. 'Penda...Penda,' he whispered, but only a hissing echo replied. Adan found him by touch and dragged him from the brink. Hirnac, picking up the still-burning torch, said quietly, 'Where's Thomas?'

They found him, half-conscious, huddled, moaning, lying face down in the crook of ledge and wall. Adan helped him up, then clutched his arm in fear, watching a dense, intangible shadow, that invaded every crevice, rising from the void below.

'What's that?'

'It's searching,' said Rædwulf. 'Searching.'

The shadow evolved into a diffuse, glowing haze, and Adan, Rædwulf and Hirnac, sensing its power, knelt again, shielding themselves; but Thomas, dazed, staring into space, taking three stiff paces towards the weird, shimmering cloud, bowed in submission. It enveloped him, gave an intense flash, and shrank; a high, piercing, eldritch shriek shattered the silence, and he reeled, as from a heavy blow. The light vanished, the echoes died away, and Rædwulf spoke from the dark.

'We must find him.'

They made their way down the tortured, twisted steps, searching amongst the ruin until Adan, giving a sudden cry and beckoning to the others, slid down, almost to lake level. Hirnac raised the torch. Penda lay buried, only his right forearm exposed, his hand clutching a rock; the ring had shattered. Rædwulf knelt, and taking the hand in his, whispered, 'I'll have Redcap's head for this.'

Adan met the desolate grey stare and said, 'Rædwulf, Rædwulf; we must leave.' Rædwulf stood up, making a sudden, wild gesture. 'Why? Why leave, when we can all stay here forever, trapped like so much carrion? No cause is worth this!'

Straining against Adan manhandling him towards the stair, he gave a savage, bellowing cry that thundered around the cavern. *'I'm coming for you, Redcap! Do you hear me? I'm coming for you!'*

The men scrambled through collapsing, smoke-filled caverns, never knowing how many prisoners lay dead or dying in the dungeons, and crawled outside at dusk, grimed, sweating, despairing. When they reached the thicket, Hirnac threw the extinguished torch aside and lit a fire. Rædwulf knelt beside it, his face buried in his hands, shoulders shaking as he wept, his companions too exhausted to keep watch.

\*

Sinister moorland stretched to the horizon under the waning moon, refreshing smells came on the breeze, and Soulis stood looking at a tiny hamlet huddled in a dusky glen. His half dozen guards returned, bringing a sack of looted food, a few bottles of ale, and a terrified woman, her wrists bound with tight thongs. They pushed her to the ground at his feet, and he raised her chin with his sword.

'Well, my little one, is this how you greet your rightful lord?' She made no reply, and Soulis snarled. 'Answer me, or it'll be your life.'

She glanced at the sword, stared at his cruel, twisted mouth and savage eyes, and struggled to whisper, 'Good evening, sire.'

Soulis, greeting this with derisive laughter and taunts, turned to his guards, strutting, bowing to them, making obscene gestures. 'Do you hear the little one? Good evening, sire, good evening.' He crouched close to her, again resting his sword against her neck. 'Now listen to me, little one,' he said, gesturing at his injury. 'I need a doctor, see? And if I don't find one, I will kill you, and your folk, and burn your hamlet down by morningtide.'

'There is no doctor here,' she said. 'We rely on old wives' tales and country medicines, although sometimes, perhaps twice a year, a travelling healer comes to us. Wyrtræd, he calls himself, but we haven't seen him for many months.'

His heavy breath sickening her, he caressed her face with his. 'Where is he, pretty one?'

She whimpered, 'I don't know.'

He dropped his sword, sudden pain crippling him; sweating, he clutched his arm for minutes before regaining his composure, then in fury dealt her face a heavy blow. 'You dare refuse me aid?' He beckoned to his guards. 'Play with this little thing, and when you're tired of play, kill it.'

They did.

Amused, Soulis watched them impale her dismembered body on improvised stakes. Then he pointed towards the hamlet. 'Torch it.'

He watched the burning buildings, memorising every detail: how high the flames were; which way the wind blew them; the thickness, smell and direction of the smoke; the loudness of the screams. It excited him. He waited until his guards returned, abasing themselves before him, and gave an order.

'Bring me this... Wyrtræd, on his knees. He will heal me, then die. Go.'

Three Spriggans loped away, and Soulis, for the moment too weak to follow, traced an arcane symbol over the fire and said, in a low voice, *'Now I summon those beyond the Divide: and they shall answer me.'* Hidden observers withdrew into the night.

CHAPTER SEVENTEEN

# The Messenger

Thomas climbed to a hilltop where Rædwulf, Hirnac, Adan and a crowd of ordinary people stood around a stout rowan tree under a coppery sky, waiting, expecting him to do something; a plain girl he knew from home, wearing a short veil over her brown, plaited hair, a coarse linen dress and an apron, stood behind a huge bronze cauldron.

'Molly,' he whispered.

She answered, not in her voice, but in Læren's. 'This Faerie gift is for you.'

'Why are these people here?'

'They're waiting for Penda,' said Adan. 'He's had a long journey but will arrive soon.'

Thomas bowed his head. 'He's dead.'

'Soulis isn't,' said Rædwulf. 'Nor Redcap; you must decide their fate.'

A tall, bearded man stepped forward through the crowd, giving a vacant stare from dark eyes, then that sudden, close-lipped, benevolent smile Thomas remembered.

'It's up to you, Thomas,' said Penda. 'It's for you.'

\*

Soulis watched the breaking dawn, breathing in thick smoke from the green fire. Finnian, standing beside him, spoke with convincing humility, choosing his words, planting ideas Soulis thought his own.

'Sire, the wind sends news: the Earth grieves for the stripling, and the Gate cannot open without the Horn and Sword, which again, have slipped through your fingers. Thomas Learmont and his men have taken them, their intentions unknown, but men are fallible, Learmont being no exception.'

'So, we must force his hand,' said Soulis. 'He would protect his kin from threats, real or imagined; therefore, we will start rumours of a planned attack on Ercildoun. Wait for us there, but remain discreet. We shall welcome him home; teach him what justice means, the Horn and Sword ours for the taking.' Finnian withdrew. Soulis sprinkled dried leaves into the fire and walked around it, chanting,

*I shall hold court in Ercildoun,*
*In Thomas Learmont's own hall.*
*I am Soulis, the Immortal.*

He raised his left arm heavenward, his cry carrying for miles. 'I will destroy thee, Ercildoun, village and man!'

With shadows surrounding him, he walked towards the sunrise, unaware of someone watching him from a granite outcrop.

\*

Rædwulf awoke at dawn and looked around for Penda before remembering the bitter truth. His companions were asleep, the horses dozing; the fire had burned down to embers, and the thicket lay silent under an overcast sky.

Hollow, broken, his amulet glinting in the dull morning light, he stood at the eaves, looking at the hills, reliving each moment over and again. He lifted his gaze to a raven calling from the nearby heights; quiet as the soft breeze blowing through his hair, he whispered, 'Take the news to the Old Ones, Master Raven; take the news. The Blācencynn are all dead.'

'Not so, Rædwulf.' Thomas approached him, his untidy hair blowing across his face, his bloody tunic torn, his fierce, pleading eyes suggesting fear. 'Not so. You are Blācencynn and must avenge your kin.'

Rædwulf looked at the hills again. Softly, he said, 'I once said I would have no comfort until I avenged my kindred, but I find none. I've nothing left, Thomas, nothing left to give.'

Thomas stepped forward again, his green eyes searching, piercing, his impassioned tone imploring. 'I don't believe you. What of the Seelie Court? What of Raldis… and Læren? The frightened child stood before you, asking what she should do if the Spriggans attacked. She was looking at Raldis but was asking *you*, Rædwulf.' He mastered his tone. 'You said you'd have Redcap's head—well, you won't find it here.' He met the desolate eyes. 'What would be the cost, Rædwulf? What price if you did nothing? We need you. In God's name, Rædwulf, I need your help.' He now sounded afraid. 'This thing clings to me, this thing I cannot handle. Why did it come to me? Why?'

Rædwulf sat down, looking at his clasped hands. 'Because you stood dazed and had no defence,' he said at last. 'Be warned, Thomas, it will use you; and overpower anyone who tries controlling it.'

## The Messenger

Thomas sat down, rubbing his thumb against his fingers. 'What now, Rædwulf? Where do we go?'

Rædwulf gave a weak smile. 'That depends on Redcap.' He glanced towards the trees where Hirnac and Adan now stood, listening to the conversation. Adan, leaning on his bow, shifted his position, giving Rædwulf a long, thoughtful look, summing up his intentions.

'Lord Blācencynn,' he said, 'Soulis' death has not paid the debt, and we have yet to take vengeance. We must go to the Mereburg before Redcap opens the South Gate and stop him from attacking the Seelie Court.'

Rædwulf drew a slow breath. 'I don't dispute you, Adan, but if I could stay, just for another two days…'

'Lord Blācencynn,' said Hirnac, 'might I suggest we wash our clothes? We are all bloody, and the smell attracts wolves.'

Thomas, still staring into space, nodded. 'That's true enough; but we shouldn't stay here.'

*Bloodied:* Rædwulf, dried blood on his right hand, pressed his clenched fist to his mouth, vowing to himself that, whatever the cost, he would hunt Redcap down to the very ends of the Earth. He sighed. 'There's a tarn we can reach by noon if we leave now.'

Borderlands

\*

Desperate, angry villagers gathered in the small farmhouse, crowding around Moris and his wife, Judith.

'Soulis has stolen all we had, Moris,' said one, 'and now we dare not work our fields; but worse, he has taken our children, our very futures.'

'Aye,' said another. 'How long do we wait before he takes our women, too? How long before he burns down our homesteads? Present our case to the Sherriff at the court of assizes next month, Moris; let him bring Soulis to account.'

'We cannot wait that long,' said the blacksmith, a brawny, fair-haired man. 'We must confront Soulis ourselves—demand he return our children and pay us compensation.'

All gave an intimidating roar of 'Yea!' and elected Moris as their spokesman. He cleared his throat.

'Friends, we can't all go.'

The blacksmith folded his arms. 'Then I suggest we draw lots.'

'We don't have the straw, John,' said Moris, 'even for that.'

## The Messenger

Judith, a strong, level-headed woman in her thirties, said, 'We may not have straw, but we've stones aplenty.' She withdrew, returning half an hour later, and handing Moris a small bag, whispered something to him.

He held it out, saying aloud, 'I invite those with few commitments, who are prepared to take the risk, and still have riding horses, to step forward. He who draws a green stone shall come with me tomorrow, and he will not turn aside.'

Ten men came forward, four drawing green: Moris' new-wed, scrawny nephew Jacob; Robbie, a near neighbour; Andrew, a tough, strong-minded labourer; and John. The men left, promising to meet Moris at the nearby crossroads the next day.

He drew up a chair and sat, dreading the morning. 'I don't know what will become of us,' he said, 'but we must try.'

Judith knelt beside him. 'Find the children, if nothing else, Moris; bring them home. If Soulis comes with swords, we'll meet him with scythes; but if he comes with fire, then I'd burn down our house myself, rather than watch him do it.'

He kissed her hand. 'The angels blessed me when I married you.'

## Borderlands

\*

Oblique dawn light came through thin clouds, the only sound the high mew of an eagle drifting aloft; nothing moved across the land, and a breeze ruffled the tarn surface.

His companions sleeping, Hirnac sat beside the small fire, watching the expanse of grassy moors and high rocks standing sentinel against the sky. He checked what little rations they had and shook Adan awake.

'Sire,' he said, 'We've not enough supplies to reach the Mereburg.'

Adan propped himself up on one elbow, thinking. 'We could forage or find provisions from settlements along the way.'

'If Soulis hasn't raided them first.'

Adan raised an eyebrow. 'Yes, indeed.' He paused, thinking again. 'Alright, Hirnac, wake the others; Thomas' snoring is giving me a headache.'

Rough, fragmented paths led them across open, grassy land punctuated with granite crags; they camped at dusk in the lee of a hill, and Hirnac lit a fire. Having eaten some of their meagre rations, they settled down to sleep, with Adan on watch.

# The Messenger

Rædwulf awoke to sounds of bleating sheep and approached Hirnac, who was standing on watch in the growing daylight.

'Where are we, Hirnac? How far is the Mereburg from here?'

Hirnac leaned on his bow, watching the horizon. 'I'm not sure, sire, in all fairness. Adan will know more, but we should have a clearer idea if we climb yonder ridge.' He nodded towards a steep bluff on the horizon.

Rædwulf followed his gaze. 'That's well over ten miles away, Hirnac, even as the crow flies, and we've little food left.' He fell silent, thinking, then said, 'I'll wake Adan and Thomas. The sooner we start, the sooner we'll arrive.'

Detours around steep hillsides and peat bogs hampered their journey, and they were not halfway when Adan pulled rein, pointing to the right. 'We're not alone,' he said. 'Look, a horseman's coming this way.'

'Here?' said Rædwulf in surprise. 'We're miles from anywhere. Where could he have come from?'

'He's riding fast,' said Hirnac, 'as if he knows what he's looking for.'

'Or who,' remarked Thomas, watching the horseman halt, change direction, and approach them.

'Don't dismount,' said Adan, 'until we know his purpose.'

The horseman stopped a few yards away, his anxious, searching hazel eyes looking at each man in turn, while they gazed at him with suspicion. He was a young man with a few days' growth of beard, wearing good clothing and a felt cap over his fine, brown, shoulder-length hair. Adan walked his horse a few paces forward and called out, 'Declare yourself.'

The man made a disarming gesture. 'I am Douglas Campbell, messenger to the Laird who aided you some days ago, and I'm looking for Lord Ercildoun.'

Thomas, hood pulled up, spoke more sharply than intended. 'Can you prove it?'

'I have this, sire,' said Douglas, holding out a twisted leather strap.

Thomas rode to his side, took the chafed strap from him, examined the twine stitching a third of the way along its length, smiled, and turned to Adan.

'A repaired stirrup strap,' he said. 'We need not doubt this man's word.' He turned to the messenger. 'I am Lord Ercildoun; why do you look for me?'

'I have news,' said Douglas, still breathless, 'and have ridden for miles, looking for you, but I lost all sense of time in the fog; the paths led me astray, to hills instead of glens, glens instead of hills.'

Rædwulf nodded towards a grassy space beneath a crag. 'We can sit over there. When did you last eat?'

Douglas bowed. 'This morning, sire, so I don't need feeding, but I would thank you for a drink.'

They sat in a circle, Hirnac handing Douglas a flask. Rædwulf folded his arms.

'You said you've ridden far to find us,' he said. 'We've little spare time, so what news, Douglas Campbell?'

'Lord Soulis is on the move. I saw him, lord, surrounded by twisted shadows, standing near a fire that burned green flames, conjuring darkness.'

Rædwulf, staring at him in disbelief, whispered, 'It's not true,' then in a more heated tone, 'It can't be true! The Caves collapsed, burying him with all his sprites and demons. It can't be true.'

The messenger drank again, then shook his head. 'No, sire. I heard him casting spells against Ercildoun, village and man.' He looked at Thomas, who sat staring at him. 'That's where he's going, sire,' said Douglas, 'to Ercildoun, with those awful shadows, even as we speak, intending to destroy it.'

Taken aback, Thomas stood up and walked away, his hood pulled low, and Adan, swapping a meaningful look with Rædwulf, leaned towards Douglas. 'Have you told the Laird?'

Douglas nodded. 'Yes, lord, he sent me to find you, with the leather strap, to prove my word.'

Rædwulf frowned. 'When did you see Soulis?'

'I'm not sure, but he's on foot, so it may take him days to reach Ercildoun. I believe he's injured, and I don't think he can use his right arm.'

Rædwulf went to Thomas, who stood, fists clenched, scanning the horizon. 'We can't help them, Thomas,' he said. 'Soulis would be there long before us.'

Thomas stared into his eyes, said, 'I don't hear you,' and marched to Adan, fixing an intense gaze on him. 'Will it take us long to reach Ercildoun?'

Adan led him away. 'I don't know, Thomas.'

'How *long*, Adan?'

Adan glanced at the ground, took several breaths, and met the pleading gaze. 'Ercildoun lies beyond the veil from here, Thomas. It could take us months to reach it, or no time at all. It's impossible to say.'

Thomas spoke through his teeth. 'You can't mean that.'

## The Messenger

Adan pointed to the distant bluff. 'The Mereburg is but half a day's journey beyond those hills, Thomas. Half a day. If we reclaim it, if we kill Redcap, Soulis will find no sanctuary there. His life will be nothing but aimless wandering, without a friend or shelter, a fitting end to an evil creature.'

Thomas, his piercing eyes fierce, his tone heated, grasped Adan's tunic collar. 'Remember what you saw at that settlement, Adan? I won't let Ercildoun share that fate. I won't let it happen, do you hear me?' He lowered his tone to a threatening, distorted whisper, his eyes darkening. 'The Flame will not allow it.' He mastered himself, releasing the collar. 'I know Ercildoun can't compare with grand Elf halls and culture,' he said. 'The folk scratch their humble living from the land… but it's still my home.'

Adan beckoned to Rædwulf, Hirnac and the messenger. 'Douglas Campbell,' he said, glancing towards Thomas, 'your news has both troubled and helped us, and we thank you. We'd give you food for your journey home, but we've little to spare, so must send you on your way as you are, with greetings and our thanks, hoping you understand.'

Douglas, giving a smart bow, mounted his horse. 'I thank you, my lord, for allowing me to rest with you, and may God bless your progress.'

He rode away, disappearing between the folded hills. Adan sat down, thinking, looking from Rædwulf to Thomas, then at the hills.

'Open the Faerie paths to Ercildoun, Adan,' said Thomas. 'You must open the way.'

Little passed Rædwulf unnoticed; he gave Thomas a thoughtful look. 'I wonder, Thomas, whether this is less about defending your people and more about protecting someone in particular?'

Adan moistened his lips. 'We've other things to consider. Would you have us go with you, Thomas, assuming what Campbell said wasn't a mere smokescreen? We might wait for Soulis, maybe for months, if he arrives at all, leaving Redcap free to open the South Gate, exposing Bright Faerie to every mortal evil: corruption, disease, death.'

Thomas, standing feet apart, his eyes revealing more than he intended, sounded defensive. 'I won't abandon my people, Adan. If you go to the Mereburg now, you'll go without me.' Turning on his heel, he walked away, Hirnac calling after him.

'You'd let Redcap destroy us, Thomas. Don't you *care?*'

## The Messenger

'Maybe it isn't Thomas driving us, Hirnac,' said Rædwulf quietly, 'but the Flame driving him, though I doubt he knows it.'

Adan did not move for almost five minutes. Then, as though thinking aloud, he said, 'Either we separate or not; going together, either to Ercildoun or the Mereburg, risks destruction of the other. What do you think, Blācencynn?'

Rædwulf sat beside him. 'We can't force Thomas into anything. We've seen what that power can do when threatened, making no distinction between friend and foe, but I assure you, Campbell did not deceive us.'

Adan thought for a while longer. 'Hirnac?'

Hirnac glanced towards Thomas. 'By going with him, we'll give Redcap his chance to open the South Gate.'

'And it won't close without the power,' said Rædwulf. 'Learmont has us over a barrel, Adan. We can't do anything without him.' He stood up and beckoned Thomas to join them. 'You leave us little choice, Learmont,' he said, 'but to go with you, and maybe stop Soulis in Ercildoun.'

'But remember, Thomas,' said Adan, 'we cannot know what we'll find there. You should prepare yourself for the same horrors we saw at the settlement we visited.' He climbed the crag, stood scanning the land, and gestured to a track not visible before, leading northwest. He called to him, 'There's your way, Thomas.'

\*

Hermitage Castle stood shadowed and silent under a cloudless blue sky, but the warm sunshine could not melt the ice on every wall.

The nervous farmers surveyed the gloomy, deserted courtyard beyond the huge, open iron-bound gate, and Robbie shuddered.

'This is evil, Moris. Must we go in?'

'If we want justice,' said Moris, no less afraid.

They rode through the gate into a timeless zone, drawing rein in the empty castle forecourt, but did not dismount.

'We've had a wasted journey, Moris,' said Robbie. 'There's no one here.'

Jacob almost squeaked. 'No one here? Can't you see them? They're all around us.'

The men now sensed peripheral shadows, heard muffled voices and sounds of activity; the gate began closing behind them.

## The Messenger

'Out!' shouted Moris, turning his horse, 'For God's sake, before we're trapped!'

\*

For days, Thomas allowed his comrades little rest. The weather became dull and damp; weary, hungry, thirsty as their horses, their pace slowed. Adan, riding at his side, protested.

'If we don't rest, Thomas, the horses will drop dead in two days.'

'If we don't rest,' retorted Thomas, 'we'll reach Ercildoun in one.'

They stopped at dusk in a dell hidden in the pasture, and Rædwulf, standing with Thomas on the lip of the hollow, gazed across the fields. 'I think we should camp here,' he said.

Thomas nodded, saying, 'We're almost there, but we can't approach Ercildoun now. They will have shut the gate… if anyone's there to close it.'

Rædwulf threw him a sharp look. 'Do you think Soulis is already there?'

'I don't know, Rædwulf. I dread we might find everything burned and everyone hanging from the trees.'

Rædwulf grasped Thomas' right shoulder and said earnestly, 'You don't know that. None of us know that. You said yourself we'll take vengeance if Soulis is there, and we will, Thomas, either there or at the Mereburg.'

Thomas, holding Rædwulf's gaze, nodded, then returned to the comforting campfire, Rædwulf taking the watch at nightfall.

Thomas awoke at midnight. Adan and Hirnac were both asleep, the weather cloudy, windy, and warm, but the shadowed dell seemed sinister in the firelight. He saw Rædwulf, standing on the dell bank again, gazing northward; he approached and stood behind him, neither man speaking for a long while, until Rædwulf gave a long, unsteady sigh.

'Why did we leave him?'

He returned to the campfire, but Thomas stayed where he was, watching the silent fields. A sudden, distorted feminine voice came from nearby.

*'You will need to fight hard in the morning.'*

Thomas spun around but saw no one, and a strange, menacing wind hissed through the meadows.

## Chapter Eighteen

# Hired Hands

Ercildoun lay undisturbed, its gate open, only the river gurgling along its channel breaking the dawn hush. A few hens pecked their way across the quiet, rutted street, and one or two dogs crept between the silent, shuttered houses as Thomas and his companions rode into the village. With no sign anywhere of Soulis, nor of anything to cause alarm, they dismounted at the preaching cross. Their thirsty horses guzzled water from a nearby trough while Thomas checked his saddle girth.

'Tom!'

He turned towards the voice, and a young, nondescript maiden ran forward, stopped, and again ran forward, seeming as if she might embrace him. She had shining, lively eyes and an engaging smile; wore a short veil, an apron over her faded yellow linen dress, and no wedding ring.

Thomas gave her a deep, affectionate smile. 'Hello, Molly.'

Molly, touching his beard, withdrew her hand. 'You've changed, Tom.'

His smile deepened. 'You haven't. What news in Ercildoun?'

'These are strange days, Lord Ercildoun,' she said, looking at her shuffling feet. 'We heard that some farmers, from a place called Hermitage, arrived a couple of days ago, asking for you. They're staying at the inn.'

Brief surprise showed in his eyes. 'Hermitage?'

She ignored this, dropping her voice to a whisper. 'Then a strange woman called at the house yesterday evening, saying she had left something in Harper's barn for you.'

'But it's derelict,' said Thomas, glancing along the road. 'She must have meant Paget's.'

Molly seemed sheepish. 'No, Tom. Mother and I checked, although told not to.'

'What did she bring?' asked Rædwulf.

She neither looked at him nor noticed his guarded tone. 'A cauldron, sir. A huge one.'

Rædwulf, twitching an eyebrow, looked at Adan. 'What did she look like?'

'I can't say,' said Molly, glancing at him. 'A veil hid her face, but she seemed quite tall.'

Thomas frowned. 'Is she still here?'

Molly shook her head. 'She couldn't wait, but said you should all lodge with us, no questions asked, though we've little space.'

'I was going to my house,' said Thomas.

'Have you *seen* it?' said Molly, raising her brows. 'You can't reach the door for the brambles.' Ignoring his bewilderment, she looked at the ground. 'Tom, I think you should go to the barn. This woman sounded, well, sort of anxious.'

He thought for a while. 'That can wait for now. Can you feed us?'

'Aye, we'd be glad to,' she said, smiling. 'Follow me.'

The farmhouse stood at the foot of a steep, wooded hillside further along the road. There was a wooden bench at the house front, another at the back; outhouses and a wood store lined one side of the yard, vegetables grew amongst herbs and flowering marigolds in the back garden, and a mature oak tree stood close to a low knoll near the rear dry-stone boundary wall.

A large room, partitioned sleeping areas on one side, a platform on the other where Molly slept, occupied almost the entire house. It smelt of bacon, wood smoke, thatch and the scattered straw on the floor; hams, sacks of root vegetables, bundles of herbs, tools and a lantern hung from the beams; a candle box stood on a shelf, a blanket box beneath, and dim light came from the burning candle on the table. A woman, an older version of Molly, wearing a large apron over her brown linen dress, and a full wimple, sat beside the fire, stirring a pot. Molly could not suppress a smile.

'Mother,' she said. 'Mother, he's here.'

The woman dropped her spoon, stood up, and smiling, approached Thomas, looking him over.

'It's been too long since Tom Learmont came under this roof,' she said, then threw her arms around him. 'I'll swear you've grown at least a hand span, but you've lost weight, lad.' He hugged her, lifting her from the floor, and she gasped. 'You've not lost your strength, though, have you?'

He gave a soft laugh. 'Nell, you've a heart of gold.'

She disentangled herself. 'Save your charm, Tom, please.'

He laughed again. 'Is Keith here?'

She nodded towards the far wall. 'Tending the sow, but he'll be here for his meal, and before you ask, Molly's brothers are in the fields guarding the sheep.' She stepped past him and assessed Rædwulf, taking in his grey eyes, his shoulders, his overall bearing. 'This must be Rædwulf, the copper-haired healer,' she said, and moved to Adan. 'You are strange,' she said. 'Here, yet distant.' Studying Hirnac, she remarked, 'Ah, yes, this must be Hirnac Strawfax.' She returned to the hearth and resumed stirring, saying, 'Lads, please pardon me, but I just wanted to know *what* is under my roof.'

Unused to being referred to as 'lad', Rædwulf coughed, glancing towards Molly. 'Your caution is wise, Goodwife, and your comments perceptive.'

Nell shrugged. 'Mere observation, sir. Make yourselves at home and we'll have breakfast once my husband's here.'

Keith, a short, stocky, lame man with peppery hair and an honest, weathered face with his daughter's freckles, gave his guests a perfunctory glance.

'Put your weapons aside, lads,' he said. 'Nell and Molly dislike them, and you'll not need them here.' He continued speaking during the meal. 'We've one spare corner you can fight over—if we turf out the dogs first—and you can stable your horses in the yard.'

Rædwulf smiled. 'We'll just sleep in the middle, here. After spending days in the wilderness without shelter, a wooden floor with a roof above is comfort indeed.'

'Tom,' said Molly, touching his arm, 'I can move from my bed-space and sleep in the byre if you need more room.'

He smiled. 'No, Hen, there's no need. We'll be content in here.'

Thomas drew strength from Molly, and he gave her a reason for being; they adored each other. Her girlish responses to his affectionate, playful teasing made a welcome distraction for Rædwulf, who was not above joining in.

'Molly,' he said, 'do you know moorland spiders are larger than this plate?' Unimpressed, having heard similar before, she stared at his deadpan expression. He leaned towards her, sparkling roguishness in his eyes. 'Mmm,' he said, raising an eyebrow, 'they eat mice,' then whispered, 'and the mice are big as cats.'

'I would imagine then,' she said, blushing and trying to suppress a smile, 'the cats must be big as wolves.'

'Oh, much bigger,' he said, winking.

'You're just like him,' she exclaimed, pointing at Thomas. 'Anyway, what's wrong with spiders?'

He scowled, almost cringing. 'They scuttle.'

'Well, they don't bother me,' she said, picking up some empty plates. 'They catch flies and help keep the house clean.'

Thomas, leaning across the table towards Rædwulf, whispered, 'It's true. She once kept one, big as your hand, as a pet for weeks.'

Rædwulf gave him a steady look. 'Then I'll know who to scream for if I find one lurking in my cot tonight,' he said and, ignoring the Learmont grin, turned to Keith. 'Goodman, may we offer payment for your hospitality?'

Keith shook his head. 'No, sire, we will take no coin for a charitable deed.'

'Perhaps we'll pay you in kind,' said Rædwulf. 'May we help with some chores?'

Keith smiled. 'Aye, sir, you may indeed, if you can chop firewood.'

Rædwulf gave his wry smile. 'Yes, Goodman, I can chop firewood.'

Keith pushed his empty plate aside. 'Tom, you can shift some straw bales from one outhouse, if you would be so kind; and if your other friends can help me in the vegetable garden and assist Molly and Nell in the house, I think we'll call it quits.'

He took Rædwulf to the wood store. 'Fill that,' he said, indicating a large basket and an axe. 'It will take you a while.'

Rædwulf stripped off his cloak and tunic, selected one hefty log, and with force, soon reduced it to matchwood, hard work on a warm day. His loose sweaty shirt hampering him, and believing himself unobserved, he flung it off and began on the next log; then he saw, not firewood, but the necks of his every foe, and bringing the axe down, he chanted with each heavy blow: '*I am Rædwulf; I am Blācencynn.*'

He stopped, wiped sweat from his forehead, shook his damp hair from his face, and saw Nell standing some distance away, watching him, her appraising glance noting every detail: the wood fragments caught in his beard and chest hair; the trickling sweat; his gleaming amulet; his fierce, piercing eyes and slow, deep breathing; the axe he held, the basket half full of firewood and the debris at his feet, and he read the '*If only*' in her eyes. Unabashed, she approached, picked up his shirt where he had thrown it, and handed it to him. 'Sire, I am but a humble farmer's wife,' she said in a steady voice, 'but hoped my noble guest might respect my maiden daughter and wear his shirt.'

With a teasing twinkle in his eyes, and giving a slight smile, he put the axe down. 'Don't worry, Goodwife; I'll only seduce her if she lets me.' Reaching for his shirt, he added, 'Perhaps a humble farmer's wife would forgive a lord in exile.'

'It seems you've fought many battles, sir,' she said, noting the marks on his forearm.

'Battle wounds, Nell, don't leave small scars.'

Thoughtful, she said, 'I think you're something more than a healer. Tell me, sire, what are you, in fact?'

He held her gaze. 'Something you wouldn't understand, Goodwife, but nothing that will harm you.'

Her gaze softening, she pointed to a small shed. 'I'll send a tub of hot water to the outhouse there if you want a bath; and we've ale, if you're thirsty.'

'I may need both,' he said, giving a slight smile. 'Thank you, Nell.'

\*

Washed, combed and dressed, he met Thomas in the yard mid-morning and glanced at the basket he held.

'Blācencynn,' said Thomas, nodding towards a roof peeping between the trees, 'Keith made this for Little

Sarah, who lives in that cottage. Everyone's busy, so if you're free, could you take it?'

Rædwulf shrugged off a fleeting doubt. 'Well, alright, I won't be a minute.'

Sheets draped on racks outside the run-down cottage should have warned him, but he knocked on the closed door, called, 'Is anyone home?' and waited, looking back towards the farmhouse. The cottage door behind him opened.

'Who are *you?*'

A small, though hefty, young wench, buxom beyond his belief, stepped in front of him. She had hazel eyes and untidy brown hair; she reeked of lavender, and her tight red dress left nothing to his imagination. He could not miss the strands of wispy hair on her chin or the crude application of rudimentary cosmetics, nor mistake her calling. He almost dropped the basket.

'Oh... *no.*'

She took the basket and, placing it beside the door, gave him a hungry look. 'Where are you from?'

He backed off. 'Somewhere you wouldn't have heard of.'

'You must be the handsomest man there.'

'I wouldn't know,' he mumbled, backing again, but she pulled him inside by his belt and closed the door.

'I don't always entertain before noon,' she said, stroking his beard, 'but I'll make an exception for such a bonnie gentleman.' Too polite to insult her, or push her off, and too proud to run, he resisted. 'Oh, you're shy,' she said, exploring his tunic fastening. 'Never mind, I'll soon cure that.'

Outmanoeuvred, propelled, cornered, he toppled back onto the bed, and she straddled him before he could move.

'Madam,' he protested, 'this doesn't seem such a good idea.'

'There's no rush, my handsome,' she crooned, her deft fingers unfastening her bodice and his belt. 'Just relax, and let me do my job.'

He gave a muffled yelp, halfway between panic and submission.

*

Keith, seated on a bale in the hay shed, watched Thomas lifting bales onto a small barrow for a while; he rubbed his lame leg and folded his arms.

'So, you've turned up again, Tom.'

Thomas looked at him. 'This isn't just a social call, Keith.'

'Your visits seldom are, although Molly's happy you're here.'

Thomas, loading hay on the barrow, said, 'I know,' and threw him a sharp, defensive glare. 'I'm not making love to her, Keith, if that's your worry.'

Keith stood up. 'We'll always welcome you in this house, but neither your status, nor paying my medical bill, give you rights. You're a rascal, Tom Learmont, and as long as I've breath, you will never marry my daughter.' He held the intense gaze for a moment, turned, and walked out.

Nettled, Thomas stared after him, kicked the barrow, marched outside, and sat hunched and glowering on the bench. Molly, a daisy chain around her neck and marigolds in her plaits, brought him bread, cheese and a jug of ale and sat beside him.

'Has father given you another of his… talks?' she said. 'You're always angry afterwards. I've brought you some food and ale.'

'I'll have the ale,' he said and took a deep draught.

## Hired Hands

'Not so fast, Tom,' she said, touching his shoulder. 'It's very potent.'

He lowered the jug and looked at her. 'That isn't for you to judge, Molly.'

'Please, don't be angry with me.'

'I'm not, don't worry.'

'Where've you been all this time?'

This surprised him. 'All this time? I was only away a few weeks.'

'A few weeks?' she said, her tone almost angry. 'Tom, you said you would spend May Day with us. I made this dress, I put flowers in the house… but you never came. First, I counted the days, then the weeks. Five harvests I've counted since we last spoke together.'

Stunned, ashamed, he whispered, 'I'm sorry, Hen, I was… elsewhere… I never meant to break my word.' He lifted the jug again.

She smiled. 'I would forgive you for anything, Tom, you know that. I've waited for you at the crossroads every morning since you left, hoping you'd come back.'

He paused, with the jug almost to his lips. 'I'm not staying, Molly.'

'Not staying? What do you mean?'

'What's the matter with you? Did I not make it clear enough?'

'Where are you going?'

'Far away, Molly.'

She leaned forward, hopeful. 'You'll come back soon, though, won't you?'

'I don't know.'

'We'll never see you again?'

He set the jug down and gave her plaits a habitual tug. 'Dearest Molly, I never said so.'

'But that's what you mean,' she said, clutching his right hand. 'Oh, Tom, you can't leave us; you can't.'

'You were ever my friend, Molly,' he said, wiping away her tears. 'Of all your qualities, it's your strength and courage I admire the most; and you'll need them, Hen.'

She saw a troubled light in his eyes. 'I was right,' she said. 'You have changed, and it's not just the beard. I can see something, Tom, working behind your eyes, as if it burns your very soul.'

Hirnac glimpsed them through the open door, Thomas seated on the bench staring at the ground at his feet, holding Molly on his knee while she, nestled against him, stared at her shabby clogs peeping from beneath the frayed hem of her faded dress.

# Hired Hands

\*

Foul candles burning on an altar cast macabre shadows around the dark chamber, and the herbs strewn on the floor gave noxious smells. A grotesque figure, its face aglow in the unpleasant light, venom drooling from its mouth, took a cap from a bowl full of human blood, raised its arms, and spoke, its wheezing voice harsh.

'I am the Prince of Spriggans, calling all brethren, all servants and slaves, to the South Gate; the Seelie Court shall fall.'

He placed the cap on his grizzled head and, taking a long draught, drained the bowl.

## Chapter Nineteen

# Harper's Barn

It was not yet mid-day when, without knowing why, Thomas entered the stables, glanced at the quiet horses feeding in their stalls, took a knife from where he had hidden it, tucked it into his right boot, and left the house, needing neither cloak nor tunic on a hot day.

At ease, greeting people with a confident, charming grin, he strolled through the village, following a shady, deserted lane, the path strewn with wispy, wind-blown hay. The air smelt of livestock, trees and grass; of home.

Faint voices amongst loud birdsong came from behind him, but, finding no one there, he stopped at a field entrance, studying Harper's barn, its skewed walls, the saplings and grass growing on its sagging roof, the faint trail in the turf leading to the half-open door rotting at its base. Musty smells greeted him within. Sunlight from the doorway showed a broken cartwheel propped against a treacherous ladder leading to the hayloft; the old, rusting implements hanging or leaning against the walls; and a huge cauldron, half-hidden in shadows, lying on its side as though dropped in a hurry. Fascinated, he approached it—and reeled from a sudden, heavy blow across his back.

Winded, confused, he glimpsed someone armed with a hayfork lunging at him. He grabbed it from his assailant and recognised him.

*'Finnian!'*

Finnian exposed his fangs. 'Yes, it's Finnian, here to take you and your so-called friends to my master, for he gives rich rewards; he knows everything about you, Thomas Learmont, and you know his name.' Giving a peculiar, snickering laugh, he sneered at the helpless gaze. 'Yes, Lord Scarecrow, Soulis will kill you; but I'm not prepared to wait.'

Another heavy blow wrenched the hayfork free; Thomas, knocked sideways, leaned against the wall, groggy, his mouth bleeding. Finnian threw him onto the cauldron before he could recover, kicking him and laughing at his involuntary yells of pain.

'Look how well you bleed, Scarecrow. Would the Lady favour you if she knew how well you bleed? I wonder what the ugly little farm wench would trade for your life? Who would defend her? You?'

Thomas rolled away, leapt up, and slamming Finnian against the wall, met his eyes, threatening green to evil blue.

'What did he promise you, weasel? The Flame's power?'

'The power is nothing without the Sword and Horn, but it burns within you, Scarecrow, and will keep burning until it leaves you… on your death.'

Finnian crumpled from a vicious punch that broke his nose, and Thomas hauled him up, shaking him in fury, spitting expletives; but Finnian kicked him in his abdomen and he fell; lay, coughing and vomiting, under hailing blows and hissing insults.

'Afraid, Learmont? No stomach for a fight? Where's your famous courage? Did you perhaps leave it at a harlot's door?'

Thomas, retching, his nose and mouth dripping blood, somehow staggered to his feet, and snatching a sickle from the wall, attacked him.

'Little shit weevil! I'll show you stomach!'

Thrown against the wall, he dropped the sickle and launched himself at Finnian again. They fell, clamped, tumbling across the floor, kicking up straw and dust, trading clouts and insults, each trying to destroy the other: Finnian fighting to kill Thomas; Thomas, for Molly, for everything.

Wedged against the wall, avoiding blows, he pulled the long, thin blade from his boot—Finnian's knife—and stabbed; stabbed again, but the unyielding creature forced him down again, twisting his right arm with one hand, strangling him with the other.

A surging nausea Thomas did not understand almost overwhelmed him, and like a thunderbolt, something threw Finnian across the barn. Again, Thomas fell on him, stabbed, rolled away, shoved the knife into his belt, and picked up the hayfork. He stood waiting, levelling it when Finnian leapt forward, and pushed him down, thrusting the deadly prongs through him into the floor. He drew the knife again and cut his throat.

'Here's some stomach! I'll string my lute with your filthy gut, and Adan's bow as well!'

Breathless, he stepped back, watching the body transform, the hay fork now embedded in a grey, contorted, anthropomorphic stone.

Bruised, exhausted, light-headed, blood in his mouth, his every breath hurting, the gory knife still in his trembling hand, he leaned against the barn wall.

'*Molly.*'

## Harper's Barn

\*

Naked, dazed, his lip sore where Sarah had nipped it, Rædwulf lay sprawled on the floor where she had left him; gone, he assumed, to touch up her awful facial daub. Annoyed by his own gullibility and growling *Learmont, you git,* he hauled himself up on his elbows, dressed, and fled to the farmhouse. The sight of Molly seated outside repairing Thomas' tunic somehow comforted him.

'Good Heavens!' she said, surprised at his dishevelment. 'Have you crawled through a hedge?'

'No,' he said after a moment. 'I… took a slight tumble.'

'Into a lavender bush, from the smell of you,' she remarked, resuming her sewing.

His eyes twinkled. 'I could dive into the river to, you know, wash it off.'

'Oh, I wouldn't do that, sir,' she said, rethreading her needle. 'The river's dangerous, didn't you know?'

'I've met with worse,' he said, giving a slight shrug, and gestured at the garment. 'Thomas and your father seem to clash.'

'My father thinks Tom Learmont has too much of a roving eye.'

'Yet they respect each other.'

'There's no doubting it,' she said, without breaking concentration and adjusting the garment on her lap. 'If Tom hadn't paid for the best medical care, my father might have lost his leg.' She paused, gazing into space, her hands in her lap, speaking as though to herself. 'As long as Tom's here, and I can see him, even from afar, I'm happy, but then he'll wander off, leaving everything drab.' Blinking, she returned to her task.

'A lord's duties,' he said, 'may take him far afield.'

She shrugged. 'Yes, I suppose they would. Are you married, sir?'

He took a breath. 'I'm widowed.'

'I'm sorry to hear that,' she said with genuine sincerity. 'Do you have children?'

'No, Molly, she died in childbirth.'

'Death is no stranger here, either,' she said. 'We buried my eldest brother and younger sister within days of each other, so we're just thankful seeing every sunrise.'

With a soft twinkle in his eyes, he said, 'You have a healer's soul, Molly.'

'You're a fine gentleman, sir,' she said, looking at his amulet. 'I'm sure there's a fine lady somewhere who would be glad to be your wife.'

He gave a faint smile. 'Maybe. Please excuse me, good maiden, but I need to speak with Thomas.'

'Oh, he's not here. He left the house a while ago.'

Unsettled, he entered the house while she continued her sewing. Looking up when a shadow fell across her, she gasped.

Thomas, his right arm raised against the farmhouse wall, stood looking at her, saying nothing; his torn, blood-spattered shirt, his injured face, the pained remorse in his eyes were enough. He eased himself onto the bench beside her while she tried wiping the blood from his face and hands with her veil, reproaching him.

'You always do it, don't you? You always seem within arm's reach of trouble. Why must you always fight so?'

He glared at her. 'You should be glad I did.' Wincing, he closed his eyes. 'Rædwulf: I need him, Molly... find Rædwulf.'

She rushed into the yard where the men stood talking together. 'Help him,' she said, pointing towards the house front. 'Help him, please.'

Her bloodied veil told Rædwulf everything, but hiding his concern, he said only, 'Adan, Hirnac, come with me.'

Thomas sat, his eyes still closed. 'Ye gods, Learmont,' said Rædwulf, giving him a brief diagnostic look. 'What on Earth happened?'

Thomas grimaced. 'Finnian happened, Blācencynn; he almost killed me.'

'What's he doing here?' Rædwulf exclaimed, then added in a more controlled tone, 'Well, you can tell me later, and I'll ask Molly to find some herbs.'

Thomas managed a smile. 'I think I've scared her.'

'You haven't reassured us, either.' Rædwulf helped him up, and with Thomas between them, he and Adan took him into the house.

The injuries alarmed Nell, but Keith had scant empathy. 'Perhaps, Tom,' he said, 'this'll teach you to not pick unnecessary fights?'

Rædwulf glared, giving a riposte he straightaway regretted. 'Give him a bed, Goodman, and hold your tongue,' adding in appeasement, 'I'm sorry, but I cannot examine him in here.'

Keith took a moment, then nodded towards a partition. 'In there.'

Adan and Hirnac took Thomas into the room, but Nell stopped Rædwulf before he could follow, her anxious eyes searching for reassurance.

'Please, sire,' she said, 'tell me, will he recover?'

His hesitation troubled her. 'I don't know, but I'll do my best, Nell.'

Adan stayed by the door while Rædwulf examined Thomas, and Hirnac took the shirt to Molly for repair.

'This is *filthy*,' she said, holding it up to the light.

'She's angry with him,' whispered Adan.

'And worried,' said Rædwulf.

The injuries concerning him, he went to Molly, now seated beside the hearth, assessing the torn garment.

'Any willow trees nearby?' he said.

'Yes, sir, by the river.'

'Any elder trees in flower?'

'I believe so, up by the fields.'

He held out a small, deep, wooden bowl. 'Would you fill this with willow bark for me, and your apron with elder blossom? Hirnac and Adan will go with you.'

Polite as ever, she said, 'Thank you, sir, but I don't need any guides.'

'We'd like to explore the village, if we may,' said Adan, giving Rædwulf a subtle smile.

Molly hesitated, nodded, and went to fetch her shawl while they waited outside for her.

'Sire,' said Hirnac, staring at Adan, 'why should we go with the maid?'

'Because,' whispered Adan, 'if Soulis or Redcap can send Finnian after us, they could send others.'

'What about those men from Hermitage?'

'If they mean us harm, they wouldn't have announced themselves,' said Rædwulf.

Adan nodded. 'We're making sure there's nothing else lurking here, watching us,' he said.

'Without our weapons?' Hirnac protested.

'Yes.'

Hirnac surveyed the trees and hills beyond the village. 'Rædwulf, that leaves you alone to defend the farmhouse, should someone attack it.'

Rædwulf, glimpsing Nell and Keith through the doorway, whispered, 'That's my problem, but I could say the same to you. Stay hidden—and hide Molly.'

She approached, carrying a small basket. 'I thought this might be useful,' she said, dumping it at her feet. Hirnac offered to carry it, but she refused. 'I can manage, sir, but thank you anyway.'

Rædwulf smiled at her, and noting her telling blushes, said, 'Accept help, sweetness, when it's offered.'

## Harper's Barn

Molly led Adan and Hirnac away, leaving Rædwulf thinking he should leave soon, if only for her sake. He glanced at Nell, now standing beside him.

'I don't like her leaving the house after what's happened,' she said.

'She'll come to no harm; besides, she needs something else to think about.'

'You mean you can read her mind?'

He faced her. 'No, I read people,' adding in an undertone, 'and sometimes wish I couldn't.'

Nell followed him into the house, where he paused. 'Goodwife, could you spare some yarrow from your garden, and tallow if you have any, and heat some water and ale?'

'You may use all the herbs in our garden,' she said, 'and anything else we have to hand; but may I speak with Tom alone?'

He hesitated. 'Wait here.'

Thomas, lying almost naked on the bed, seemed asleep; Rædwulf, pulling up a stool, sat down and hissed, '*You utter bastard!*'

Despite his pain, Thomas smiled. 'Ah… you met Little Sarah?'

'Thunderer's *balls*, Thomas. I'd rather take my chances in a bear pit than spend another *minute* with that woman. I'll bet she eats men for breakfast.'

Thomas glanced at him. 'Rædwulf, your protests deafen me.'

'*I* am six foot four; warrior lord of the Blācencynn. How could a five-foot tall… *barrel…* overpower *me?*'

Thomas closed his eyes again. 'I admit she makes a kick in the teeth seem subtle, and from experience, know she's a little over-zealous. The village men hide if they see her loitering, but she's not so bad, underneath that facial hair. I thought you needed, well, a distraction.'

Rædwulf stood up and growled, 'By rights, I'd knock you into next week if you hadn't already had the crap beaten out of you.' He flung a blanket at him. 'Cover yourself up, Learmont. Nell wants a private word with you.' He went to the door, beckoned her, said, 'Keep it brief,' and left.

She sat on the stool, looking at his injured, swollen face. 'I don't think Molly can stand much more.'

He opened his eyes. 'What's that supposed to mean?'

Nell shook her head. 'You break her heart whenever you leave home; mend it when you come back, only to break it again. You're tearing her apart, Tom.'

Cut to the quick, he closed his eyes against his tears. 'Spare me, Nell, I beg. Don't kick me when I'm down.'

'I've known you all your life, Tom, but I've never seen you weep.'

He whispered, 'Perhaps I'm human, after all.'

\*

Rædwulf foraged in the garden and the woodland beyond, gathering any medicinal herbs he could find, then sat beneath the oak tree and fell asleep until Keith prodded him.

'Wake up, lad. Molly's back.'

Molly, watching Rædwulf preparing a cordial, frowned. 'You're expecting him to drink that stuff?' she said. 'It smells appalling.'

'It tastes worse, believe me,' said Rædwulf, 'but I wouldn't give him anything I wouldn't take.'

'Don't worry, good maiden,' said Hirnac, 'he knows what he's doing.' He followed him and Adan into the room. Thomas took a mouthful of the concoction and coughed.

'Good God, that's vile.'

Rædwulf nodded. 'Mmm, it's potent stuff. It will stop the pain, but you'll need another dose at nightfall.' He began smearing ointment on the cuts.

Thomas flinched. 'Ah, that stings.'

Rædwulf put the ointment aside. 'Then it's doing its job. It looks as though he kicked and stamped on you. I thought at first you'd fractured at least one rib, and I'm surprised the injuries aren't more severe, if I'm honest.' Pausing, recalling that the power protects its servants, he whispered, 'Or am I?' 'Alright, Thomas,' he said aloud, 'now perhaps you can tell us what's going on? What is Finnian doing here?'

'Looking for us,' said Thomas, putting the cup down, 'or rather, was.' He paused, staring at the wall in sudden disbelief. 'I killed him, Rædwulf.'

Rædwulf shrugged. 'Well, clearly, or you wouldn't be here talking to us now.'

Thomas lay back. 'Soulis sent him.'

Adan leaned against the partition. 'After all you've told us, I would have thought Finnian was Redcap's lackey.'

Hirnac glanced at Thomas. 'What if Soulis is already here, hiding, watching us?'

Hand on chin, Rædwulf walked to the far wall. 'Then we'd already know about it. Everything Finnian said was misleading, but evil as they are, Spriggans are not traitors. I suspect he intended taking the power, and deceived Soulis, while spying for Redcap. You did well killing him, Thomas.' He gave him a sidelong, thoughtful look. 'I suspect you met Finnian at the barn where the woman left the cauldron for us.'

Hirnac bit his lip. 'Who would bring such a thing?'

'I'd hazard a guess,' said Rædwulf. 'Is it big as Molly said?'

Thomas wrapped his arms around his knees. 'You wouldn't believe that you could almost swim in it, but I'll show you—once she's repaired my shirt.'

Rædwulf found Molly sat in the yard, washing the shirt in a water tub, and she gave him a weak smile. 'I've mended it, and scrubbed out the worst stains as best I can, sir.' She paused. 'He scares me, sometimes; that he always fights, I mean,' she added, answering his sharp look. 'I've told him it solves nothing, but he just ignores me.'

He crouched in front of her, looking at the wilted flowers in her hair, and now understood why Thomas so adored her, his insisting they divert, risking everything. 'Listen, Molly,' he said, his tone soft, though earnest, 'listen to me: evil things sometimes roam the world, and he just happened to… meet… one of them today. He had no choice, Molly; he had to fight.'

This horrified her. 'A demon?'

'Not quite.'

She swallowed, looking at the shirt in her hands. 'Will he die?'

He gave her a kind, reassuring smile. 'Not today, good maiden.'

'It's still very damp,' she said, handing him the garment, and lowered her gaze. 'He said he can't stay. Is it true?'

'Yes,' he said, standing up. 'We'll leave soon, but he'll come back if he can.'

He turned away, but she, taking an unsteady breath, said, 'Thank you for helping him, sir.'

'You're very welcome, I'm sure,' he said, smiling, 'but remember, you helped him too.'

## Chapter Twenty

# Strangers

His pain gone, and bleeding stopped, Thomas took his companions to the barn, its door barred shut, as he had left it, and they entered, kicking clouds of dust from the straw. The late afternoon sunlight coming through the open door shone onto the hay fork still embedded at an angle in the stone, the blood-spattered wall and the immense cauldron. Adan threw Thomas a quizzical look.

'What's this for?'

Thomas stood with one hand on the cauldron, remembering his dream in vivid detail: Molly, standing behind it, the people crowded around it, Penda standing before him. He faced Adan and said, 'Vengeance.'

Rædwulf looked thoughtful. 'We should keep watch tonight. Now, where are you going?'

Thomas paused in the doorway. 'I've people to meet. Stay put, and I'll bring those farmers here.'

Rædwulf raised an eyebrow. 'We'll see you later, then.'

Alehouse, whorehouse, or den of thieves, depending on a customer's need or want, the inn, a long, low, thatched building, was situated amongst beech trees near the village gate. Thomas, his hood pulled down to his beard, planning how best to approach the strangers, marched to the door, snatching aside the curtain hung across it. He stepped into the fug of strong ale and wood smoke; Moris and his comrades fidgeting in a far corner of the gloomy, crowded common room drew his immediate attention. His hood drawn low, he approached them, noting that Moris wore a small, silver-gilt brooch, but they ignored him.

After five minutes, Thomas said, 'Well? What did you want? Speak up.'

Moris gave a salutary grin, exposing uneven teeth; he looked Thomas up and down and cleared his throat. 'We're waiting for Thomas Learmont.'

'You're looking at him.'

Andrew sniggered. 'Oh, anyone can say that. How do we know we can trust you?'

'You don't,' said Thomas, unmoved, 'but my word should be good enough.'

Moris digested this, studying Thomas, assessing the risks, then whispered, 'We're from Hermitage. I'm

## Strangers

Moris, and we,' he gestured to his companions, 'are looking for Soulis; the maiden told us to come here.'

'Maiden?'

'Yes, lord. Dressed in wool, a shawl hiding her face, much as your hood hides yours.' Moris moistened his lips and drew Thomas aside, whispering, 'We went to Hermitage Castle, intending to put Soulis on trial, but found the gates open, the place dark and abandoned, and the sun couldn't melt the ice on the walls. Shapeless forms moved in the shadows and patrolled the ramparts, and we heard voices from things we couldn't see.' Again, he looked towards his men. 'It fair terrified us, I'm not ashamed admitting, so we started for home, meeting the maid on the way. "Find Lord Thomas Learmont in Ercildoun," she said, "and you will find Soulis." Then she walked off and sort of faded into the hedgerow.'

Thomas, grasping this in a split second, nodded towards the door. 'We shouldn't discuss this in here. Come with me.'

\*

Moris' companions stared at the cauldron in disbelief, and Robbie snorted.

'Have we come this far just for an oversized cooking pot?' He nodded towards Thomas and, in a low voice, said, 'This *lunatic* might do anything.'

'Don't question the man,' said Moris. 'Perhaps he knows more than we do.'

'I do indeed,' said Thomas, glaring at Robbie. 'Soulis is coming here, so we'll wait for him, together with this… *cooking* pot.'

Robbie stared at him, astonished. 'He's coming *here?*'

'We'll have him,' said Rædwulf, his tone heated, 'and boil him alive as a fitting punishment.'

Thomas fixed his penetrating gaze on Moris. 'Now that you know our purpose, wait at the inn; we'll send you a message when we're ready.'

Adan watched Moris and his comrades walk away. 'Why are they here, Thomas?'

Thomas faced him. 'The same reason we are, Adan. We just need to wait.'

'How long for? You forget Redcap destroyed my hall and people, Thomas. I want vengeance, too.'

Thomas ran his fingers over the cauldron. 'And you shall have it once we've dealt with Soulis.' He grimaced, his pain returning. 'Go back to the farmhouse; tell Nell and Molly not to worry.'

## Strangers

'They're cooking us a meal, Thomas,' said Hirnac.

'Then tell them to keep it warm; I'll stay here and guard the cauldron.'

'Why?'

'Because I'm not sure I trust those men.'

They could not dissuade him. Adan and Hirnac left, and Rædwulf stood in the doorway, watching the sun touching the western horizon.

'I can tell you're in pain again, Learmont,' he said, 'and you need sleep. I'll bring you another draught, if you insist on staying here.'

Thomas, leaning against the cauldron, sat down, eyes closed. 'They're talking.' Rædwulf stared at him in alarm. 'They're talking,' repeated Thomas. 'People talking in a closed room, but I can't quite hear the words.'

Rædwulf kneeled beside him, searching the ashen face. Thomas, jaw and hands clenched, garish shadows staring beneath his closed eyes, seemed asleep.

'Listen, Thomas,' said Rædwulf, 'This is the power working. Don't suppress it, or it will overcome you. Accept it.'

Thomas dozed until dusk, when he again became restless, grimacing with pain.

Borderlands

\*

The Hermitage men sat crammed around a table in deep discussion. Moris drank, wiped his mouth, and set the mug down.

'We've only a madman's word they mean to kill Soulis,' he said.

Robbie frowned. 'Those men seemed bent on revenge, Moris.'

Moris sat back. 'Revenge for what? They know nothing of the damage Soulis has done. Yes, they talked well, but they didn't seem like lords to me. They're unarmed, their clothing's tatty and old-fashioned, and it's clear Thomas Learmont's taken a thorough beating. I didn't like his eyes, and the others looked like outlanders, mercenaries maybe.' He shook his head. 'That redhead, I've never seen the like; he's wild, uncultured, his accent's thick as porridge, and did you see the pendant at his neck? But he told us the means for killing Soulis and it lies in that barn.' He stood up, walked around the table, fingertips on his chin, and faced his comrades. 'Robbie, go out at dawn and find the strongest cart you can.'

Robbie smiled. 'There's one in the inn yard, but whether the innkeeper will lend it to us is another matter.'

'The redhead said they would boil Soulis alive,' said Moris, looking at John. 'Hot water's too good for him, and as you're the blacksmith, find as much lead as possible.'

John stared at Moris. 'What, here?'

'Don't argue,' said Moris. 'The village blacksmith might have some scraps.' He turned to Andrew. 'Find a draft animal, horse or mule.'

Jacob put down his mug of ale. 'Moris, can we find all this here?'

Moris leaned forward between Andrew and Robbie, grasping the back of each chair. 'Folk will lend or sell anything for the right price, Jacob. That barn is unguarded; the door's barred on the outside.' He sat down, thinking, pulling at his bottom lip with thumb and forefinger. 'We'll take that cauldron before those men can stop us, and Soulis will stand trial in our own fields.'

## Chapter Twenty-One

# Sudden News

The low moon floated in a star-spattered sky, and Rædwulf, sensing a slight movement in the shadows near the farmhouse and hearing faint, crunching footsteps, crept forward; a Spriggan, hunched, menacing, indistinct, came lurching from the dark.

Rædwulf reached for his Sword, remembered it was not there, stifled a curse, drew his dagger and hid in the shadows, watching the figure approach. He lunged; taking a fierce hold, not sparing his strength, he pressed his blade across the creature's neck and whispered into its ear, 'Make one move, make a single twitch, and I'll kill you.'

It gave a faint gasp. 'Don't hurt me!' It was a woman. Confused, he released her and stepped back; she, a large shawl covering her head, sputtered, 'What are you *doing?*'

He could not control his sharp tone. 'Did I hurt you?'

'A bit,' she said, rubbing her arms, her voice quavering, then peered at him. 'Are you who I think you are?'

'That depends on what you think.'

'It is!' she said with obvious relief. 'Lord Rædwulf, thank the stars.'

He suppressed a smile. 'Lady, you have me at a disadvantage.'

'Oh, forgive me, kind sir.' Taking off her shawl, she revealed her gleaming hair and radiant face.

'Læren!' he said, wondering why seeing her lifted his heart.

She swallowed. 'You scared the very daylights out of me.'

'I'm sorry, Læren, I'd never want to frighten you, but in the dark, you looked like a Spriggan. Why are you here?'

'Looking for you.'

Ever astute, he said, 'So, where's Raldis?'

'Raldis?'

'I wasn't born yesterday. She seldom lets you out of her sight.'

'Oh, somewhere nearby,' she said, giving a guilty shrug.

He made a shrewd guess. 'Did you ask a certain laird for help? Or rescue Adan and Hirnac from prison?'

'Oh,' she said, sounding sheepish. 'So, you know.'

## Sudden News

He drew a long, pensive breath. 'You've been preparing our road, yes?' Taking her silence as a confession, he warned her, 'Læren, if you've spied on us—'

'We've watched Soulis, not you, although we've tracked your movements. That's how we knew you'd be here.'

'You would do well, lady maiden, not to lurk in the shadows. I could have been anybody, or anything, and I almost stabbed you.'

She ignored this. 'I need to speak with Lord Ercildoun.'

'I'm not sure you should. He's tired, injured, none too pretty, and may be unpredictable. He may think you've been meddling, so it would be wise if you didn't tell him what you've been doing.'

Her voice tremored. 'I can't help that; I said I would meet him, so I shall.'

'Can't this wait until morning?'

She came close to him. 'There isn't time. This is important, although if you're there…?'

'He won't scold you?'

She looked at the ground. 'Sort of.'

'Alright,' he said, 'Wait for me here, bright maiden; I need to fetch something. I'll come back soon with some friends… and a lantern.'

*

Thomas sat propped against the cauldron, eyes shut, holding the bridge of his nose. Rædwulf hung the lantern from a peg and crouched beside him.

'There's someone here to see you.'

Thomas looked up, said, 'Alright,' and closed his eyes again.

Læren, her shawl again over her head, kneeled beside him, Adan and Hirnac facing her, Rædwulf leaning against the wall beside her.

'I'm rather tired,' said Thomas, 'so, whatever you want to say, be quick about it.'

'My lord,' she said, 'Redcap will attack the Seelie Court soon.'

Thomas recognised the voice he had heard in the hollow; his mind racing, he opened his eyes and snatched the shawl away. 'You're rather far from home, Læren.'

She hid her alarm when she saw his injured face; Raldis, noted Rædwulf, had trained her well.

## Sudden News

Thomas frowned. 'You seem shaken.'

She sat down. 'Rædwulf mistook me for a Spriggan.'

'Good God! Can't he tell the difference?'

'Anyone could have made that mistake in the dark,' she said, in blatant accusation. 'Even you.' She lowered her tone. 'We've followed Soulis, watched his movements; we saw him interrogating a captive from one of his raids.'

'We?' he barked.

'Dagan, me and...' she glanced at Rædwulf, 'and Raldis.'

Rædwulf, stroking his beard, glanced at the door. 'Where are they?'

'They're waiting in the trees, by the river there.'

'Soulis is coming here, Læren,' said Thomas.

'No,' she said, 'he isn't.'

He frowned. 'What do you mean?'

'You haven't heard?'

'No; what?'

Her words seemed leaden. 'Redcap reads the wind,' she said, 'and we listen for the news it brings. He has summoned his brethren and all his creatures to the Mereburg. Do you understand, lord? *All* his creatures. It's rumoured Soulis will lose his soul by meeting Redcap's eyes, that he has rebelled against him, but he cannot ignore the summons. He isn't coming here, lord; he's going to the Mereburg.'

Thomas, remembering her brooch, the design woven into his shirt and engravings on the Horn, now hidden in Keith's stable, glanced at Adan. 'What's your link with the Mereburg, Læren?'

She took a deep breath. 'I'm from there.'

'Then you must know Adan and Hirnac.'

'I've only seen Lord Adan from a distance before; I don't know Hirnac.'

Thomas shifted his position, resting his left arm across his knee. 'Who made the cauldron?'

'We did,' she said, meeting his eyes, 'and Raldis brought it here.'

'Why?'

Læren faltered, staring at the floor. 'To use with… with the power; to kill.' She looked at Rædwulf. 'We know what happened to Penda. All the Earth speaks of it. I'm so sorry.'

All eyes on him, he growled, 'Sympathy wins no battles.'

Crushed, angry, scrambling to her feet, she looked into his cold eyes. 'How can you be so ungrateful? So… *cruel?*'

## Sudden News

'Don't speak to me of cruelty, Læren, until you've seen it.'

'I *have* seen it,' she said. 'Spriggans herding women and children like cattle to the Caves; men hanging from the trees, like autumn fruit. And we saw Soulis standing on the hill above the Caves, declaring lordship over all lands. He's sent Spriggans to find Wyrtræd, to heal a festering wound, and, and… he's summoned the dead.'

His icy gaze melted. 'Why did you ever leave the Court?'

'Because it didn't seem fair that we should cower behind the palisade, while you…' She paused, her jaw clenched, swallowed, then whispered, 'We've done what we can, but my Lady has now recalled us, and we can't help you anymore.' She hung her head. 'I just can't do any more.'

It was a discreet cry for help he could not answer. He lifted her chin, said, 'You don't need to,' and kissed her, a mere brush of his beard against her forehead.

Surprised, bowing her head again, she whispered, 'Why did you do that?'

He gave a pleasant, reassuring smile. 'Because I didn't think you'd mind. Go home, bright maiden.'

She curtseyed, saying, 'Be careful, lord; you must all be careful.'

'Rædwulf,' said Hirnac, pointing towards the door in sudden warning.

Rædwulf turned. Raldis, stepping across the threshold with Dagan, curtseyed. 'My lord Adan,' she said, 'you may need these.' Dagan bowed, presented Adan and Hirnac with new arrows, and withdrew. Raldis, beckoning to Læren, said, 'Wait with Dagan in the lane.' She watched her follow him into the night, then faced the men. 'So,' she said, 'it has happened: a mortal man has kissed the maiden, sealing her fate.'

Rædwulf approached her, his eyes cold. 'Why did you allow her to come with you?'

'It wasn't a question of "allowing" her to come,' she said, 'but of stopping her from coming alone.'

'Not on our account?'

'No, lord,' she said, then whispered, 'on yours.' She turned and disappeared into the dark, leaving him embarrassed and silent.

'Rædwulf,' said Hirnac, 'if Soulis finds Wyrtræd—'

Rædwulf folded his arms. 'I'm sure that, once healed, Soulis will kill him.'

## Sudden News

'But isn't he a friend of yours?'

'I never said that. He's an acquaintance. I cannot meet him without serious conflict, but I'll put any differences aside, under the circumstances.'

'But we've no means of warning him.'

Rædwulf shrugged. 'There are many ways of sending messages, Hirnac.'

'If it's true that Soulis has summoned the dead,' said Adan, 'we've little hope. All Bright Faerie cannot withstand such a foe.'

Rædwulf stared at him. 'Then so be it.'

Thomas leaned back against the cauldron, and something spoke through him. '"*Redcap reads the wind,*" but only when it blows.'

Rædwulf kneeled beside him, proffering a flask. 'Drink this, Learmont. It'll help you sleep, or at least to rest, if sleep is impossible. We can't do anything until daylight, so come back to the house.'

Thunder awoke Thomas at dawn, and he sat, listening, but the house was quiet; the thunder, rumbling into the distance, did not recur, and he fell asleep again.

\*

Molly, following an old road home from delivering food to her brothers, often stopping to admire the fragrant wayside wildflowers in the morning sunshine, saw Moris driving a loaded two-wheeled cart, his men riding alongside, leading his horse.

She ran forward, shouting to them. 'Who said you could take that?'

Moris reined in. 'We need no permission, wench. Women shouldn't meddle with men's business, even if they could understand it. Go back to your hearth.'

Angry, her cheeks flushed, she did not budge. 'That cauldron belongs to Tom Learmont and his men. You've no right taking it.'

Andrew laughed. 'Why would they want a cooking pot?'

With her fists on her waist, Molly stood in front of the horse. 'Why do *you* want it, then?'

The men laughed. 'Oh, run back to your hearth,' said Robbie. 'This is serious business, not something a simple wench can understand.'

She folded her arms. 'I'm not moving, and neither are you.'

'Stand aside, wench,' said Moris, 'before the horse tramples you.' Molly, glaring at him in silence, did not flinch. 'Move *aside,*' demanded Moris, but she remained defiant. Exasperated, not wanting to alarm or hurt her, he looked at Robbie, who dismounted and, lifting her without ceremony, put her down on the roadside as Moris twitched the reins. The cart moved forward at speed, and Robbie remounted, calling to her as they passed.

'Run along home, little wench.'

Furious, worried that perhaps Thomas and Rædwulf had already left, she picked up her skirts and ran home across the fields. She barged into the house, almost colliding with Rædwulf. Scarlet-faced, she stood in the doorway, breathless, her dress and apron snagged from brambles and gorse, her hair in disarray. 'They've taken it!' she exclaimed, before the bemused men could say anything. 'They've taken it. Why would they do that, Tom? Why would they steal?'

Thomas went to her in a heartbeat. 'What, Hen? What have they taken? Who are "they"?'

'Those Hermitage men. They've put the cauldron on a cart and taken it. I tried stopping them, but they laughed at me.'

Rædwulf closed the door. 'When?'

'I'm not sure. I saw them on the drover's road, perhaps half an hour ago, and I've run all the way home.'

'Good God, Hen,' said Thomas. 'That's all of two miles.'

Still outraged, she ignored him. 'I knew there was something amiss,' she said. 'They wouldn't listen to me.'

Thomas looked at Rædwulf, then at Molly. 'Where were they going, Hen?'

She shook her head. 'I don't know, Tom, but they were heading south.'

Nell, bringing in firewood, gasped when she saw Molly; Rædwulf, giving Nell a reassuring smile, took her aside.

'Don't fret. She's unhurt, and will recover soon enough with rest and light duties, but she needs a drink. Tell Keith we need our weapons now, but would you allow us a few moments to ourselves?'

Nell nodded, said, 'Of course, sire,' and took Molly outside.

'So,' said Adan, 'they've taken the cauldron, but where?'

'Hermitage, I guess,' said Rædwulf.

Thomas sat down, glowering, his guilt and anger simmering like a pot on a fire. 'How dare they?' he said, struggling to control his tone. 'It wasn't thunder

## Sudden News

I heard but the cart rumbling past the house. I could have, would have, stopped them.'

Rædwulf sat down and leaned his forearms across his knees. 'It makes no difference where the cauldron is,' he said. 'It's where Soulis and Redcap are that matters. Soulis is going to the Mereburg, Thomas. And so are we.'

\*

Rædwulf entered the stable and, watching Keith grooming their horses, stroked the nearest. 'Goodman,' he said, 'this one is for you, for your kindness.'

Astonished, Keith said, 'Sir, we can't accept so good a beast. It should belong to a lord.'

'Then sell him to a worthy one. This was my brother's horse, Keith, my brother's.' He turned away, but Keith spoke.

'How did you meet Tom?'

Rædwulf faced him. 'Through a mutual friend; why do you ask?'

Keith stroked the horse's muzzle. 'You're not like some unsavoury associates he meets—you know the kind: harlots and reprobates.'

'I've had my moments too, Keith, and he's better than you think. Perhaps there's worse than a likeable gadabout you should worry over.' Holding the thoughtful gaze, Rædwulf walked away before Keith could answer.

Molly, gathering herbs in the garden, saw Rædwulf climb the knoll; facing north, he stood, radiant in the light coming from the crystal, holding the Sword at an angle before him; a powerful, somehow threatening stance, so at odds with the gentle healer she admired. He chanted into the wind, using a strange, guttural, savage dialect, but she understood the last few words: *Penda, I will avenge thee.* He sheathed the Sword and approached her. His burning grey stare unsettling her, she looked at the ground, whispering an accusation.

'You let us believe that you're a healer, but you're a warlock who conjures demons and storms. How could you deceive us so?'

'You know nothing of me, sweetness,' he said. 'I'm a warrior; I don't conjure evil, I fight it, and I expect to die in battle one day—however gentle the healer might seem.' He turned away.

'Sir,' she said, 'I've never known Tom so preoccupied, so… distant. Why has he changed?'

He met her pleading eyes with compassion. 'Because he's afraid.'

'But he isn't afraid of anything.' Molly lowered her gaze, then looking at him again, said, 'Sir, please, if you don't mind my asking, keep him out of trouble?'

'I'm only a man, Molly,' he said, giving a slight smile, 'and don't know if I can keep myself safe, let alone Thomas Learmont. Forgive me, but I can't promise anything.'

He walked away, passing Nell coming from the hay shed, and she, reading Molly as only a mother could, approached her. 'He's a remarkable man,' said Molly, watching him enter the house.

Nell smiled. 'One who might send any maid giddy, but he's not worth putting on a pedestal, and I somehow doubt he'll visit us again. Come, daughter, we'll bid them farewell.'

\*

Thomas, his hood pulled low, fingering his horse's mane in grim, preoccupied silence, stood at the roadside with his already-mounted companions. Keith and Nell stood watching from the doorway.

'Tom,' said Molly, now standing beside him, 'I have a small gift for you.' Baffled, he pulled back his hood and stared at her. 'From our garden,' she said, placing a small white pebble in his palm, 'to remind you of home.'

Moved to his core, he pocketed it, but Keith snorted, 'Molly.'

Weary of the constant disapproval, and knowing he might never see her again, Thomas glared at him. 'You might forbid my marrying your daughter, but with due respect, Keith Goodman, so help me, you will not deny me this.' In defiance, he embraced, and for the first time, kissed her—the gentlest, most meaningful kiss he had ever given. 'Stay strong for me, Hen,' he whispered. 'Stay true.' As he mounted his horse, Rædwulf gave Molly a brief, reassuring wink, and Nell raised one hand in adieu.

'We'll wait for you every eventide, Tom.'

'You may not see me for years, Nell,' he said, 'if ever,' and with his gaze lingering on Molly, he rode away with his companions.

## Chapter Twenty-Two

# A Convenient Truce

Afternoon shadows stretched across open, silent land. Moris led his men along the broken road that stitched its way through the heather, the lumbering, lurching cart giving alarming creaks with its every pitch and yaw. Robbie drew a long breath.

'We're losing the way, Moris. The horse is near spent, the cart's already leaning, and it must overturn if we go further.'

Moris drew rein, throwing him a brief, sidelong glare. 'We can't turn back, Robbie, not now.' He paused, considering their options, then gestured to higher ground two miles ahead. 'We'll spot anything moving from yonder ridge.'

Unconvinced, Robbie turned his horse aside. Moris drove forward, and his men, expecting trouble, followed. He stopped on the further ridge crest. A tall man, his hair gleaming like molten copper in the evening sunlight, his hands hidden beneath the cloak drawn close around him, stood a cart's length ahead. Even at this distance, Moris saw the glinting steel-grey eyes, and standing on the cart, called out, in pure scorn.

'I recognise you. Out of our way, redhead; you won't stop us.'

Rædwulf, lord of warriors, approached the horse. His tone low, measured, intimidating, he replied, 'You might have forced the maiden from your way, *master yeoman*, but you will not pass me.' He drew his cloak aside, revealing the Sword in his hands, its tip resting in the turf at his feet, the hilt crystal glimmering in the sunlight, but the men laughed in his face.

'Away!' called Moris. 'We can pass you on either side with ease! You will not hinder us!'

With a glance, Rædwulf summoned his companions from a nearby granite outcrop, and they took positions: Adan behind the wagon, Thomas beside Rædwulf. Hirnac walked to the cart horse and ran one hand through its mane, whispering to it, while it nuzzled his right shoulder. Moris sat down and twitched the reins, but the horse did not move. He tried again; again, the horse refused.

'You will neither scorn nor obstruct us, Moris,' said Thomas, his tone low, calm, anything but reassuring. 'A fixing spell is upon both horse and cart, and neither will move until we say.' He glanced at both. 'That's Mother Scott's old nag, and the cart's been standing in the tavern yard for years.'

Moris climbed from his perch and faced him, unintimidated by the intense, steady gaze. 'What of it, Learmont? Do you imply we stole them?'

Thomas walked a slow circuit of both cart and horse, giving them a long, appraising glance. 'Did you not? You stole the cauldron, didn't you? You should beware of handling Faerie gifts.'

This rattled Moris. 'We are not thieves, Learmont. We paid a fair price for them: three silver coins for the horse, six for the cart.'

Thomas gave a disquieting laugh. 'You were overcharged on both.' He returned to Rædwulf and gave another quiet, unsettling laugh. 'You don't know what I'm capable of. Should the fit take me, I could cause the earth under you to open, and you all to fall into it.' He turned, walked towards Hirnac, paused, and went back to Moris, speaking now as a negotiator. 'We are not foes. If we bring you Soulis, you shall have your vengeance, as we will have ours.'

Moris did not hide his disdain. 'Yours? Why would you, and your strange friends, want vengeance,

Learmont?' Walking first to Hirnac, then Adan, he continued speaking, his tone unchanged. 'We need no help with either finding Soulis ourselves or taking him and the cauldron to Hermitage.' He faced Rædwulf. 'We must thank you, redhead, for telling us how to kill him.' His tone became thick, resentful. 'You cannot know, or ever understand, the hurts he has done: he has stolen our grain and livestock, terrorised our women and old men.'

Rædwulf, surprising everyone, grabbed him by the collar, almost choking him, and slammed him against the cart. Fixing him with a cold, wolf-like stare, he hissed at him, his tone a savage whisper of stifled fury.

'Who will greet you when you go home? Who will honour you? Your wife… brother… *children*? Will you even *have* a home? When have *you* ever murdered your own priest? You know nothing… *nothing.*' Shoving Moris hard against the cart, he walked away, leaving Moris feeling his neck for damage.

'Understand, yeoman,' said Adan, 'that he watched his brother die and has lost everything he ever had.' He shifted his grip on his bow. 'We will aid you,' he said, meeting the stunned gaze, 'as *you* will aid us.' It was a command, but Robbie drew him aside and whispered

## A Convenient Truce

to him; shocked, Adan approached Rædwulf, who sat, looking at the country beyond the ridge, and crouched beside him. 'Thomas is right, Rædwulf. These men are allies; but they're simple, with little idea of things beyond their own fields.'

Rædwulf gave a long sigh, his eyes matching his bitter tone. 'I will make no apology, Adan. I've had nightmares where the High Priest stands before me, emaciated, broken, looking at me—*pleading* with me—for life, when I can offer him only death.'

'Listen, Rædwulf, please. Think of what they've lost: their grain, their livestock. They will have no harvest, nothing for the winter, nothing to plant in spring. They, and all their folk, could starve before the year is out. Save your anger for Soulis.' He lowered his hand and sat down. 'He's taken their children, Blācencynn.'

Rædwulf, staring at his feet, did not reply. The sun was now touching the gleaming horizon, the hazy sky afire and all the land bronzed. He stood up, and beckoning to everyone waiting beside the cart, gestured to the open fields, woodlands and river below the escarpment.

'Evil walks out there,' he said. 'We will help you take the cauldron home, where you will guard it until we bring you Soulis.'

'We can't go further today,' said Adan. 'We'll overnight here.'

'And move on soon after dawn,' said Thomas.

\*

Intermittent fever had delayed Soulis. With all his rations gone, and Finnian sending no news, he now surveyed Ercildoun from the trees on the hill, watching the mist rising from the river. Bright evening sun and dark shadows painted the streets and byways, and people coming home from the fields fastened their doors against the night. He waited until moonrise, gestured towards the farmhouse below, where Molly, Nell and Keith lay sleeping, and spoke to the shadows gathering around him.

'Light a fire. Bring me all who live in that cottage and burn it down.'

Left in stark silence, he knew he was not alone. Patient, inscrutable darkness analysed him; the rising half-hooded moon watched him from between the overhead branches; the white fire gave no warmth, and everything remained dark.

## A Convenient Truce

The moon reached its zenith, and the guards had not returned. Soulis picked up a burning branch from the fire and followed the grey downhill path, looking for them. When he entered a woodland grove, he saw faces glowering from the surrounding ancient yews, and an indistinct figure stood, as though waiting, beside a weathered standing stone. Soulis spoke with utmost contempt.

'I am the master of shadows and command thee: lead me to Ercildoun.'

The figure faced him as though scrutinising him, then, at a slow, steady pace, walked away, leading him into the mist.

\*

Thomas and Moris stood sentinel in the grey dawn, watching the sun climb beyond the eastern hills, the light flooding the silent expanse below: fields, woods, the high, bleak moorland. They smelt the heather, and the campfire; heard their horses grazing. Moris glanced at the cart behind them and took a deep breath.

'I think we'll need to keep to the valley,' he said, 'or fly. I just hope the wagon lasts the distance.'

'So do I, Moris,' said Thomas, walking to the camp, 'for your sake.' Waking Adan, he drew him aside. 'I'm worried, Adan,' he said. 'Worried that we'll never dislodge Soulis if he reaches the Mereburg first.'

Adan met the green eyes. 'It isn't far from Hermitage. Trust me, the ways are open.'

Thomas hesitated. 'The Mereburg: I fear its very name.'

Adan held his gaze. 'I doubted you when we first met,' he said, 'wondering what your motives were. I doubt you no longer. We need you, Thomas.'

'No, Adan, you need only the power within me.'

'Of course we need you,' said Adan and, nodding towards the camp, added, 'We'll have breakfast before we leave.'

Robbie inspected the cart, shaking his head. 'It's overloaded, Moris. We should have brought two carts.'

'Well, we've no choice now, have we?' said Moris, giving him a brief glare. 'It is as it is. We'll keep to the burnside where the ground's level.'

Thomas sat, knees up, throwing his dagger into the turf between his feet. 'The cauldron doesn't swim,' he remarked. 'If it falls in the river, we're in trouble.' For the sixth time, he withdrew the dagger but paused in mid-aim, frowning. 'Something isn't right. Something doesn't fit, and I don't know why.' Throwing the knife into the grass again, he stared at the hilt while Robbie and Andrew began harnessing the cart horse and Moris gave the command.

'Fall in, we're ready.'

With Thomas and Hirnac controlling the horse, each with one hand on its harness, Moris guided the veering cart, now as much as a foot higher on one side, downhill, the cauldron ringing and rattling behind him. Adan led the procession along the riverbank; the morning was already hot, the sky hazy, the flies swarming.

'Hot, isn't it?' said John, mopping his forehead.

'Pure folly's what it is,' remarked Robbie.

\*

Soulis followed the shadowy apparition all night, certain the path led to Ercildoun, but now he stood on an exposed hilltop, confused. The pale morning sun rested on the horizon, and the silent, dripping woodland eaves behind him stood sentinel in the dawn. He saw the grey path winding downhill through the turf and vague forms around him coming and going in the wafting fog.

In sudden pain, he clutched his wounded arm, teeth clenched, sweating, shivering for minutes until the pain subsided. He tottered along the path, the crowding shadows disappearing whenever he looked towards them, his night guide vanishing in the lifting fog. The day became hot and hazy, and the clear path meandered between hills and rocks over a wide, unfamiliar land.

Weary, pain-wracked, he stopped beneath a high rock formation to rest; whispered conversations all around him kept him awake, and he sat up, but nothing moved amongst the rocks. He could not see the path anymore but saw food and drink laid out on the grass nearby: bread, meats, cheese, fruit, wine and ale, fit for a lord's table. Neither knowing nor caring where it had come from, he ate and drank all of it and slept until evening.

\*

A waterfall thwarted any plan Moris had of following the river, forcing him across difficult terrain. Unseen pitfalls, rocks and trailing roots that might snag the unwary lay hidden in the tussocks and thick heather, and swarming midges and stinging horseflies, relentless as the afternoon heat, made riding almost unbearable.

## A Convenient Truce

Mist crept from the land, and the incessant creaking of the wagon set every nerve on edge as the sun crept closer to the horizon.

Robbie waved away the punishing flies. 'We're too slow, Moris.'

Moris stared ahead. 'We're almost there, Robbie.'

'It'll be evening soon,' he retorted. 'We'll never reach home before dark.'

Adan drew rein. 'I agree, but we can't rest here; we might camp on yonder ridge. We'll be there by nightfall.' Thomas came alongside him and in silence followed his gaze across the bleak, high, grassy expanse.

'You've not said a word since this morning, Learmont,' whispered Adan. 'Why so quiet?'

Thomas looked at him. 'My eyes burn me, Adan,' he said. 'All I see, in my mind's eye, is a wide, dark water… and I'm drowning.' Holding the concerned gaze, he turned his horse aside.

The sun dropped behind the hills; flying ants joined with the swarming midges, an owl floated across the way ahead, and even Adan struggled to see through the hazy twilight. Behind him, Moris nursed the jolting cart over hummocks and tuffets, climbing a long slope to the mile-wide ridge crest.

Ancient, dusk-shrouded standing stones, all plastered with moss and lichens, encircled a blossoming rowan tree. One stone stood taller than Rædwulf; another, no higher than his breastbone; others smaller, upright or leaning, or half-buried in the turf. Moris drove the cart towards them, but the off-side wheel, warped beyond hope, shattered against a hidden rock. He leapt clear of the toppling cart, but the squealing horse fell with it; the rolling cauldron, clanging like a death knell, came to rest under the tree.

Bruised and dazed, Moris picked himself up; his men talked amongst themselves in fear, and Rædwulf, jumping off his horse, growled, kicking the wreckage in frustration. Thomas gave a chilling, almost calculating laugh, and Andrew turned on him.

'You knew this would happen, didn't you? You knew... you *fucking* knew!'

\*

*'Find Wyrtræd.'*

The clear, insistent voice woke Soulis to a murky dusk. A small watch-fire he had not set burned nearby, but he saw no one.

'I hear you,' he sneered. 'I am the demon-master, commanding the power, and do not fear you. Watch now how I summon shadows.'

He walked widdershins around the fire, holding his left hand over it, and chanting.

*I am the lord of demons; they will lead me to Ercildoun and bring me Wyrtræd, the healer.*

He halted, eyes closed, his hand poised over the flames, taking slow, deep breaths. Someone gave a quiet sigh; slow, shuffling footsteps paced three times around the fire, and he opened his eyes. An undefined darkness shape-shifted into a human shadow that faced him across the fire for several moments before retreating a few yards and halted, prompting him to follow a shining path into the night.

\*

Jacob, awaking in the silent small hours, saw Thomas walking around the circle, stopping at each stone for a moment before moving on. As he approached, Jacob said, 'What are you doing?'

Thomas took one breath and, in a peculiar voice, said, 'Ask nought of something you don't understand.'

He resumed his slow march to his sleeping companions and sat near the tree, brushing dirt and dust from his right hand.

Adan and Hirnac awoke at dawn; Rædwulf, sprawled fast asleep on his blanket, snored on. Hirnac tended the horses and returned to find him now awake, warming his hands over the fire, and Thomas helping Moris pile the heavy sacks nearby.

'What's this lead for?' said Thomas, handing one to Moris.

Moris looked him in the eye and almost sneered. 'For Soulis. We'll take it home, and once it's melted, we'll make him such armour you've never seen the like of. You have only to find him.'

'*We've only to find him,*' echoed Thomas, watching Moris walk away. 'Oh, my friend, you make it sound so simple.'

*

Rædwulf took his companions to a point beyond the circle and looked at the pathless moorland: trees, rocks; a standing stone at the foot of the slope below them; a burn trickling over a low waterfall into a nearby tarn;

thick hazel and alder clothing its steep banks. At first, they sat silent, knowing they must soon leave Moris and his followers on trust.

Adan nodded towards the circle. 'It's time we told those men our intentions, though I doubt they'll be happy.'

'Should they come with us?' said Hirnac.

'I've considered that,' said Rædwulf. 'But only Moris, John and perhaps Andrew have enough strength of mind.'

'And they'd hinder us,' remarked Adan. 'We need them here.'

'I doubt the others would stay without them, anyway,' said Rædwulf. 'Nor do I want more innocent deaths on my conscience. No; they're safest here.'

Hirnac frowned. 'Then should one of us stay with them?'

'This needs all four of us,' said Adan. 'We mustn't separate.'

Rædwulf flexed his arms. 'Adan, can you lead us to the Mereburg?'

Adan nodded. 'Yes; there's a direct path from here, but seeing it or not depends on how one looks at it. We'll reach it before nightfall—if we leave now, or at least after breakfast, and don't stop on the way.'

Rædwulf, hands clasped across his knees, nodded. 'Alright. I suggest we take some things with us, or rather, I take: a harness strap, some rope, an empty sack… and the cart horse.'

Astonished, Thomas said, 'Why?'

'Because, Thomas Learmont, we might need them.'

'But the horse startles at nothing, Rædwulf; it's only fit for the pot.'

Rædwulf raised an eyebrow. 'We'll see.'

\*

The grumbling farmers made it clear they resented being left to guard a cauldron they thought bewitched, in a circle they believed cursed. Moris, seated with Rædwulf and his companions beneath the tree, shifted his uncomfortable position, resting his right forearm across his knee and flexing his fingers. 'We've only your word that you'll come back, and Heaven knows when,' he said. 'Look how exposed we are. You can't expect us to stay here waiting when we have homes, wives and trades to attend, even if you haven't.'

## A Convenient Truce

Thomas scowled at him. 'You may have none of them if you leave here without us, which I'm sure you won't. You're protected only if you remain here.'

'We know you don't trust us, Moris,' said Adan, 'and why should you? But we also know you could not overpower Soulis, even if you found him. He has signed a pact with Robin Redcap, Prince of Spriggans, that, by its very nature, has made him unassailable.'

Moris shifted position again. 'Robin Redcap; it's said he governs all evil sprites, that he brings plague, famine and woe.'

'Soulis draws power from him as one draws water from a well,' said Rædwulf. 'We aim to drain that well, so to speak.'

'Redcap has ensconced himself,' said Adan, 'on an island without bridge or causeway. You may know it as Grimsmere.'

Moris looked at them with respect. '*There?* I've heard tales: it's home to the worst sprites and banshees; no one dares approach it.'

Adan and Hirnac said nothing, but Rædwulf did. 'We dare; and watch your tongue, Moris, for some sprites may be closer than you think.'

'As for trust,' said Thomas, folding his arms and meeting Moris' gaze, 'remember we are trusting you, and your men, to remain here, guarding the cauldron, until we return.'

Moris looked away, then met his eyes. 'What if you don't return? We cannot stay here forever and a day.'

'Assume the worst,' said Rædwulf, 'if we're not back by the full moon, three or four nights hence.'

Within an hour, they had mounted their horses, ready to take their leave of Moris and his men. 'We wish you all Godspeed, Blācencynn,' said Moris, glancing at the amulet, 'if that means anything to you. God willing, we will meet you at full moon.'

'God willing, indeed,' said Thomas. 'Whatever you do, Moris, don't touch the cauldron.'

Half doubtful, rubbing a thumb along his lower lip, Moris watched them go.

\*

Although he followed on its heels, Soulis could not overtake his dark guide. It stopped, as though studying the clear, straight path leading towards a ridge in the middle distance. Fevered and confused, Soulis scanned the empty, open expanse.

Dull, distant hills floated above the dawn mist; crows called from trees growing in crevices on a tall, distorted crag nearby; invisible, chittering beings crowded him, and his guide turned towards him, its face a featureless grey mask.

Soulis spoke, in both fearless command and contempt. 'Take me to Ercildoun or the dead will drag you to hell,' but pain overwhelming him again, he fell, lying in fevered sleep for hours.

## Chapter Twenty-Three

# The Mereburg

Shadowy forest eaves half a mile ahead stretched across quiet, mist-bound land, and Rædwulf glanced back towards the circle, now miles away, where Moris and his brethren were waiting. Thomas switched the reins from one hand to another.

'I don't like it here, Adan,' he said. 'God alone knows what's watching us.'

Adan shrugged. 'We've no choice, Learmont.'

Thomas snarled.

Every move an effort in the unquiet, stifling air, they followed a narrow path, pushing through the misty, deep green twilight, ferns, holly and brambles; reaching a ridge crest, they peered through the thick fog beyond. A faint, resonating pulse came from the earth, and Hirnac shuddered.

'A strange homecoming, sire,' he said. 'Do you hear it?'

'No, but I sense it.'

'The earth,' said Thomas. 'The earth awakens.'

'Neither mist nor dark can hide them,' said Adan. 'Follow me. I know my way, blindfold.'

Rædwulf snorted. 'You may as well be.'

They rode slowly for miles, seeing nothing; heard only the dull, rhythmic throb now coming from the air. Adan reined in, signalling a dismount, and crouching in the dense undergrowth, they gazed down at the placid lake, only half seen between shreds of breaking mist.

Thomas stared in disbelief at the Mereburg floating on clouds, and Adan smiled.

'Whatever happens,' he remarked, 'Soulis will need a boat. The lake is fathomless. I wonder, Thomas, if you've ever seen water so broad?'

His defensive reply, almost suggesting embarrassment, surprised them. 'Well, not since I swam across Loch Tay, for a bet.' After a pause, he confessed, 'Not something I'd want to repeat.'

'Did you win your bet?' said Rædwulf.

Thomas gave a sudden, broad grin, hinting mischief. 'What do *you* think?'

Adan, gesturing at a path winding down towards the lake, breathed a command. 'Come on. We can't waste time.'

## The Mereburg

\*

Midges tormented Moris and his followers, who sat nervous and uncomfortable beside the small fire; their horses stood dozing, low mist drifting across the circle, silent under the pale sun.

'Do you notice the quiet?' said Andrew. 'Not a creature dares come here. Why should we stay, Moris? We can almost see our rooftops; we should go home, bring a stronger cart, take the cauldron, and find Soulis ourselves.'

John, studying the cauldron with deep respect, said, 'Whoever made that is a master of his craft.'

Robbie snorted. 'We may as well be guarding a shovel, if you ask me.'

'This is a cursed place,' said Jacob, his arms around his knees. 'I know the tales told of it: witches come here, demons haunt it, and the stones transform into evil things at each full moon.'

*Full moon:* the deadline. Moris looked at the standing stones and the moor beyond, remembering Thomas' threat, but, priding himself that he always put others' needs first, and flicking a glance from John to the cauldron, he said, 'Alright. We'll go. Andrew, put out the fire. Robbie and Jacob, prepare the horses, and John: upright that thing.' Andrew tried quenching the fire; it burned brighter. John grasped the cauldron; it scorched his palm. The horses would not move. Moris, thrown back several yards when trying to walk between two standing stones, picked himself up and faced his frightened men.

Thomas Learmont had closed the circle.

*

The pulse now an almost-audible thud, Adan and his companions tethered their unsettled horses in a dark glade near the lakeshore. Rædwulf wound the rope around his waist, fastened the sack to his belt, and taking each step, each breath, with care, followed his companions to a low cliff overlooking the wharf ten feet below. Torches burned along its length, and a single boat, half-hidden in drifting mist, lay moored at the far end. Three indistinct figures stood in the shadows on the shore, listening, watching, with their every faculty, and Rædwulf, watching them through the fronds, hissed in disgust.

'They'll hear anything moving within a hundred yards.'

'Quiet,' breathed Adan. 'We'll approach them from behind. Move.'

They crawled forward and, crouching behind festoons of ivy five yards from the wharf, watched the three featureless figures. Adan nocked an arrow and, taking careful aim from between two close-growing trees, loosed it, the faintest hiss marking its flight; one guard fell dead from the wharf, the torchlight revealing its contorted face. Adan and his companions ran forward; Hirnac killed a second guard, and Rædwulf engaged with the third, an agile, quick-minded thing that ran forward wielding an axe. Caught off balance, Rædwulf fell, rolled, and turned; saw the axe coming down in a deadly arc; but another blade met it with force, throwing the guard into momentary retreat, with Thomas in pursuit. Rædwulf attacked the Spriggan from behind, the Sword shattering the axe handle, and the guard reeled.

Thomas gripped its hoary arm, trying to stab, but the Spriggan squirmed, and Thomas, his arm grasped in a fiercer twisting hold, yelling in pain and dropping his sword, wrestled the Spriggan along the jetty. Adan raised his bow.

'Adan, wait!' yelled Rædwulf, restraining him. 'You've no clear mark.'

Thomas and Spriggan fell into the cold, dark, disorienting water and sank, rolling over each other, to the lakebed. Trapped under his foe, the numbing water half blinding him, Thomas drew his knife, stabbing the creature until its terrifying weight had gone. He surfaced, floundering, found his feet, waded ashore, and retrieved his sword.

'You'll kill yourself one day, Thomas Learmont,' said Rædwulf, his tone steady as his eyes, 'unless you learn to look where you're going.'

Sodden, silent, Thomas glowered at him through his curtain of dripping hair.

Hirnac hauled the boat ashore where Adan, Rædwulf and Thomas stood abreast in silence and the deepening dusk, watching the darkness encroaching from the Mereburg. Not a leaf in the forest moved. Rædwulf ran one hand through his hair.

'Now we come to it, Adan. Now we take payment. A few yards are all that stands between us and vengeance.' He turned to Thomas. 'We only need a competent oarsman.'

Thomas took the point. 'If you're suggesting I row us across,' he said, 'then we'd better make it quick. Just looking at a boat makes me feel ill, and I'm useless with a paddle.'

*

Livid light from candles burning in upturned skulls on the altar cast looming shadows everywhere. Robin Redcap, the blood oozing from his damp cap, poured more from the bowl in a wide circle on the floor. He placed four lanterns offset from the cardinal points, another in the middle, and danced around the perimeter, chanting,

*The brethren gather, for the South Gate shall open at moonrise,*

*No Faerie charm will hide things approaching.*

*I shall see them, I shall kill them,*

*All Faerie lies bare to me.*

The ground shuddered, shaking the lanterns, and the shadows danced; a piercing, euphoric shriek from the rock, becoming faint mocking laughter with distance, carried far across the lake. The boat rolled on the surging water, almost pitching Rædwulf into the depths, before righting itself. Thomas, dropping the oars, clutched the gunwale, looking at his companions in alarm as the laughter swept over them.

Adan, understanding the signs, murmured in dismay, 'He's opening the South Gate.'

'Why now?' said Hirnac.

'Perhaps he wanted to destroy the Sword and Horn first,' said Adan, 'but has become impatient.'

'And we're delivering them,' said Rædwulf, staring ahead, 'almost into his lap, with little choice but to walk into his snare.'

Thomas began rowing again, taking his time, often glancing over his shoulder at the Mereburg.

'Adan, where do we land?'

Adan leaned forward, staring at the island, a menacing massif looming through the mist. 'Keep going, but take care,' he said. 'Fallen branches may lie half submerged, and there are rocks beneath the surface near the shore.'

'That sounds very reassuring,' snorted Thomas.

Hirnac, seated as look-out at the prow, pointed towards figures pacing a wharf, mere shadows in the faint lamp light.

'Look there,' he said. 'They've built a quay.'

'Use an inlet on the far side, Thomas,' hissed Adan. 'But take care; we're coming to the shallows now, and everyone keep quiet. I doubt those creatures can see us, but they may well sense us.'

Carefully but clumsily, Thomas guided the boat around the island, and Rædwulf spoke, his voice no louder than a sigh.

'There it is.'

The boat grounded on pebbles. Thomas shipped the oars and followed his companions along a faint path, through deep, brooding silence, their every breath and footstep echoing; they glimpsed intermittent lights through the trees ahead. Thomas' eyes were burning again, and he was aware of a soft, surrounding murmur. He had felt exposed when he stepped ashore but said nothing until they stopped on a high bank to consider their options. He leaned back against a tree, pulling his hood low over his face.

'He knows we're here, Adan.'

Unruffled, Adan faced him. 'I know. What's important is *we* are here.'

'Penda closed the North Gate, Thomas,' said Rædwulf. 'Now you must close the South.'

Thomas stared into the steady grey eyes. 'How?' he said. 'Adan has the Horn. You have the Sword. I have only my hands.'

'Then use them,' said Rædwulf.

Adan turned to them. 'Follow me to the Hall. I'd bet anything Redcap's there.'

They climbed down the bank, then stopped, looking at rough slabs paving a steep uphill path, skull lanterns hanging from the branches lighting the way. A loud screech came from somewhere amongst the trees, shadows flitted between them, and the irregular pulse, inducing tension and self-doubt, jarred every nerve. Thomas grasped his sword hilt but did not draw the weapon, and a faint grey light in the sky ahead heralded the rising moon.

Adan led them to the hazy summit, and they inched forward on their knees, every few minutes glancing at the surrounding forest. They surveyed a stone fortress built in the dell below, its battlements at their eye level. Adan gasped, and Hirnac, swallowing a cry, whispered, 'Oh no. What have they done?'

An unpleasant light came from the building. It seemed unguarded, and the pulse changed again, became rhythmical, regular as breathing. Rædwulf spoke in surprise.

'Where are they?'

'Hidden,' said Adan, 'awaiting Redcap's orders.'

Persistent, troubling inner murmurs blocking his every thought, Thomas lay, sensing something, and the trees crowded him.

'He will lure you, if he perceives the power, Thomas,' hissed Rædwulf. 'Forget about the Flame.'

Thomas stared ahead, aware only of the fortress. 'No,' he said, 'something else draws me.' He stood up and remained still for some minutes, his heart beating with the pounding air, his gaze fixed on the building.

'Stay here until I come back,' he said.

'Whatever you're up to, Learmont,' replied Rædwulf, 'have a care. That creature is deadly.'

Knife in hand, expecting anything, Thomas walked down a long flight of stairs into the dell and along a narrow tunnel; skull lanterns burned in every niche, and water trickling onto the floor made his footing treacherous. A slippery stone stair brought him to a cave; puddles reflected the macabre wall-mounted lamps, and he sensed a primitive, all-pervading evil coming from behind a heavy, locked door. He pushed at it, taking a slow breath with each shove, until it opened to a vault beyond.

A column of pulsating dark light, rising towards another descending from the roof above, cast a grotesque shadow on the far wall. The ground shook, the air trembled, and Thomas' voice echoed around the chamber:

'Prince of Spriggans, why sit you waiting? Soulis comes hither, hungry for power.'

The shadow moved; a contorted form with narrowed eyes appeared from the dark.

'I don't see you,' rasped Redcap, 'but I know the Flame is here. Soulis wants power, say you? He can want, for he cannot meet my gaze without forfeiting his soul.'

'Prince of Spriggans, why stand you waiting? The Healer wants your blood.'

Redcap danced around the circle, laughing. 'None can kill me!'

'The power stands before you, Prince of Spriggans. Why do you wait?'

Suspicious of a force greater than his, Redcap drew his vicious blade, ran from the chamber, and stood near the stair, listening. Thomas pounced from the shadows, striking at him, missed, then spun around to strike again; but Redcap leapt, turning in mid-air, bringing down his blade. The knife, knocked from Thomas' hand and chinking against the rock, was lost in darkness.

Thomas yelled, leapt aside, drew his sword, and facing Redcap, whispered through his teeth, 'Soulis moves against you, Robin Redcap.'

Redcap, standing on the bottom step, snarling, leering, licking the dripping venom from his fangs, gave a harsh, mocking, malevolent reply. 'I gave him immortality and hold the keys to his treasury. He will lose everything if he destroys me, Thomas Learmont.'

'Your blood-craving magic,' spat Thomas, 'corrupts all it touches, all it cannot have.'

Redcap, crafty, malicious as before, goaded him. 'You cannot hide the Flame from me, for I sense its power in you. It eats at you, Learmont, seeking to overturn your mind. Share that burden, Learmont. Join your power with mine, and I will destroy Soulis.'

Thomas did not change his tone. 'The Flame does not share its power, Sprite; no one governs it. It destroys all who act against it.'

Redcap gloated. 'The pillars are joining, Thomas Learmont. The Seelie Court will fall, and everyone there will die, when the Gate opens at moonrise.' He gave a high, cruel, soul-piercing laugh. 'There's nought you can do, Thomas Learmont. Only a Spriggan's blade can stop it.'

Thomas ran at him, but Redcap retreated a short way up the stairs, stopped, spat, and taunted him. 'Come and kill me, Learmont! Come and kill me, if you can!'

Thomas leapt forward again, striking at him, but the wall deflected the blow. Again, Thomas lunged at him, again Redcap retreated, almost to the stairhead, before bringing his dagger down, shattering the sword. Thomas, staggering from the blow, lost his footing, fell, and rolled to the bottom step where he lay stunned, the power no protection for the unconscious. Redcap leapt down the stairs, giving a triumphant shriek.

'You cannot kill me, Learmont! No puny elf-blade can touch me! I have only to kill you, Thomas of Ercildoun! I've only to bite your life away to take the power!'

He crouched over him, slavering, poised to give a lethal bite, holding his knife ready to stab—but another shattered it. Someone threw a hood over his head, blindfolding him; bound rope around him, and pressed a blade against his neck. He squirmed in vain to free himself and screeched.

Rædwulf breathed into his ear, 'Shut up, or I'll cut your miserable balls off. March.'

Giving Redcap a savage kick, he dragged him to the ridge where Adan and Hirnac tied him to an oak tree.

Rædwulf stepped back and said, 'What tidings in the wind today, *Robin Redcap?*'

'Come, my lord,' said Adan, in mock defence, 'one cannot receive news from a messenger who makes no call.'

Redcap gave a shrieking laugh through the hood. 'Nought will stop the South Gate opening at moonrise, now that Learmont lies dying at the chamber door.'

Rædwulf and Adan looked back and saw the moon's rim already peeping above the distant hills. Hirnac ran down to the fortress; Rædwulf, facing Redcap again, spoke with murder in his voice.

'Well now, my merry fellow, what shall we do with you?'

\*

Hirnac found Thomas slumped and groaning on the bottom step; helping him up, he recoiled, alarmed at the burning blue light in the darkened eyes. Something drew Thomas against his will into the chamber, the weird lamplight casting his shadow on the walls, and he watched the mesmerising pillars, now a hair's breadth from joining. Twisted faces peered from every niche, the air quaked, and the voices in his head clamoured *Close the South Gate.*

*

Adan pulled the ropes around Redcap's torso and neck, tight enough to choke him, and Rædwulf, giving a sinister smile, spoke through clenched teeth.

'The Healer demands a fee, Redcap, a fee for his slaughtered kinfolk; a fee for one who sleeps in the Flame's ruin.' He snatched the hood from the grizzled head and, not without personal risk, forced the thick leather strap between the fangs, preventing any bite. His smile gone, his piercing eyes cold, he rested the Sword against the hoary neck. 'The Blācencynn wrapped spells for your ruin around this blade, Robin Redcap. I will kill you.'

Redcap squirmed, shrieking through his gag, and Adan drew his own sword.

'I, Lord Mereburg, call in a fee for all my kinfolk slaughtered in the darkness, for every head hanging from the trees, and for my ruined hall. All your blood cannot pay me.'

In sudden bloodlust, they stripped Redcap naked and struck him, over and again: shoulders, limbs, torso.

## The Mereburg

Redcap shook like a sack of wool with each blow, but he did not succumb. Rædwulf, a frightening triumph burning in his eyes, pressed himself against Redcap, pushing and twisting the Sword through the torso; through, through, and through, into the tree behind.

'I take only my due, Robin Redcap,' he snarled. 'All eternity you will be a mere shadow, for women to scare their children with.'

Glassy-eyed, blood gushing from his mouth, Redcap slumped forward. With a single blow, Rædwulf severed the head, and revelling in the blood spattering over him, held it aloft, yelling in triumph, *'Penda, I avenge thee!'*

Adan sheathed his sword. A sudden silence came, a brief stillness as though all the trees awaited a final blow. Without warning, the ground surged and the air throbbed; contorted, screeching beings, forming from the shadows and darkness between the trees, surrounded Adan and Rædwulf, who, taken unawares, raised their weapons to defend themselves. Rædwulf, between Adan and the lunging horde, met each lethal blade with savage blows from his own. His foes retreated but advanced again. Adan, standing between Rædwulf and Redcap, loosed every arrow he had, then drew his sword again, killing any foe within his reach. The Spriggans, gibbering and shrieking, rushed forward, pushing Rædwulf to the quaking ground. Fighting and kicking with all he had, he yelled, 'The Horn, Adan! Sound the Horn!'

Adan, leaping aside from the Spriggans, blew the Horn three times, the sound changing with distance—loud, penetrating thunder at the Mereburg, a bittern's boom over the lake, a wolf's howl across the forest and the land beyond; musical as panpipes at the Seelie Court—and the part-cowled moon hung above the horizon.

\*

Voices surrounded Soulis, waking him.

*'The South Gate is open. Go to the Mereburg, Lord Soulis, and claim Lordship of all Faerie, for Robin Redcap hath betrayed thee.'*

Soulis stood up, staring into the night. He heard wolves howling, and a strange nearby watch-fire burned without heat: ice-fire. His guide, a wafting and re-forming shadow, stood waiting just beyond the firelight. The earth trembled, and the hazy moon rode the distant hills.

\*

## The Mereburg

Black clouds hung low over the night-bound Seelie Court, the ground thundered, and a fierce gale thrashed treetops back and forth in the nearby woodland. Three veiled women, standing in a lamp-lit woodland clearing, their hands joined over a spring, began walking sunwise around it, staring at the water.

'Great Mother,' said the tallest, 'we three Daughters of Earth, standing by the Well of Fate, hear the Mereburg call. Bright Faerie will fall if two sons of Earth and two of men cannot close the South Gate.'

'Great Mother,' called the second, her voice clear against the thudding earth, 'shield these mortal men from the darkness that now overcomes them: Thomas Learmont, for we love him...'

The third took several shallow breaths before she called out, 'Rædwulf Blācencynn. For I... for we... love him.'

Dagan and Cynwæd ran up the heaving steps to the billowing Faerie banner, and lightning on the horizon revealed shadows marching from the dark horizon.

'Take the standard down!' yelled Dagan, grabbing the shaking flagpole. 'They can't find us if we take it down!'

Borderlands

*

The columns of dark light were now touching, tip to tip. As through a window, Thomas saw the bright banner of the Seelie Court fluttering in a strong wind, its mast, the entire enclosure, shaking, and three women standing around a wellspring, their hands joined as though in ritual. Dumb, frozen, he watched them lift their veils: Raldis; Læren, whose troubled gaze had haunted him since their meeting in Ercildoun; and the Lady, whose beauty had bound him in an unbreakable spell, but she was now aged beyond old, gnarled as an ancient oak, and angry humiliation deluged him.

Heavy footsteps came from the stairs, loud shrieks echoed off every wall, and Hirnac gave a despairing yell as he fought the hordes on the threshold.

'They're opening the Gate, Thomas. They'll destroy Bright Faerie. Don't let them kill us, Thomas! Don't let them kill us all,' but Thomas did not respond. Entranced, he stared at Læren, taking an involuntary step back when her features transformed into Finnian.

*'Better be blind, Thomas Learmont, if thine eyes offend thee.'*

## The Mereburg

A distinct, deep rumbling, growing until it overpowered everything, swept through the chamber. Hirnac, fighting off the onslaught, cried out in one last hope.

'The Horn, Thomas! Adan has blown the Mereburg Horn!'

Wrapped in shadow, Thomas awoke as though from a dream. His eyes burning, conflicting forces almost overwhelming him, he watched the column, thick as his arm, rising from floor to roof; his weird, distorted tone gave the surrounding stone a voice:

*'The South Gate shall close.'*

He took Finnian's knife from his boot, for a moment stared at the column, and scythed through it. The knife melted in his hand, and the column collapsed. The shaking chamber floor and walls split open, choking clouds of mortar fell from the roof, the falling lanterns ignited the herbs and straw spread on the flagstones, and fire spread along corridors above. It trapped the sprites, their terrified, tormented screams echoing through the fortress.

\*

Pinned to the ground, unable to fend off the assault any longer, Rædwulf closed his eyes in despair, awaiting the end, but the surrounding shrieks became screams as opening fissures pulled every Spriggan into the earth. He realised he was free and staggered to his feet, listening to the cries.

'Hear them scream,' said Adan, 'as we did before.'

\*

The clouds over the Seelie Court dispersed, the wind dropped, and the ground became still. Dagan and Cynwæd stood beside the now inert banner, watching the lifting darkness, and Dagan gave a deep sigh.

'That was close.'

\*

Hirnac picked himself up and, glimpsing Thomas leaning against the far wall, half-hidden in smoke and waist-high flames, called, 'Thomas! Over here!'

Thomas, choking on the acrid fumes coming from the burning herbs, gasped. 'Go back!'

*The Flame protects itself.* Power, and unbearable, overwhelming pain, surged through him, and he fell to his knees. Hirnac cried out again. 'You can't stay in there!'

Wreathed in smoke, Thomas gave a rasping yell. 'Go *back*! You can't help me! Go back to Adan!'

Alarmed, Hirnac shouted, 'You can't give up, Learmont. Don't give up now!' His voice echoed around the chamber: *You can't give up now!*

The shaking ground pitched again. With the chamber falling around him, Thomas struggled to his feet and leapt over widening fissures, through rising flames and thickening smoke, to the doorway. Without ceremony, Hirnac grabbed and hauled him up the shaking stairs, the roof and walls crumbling around them, and the chamber below collapsed.

They reached the ridge foot and looked back, smoke and soul-rending screams streaming from the burning building. Thomas, taking a deep breath, murmured, 'The South Gate is closed,' and sat down, giving a long sigh. 'What can I say, Hirnac?'

'Say nothing, Thomas Learmont,' Hirnac retorted. 'You can explain to Rædwulf and Adan—if they're still alive.' He turned away before Thomas could reply.

Adan and Rædwulf met them near the oak tree, wanting to know about events. Thomas proved reticent, but Hirnac, having no such qualms, recounted it all. Worried, exasperated, annoyed, Rædwulf took Thomas aside.

'I know you're not a coward, Thomas Learmont,' he said in a heated whisper, 'but you're an utter liability! Your only task was to close the Gate. What would we have gained, what did you hope to *achieve*, by staying in that chamber?'

Thomas gave as heated a reply. 'Fire almost trapped me, Blācencynn. I couldn't move, breathe, or see a way out.'

'We were fighting for our lives up here, Learmont, and for yours, and you almost gave up? There's no room for self-doubt, Thomas, for any of us.' He turned, but faced him again. 'We're not finished yet. There are miles between us and the circle, and you still have a task, but *if* you can't do it for the Blācencynn, the Seelie Court, Penda, or even for yourself,' he snapped, 'then do it for the lady maiden. Do it for her. I've known some brave men who've had *half* her courage.'

He began walking away, but Thomas, stung by the taunt, shouted after him. 'You don't know what I saw through that Gate, Blācencynn.'

Rædwulf turned back, giving him a guarded, suspicious look. 'What did you see?'

Thomas sat down, bowing his head almost to his knees. 'Raldis… Læren… and the High Lady, but she as a crone.'

Now calm, Rædwulf sat beside him. 'Because that's what she is. Truth cannot hide from either the power or the Blācencynn, Thomas. I've always seen her like that.' He lowered his tone. 'I'm not a fool, Learmont. I know you lay with her at court, and I've wondered why, and now I know. She deceived you into believing her beautiful, and perhaps you'll never see her like that again.' He gave a wry smile. 'Once the veil lifts, Thomas, there is no disguise.'

'Then why,' said Thomas, staring ahead, 'were Læren and Raldis as I remember them?'

Rædwulf shrugged. 'I guess because Læren cannot yet disguise herself, and Raldis has no need.' He stood up.

'That's not all,' remarked Thomas. 'I saw Finnian as well.'

Rædwulf raised an eyebrow. 'Now, that surprises me. Did he say anything?'

Thomas replied without looking up. 'Well… yes… that I should blind myself.'

'Or,' said Rædwulf, unruffled, 'you should just… turn a blind eye?'

'Why was he not in his true form?'

Rædwulf, staring at the trees, sounded thoughtful. 'I'm not sure; maybe he could not discard so ingrained a disguise.'

'I've a wicked headache,' said Thomas, pressing one hand to his forehead, 'and my eyes are sore.'

'That could be from all the smoke.' Rædwulf gave a beckoning nod. 'We'll move back to the mainland, then eat and sleep—we all need it.'

He approached the oak tree, and picking up the severed head, gave a grim smile. 'Well, my handsome friend, I've a nice little task for you.' He put it in the sack on his belt, and glimpsing a folded parchment on the ground, picked it up, somehow knowing that this was Soulis' contract.

'This might be useful,' he said, tucking it under his shirt, 'but we'll examine it in daylight. It's time we returned to the mainland.'

'I agree,' said Adan, 'but we should make sure Spriggans aren't waiting at the wharf. Follow me, and stay alert.'

A peculiar, grim stillness filled the forest; Adan led them along another rough-paved path, dimly lit by the grinning lanterns hanging in the trees. Hirnac shuddered.

'These awful lamps make my skin crawl, sire,' he whispered. 'Can we not destroy them?'

Adan thought about this. 'Clouds hide the moon, Hirnac. They light our way, well enough.'

'I don't like this quiet,' said Hirnac. 'It feels like the land of the dead.'

'Nowhere I haven't walked before,' muttered Rædwulf.

They found the mist-bound wharf deserted and a crude, two-berth log boat beached beside it; more macabre lanterns burned, either on posts along its length or in the trees.

'You and Thomas stay here,' said Adan, 'while Hirnac and I fetch the boat.'

Rædwulf and Thomas watched them out of sight and, ill-at-ease, waited, alert for any Spriggans still lurking in the dark. Thomas walked the length of the wharf and stared, sickened, at the skin and plaited hair still attached to the skull lantern hanging from the tallest post. Rædwulf, hearing his gasp and understanding his thought, approached him.

'It isn't her, Thomas.' Thomas blinked, stared at him, and looked at the skull again. 'It isn't *her*,' repeated Rædwulf. 'It's too small, Thomas. Don't you see? These are the children Soulis stole.'

Thomas stared at the lamp. 'Those farmers would pay the very devil to kill him,' he said. 'We should tell Moris.'

Rædwulf stepped towards him. 'And achieve what? Would you watch grief and anger drive blameless men to madness or crush them to despair? Either would be an injustice.'

Thomas met the burning grey eyes. 'Good God, man; they've every right to know.'

Rædwulf returned the stare. 'I don't dispute that, but we'll tell them afterwards—if at all.'

Thomas dropped his gaze and his tone. 'Hirnac was right; we should destroy all these lamps, and I don't like this silence either… it smothers me… And Soulis could still attack Ercildoun.'

Rædwulf looked at him sidelong, as though hinting something. 'It isn't unprotected, Thomas; nor is she.' He turned away and stood watching for Adan and Hirnac to return.

*

Moris stood beside Andrew, the fire burning behind them, the cauldron still on its side, the standing stones hidden in dawn mist. Andrew wiped perspiration from his forehead.

'Nothing's changed since we heard the wolves last night, Moris; although, for a moment, I saw a stag watching me—massive thing it was. It disappeared before I could call out, but I'd take any oath it was here. Nothing moves or calls. It's unnerving.'

Moris gave this some thought. 'Do you think we're still trapped here?'

Andrew gave a resigned sigh. 'We won't know unless we try leaving.'

'Wake the others,' replied Moris. 'We'll find out soon enough.'

Moris chose Andrew and Robbie to go with him to the perimeter. Andrew, wary of the standing stones, crept forward, and when almost between them, recoiled, charged energy surging through him. He shook his head.

'There's no way through it, Moris. Whatever those men did, we can't leave here.'

'It was Learmont,' said Jacob. 'I saw him, walking around the circle.'

'Learmont?' replied Moris, surprised, then smiled. Despite himself, he had a new, though reluctant, respect for Thomas. 'The crafty git.'

\*

Hirnac awoke two hours before mid-day; the small fire was now a mere column of smoke, and thin mist drifted between the trees. He heard his companions snoring, humming bees working the woodland, and a thrush twittering nearby. Dull, distant hoof beats came through the forest, and alarmed, he awakened his bewildered companions; they waited, weapons drawn, expecting the worst. The horseman, the sunlight glancing off his antlers and pelts, broke through the surrounding undergrowth, stopped, dismounted, and approached Adan.

'Lord Mereburg,' said Cernunnos, 'the men at the stone circle are uneasy; they have tried leaving it once already, and may well try again.'

## The Mereburg

'I closed that circle,' said Thomas with some force. 'They can't go anywhere until we go back; not until full moon.'

'Full moon is almost on us,' replied Adan. 'The enchantment won't last longer than another couple of days, Thomas, and once they realise… don't you see? They'll try again, and again, until they escape.' He turned to Cernunnos. 'Lord Hunter, what of Soulis? We were waiting here for him; have you any news?'

'He might be anywhere,' said Cernunnos. 'Nearby, or further away than you think.'

Rædwulf stared at him, then looked at Adan. 'Either we stay here, waiting for him,' he said, 'or go to the circle. We can't do both.'

'No, we can't,' said Adan. 'At least, not if we stay together.'

'Meaning?' asked Thomas in a guarded tone.

'I don't trust those men, Thomas,' replied Adan, 'any more than you do.'

'They are not bad people,' said Rædwulf, 'but they're superstitious, and it wouldn't surprise me if they try to find Soulis for themselves, as they first intended.'

'Soulis may not come here,' said Hirnac.

'The elf maiden said Redcap has summoned all his creatures,' said Adan. 'Soulis must respond.'

'Redcap is dead,' said Rædwulf.

'Maybe so,' said Cernunnos, 'but you cannot override the summons.'

Thomas walked away to a vantage point out of sight of his companions where he sat for ten minutes, looking at the dark, silent Mereburg and the jetty below him. Rædwulf sat beside him, was silent for a while, then looked at him.

'I want to examine your eyes, Thomas. Hirnac said he didn't like what he saw in them.'

Thomas hesitated, then nodded. 'Very well.'

Rædwulf, finding nothing wrong, sat back, stroking his beard. 'I'm sorry about what I said, Thomas, but I was angry.'

Thomas shrugged. 'You were within your rights.'

Rædwulf took the parchment from beneath his shirt and, holding it up to the light, frowned. 'I thought I could read most things, Thomas, but I don't understand this.'

Thomas studied it: the faint traces of elegant script beneath the distorted, crude lettering and unreadable phrases peppering the page. 'It looks like bastardised Latin,' he said, 'but the signature is clear enough.'

## The Mereburg

Rædwulf nodded. 'Yes, that I could read.'

'What do you want it for?'

'Barter.' Rædwulf tucked it under his shirt again. 'I worry Moris and his men will lose heart. They trust us less than we trust them, and they're right fearing that circle; whatever force it has can't escape either. I suspect there are spells twisted all around that cauldron, that it could now kill anyone who touches it other than us, so Adan, Hirnac and I must go back before they try taking it.'

Thomas stared at him with sudden misgiving. 'While you leave me here alone, unarmed, waiting for Soulis?'

Rædwulf gave a measured reply. 'He never saw you at the Caves. Tell him he'll find Wyrtræd at the circle—anything to draw him there.'

'You forget, Rædwulf, that I cannot tell a lie.'

'I'm not asking you to. Of us all, you have the best defence, but remember, you cannot afford injury; the power doesn't protect the weak, Thomas. Don't doubt yourself. He can overcome you if he has even a hint of who you are.'

'I thought perhaps you, at least, would help me.'

'I can't, because he'll recognise me, and despite what the Hunter said, there's still a chance Soulis will reach the circle first; and if he finds those men unguarded…' He let the sentence drift. 'He's a wounded beast, Thomas. Those farmers don't know what danger they're in.'

Thomas remained silent for perhaps a minute, then said, 'Sometimes, the power overwhelms me; sometimes I no longer exist. I thought it would leave me once the Gate closed, but still it churns. It scares me, Blācencynn; I want rid of it.'

'It won't leave you, Thomas,' said Rædwulf, 'until… well, until it decides otherwise.' He nodded towards the glade. 'We must prepare things, Thomas. We need to move.'

Adan and Hirnac were already breaking camp and the horses were saddled; Rædwulf led Hirnac aside, whispering to him, and Adan handed Thomas a package.

'Your rations, Thomas,' he said, 'enough for a few days.'

Thomas watched them mount. 'I will meet you at the stone circle, with or without Soulis,' he said. 'Bury me in Ercildoun if I fail.'

Rædwulf gave a droll smile. 'I will—if I live long enough.'

Thomas watched them go. Cernunnos, now mounted, his steady, soul-penetrating gaze on Thomas, spoke with a warning undertone in his voice. 'The Flame is a dangerous mistress, Thomas Learmont, more than once almost destroying you. Remember: fear sharpens the senses.' He made to turn.

'Lord Hunter,' said Thomas, 'Spriggans transform to stone on death, but Redcap didn't. Why?'

'Because he formed from ideas, Thomas Learmont, and one cannot destroy ideas, whatever their source. Perhaps other Redcaps are waiting to take his place.'

He rode away, with Thomas calling after him, 'Wait—do the others know? Does Rædwulf know?' But Cernunnos disappeared among the trees, leaving Thomas staring after him and then at the path his companions had taken, powerless to warn them.

He ate and drank some of his rations, covered the fire, returned to the lake, swam to wash the grime and sour, smoky smell from his clothing, then sat in the hazy sunshine, watching the dark Mereburg drifting beneath a hot, milky sky. He heard the low, persistent, tormenting voices again; felt exposed, abandoned, fearing the power could, as he now suspected it had Penda, betray him to his death.

## Chapter Twenty-Four

# The Oarsman

Drifting mist made the silent land seem unreal, the sun a brass disc, the sky planished copper, and the standing stones hunched, frozen beings. The farmers kept an anxious, sleepless vigil throughout the night and the following morning; Robbie began his patrol in the afternoon, unsure of what to expect, or what he was watching for. He gave a sudden call, pointing towards the south-east.

'Look! Horsemen! Three horsemen, riding like the wind, by God!'

Adan, Rædwulf and Hirnac rode into the circle, dismounting almost before their horses stopped. Moris glanced around, confused.

'Where's Learmont?'

'Waiting for Soulis at the Mereburg,' said Adan, unfastening his saddle girth.

'Alone?' said Moris, astonished

'It's a calculated risk, I'll admit,' said Rædwulf, giving a slight shrug, 'but one we wouldn't have taken at all if you hadn't tried leaving the circle.' He saw the guilty flash in Moris' eyes, whispered, 'Don't assume nothing watched you in our absence,' and turning, stared at the cauldron.

'It's brooding,' said Moris, 'and we think it's watching us. See how it glares.'

Rædwulf glanced at him. 'It's the hub of a wheel,' he said, 'focusing power from every standing stone.'

'So much for power,' said Andrew, 'when we're stuck with pounds of lead we can't melt down.'

'We might build a furnace,' said Robbie.

John stared at him. 'A furnace? With what? It'll be useless without charcoal or bellows.'

Practical as ever, Rædwulf nodded towards Andrew, Robbie and Jacob. 'You might improvise bellows from the leather jerkins your comrades wear. We'll help you build the furnace and hope it's finished before dark; and you won't need charcoal... if Hirnac tends the fire.'

John snorted. 'I can tell you're not a blacksmith. What shall we use for the crucible?' Rædwulf looked at the cauldron, and John, understanding the hint, spluttered, 'You're not suggesting we use *that*? Look what it did to my hand when I tried righting it.'

'The injury's superficial, John,' said Rædwulf, glancing at the outstretched palm, 'and will soon mend.'

'How would you know?'

'Experience.'

John fizzed. '*You* try touching it then.'

Unconcerned, Rædwulf pulled the cold cauldron upright, remarking, 'I wonder why you touched it at all, after Thomas warned you against handling a Faerie gift.' He stroked his beard, thinking aloud. 'Soulis has an open wound that needs treating, and Thomas will lure him here on the promise of finding a doctor.'

Moris flicked him a doubtful glance. 'You know of one?'

Rædwulf shrugged. 'Yes. If all goes well, he'll meet us here.'

'Ah, but do you trust him?' said Robbie.

Rædwulf stared at him. 'Implicitly.'

'Soulis will see that cauldron the moment he sets foot here,' said Moris.

Rædwulf faced him. 'I don't care.' A sudden, fierce light erupted in his eyes. 'I'll have his *blood* before this is over.'

\*

Most torches along the jetty had burned out, leaving one dying at the far end, and a subdued, crimson dusk hid the Mereburg across the steaming lake. Thomas patrolled the shore, then sat near the boat, watching the still, silent forest, and fell asleep.

He was jolted awake by deliberate, heavy footsteps which trod along the jetty, stopped, and returned; a man uttered a low moan, and a loud thud came from the boat. Startled, Thomas saw nothing in the darkness, heard only rippling water; he was alone.

\*

Soulis awoke after midnight. Strange shadows stalked around the forest glade in the cold light from the comfortless watch-fire, and his guide, standing beneath a yew tree, turned away. Soulis crawled after him to the lakeshore. His guide left him, and he stood up, uncertain, sensing openness, a glowering, threatening stillness; he smelt a miasma of damp air, earth and leaves, and the water glimmered in the torchlight. A cowled figure, a faint blue light tracing the folds of its cloak, sat in the boat as though waiting for him; sensing a threat, Soulis crept to the stern and drawing his sword, spoke, his voice harsh, jagged.

## The Oarsman

'I am Soulis, Lord of both Mereburg and Blācencynn, and hold my blade at your throat. Declare your purpose.'

Thomas smelt the festering wound, heard the rasp of the weapon drawn from its scabbard, and saw the glinting blade, something he had not bargained for. Afraid, and for the moment nonplussed, he thought fast. Unarmed, the power latent for now, knowing his life depended on his answering without hesitation, or lying, and swallowing his fear, he replied in a low, even tone.

'I am the oarsman of Grimsmere.'

Soulis boarded the boat and, holding his sword within an inch of Thomas' throat, answered with contempt. 'Know this, Oarsman, shades guard, guide and obey me, and so will you. Take me to the Mereburg, for my slave Redcap has betrayed me; I will take vengeance upon him, and all Faerie.'

Thomas said nothing. Ever aware of the sword hovering near his throat, he punted the boat off the shingle, and although it moved almost of its own accord, he began rowing towards the island, the only sound that of the creaking oars. At length, he spoke, his tone unaltered.

'You do not need your blade here.'

Soulis spoke with undiluted spite. 'I know not what menaces me, but menace there is; I sense it. No, I shall not sheathe this blade, Oarsman, until I have Redcap's head.'

'You cannot kill him.'

Soulis almost screeched. 'I have every right to punish traitors and to wield the Blācencynn Sword and Elfin Horn; and once I find them, Oarsman, all Faerie will open to me.' Pain overcame him again, and he sat rigid, pressing his disabled arm against his chest.

'You should have that treated,' said Thomas gravely, 'before it becomes much worse.' He glanced towards the Mereburg; saw the wharf not far away, and the strange, diffuse pale light coming from the island summit.

Soulis looked up. 'I have sought, and sent for, the healer Wyrtræd, yet he eludes me.'

As though unaware, Thomas spoke with a hint of menace in his voice. *'Let maidens guide you.'* He stopped rowing, and the boat floated motionless on the glassy water. With the glinting blade at his throat, Thomas tried to gauge what Soulis might do. *Bite,* he thought. *Take the bait, dog, now, while there's time.*

Confused, Soulis made no reply but sat staring at the featureless oarsman, who spoke again: the same tone, the same unnerving timbre. 'Do you know the Northern Lights?'

## The Oarsman

Soulis, glancing northward, seeing nothing through the misty darkness, remained silent. Thomas gave a quiet laugh. 'No? Folk see them sometimes: spirits of maidens turned to stone for dancing on the Sabbath.' He resumed rowing, speaking in the same quiet tone. 'Or of women that go dancing across the sky, beautiful, but frightening as death, seeking men's souls.'

The boat slid beneath the overhanging trees, coming to rest on the shingle by the wharf, but before Thomas could move or speak, he felt the weapon snag on his cloak and the blade pressing against his chest. Soulis gave a brief, sneering laugh.

'Now, *Master Oarsman,* you shall guide me to my hall and bear witness to the justice I dispense, and if that doesn't sicken you, you will lead me to Wyrtræd.'

Thomas, having neither space nor means to fight, had no choice but to lead Soulis along the misty path, all the time aware of the blade at his back, the burning lanterns giving a dim, unpleasant light. Soulis, groping, stumbling, supporting his weight against trees, stopped and stood looking at the path ahead, listening to a silence deeper than the dark; he recognised the hanging skulls in the trees as the children Finnian had demanded—and did not care.

He faced Thomas, whose form remained vague in the darkness, despite the lamplight, and said, 'Many of my kindred await me, yet I don't hear them. Where are my people? *Where are my people?*'

Thomas murmured, but his voice echoed, as though coming from a cavern. 'They belong to themselves.' His gaze dropped to the glimmering sword, then lifted to the surrounding forest where pockets of mist hung in the hollows. The path, dipping into mist, rose to the glowing summit. Undeceived, Soulis spoke.

'Well, now, Oarsman, I no longer need a guide, nor do I need you to ferry me to the mainland, for the boat will move as I command.' He circled Thomas and faced him again. 'What use would a mere mortal be to me? For I don't doubt that mortal you are. I would bind you for my sport, if I had use of both arms, and the time, but I have neither, so I fear your death will be quick. Now, that is a pity.'

He stepped forward, cornering Thomas against a tree, scanned his now iridescent form, peered at the shadowed features, and sniggered. 'Now, let us see you, my handsome friend,' and lifting the hood from Thomas' face with his sword, he whispered, 'Here it shall end for you, mortal. Here you shall bleed.'

With Soulis standing beyond his arm's reach, Thomas felt the cold steel against his face; saw shadows moving within the drifting mist; met the maniacal gaze. Soulis raised his sword. Thomas braced himself.

A distant, drawn-out call came from the path ahead: *'Sou-lis.'*

Soulis glanced around, but there was silence. He faced Thomas again, again raised the sword, making to stab.

*'Sou-lis.'*

He turned, and as though drawn against his will, walked towards the light that now set the sky aglow and disappeared into a misty ditch. Thomas leaned against the tree, taking deep breaths, collecting himself, watching the diffuse light. It drew him unawares towards the hollow, but he stopped on the brink, realising the danger in time, and looked around at the sentinel trees. He returned to the wharf and stood peering through the silent dark, listening, expecting pursuit, but there was none.

A quiet, distinct sigh came from his right, and he spun around; perhaps it was only the fitful moonlight, only shadow-play, but he swallowed a cry: Penda, older than in life, white strands in his black hair and beard, stood just feet away, his staring eyes blind. His voice came from the trees: *Leave or die*, then he faded from view.

Afraid, unable to move, Thomas heard Rædwulf warning him: *Die… and the power will go to another mind.* The mist lifted a little, and a thin moonlight shone onto the lake, creating a pale track across the water to the mainland. Thomas looked back, wondering whether Soulis was already returning, knowing that they each needed the boat: a boat. He jumped down to the log boat, heaved it into the shallows, clambered aboard and, struggling for balance, paddled it beyond the wharf. He glimpsed something on the water's surface, half a boat length ahead; realising too late it was a large, half-submerged branch, he collided with it and slid off the capsizing boat, the cold depths taking his breath away.

He fought his way to the surface, gasped, looked around to find his bearings, and started swimming fast along the pale moonlight track towards the mainland.

\*

Wary, sensing a strange, surrounding force, Soulis limped towards the summit, the hazy light revealing a naked, headless, twisted corpse tied to an oak tree. He stared at the red cap placed over the severed neck, the savage, distorted rune carved deep into the torso, the ruined fortress in the dell beyond, and understood he was free of the contract—and who the oarsman must have been. With icy triumph, he lifted his sword to the heavens and gave a weird, savage cry: *'I see you, Thomas Learmont! You cannot hide!'* The silence deepened, as though the entire world lay listening.

\*

Halfway to shore, Thomas heard the cry echo across the lake. Benumbed, his pace becoming ever laboured, he was slowly sinking, slowly falling asleep. It was just a matter of time.

\*

*'Wake up, Hen.'*

Startled from deep sleep, Molly lay watching light shimmering like surface reflections across the wall. She turned over, stifling a yell when she saw Thomas, bathed in moonlight, at her bedside, his hair dripping, his face ashen, his eyes gazing into the distance; she had never seen such fear. He retreated to the far wall, his fading form leaving only the dim glow from the rush lights, and she gave a peculiar, despairing, hollow cry.

\*

Suspended, drifting, peaceful, Thomas saw fleeting visions: his companions, Molly, Raldis, Læren; the Seelie Court, Ercildoun; the High Lady and every woman he had shared a bed with. He heard Rædwulf rebuking him, *'Do it for the lady maiden,'* and Hirnac yelling, *'You can't give up now.'*

Released from his reverie, Thomas surfaced near the jetty, its form ghostly through the mist, and he floundered ashore, making his unsteady way to the glade. Drenched, shivering, his hair dripping into his eyes, his hands benumbed, and the moonlight giving little aid, he untethered the horses. Leaving the draft animal tied to the jetty, he mounted his horse and, somehow knowing he could not lose his way, rode fast, reaching the forest eaves at dawn.

\*

## The Oarsman

Soulis reached the wharf, saw the empty boat, tinged with blue light, its oars set for departure, then turned about, sword outstretched to attack, but nothing moved amongst the trees and a voice came from all around him: *Find Wyrtræd.* He climbed aboard, and the boat moved onto the lake, the oars creaking, yet he saw no oarsman, and he called out in defiant triumph.

'No longer will you menace me with empty threats, Robin Redcap, for your face and gaze are gone, lifting your curse. My soul is my own.' He faced a vague shadow in the prow. 'What say you, *Master Oarsman?*'

There was no reply. The boat grounded on the shingle, the oarsman faded, and languid mist hung amongst the trees in the pallid dawn. Soulis disembarked, saw the horse, gold glinting on its harness, untethered it, and scrambled into the saddle. The horse ambled forward through undergrowth and mist, something unseen guiding it, and Soulis gave an imperious cry.

'I am Soulis! None can touch me!'

He drew rein at the forest eaves and, as though held there, fixed his gaze northward, the land brooding in a sombre light. Unprompted, the horse walked on until the afternoon, when it stopped. Soulis dismounted, tethered the animal, then lay in a broken, fevered sleep.

Borderlands

\*

Clouds hid the hilltops. Thomas rode across the silent land, watching for signs of pursuit, but saw none. Then he saw a sudden, frightening image of a contorted, grotesque shadow leading Soulis on a pure-bred stallion, following, gaining on him. Thomas reined in, alarmed.

*'Oh no.'*

He kicked his horse and rode like a man possessed, often glancing back, paying too little heed to what lay ahead; the horse, scrambling up and down hills, came to a sudden halt, refusing the steep descent, and fell on its haunches. Thrown off, Thomas slid and rolled at speed down the hillside, through rending gorse, grasping in vain at anything that would stop him; hitting the ground with force, he lay bleeding and insensible in the heather.

\*

Stealthy shadows, formless, threatening, attached to nothing, moved around Soulis as he tried to sleep, advancing, retreating, advancing again. He sat up, saw no one, but a faint, mocking sound came on the wafting breeze. He stood up, laughing.

## The Oarsman

'I fear not you! You can't kill me! I am Soulis!' Fever swept over him, again bringing him to his knees, and the gloating shadows returned, one tall and silent, the other squat and headless. He opened his eyes, found he was alone, staggered to a stand, then mounted the horse, which walked on, led by unseen things.

## Chapter Twenty-Five

# Waiting

Flickering firelight made the stone circle seem sinister in the brooding dawn, and the cauldron squatted over the cold furnace like a malevolent toad.

Moris and his followers stood whispering together, Adan stood tense, surveying the empty horizon for any approach, and Hirnac, surrounded by debris, sat weaving something from the rowan leaves and blossom.

At length, Adan left his position and, crouching beside him, spoke in a secretive tone. 'Nothing moves, Hirnac, everywhere's deserted, and it's small wonder these men fear this place; it unnerves even me.'

Hirnac glanced at the cauldron. 'The power affects everything here.'

Adan nodded towards Rædwulf, fast asleep by the fire. 'Does *he* know?'

'Yes,' replied Hirnac with some confidence, 'or he wouldn't dare sleep here.'

Adan raised an eyebrow. 'Brave man.'

Groggy when he awoke, Rædwulf accepted breakfast, then wandered away to a high rock overlooking the tarn; he smelt peat smoke from the campfire, wild thyme and heather; stood in the stifling heat, remembering the Court, the Caves, Ercildoun and Molly; Læren, standing in the barn, frightened but brave. He had almost quailed, her fury shaming him, but he admired her courage, had pitied her and now missed her.

Midges settling on his face awakened him. He watched the rill percolating through moss and waterside plants into the deep pool; the clouds, bankside trees and hazel were mirrored in its dark, glassy surface: a grimy window to that Other Realm. He stripped his shirt off, spear dived, and lay, floating between worlds, staring at the iron-clad, battlemented heavens; drifted, and stood shoulder-deep beneath the falls. Facing outward, arms outspread, wrapped in cool, cleansing water, he closed his eyes, bracing himself for something he knew might destroy him. He stayed there until numb.

Moris berated him on his return. 'You've a fucking nerve, Blācencynn, gallivanting off like that!'

Rædwulf merely smiled. 'Cold water in the morning, Moris, clears the mind better than anything.'

## Waiting

Moris was not reassured. 'What would have happened had Soulis arrived?'

Rædwulf shrugged. 'But he didn't.' Nodding towards Jacob, who sat yawning, he said, 'Have you, or your men, slept?'

Moris shook his head. 'It's hard sleeping here.'

'Then sleep now,' came the steady reply, 'while Adan, Hirnac and I keep watch. Nothing will harm you or your men… for now.'

Moris nodded and informed his men, but few slept, and a slow, sultry breeze stalked through the grass and heather. Rædwulf paced around the circle for a long time, smelt hot stone, heard the incessant drone of midges and flies, the occasional distant mew of a bird hunting in the relentless ochre sky. Moris, playing an idle dice game with Adan, stood up, raising one hand to waist level.

'I'm out. I'll owe you, Lord Adan.'

Surprised, Adan raised an eyebrow. 'Twopence too high a stake, Moris?'

Moris smiled. 'I said, I'll owe you.' Approaching Rædwulf, he said, 'Ready, my lord?'

Rædwulf shivered, despite the stifling heat. 'Yes. No. No, I'm not. This place is wrong.'

Moris glanced behind him. 'Sire, what if Soulis doesn't come?'

Rædwulf ran a hand through his thick hair. 'I'm seldom worried, Moris,' he confessed, 'but I'm troubled now.' Moris returned to the fireside, leaving Rædwulf standing on the circle boundary, watching the empty landscape. The daylight faded, though the sun climbed to beyond noon, and he whispered, 'The power's rising. It's time you were here, Learmont. Time.'

\*

Suspended in darkness, aware he was trying to fend something off, Thomas heard an impatient voice close by.

'Keep still. I swear, I've never met such a fidget. Keep *still*.'

Thomas opened his eyes to clouds that seemed low enough to touch. Head throbbing, his sides aching, struggling to sit up, he saw a strange man, who he thought for a moment was Wyrtræd, kneeling beside him; but there was something odd about him; something 'other'. He had wild red hair, was clad in brown and made abrupt, wild movements.

## Waiting

'Will you keep *still!*' the man repeated. 'I cannot dress the wound if you insist on fidgeting.'

Alarmed, Thomas looked around. 'Where's my horse?'

'Hard by, my friend, so you can be on your way once I've done this.'

Thomas winced, holding his left side. 'Is it morning or afternoon?'

'It's afternoon,' was the calm reply. 'I think you've cracked some ribs, but no matter, I've strapped you tight, though this wound is nasty. You may feel light-headed for a while.' He smeared the injury with something which brought brief, searing pain, then numbness. 'There,' he said, applying a bandage. 'From now on, I'll tend the wild creatures of the moors. You're an exception.'

Thomas lay back. 'On whose orders, Brown Man?'

'My own. You've no time to rest, Thomas Learmont. Soulis is a mile away.'

Thomas stood up, despite his pain. '*How* far?'

The man fetched Thomas' horse. 'A mile and coming closer the longer you delay, but don't worry, I won't help him.' He looked the horse over, stroking its neck, remarking, 'Beasts know how to land if they fall. Your horse isn't hurt.'

Thomas, scrambling into the saddle, looked at his strange benefactor, who gestured towards the land ahead. 'North is that way, my friend; this time, look where you're going.'

'I will. Thank you.' Thomas gave a slight, acknowledging nod and kicked the horse to a gallop faster than the breeze.

\*

The hazy sky became a crimson pall, the air oven hot, and the low mist lifted, revealing the cauldron, coppery in the firelight. Moris' men walked back and forth, their constant muttering and restlessness disquieting Rædwulf, Adan and Hirnac. Rædwulf, standing in his shirtsleeves on the south-east edge of the circle, watched the fading light. Moris approached him, gave a long sigh, and ran a thumb along his lip, a sign, Rædwulf now recognised, of nervous tension.

'What can we do, Blācencynn?' he said. 'What can we do? My men say Learmont's dead, that Soulis is free to kill and destroy at will; that he won't come here.'

## Waiting

Rædwulf faced him, his steady grey eyes meeting the restless gaze. 'I told you: Soulis has no choice now we've laid the snare.'

'Using Learmont and the healer as bait,' said Moris, 'you're risking their lives, Blācencynn.'

Rædwulf spoke into his ear. 'I'm risking all our lives, Moris. I know the circle is small, but I warn you: once Soulis arrives, you and your men *must* stay within it, whatever you might hear or see.'

'Then he will cast spells on us all,' replied Moris, 'and turn us into dreadful things.'

'He'll do nothing of the kind but will take what we offer him.'

Moris snorted. 'Such as?'

'His heart's desire.'

Robbie called from a short distance away, gesturing to the south. 'Over there! Over there! A horseman!'

John ran to his side. 'I can't see who it is,' he said. 'He's too far away. It might be Soulis.'

Moris, Adan, Hirnac and Rædwulf stood beside him, peering through the murky dusk. 'No,' said Rædwulf, 'it isn't. Learmont's here.' He turned, calling across the circle, 'Make ready, make all ready!' Facing Moris, he said in a menacing undertone, 'This is where our vengeance begins. Do you all know what to do?'

Moris hesitated, met the fierce grey eyes, and nodded. 'Aye, and I will say this to you, Blācencynn, and your companions: we thank you for helping us.'

Rædwulf, giving a slight smile, nodded, then walked away. Robbie and Moris stayed where they were, watching Thomas riding at a dangerous pace towards them.

'He's riding as if the very devil's after him,' remarked Robbie.

Moris raised an eyebrow. 'Maybe it is,' he said and went to Rædwulf.

Dizzy, weary, in pain, Thomas reined in when he reached the circle, almost sliding off the horse, then limped to the fireside. Rædwulf, Adan and Moris glanced at one another in concern as he approached. The firelight on his ashen face made him look like the walking dead.

'We're relieved you're here,' remarked Rædwulf, 'but you've lousy timing.'

Thomas glared at him. '*You're* relieved? He had me at sword point; I barely escaped, almost drowned, almost broke my neck, and you say you're relieved! I've a vicious headache and feel a mule has kicked me in places I never knew I had.'

## Waiting

Rædwulf suppressed a smile and made a disarming gesture. 'All in good time, Learmont. Sit here with us and eat something while I examine your injury. Moris, would you join us, please?'

With reluctance, Thomas agreed and, without mentioning Penda, recounted events while Rædwulf removed the bandage.

'Whatever he dressed the wound with, he knew what he was doing,' he said. 'It's clean enough, and well staunched, although there's some swelling and I think it'll leave a scar; but that'll fade, given time.'

Thomas hissed. 'We don't *have* time, Rædwulf. Soulis isn't far away, and I doubt we'd be ready if he arrived now.'

'We've not been idle, Thomas,' said Adan. 'Moris and his men have done their bit, as we've done ours. We were waiting only for you.'

Thomas sat hunched, chin on fist, the flickering firelight gleaming against the dark, and at length, he looked at Rædwulf. 'It's not just Soulis we're dealing with. Redcap's spirit is guiding him.'

Rædwulf gave his inimitable shrug. 'Well, it's unlikely that Soulis can move anywhere in the dark, whoever leads him. You need sleep, Learmont, and so do we.'

Thomas looked at the cauldron; it seemed larger in the firelight. 'That thing,' he remarked, 'seems almost alive.'

Rædwulf, exchanging a meaningful look with Moris and Adan, whispered, 'It draws the power to itself, Learmont, as do you.' He looked at Moris again and sighed. 'Alright, gentlemen, this is what we'll do: I'll speak with the doctor when he arrives, and I'll attack Soulis once he's healed. Don't intervene unless he overpowers or kills me.'

Aghast, Adan stared at him. 'We can't stand by while you face him alone. Why risk your life like that?'

'Have you so little faith, Adan?' said Rædwulf, his tone sharp as his blade. 'I'm stronger than you think, and,' he added, lowering his voice, 'you've more to lose.'

Adan turned to Hirnac. 'Hide the horses; keep them calm; above all, keep them quiet; then we'll both take sentry and give warning if anything approaches.'

Moris nodded. 'We'll keep watch too, and John will light the furnace at first light.'

As they walked away, Thomas glanced at Rædwulf. 'They're talking again, Blācencynn, voices in my mind that won't let me be, and whispers on the breeze torment me.'

## Waiting

Rædwulf studied him for a moment, then said, 'It's the power possessing you, Learmont. I sense it, and your eyes are darkening.'

Although exhausted, Thomas could not sleep. He tried thinking of Ercildoun, of Molly, of ordinary things, but all his memories became waking nightmares; the inner voices tormented him until Thomas Learmont was no longer there.

## Chapter Twenty-Six

# Wyrtræd

Morning blazed along every horizon as Soulis, fevered and torpid, rode between the silent, watching hills, his horse picking its slow way around tussocks, rocks and furrows, its hoof beats dull on the peaty ground. The silence deepened, and the horse stopped.

A raven's harsh call startled Soulis from his inertia; he dismounted and, sword drawn, with the horse following him, he crept towards wispy peat smoke rising from behind a ridge not far ahead and reached a natural embayment at its foot. He saw the raven perched atop a tall standing stone, and a shirtless man sat cross-legged beside it, staring at the fire.

He wore a wolf-pelt around his shoulders, a length of cat fur, tail still attached, around his upper right arm, and a raven's skull talisman around his neck; a wide-brimmed green hat with a rowan blossom band overshadowed his features. A heavy rowan wood staff, inset with a gypsum crystal, and tied with a plaited leather thong ornamented with a boar's tusk, lay on the ground beside him.

The ashy daub plastered on his bare skin, his beard and his long, straggled grey hair disgusted Soulis. He noted with disdain the tatty sheepskin trousers, the bark shoes lined with grass and the two silver birch bark bowls, full of herbs and moss, near the fire. The healer, his outlandish, intimidating air reminding Soulis of the High Priest, spoke without looking up.

'I am Wyrtræd. Pray, sit beside me and I will heal you.'

Soulis dithered, wondering whether to threaten this thin old man, then drew his sword but could not lift his heavy blade. The healer spoke, the undertone somehow menacing.

'If you want treatment, stay. If you wish still to suffer, go.'

As though under a spell, Soulis dropped his sword and kneeled, studying Wyrtræd, staring at his shadowed face. At length, Wyrtræd leaned back, stretched out his long legs, and sighed.

'I must examine your injury; take your shirt off.'

With help, Soulis complied, wincing under every exploratory touch.

## Wyrtræd

'Mmm,' said Wyrtræd, 'you've a severe infection, and a fever born of it that should have killed you. I find it puzzling that it didn't.'

Rattled, Soulis sneered. 'I would not expect a ragged little healer to know who sits before him. I am Soulis, and naught can kill me.'

His eyes glinting beneath his hat, Wyrtræd lifted his slow gaze. 'Don't depend on it. You've a lot of poison there that needs drawing out, or, if you like, I can amputate your offending arm. There'll be agony for you either way. Or, do nothing, and spend all eternity wandering the wilds, in fevered pain, neither alive nor dead. Which shall it be?'

Soulis stared at him, and at the implements and herbs at hand. Wyrtræd, conveying a quiet, smouldering menace, without taking his eyes from Soulis, drew a broad knife and turned it between his fingers.

'Which shall it be?'

Soulis held out his arm. 'Heal me. Heal me, and I will give you all these lands.'

Wyrtræd stopped turning the knife and stared at it. 'We will discuss my fee later,' he said. 'For I have something I would offer thee in return, as a token of trust between us.'

Soulis became suspicious, dangerous. 'What could a mere country healer offer me? Grain? A few herbs, perhaps?'

'Something you have long desired. No matter, you shall receive it this eve.'

Now fearful, Soulis watched Wyrtræd, who seemed in no hurry, hold the blackening blade over the fire; who, with surprising strength in one so scrawny, grabbed the diseased arm and made a deep cut, saying, 'Now, this will hurt.'

Soulis screamed, and continued screaming almost without pause. Wyrtræd spoke through clenched teeth.

'Keep quiet. Every brigand for miles around will hear you.' Again, Soulis screamed, and then swooned.

Patient, methodical, Wyrtræd completed the task, bandaged the arm, dressed Soulis, then stood up, knife in hand, looking at the sprawled form.

'Well, now, my immortal Lord Soulis,' he said, his slow, somehow unpleasant smile matching his tone, 'what are you prepared to pay?'

He led the horse away, picked up his staff, then sat beside the fire waiting, with cat-like patience, planning.

Soulis awoke in the mid-afternoon, wondering where he was, smelt a faint odour of burned flesh, and tasted a metallic tang in the silent, humid air. Thick, leaden clouds hid the sky, and the fire now seemed a deep, smoking pit. He sat up; Wyrtræd, his hat brim pulled low, his aura glowing against the tawny afternoon light, sat watching him. Vague shadows, tall, faceless, squat, headless, moved back and forth, then stood motionless behind him. He held out a small bowl of thin, unappetising broth.

'This will strengthen you,' he said. 'How is your arm now?'

Soulis, stretching out his arm without pain, stared at him, half-surprised. 'Better. Your healing powers are impressive.'

'I know.'

Soulis found the broth flavoursome, sustaining as thick stew; drank a herbal infusion; ate with relish the handful of delicious savouries and dainties the healer offered him, his strength returning with each mouthful.

'What shall be my fee?' said Wyrtræd, a vague taunt in his soft tone.

Soulis snarled, pressing his sword against Wyrtræd's neck, nicking the skin. 'There will be no fee.' He scanned the ragged clothes. 'Well, my lowly little healer, I once had a pet, just like you, and I taught it tricks. I jabbed it, it squealed, when I stabbed it, it bled, and I can do the same with you.'

The reply was soft, unnerving. 'Can you now?'

Soulis sniggered. 'I have a mind of returning to Hermitage where I shall collar and tie you to the walls of my treasury, my little pet healer, to perform tricks as I want. I command thee: prepare my horse.'

Unmoved, and bleeding from the superficial wound, Wyrtræd stared at Soulis for a moment before giving a slight nod.

'I have powerful allies, healer,' snarled Soulis. 'You shall not cheat me.'

Wyrtræd, glancing at the blade resting on his shoulder, stood up and, without concern, said softly, enticingly, 'Follow me to your heart's desire.'

With the sword held to his back, he led Soulis uphill into a dark, glimmering haze which hid everything.

And the raven followed.

Wyrtræd propped his staff against the tallest stone and faced Soulis who, levelling his sword, spat, and sneered.

'Bring my horse, healer.'

Wyrtræd, giving a slight smile, whistled, summoning an old, thin, decrepit horse from the murk, its harness an old rope halter.

Wyrtræd whispered, 'Why should a proud lord ride a cart horse, as though in shame?'

Soulis stared at it in fury. 'How dare you mock me? Where is my horse? Where is it?'

'This is your horse,' said Wyrtræd, unruffled.

Soulis snorted. 'You think I, an immortal lord, would ride this? My horse is a proud creature, with gold on its bridle. *Where* is my horse?'

Wyrtræd did not change his tone. 'There is no such beast here.'

He picked up his staff and, giving a sustained, low, nasal hum, hit the standing stone nine times, the sounds resonating as though he had struck a drum. Wyrtræd was summoning his guardians. Lightning glimmered in the clouds, thunder growled in the distance, the haze became dark fog, the raven called again, and undefined shadows patrolled the circle perimeter.

Wyrtræd gave Soulis a slow, steady stare, beckoning him. 'Follow.'

Staff in hand, he walked to an upright stake covered with a sack and faced him. 'Now,' he whispered, 'now we will discuss payment.' He snatched the sack away, revealing Redcap's severed head, its bulging dead eyes staring straight at Soulis, and gave a deadly laugh.

'Look at him; look at him well. Yes, Lord Foulguest, death awaits you. Such is my fee.'

For a moment, Soulis gazed at him; then, sword in hand and giving a sudden, murderous cry, he dealt a vicious blow, intending to kill, but his blade broke against the staff. Wyrtræd, tall and menacing, giving a soft, chilling laugh, did not move.

Soulis ran towards the north stone; a huge, crouching, snarling grey wolf, with cold grey eyes, its pelt shimmering with unearthly light, blocked his escape. Soulis fled again; a huge silvery boar with intense yellow eyes, its tusks whiter than the moon, barred the west side; a shining, wolf-sized wild cat, with fathomless, livid green eyes, guarded the east; the raven, its immense open wings emitting a pale violet light, called from the south; and Wyrtræd gave a wolfish growl: '*The circle is closed.*'

Soulis turned and looked at him in awe and disbelief. '*What are you?*'

The healer, giving a slight smile, held out a tangled length of horsehair. '*Elves tie a pretty knot, making things seem other than they are.*' He pulled the thong from his staff, levelled the Sword, flung off his hat; and Rædwulf whispered, his words savage as his eyes, '*I am Blācencynn…* and *you…* are *mine.*'

Unbowed, Soulis spoke with utter contempt. 'You cannot touch me, for I control the Flame. Do the Blācencynn not serve it?' He gave a mocking laugh. 'But I forget: the Blācencynn are dead.'

Like a predator stalking its prey, Rædwulf manoeuvred Soulis across the circle, cornering him against a standing stone, holding him there at his merciless Sword point. 'When I look at you, I see evil done and evil breathing; I see murder.'

Soulis sneered. 'Why wait? Why not strike me down if you think you can kill me?' He spat at him. 'I command the dead, Blācencynn; you can do nothing.'

Rædwulf spoke, his tone of pure venom. 'And the dead condemn thee. This blade neither gives, nor controls, the power, but defends it, destroying all from Dark Faerie.' Casting all Blācencynn ethics aside, he brought his sword down; it struck the stone, showering sparks everywhere. He attacked again, dealing Soulis savage, unrelenting blows that would have felled a bear, one each for all his murdered kindred—Penda, the High Priest, Lybbestre—but to no avail, and he stepped back.

'You're wasting your energy, boy,' mocked Soulis. 'I am not from Dark Faerie. I fear nothing.' He retreated, beckoning Rædwulf. 'Come, little man; let us see what you can do against me, lord of demons.'

Laughing, he leapt aside, goading Rædwulf, avoiding his every blow; picked up a heavy stone and threw it. Hit in his stomach, momentarily winded and the weapon falling from his hand, Rædwulf dropped; he saw Soulis looming and leapt onto him, punching him with raw animal ferocity, to no effect. Soulis kicked Rædwulf off; grabbed him, throwing him face down into the turf; knelt hard on his back; grasped the cord the amulet hung from and, lifting Rædwulf to his knees, enjoying it almost as he would a woman, tightened the cord into a garrotte: the slow killing of the Blācencynn. *'Are you mortal?'* he hissed. *'Are you?'* Rædwulf, clutching the cord, fighting for his every breath, fell.

Soulis kicked him over, and lifting the Sword, stood astride him, poised, gloating. 'I've no time for weaklings. It is I who kills you... *Boy Blācencynn!*'

\*

Sentinel trees surrounded the silent glade and nothing moved in the cold, still Grimsdene twilight. Rædwulf, lying outstretched, paralysed, helpless on a stone slab he

## Wyrtræd

knew was his tomb, watched three veiled women in dark robes standing at his feet, one measuring out a slender, silvery cord: each heartbeat, another ell. Defeated, he wept, whispering, *'No... no...'*

Radiant against the dark, Raldis materialised on his right, so close he could see the stitching on her sleeves, and she offered him her open hands. 'One hand gives life; the other, death. Choose your path, Rædwulf Blācencynn.'

He held out his right hand, could not reach her, tried again, but she faded; death-terror came on him and he whispered again, lapsing into dialect, *'Láta mér nei deyja hí,* Raldis.'

*One hand gives life...*

This time, stretching out his left hand, an effort taking all his remaining strength, he touched her right hand, and everything faded. The slab beneath him seemed suspended in churning green storm clouds; he saw Soulis standing against the lightning, holding the Sword high, and closed his eyes, giving a last, slow exhale. *I... am... Blācencynn.*

And Adan blew the Horn.

---

\* *Lit: 'Let me not die here'*

## Chapter Twenty-Seven

# The Nine Stones

The deafening Horn call reached the heavens; thunder and glimmering lightning answered, and thick cloud swallowed the crimson moon rising into a red night. Rædwulf felt firm earth beneath him, smelt turf and rain, opened his eyes; the Sword plunged, Soulis crying out with wild, malicious triumph, 'I govern all!' but he staggered, hands burned. Rædwulf, scrambling to his feet, snatched the Sword from him and sheathed it. He took a small pouch from his belt, and facing Soulis, spoke, his tone softer than mires. 'What did the healer give you, Soulis? Food? From this, perhaps?' Opening the pouch, he scattered a quantity of toxic berries, seeds and roots on the ground before him. He gave a quiet, unnerving laugh. 'There's enough poison here to kill an entire community.'

Soulis gave a twisted smile. 'You delude yourself. No poison can kill me.'

The lifting mist revealed John, pumping the wheezing bellows, every squeeze a slow, threatening breath. Shadows advancing from the murk became men, Soulis recognising Moris as that ragged, filthy farmer who had begged him for grain.

'Look at them,' spat Rædwulf. '*Look at them.* You've no need returning to Hermitage, for Hermitage hath come to thee.'

Moris took one step forward. 'We've come for our children,' he said.

Jacob, who would have attacked Soulis had Andrew not held him back, screamed, 'Where are our children, Soulis? Where are they?'

Soulis merely sneered. 'Search all you like, yeomen; perhaps you should have taken better care of those mewling bairns, whose fair heads now light the Woodland Way.'

The farmers gave an anguished cry; Rædwulf raised one commanding hand, preventing a lynching, and fixing a diamond-hard stare on Soulis, whispered, 'Tell them, Soulis.' Then, his thunderous voice frightening the bravest, shouted, 'Tell these men you sacrificed their children just to save yourself.'

Soulis, meeting those intense grey eyes with contempt, answered with pure malice. 'Prove it. This is no trial; I see neither reeve nor King's man here to judge me.

I wield a power stronger than all the earth and fear no landless lord, weak in mind and body. Do you believe you have won by killing Redcap? Nay, boy Blācencynn; I have called him here to carry your soul away.' Then said, a word with each breath, '*You… don't… scare… me.*'

Rædwulf drew the Sword and whispered, 'By meeting his gaze, you have honoured the contract. He comes for your soul, not mine. You have nothing.'

A gusting wind from nowhere blew the last shreds of mist away, revealing Thomas, cowled and iridescent in the lightning, standing beside the fire. He stared at Soulis with burning eyes and spoke, his voice changed beyond recognition. *'The Flame now stands in judgement before you, Lord Soulis, and has passed sentence: death.'*

Rædwulf levelled the Sword. 'On your knees, Foulguest,' he said, 'on your knees, and beg.'

Adan seized Soulis, a hold stronger than chains. Helpless, and in rising panic, Soulis pleaded: 'I asked only for respect amongst my peers, as you would have done. Have I not cared for your halls, and your people, ready for your return? Think what I could grant you. You won't kill me, Blācencynn; it isn't in you.'

Rædwulf spoke as a spitting snake. 'Save your breath, Foulguest, for you'll soon have such a need of it as you never imagined.' He handed Thomas the Sword, held out the open contract and snarled, 'Recognise this? You signed it, Soulis, signed it with your blood. Intact, it grants you an immortal life full of pain and woe; destroyed, death, an eternity of torment, binding you to Redcap forever. Do you plead, Foulguest? Do you beg? Will it be life or death?' Beyond speech, Soulis gave a strangulated yelp, and Rædwulf smiled. 'Then what should I do with it? Shall I burn it?' He held it over the cauldron, the parchment charring within seconds, and Soulis gave another involuntary cry. Rædwulf, his smile more vicious, said, 'No?' whispered, 'So be it,' tucked it into his shirt again, and holding Soulis' head between his hands, pulled him within biting distance, each man staring into absolute hate. His glittering eyes those of a wolf closing in to kill, Rædwulf growled, 'Look at me, Foulguest; look at the last face you'll ever see,' and pushed his thumbs against the mad, dark eyes, pushed, pushed, pushing relentlessly, bursting the bleeding eyeballs; rammed the contract into the twisted, screaming mouth to choking point; drew his knife, pulled Soulis closer, snarled, 'If I can't kill you, your tenants will,' and stabbed him.

The damaged contract took effect. Blinded, wounded and poisoned, Soulis crumpled, and Rædwulf gave

Moris a single, commanding nod. Bare-handed, Moris and his men forced Soulis down, tore his clothes, his skin; pulled out his hair and bound him with rope Hirnac had twisted from rowan bark and mud from the stream, rope thin as grass stems, tightening the more Soulis struggled. They wrapped a leaden sheet around him and hung him from the tree by his feet, before withdrawing to the circle boundary where those strange, gleaming creatures kept unceasing watch.

Without sentiment, with fire and blue light surrounding him and his eyes ablaze, Thomas watched Soulis, hanging like a grotesque, squirming pupa spinning on its thread over the fuming cauldron, gagging on the contract.

Rædwulf snarled again. 'Spit it out, Foulguest. If you want free of it, spit it out.'

Under a foreign will, Thomas, the Flame incarnate, raised the Sword at arm's length, tip down-most, to shoulder height, its crystal shimmering as if liquid fire burned within. As though summoned, nine seven-foot-tall, pale, twisted shadows, scaring almost every man there, now formed the circle perimeter; afraid, Rædwulf understood. *They are the circle.* Sparks from every stone met at the Sword's hilt. Thomas raised the weapon further, high as he could reach, power surging through him, the crystal unleashing twisting white beams brighter than the sun in all directions. Lightning answered, tearing the heavens apart, thunder echoed through the hills, the parchment fell into the cauldron, and a sudden silence enveloped everything. Thomas cried out in overwhelming pain, his strange voice matching his wild eyes.

*'Soulis, you are mortal! Redcap awaits thee!'*

Soulis caught fire, his screams giving a voice to the shaking ground and the sudden howling gale that whipped the tree branches back and forth. Nasty smells filled the air: blistering skin, melting fat, roasting meat, acrid fumes of boiling lead, and he fell into that molten mass.

Lightning struck adjacent hills, thunder hammered the heavens, and Rædwulf, leaping across the heaving ground, grabbed Thomas' right arm.

'The Sword, Thomas Learmont! Drop the Sword!' The response, a woman's strange voice coming from all around, scared him.

*Thomas Learmont is not here. I am the Flame. And I burn.*

A hot, blinding flash vaporised the tree and cauldron and threw Rædwulf and Thomas off their feet. Wolf, Boar,

Cat and Raven, and those sinister forms, vanished in cruel hail and driving rain, but the downpour soon eased. Dazed, winded, bruised, and supporting himself on his elbows, Rædwulf glimpsed Adan and Hirnac crouching with Moris and his huddled comrades, shielding themselves from the constant lightning. He stood up, pulling the undamaged Sword from the turf; he looked into the crystal, but it was now dull as glass, and he whispered, *'It's all over, my friend.'*

*'Sire!'*

With a sudden foreboding, he approached Hirnac standing beside the south stone and stopped in his tracks. Thomas lay flat, his blind eyes open to the sky, his face a ghastly pallor, and Moris stuttered, 'Oh, my God, oh my God, he's dead.'

Exhausted, Rædwulf knelt; with one hand on Thomas' throat, he detected a weak, fading pulse. His eyes closed, and murmuring *Raven, guide me*, he went searching along shadowed, silent pathways.

*

A weak light filled the cavern where Penda lay on the rubble. Thomas kneeled, and looking at the pale face, spoke to ease the unbearable silence.

'Did you call me?'

A voice echoed around the cavern. *The Blācencynn are dead, and the Caves empty.* Thomas bowed. *Take him,* said the voice. *Honour and remember him.*

A similar voice came from beside him: *Thomas!* and repeated, *Thomas.* He saw no one, but a hand pressed against his throat and he lashed out, yelling, 'I am the Flame! You can't kill me!'

\*

Thin smoke from the fire and furnace rose into a subdued dawn, and Moris grasped Rædwulf's right shoulder in a gesture of friendship and farewell.

'We owe you thanks, sire, and invite you to visit us whenever, if ever, you can.'

Rædwulf gave his slight smile. 'Maybe.' He paused, then said, 'We didn't do this alone, Moris.'

Moris hesitated, nodded, mounted his horse, and led his men from the circle, leaving Rædwulf, Adan and Hirnac shivering in the relentless rain.

Chapter Twenty-Eight

# Farewell, Fair Blācencynn

Crops lay ruined in the sodden fields and pastures; animal pens and granaries stood empty, and the womenfolk, old men and labourers gave Moris and his fellows a strange, muted homecoming; they spent the evenings by their hearths, awaiting starvation.

Jacob awoke at dawn and looked around the darkened room, listening to the rain; a cockerel crowed outside and, at first so faint it seemed only the wind gusting through the thatch, he heard livestock lowing. He opened the shutter and, listening, spoke to his wife who sat near the closed door, grinding flour from acorns and other subsistence stuff.

'Do you hear that?'

'Hear what?'

He made an insistent gesture. 'Listen.'

She opened the door and, with her neighbours, watched, in amazement, a mighty, white, red-eared bull and ram leading sheep, cattle and goats, all with young, shambling along the street to the pens for milking; granaries and haylofts held enough fodder for six months or more, the fields were thick with standing crops and every sty had its sow. No longer facing famine, the bewildered villagers danced in the rain. Only Moris guessed who had brought this good fortune and insisted they bury the first loaves in every field, and sprinkle the first milk onto the land, as thanks to Faerie.

\*

Thomas, awaking in a comfortable bed, recognised the room, smelt wood smoke, and lay listening to the rain dripping from the eaves. Rædwulf, leaning against one wall by the open window, stood drumming his fingers on the sill, watching the rain.

A modest silver brooch at his shoulder fastened his heavy, deep-blue cloak, gold braid trimmed his red tunic, and the Sword hung from his broad leather belt. He met Thomas' gaze with leaden eyes.

'Ah. Welcome back.'

'Back? Where have I been?'

Rædwulf raised an eyebrow. 'Somewhere betwixt, I think. I don't know how you survived, to be honest.

## Farewell, Fair Blācencynn

Strength of will, probably, although Moris thought you were dead.' He went to the table. 'We brought the cart horse with us,' he said, pouring ale into a cup, 'and Hirnac's taking good care of it.'

Thomas flopped back on the pillows, closing his eyes. 'I ache all over,' he said. 'My right hand seems on fire, and I have a headache. Have I slept for long?'

'Oh, a couple of days.' Rædwulf proffered him a cup. 'You'll be thirsty,' he said and stood by the window again, lifting his gaze to the sodden Faerie banner snagged around its mast. He shook his head. 'It's hard to believe it's summer. The power is returning to Earth, and I suspect that's what's causing the storms.'

Wind gusted beneath the eaves, sending dust drifting around the room. Rædwulf closed the window and, dropping a neat bundle on the bed, his curt tone surprising Thomas, said, 'New clothes—with Læren's compliments.' As a doctor in consultation, he said, 'What's the last thing you remember?'

Thomas frowned. 'I'm not sure; it's hazy as though it all happened to someone else.'

'Mmm,' said Rædwulf at length. 'Well, either you'll remember, or forget; time will tell.' He paused. 'You never told me, perhaps to spare me pain, but I know you met Penda at the Mereburg.' Again, he paused, considering something, then said, 'Soulis didn't summon the dead.'

Thomas stared at him, aghast. 'It was you!'

Rædwulf shrugged. 'Yes, it was me. Put your clothes on.'

\*

Firelight and shadows danced around the Hall, wood smoke hid the rafters, and hammering rain broke the silence. Thomas, standing with his companions, remembering the apparition he had seen through the Gate, would not look at the Lady, who stood on the dais with Raldis, Dagan and Cynwæd.

'Goodmen,' said Raldis, her voice soft as rain, 'your task is done, and you have only to name your reward. What, now, are your intentions?' The silent men looked at each other. She spoke again. 'Lord Adan?'

He looked away, then at her. 'Destroying Soulis and Redcap is reward enough, my lady. The Mereburg has gone, the dells stained, the place haunted. Neither Hirnac nor I can return until it's cleansed. We make no demand but would ask only that my Lady of Faerie give us refuge until then.' Hirnac bowed, saying the same. Raldis turned to Thomas. 'You need not ask,' she said in a grave, steady tone, 'for your path now leads to Ercildoun. You may leave Faerie whenever you wish on one condition.'

'Condition?' He lifted his guarded gaze, first to her, then to the High Lady, and found her beauty restored.

'That we recall you to Court one day,' she said, in the same tone as Raldis, 'and Thomas the Rhymer will not refuse.' She smiled. 'Why the surprise? I am but the first to call you thus. Remember the apple.'

Raldis turned to Rædwulf, meeting his despondent gaze with compassion. 'Rædwulf Blācencynn, you have perhaps lost more than anyone. What reward would you ask of Faerie?'

He bowed his head, took several slow breaths, then spoke, thinking aloud. 'I've seen things I never thought I'd see, done things I never thought I could, and now I stand destitute before you all.'

'Don't blame yourself,' she replied, 'for you did what you thought right. Few could have endured more.'

He looked at her. 'I would ask only that the Hermitage men and their kinfolk do not starve.'

Raldis smiled. 'We have made provision for them. They will not starve; and we shall reward the good

Ercildoun family who sheltered you.' She paused, then said, 'Sire, what will you do?'

He gave a slight shrug, thinking. 'Moris invited me to visit him,' he replied, 'but often are invitations forgotten in the cold light of day, however well-meant in the heat of the moment.' He fell silent, then continued. 'I may find a worthy lord in need of a blade and strength to wield it, or, as I have sometimes done before, wander the wilderness as a healer.'

The High Lady smiled at him. 'There is a home for you here, Rædwulf Blācencynn, as counsellor and Captain of the Guard.'

He glanced at his companions, then lowered his gaze, moistening his lips. 'When will you need my answer?'

'Whenever you are ready,' she said. 'Although I would ask that you attend the feast tomorrow.'

'If you are in doubt, Lord Blācencynn,' said Raldis, 'we have something here that may help you decide. Come, gentlemen.'

They followed her to the hill beyond the orchard and climbed to a cave entrance on its northern slope. Bitter draughts from within did not disturb torches burning either side, the stillness reminding Rædwulf of Grimsdene. There was a carved spiral in the lintel above the doorway, and he glimpsed others on the walls within. He looked back; a rainbow, vibrant against the slate-black sky, overarching the enclosure, stretched from horizon to horizon.

Dagan took a torch and faced him. 'Sire, prepare yourself, for this avenue may lead you to your fate.'

The narrow, winding passage led down to a lamp-lit vault, an inverse spiral gleaming at the very apex of the high, corbelled roof, and an embroidered banner, of a sword suspended over a flame, hung on the wall opposite the doorway. Rædwulf approached an alabaster plinth, the runes carved on it indecipherable in the lamplight, and felt something inside him twist.

Penda lay uncorrupted, pale as the stone, his long, black hair spreading over the pillow beneath his head, his folded hands resting on his abdomen; he wore a white knee-length tunic, and a silver clasp at his shoulder fastened a grey cloak draping to the floor. A silver buckle fastened his leather belt.

A lady, her dark, knee-length hair cascading over her blackberry-coloured gown, stood at his feet, gazing at him.

'Cerin,' whispered Rædwulf, touching her shoulder. 'Cerin, why are you here?'

She glanced at him, said, 'I had no choice, sire,' then hung her head. 'No choice.'

'This is no place for you, lady,' he whispered. 'You belong in the forest.'

'I don't have a home in the forest anymore.'

Confused, he stared at her tear-stained face, then looked at Penda. 'Who brought him here?'

She could manage only a whisper. 'Dagan and other elves tended to him. You see?'

He could not comfort her, and noting Thomas felt the same, looked at Raldis.

'I would have had this chamber sealed, my lady,' she said, 'had I known you would come here.' Cerin, staring at Penda, did not answer. Raldis spoke again, her tone low, kind. 'Go to the women's house, Cerin. If you stay in here, you will die.'

'Come back with me, Rædwulf,' said Thomas. 'Molly and her family are fond of you.'

Rædwulf looked at him with heavy eyes. 'And I of them,' he said, 'but I know how suspicious, and superstitious, village folk are. They would name me "Outlander", blaming me if the harvest fails. I'm sorry, but I don't belong there.' He gazed at the banner, the glimmering granite walls and the spiral, looked at his companions, then murmured, 'Leave me alone with him for a while.'

His companions left with Dagan and Cynwæd; Cerin, giving a silent curtsy, followed them. Rædwulf watched her walk away, and only the fluttering lamps broke the silence. Then Raldis spoke.

'She's carrying his child, Rædwulf.' Sharp, shocked disbelief flashed across his eyes, but he said nothing. 'I knew when we first met that you were more than you seemed,' she said, 'and asked that you declare yourself. Who are you, lord?'

'I am Rædwulf Blācencynn,' he said. Then, his steady eyes penetrating her very essence, he chanted, *'I am Cat, and I am Boar. I am Wolf, and I am Raven. I am Wyrtræd... I am Shaman. And I summon spirits from the barrows.'*

Awe, even fear, flickering in her eyes, she said, 'That's sorcery!'

'No,' he said and, looking at Penda, whispered, 'It's speaking with ancestors.'

She turned to leave, but he implored her, 'One moment, Raldis, please.' His searching eyes scanning her face, he said, 'The Blācencynn do not seek advice from our lords, captains, or even priests, in time of doubt, but from our women. Raldis, will you not give me counsel?'

She met his beseeching eyes with fond compassion. 'This only will I say, Rædwulf Blācencynn: As you are now, so in Faerie shall you ever be, until you grow weary and yearn for your long sleep. You cannot leave if you stay, cannot come back if you leave. Do what you think is right.' He lowered his gaze to Penda, looking at anything but her face. She spoke again, her tone almost motherly. 'Sire, I repeat what I said to Cerin: you should not stay in here. Go to the Hall and break your fast with your companions.'

He stared at the floor. 'I'm not hungry.'

'Your companions grieve too,' she said. 'You will find comfort together.'

He hesitated, digesting her words, and, his gaze lingering on Penda, followed her.

\*

Racked with grief and doubt, he went to his lodging at midnight, propped the Sword against the wall, and saw the woman whose bed he had shared before, waiting.

'If you wish to speak,' she said, her voice soft as the lamplight, 'I can listen, my lord.'

## Farewell, Fair Blācencynn

He stood, eyes closed, his palms and forehead pressed against the closed door. 'I am no lord. I have nothing, I am… *nothing*,' he ended, punching the door.

'You are Lord Blācencynn,' she said, now standing beside him. 'No one can take that from you. No one.'

He grasped his amulet to wrench it off, but with surprising strength, she gripped his hand.

'You said this defines you,' she said quietly, plaintively. 'Do not disown your forefathers' blood, fair Blācencynn, nor succumb to bitterness.' She met his eyes and whispered, 'Sometimes it's a mistake, leaving things unsaid. You can confide in me anything you can't tell others.'

At last, he broke, storming back and forth, raging against the heavens and fate; then facing the door again, he said, 'I should go; but I don't want to leave him.'

She stood close to him. 'Or her?' she said in a knowing tone. 'Only you can decide your course, my lord, but wait until daylight. Sometimes the head shouldn't rule the heart.'

He looked at her. 'I don't even know your name.'

She smiled. 'Oonagh.'

'You once favoured me,' he said, his tone soft as the shadows, his now mellow gaze searching her face. 'I would ask you, Oonagh… favour me again.'

She gave a gentle smile. 'That's why I'm here… fair Blācencynn.'

He lifted her onto the bed, taking his comfort in the only way he knew.

\*

Ribbons of bright blue sky showed between the white scudding clouds, the banner billowed in the vigorous breeze, and the air smelt of sweet herbs and earth. Læren, carrying a large basket of wildflowers, singing a whimsical tune to herself, walked across the enclosure and entered the Hall; the lingering wood smoke within shone in sunny, dusty beams coming through the open door. She selected a handful of flowers, turned, and saw Rædwulf seated on a stool, staring at the cold hearth. 'I'm leaving,' he said despondently.

She seemed stunned. 'Must you? Can't you stay, just for a short while?'

He met her eyes and gave a wan smile. 'Yes, I could stay, but a short while here, in your world, Læren, is worth decades in mine. I would begin yearning for my own lands—and crumble to dust the moment I set foot there. I cannot stay here, Sweetness.'

Farewell, Fair Blācencynn

Læren knelt before him, studying his face, noting a single grey hair in his beard, and took an unsteady breath. 'Do what you think is right.'

He gave a soft, brief laugh. 'That's Raldis talking.'

'It's true, isn't it?'

He paused, looked at the hearth again, and sighed. 'I suppose it is.' He leaned forward, memorising the loveliest face he had ever seen; saw new maturity in her eyes—and love. Only now he realised he adored her; knew she was having an inner debate. Before she could speak, he placed a gentle finger over her mouth and whispered, 'Hush, lady maiden; I already know.' He gave her a tender, lingering kiss, placed a flower in her hair, and left her kneeling by the hearth, all her joy gone to ash.

\*

Laughter, songs and loud conversation filled the Hall where flowers hung from every beam. Aromatic gusts came from the stew in the cauldron suspended over the fire, and bright lamp light threw shadows across the walls. Draughts set candle flames flickering, and daylight faded into a starry night. The Lady sat at the High table on the dais, Adan and Hirnac seated on her left, Thomas and a preoccupied Rædwulf on her right. Raldis, standing behind her, had persuaded Cerin to attend as well; the forest lady, veiled and quiet, seated between the Lady and Adan, ate and drank very little. Læren, wearing a modest pale-yellow gown and forget-me-nots in her hair, made her graceful way with the other handmaidens around the company; no longer clumsy, but adept, she filled goblets with wine or ale from the jugs she carried, according to the guest's liking, sensing someone watching her from time to time but dismissing it as fancy. Rædwulf noticed she never once smiled, or looked at him, and it hurt.

As before, Thomas played music, giving his charming smile and a teasing wink to any nearby handmaiden. Some elves began telling tales of Soulis' defeat, embarrassing Rædwulf, who remained thoughtful throughout. Oonagh, catching his gaze, gave a subtle nod. At midnight, the handmaidens gave a curtsey and withdrew. A sudden, strong voice cut through the hubbub.

'Læren.'

Silence. She turned back, saw Rædwulf, now standing at the hearth, give a slight beckoning gesture, and glancing at the other maidens, approached him.

## Farewell, Fair Blācencynn

'Læren,' he whispered, 'would you accept a handfasting to a mortal man if he had only companionship to offer thee?'

Speechless, she stared at him for a long moment; looked at Raldis, who said nothing; the High Lady smiled but also made no sign. Læren glanced at Thomas, whose warm, gentle smile and reassuring wink said it all. At length, she looked at Rædwulf, at his amulet, into his twinkling eyes, swallowed, and replied in a shaky whisper.

'If he were brave, good... kind... were his name Blācencynn, then I would. With all my heart, I would.'

He faced the dais, calling out, 'Will Faerie bless this betrothal?'

The High Lady stood up and smiled, but she spoke in a solemn tone. 'Do you understand what this would mean for you, Rædwulf Blācencynn?'

'I understand perfectly,' he said, his steady eyes fixed on Raldis, who smiled, giving a slow nod. He faced Læren again, looking first at the flowers in her hair, then into her clear eyes, and whispered, 'I cannot leave you again, lady maiden.'

The High Lady beckoned them to the dais, then called, 'Faerie blesses this betrothal.'

'Of all your deeds, Rædwulf Blācencynn,' whispered Raldis, 'this is the noblest.' She stepped from the dais. 'Come, Læren,' she said. 'It's very late, and you are weary.'

Rædwulf returned to his chair, and Thomas, smiling, muttered, 'You crafty sod.'

The guests dispersed towards dawn, leaving the Lady and Thomas alone. She led him to her bower, where they talked for a while, discussing his departure. Then she kissed him, and he could not resist.

\*

Ankle-deep morning mist drifted across the enclosure, and the banner hung inert. Thomas, the braid on his clothing glinting in the morning sunlight, sat gazing at the pebble he held, ignoring the laughing, chattering passers-by. Rædwulf sat down beside him, said nothing, but looked at the pebble in Thomas' palm.

'Molly gave me this,' said Thomas, 'to remind me of home.'

Rædwulf smiled. 'Hold a treasure close, if you have one,' he said and met Thomas' gaze. 'The girl's a treasure, Thomas.'

Thomas pocketed it. 'I know.'

'Are you leaving today?'

'I think so.'

'You've been a loyal friend and brave companion, Thomas Learmont, and I thank you for it. Give Molly my regards when you see her.'

'I will.' He paused. 'Give Læren mine.'

Rædwulf gave his slight, wry smile. 'I will.'

Thomas smiled in return.

A powerful gust of wind came from nowhere and cries of alarm carried across the enclosure: 'The banner! The banner! Look at the mast!'

The mast was now leaning at a precarious angle. Thomas and Rædwulf ran with everyone else towards it but stopped halfway. Another gust shook the mast and it leaned further, further still, fracturing where Rædwulf had hit it. He ran forward, but Thomas restrained him.

'Rædwulf, no! It's falling!'

Rædwulf wrenched himself free, ran forward again, but stopped after three paces. The mast, giving a piercing shriek, snapped and toppled like a felled tree, taking the banner with it. The alarmed elves rushed forward, calling out. The wind dropped, there was sudden, silent stillness, and the thickening, rising mist hid the sun.

Thomas stood rooted, listening to the now distant shouts. He looked around for Rædwulf, who was nowhere in sight, but he saw Raldis standing at the gate, her form and voice fading into the drifting mist.

*'The spell has broken.'*

Alone, bewildered, in threadbare clothes, he stumbled towards her over ridges and hollows, through thistles and deep turf, calling, *'Raldis!'* He stopped at a tall silver birch tree he had not seen before standing in the gateway, and he kneeled in a foggy, long-abandoned enclosure, weeping as though bereaved.

\*

Smells of mint and thyme filled the herb garden. Dandelion seeds and thistledown drifted in the afternoon breeze, and the sun cast shadows across the knoll. A huge raven, its constant, raucous calls needing no translation, fought to free itself from some twine Keith had laid to protect the beans and peas, and Molly knelt beside it.

'Oh, let me take this awful thing off you.'

The violet-black raven, its compliance surprising her, lay still and silent in her lap while her patient, gentle fingers disentangled it.

## Farewell, Fair Blācencynn

'Almost done,' she said, easing the last thread from its leg. She expected it to fly off, but it stayed, watching her with wary grey eyes, as though trying to convey something. 'Go on, shoo,' she said, almost blowing a kiss, 'before my father sees you.' The raven marched off, then flew towards the oak tree, disappearing into the glimmering green leaves.

Annoyed, Keith stomped across to Molly. 'That healer's dizzied your head, lass,' he said. 'You've been fey ever since he left. Call yourself a farmer's daughter? Nursing sick livestock is one thing, but helping a raven is another.'

'But it would have died if I hadn't helped it.'

'Aye, it would; I'd have snapped its neck.'

'I couldn't watch it suffer. Where's the harm?'

'You won't say that when it takes the hens' eggs and lambs,' said Keith. 'Evil witches' bird! It'll curse the house.'

Nell hurried to them, wanting to stop the argument, but stopped when she saw Raldis coming from the knoll.

'Do not despise the raven, Goodman,' said Raldis, her voice kind as her amber eyes, 'for perhaps it brings a blessing.' She smiled. 'You once sheltered friends of mine, brave men, who delivered the Mortal and hidden realms from evil.' Giving Keith a small coin pouch, she said, 'This is for your kindness towards them and the raven.' Looking at Molly, she whispered, 'Meet Thomas Learmont at the Eildon Tree at dawn, tomorrow.' Before anyone could answer, she turned, climbed the knoll, and melted into the afternoon sunlight.

\*

Rædwulf, with Adan and Hirnac, placed the Sword on Penda's breast; then, sealing the barrow, they left him sleeping there, forever following the winding paths of Grimsdene, beyond the borderlands.

---

# Epilogue

Evergreens hanging from the roof beams glowed in the bright torchlight, the hall full of people and seasonal goodwill. From swine herd to freeman, washer woman to goodwife, every villager was there. With typical generosity and warmth, Thomas Learmont, Lord Ercildoun, white-haired, his handsome features faded with age, ensured there was enough food and drink for all.

A servant sidled up to him, whispering, 'Sire, a white stag and hind with red ears have walked past the gate towards the cross. I saw them in the torchlight, clear as anything.'

Astounded, Thomas met the man's gaze. 'Are you sure?'

'Certain as I stand here, sire.'

A thousand thoughts flooding his mind, Thomas looked at the evergreens and his crowded hall, so reminiscent of another, half-remembered until now. He stared at his almost-crippled hands, whispering, 'I never expected this at Yuletide.' He took a slow breath. 'Fetch my warmest cloak, Simon. Meet me outside and bring a lantern.' Simon withdrew; Thomas turned towards a man seated beside him and giving him a key and a signet ring, said, 'I have received a summons I cannot ignore. As my son, you come into your own today.'

Bewildered, troubled, his son stared at him. 'Where are you going, lord?'

'Somewhere no one will ever find me. Don't follow me; on no account let anyone follow me—do you understand?'

Simon met Thomas in the frosty courtyard and handed him the cloak and lantern. 'I understand you're going away, sire,' he said, 'but when can we expect you home?'

'I'm not coming home.'

Simon bowed, and Thomas strode into the freezing night, along streets deserted under the star-frosted sky. A youth, waiting at the village cross, his face, dark eyes and raven black hair clear in the lantern light, bowed.

'I am Pelan, son of Cerin, the forest daughter, and Penda Blācencynn.'

Thomas nodded. 'You look like him. I trust your mother is well?'

'Well enough, my lord. She attends the Lady Læren now.'

'And is Lord Rædwulf—'

## Epilogue

'He remains hale,' said Pelan. 'Although preoccupied and forgetful of late. Lord Ercildoun, I bring greetings from my Lady of Bright Faerie. Do you answer?'

Faint sounds of revelry drifted on the night air, and Thomas, looking towards his hall, hesitated. 'You must choose, before cockcrow,' said Pelan, 'to either leave or stay.' He pointed to an effigy lying on the road, its features all too clear. Thomas stared at it.

'That's me?'

'Yes; whether you stay, or go, you'll never see your hall again, Thomas Learmont.'

Thomas struggled to control his tone. 'Let me take leave of someone first.'

He led Pelan not to a house, but the churchyard, which Pelan would not enter out of respect; Thomas, lantern in hand, taking slow steps, every silver-plated grass blade crunching underfoot, walked towards the church, then stopped. His breath steaming, he crouched, took a small white pebble from his pocket, kissed it and, placing it on a grave, spoke tearful, fractured words. 'I'm leaving you now, Molly. Forever. Farewell, Hen.' Pelan called to him, and they walked to a familiar farmhouse now closed, deserted, its current occupants enjoying the festivities in the hall; the frosted axe lay in the wood store, almost as Rædwulf had left it, and Thomas stood in the penetrating cold, remembering. Pelan beckoned him, and they climbed the knoll, an unseen raven watching them from atop the naked oak tree.

## **THE END**

# Glossary, Notes, Sources & Bibliography

**An Approximate Guide to Pronunciation:**

*Ā pronounced as a long 'a'; æ pronounced 'short', as in 'hat'; ǣ pronounced 'long', as in 'farther';*

*the 'r' and last 'e' in* Lybbestre *pronounced as separate letters;*

*the 'y' in the names* Lybbestre *and* Lyblǣca *pronounced as long 'u', as in yule;*

*'yr' pronounced as in myrtle;*

*the letter 'c' in the names* Blācencynn, Cerin, Cernunnos and Cynwæd *pronounced as in cat.*

*For further information, visit:*

https://oldenglish.info/advpronunciationguide.html

# Glossary

**Adan**: 'a' pronounced short, as in 'at'

**Asrai:** A water nymph or spirit from Cheshire/Shropshire, UK

**Bean-Nighe**: Type of banshee: she washes the clothes of those who are to die in battle.

**Blācencynn:** pronounced *Blāc-en-cynn:* Bright Kindred

**Brown Man of the Moors:** A Faerie being who tends and heals injured wild creatures

**Cernunnos:** The powerful horned god of ancient Celtic beliefs. 'C' pronounced hard, as in 'cut'.

**Chore:** colloquial: Thief

**Eversteel:** Metal the Blācencynn forged the Sword, Horn, Amulet and High Priest's helmet from

**Forest Father/Green Man/Woodwose:** An embodiment of Spring, a direct reference to those carved images found in Medieval churches

**Lucken Hare:** a hillock in the Eildon Hills; from *Canobie Dick and Thomas of Ercildoun*

**Lybbestre:** Enchantress, Priestess

**Lyblǣca**: Enchanter, Magician

**Ræd:** Old English: Counsel, advice

**Robin Redcap:** An evil sprite that haunted the Scottish Borders; he would drink human blood and dye his cap in it.

**Spriggan:** A type of goblin

**Wyrt:** Old English**:** Herb**,** related to the English word 'Wort', as in St John's Wort, the 'yr' pronounced as in *Myrtle*

The Old Norse phrase, *Láta mér nei deyja hí,* from the chapter 'Wyrtræd': Don't let me die here–translated by the author through the website Vikings of Bjornstad - English to Old Norse Dictionary

## *Author Notes*

The following notes summarise the materials and sources, shown in bold italic type in the paragraphs below, used for this book and its context.

### Thomas of Ercildoun

Laird; Minstrel/Poet and Prophet. (c1220–1298).

History does not record his parentage, marriage or death, and his surname, either Rymour or Learmont, is uncertain.

Folklore says he delivered his prophecies beneath the Eildon Tree and became known as True Thomas, or Thomas the Rhymer. He foretold Soulis' death and, according to one tale, killed him.

The folk tale ***True Thomas*** inspired his meeting the Elder Witch, his following a Faerie path to the Seelie Court, and his seeing the Elf Queen as beautiful when others saw her as a crone. His treatment of the jailer in the chapter 'Business' arose from the ***Fyvie Castle*** legend.

The chapters 'Black Chore Hugh' and 'Luc-Nan-Har' re-imagine the tale ***Canobie Dick and Thomas of Ercildoun***.

The stag and hind in 'The Epilogue' came from other tales of Thomas given in ***Scottish Folk Tales and Legends,*** tales which also inspired his relationship with Molly described in the narrative and the time dilation implied in the chapters 'The Messenger' and 'Hired Hands'.

**The Eildon Hills and Lucken Hare:** Melrose, Roxburghshire, Scotland

**Ercildoun, now Earlston, Berwickshire, Scotland:** Thomas built his tower here.

Glossary, Notes, Sources & Bibliography

**William de Soulis, Lord of Liddesdale, and Butler of Scotland** (1280–1320)

Folk tales allege that William de Soulis was a man of absolute depravity, although these may refer to *Ranulf de Soulis*, 1150–1207/8.

A mysterious character introduced Soulis to the 'Dark Arts', and Soulis invoked Robin Redcap as his familiar.

Legend says that local people killed Soulis in a cauldron of molten lead.

**Hermitage Castle** is in Roxburghshire, Scotland.

**Ninestane Rig** is a small hill and stone circle (nine stones).

**Faerie:**

Norse myth led to my separating elves into Bright or Dark and inspired the Well of Fate in the chapter 'The Mereburg'.

Folklore gives the Elf Queen different names, but I have used the more generic term 'High Lady'.

I have followed Brian Froud and Alan Lee's book *Faeries* by using the terms 'The Seelie Court', 'Faerie' rather than 'Elfland', and 'Spriggan' rather than 'goblin'.

I have also used some Faerie activities listed in *Faeries,* including changelings, the practice of elves leaving wooden effigies in exchange for mortal infants, and Faerie rades.

Old beliefs, also cited in *Faeries*, that elves would make ugly or dangerous things appear as pleasant, for example, disguising leaves as Faerie gold, or tie knots in people's hair and horses' manes, inspired the disguising faerie knot in the story.

British and Irish Folklore inspired the Faerie paths and roads, and red-eared animals.

*Faeries* describes Robin Redcap as the most evil of Scottish Borders goblins, hence his portrayal here as 'Lord of Dark Faerie', or 'Prince of Spriggans'.

**The Blācencynn:** A fictitious clan of hybrid Anglo/Norse extraction, the power influencing their cultural development from Norse and Germanic traditions and beliefs.

Glossary, Notes, Sources & Bibliography

I have used Stephen Pollington's Old English Dictionary ***Wordcraft*** for their nomenclature. Grim: (Grimsdene, Grimsmere) refers to Woden/Odin. Rædwulf is named after a 9th-century Northumbrian king, and Penda after the 7th-century king of Mercia. 'Yggdrasil', the 'World Tree' or the 'Irminsul' inspired the Lord of the Higher Hall pillar. The Norns from Norse Myth inspired the veiled women measuring the thread of life in the chapters 'The Blācencynn' and 'Wyrtræd'; also the Daughters of Earth and Well of Fate in the chapter 'The Mereburg'. The full moon epithet 'The Night Watchman', from the chapter 'Bringing in the May', references the Old English poem ***Exodus*** c 800 CE (lines 106–119). Prehistoric Cup and Ring marks inspired the carved spirals described in chapters 'The Blācencynn', 'Bringing in the May' and 'Farewell, Fair Blācencynn'.

I leave the amulet open to interpretation.

**The Sword and Horn:** I have used capital letters to distinguish them.

# Trees

**The Rowan:** Traditionally, a powerful protection against evil

**The Yew:** Some sources suggest the Yew was the World Tree Yggdrasil in Norse and Germanic myth, which inspired the yew tree in the chapter 'The Forest'.

# Sources

## Bibliography and Suggested Websites

**Thomas of Ercildoun and William de Soulis:**

Alexander, Mark. 2005. *(The Sutton Companion To) British Folklore, Myths & Legends: Legends of Fyvie Castle, Hermitage Castle and William de Soulis.* Sutton Publishing. ISBN: 0 7509 3920 6.

Anonymous: *Folk-lore and Legends Scotland*: *Canobie Dick and Thomas of Ercildoun.* London: W.W. Gibbings, 1889. (See Project Gutenberg, www.gutenberg.org.)

Briggs, Katharyn M. *British Folktales Myths and Legends–A Sampler: Canobie Dick and Thomas of Ercildoun.* Paladin Books/Granada Publishing (now published by Taylor and Francis Books, UK). ISBN: 9780415286022.

Hippesley-Cox, Anthony. 1975. *Haunted Britain: Legends of Fyvie Castle, Hermitage Castle and William de Soulis.* Pan Books. ISBN: 0 330 24328 4.

Ker Wilson, Barbara. 1984. *Scottish Folk Tales and Legends: Thomas meeting with the Elf Queen; his return home, and recall to Faerie.* Illustrated by David Whitton. Newtongrange, Midlothian: Lang Syne Publishers. ISBN: 0 946264 95 3/9780946264957.

Murray, James H., editor. *The Romance and Prophecies of Thomas of Erceldoune.* Felinfach: Llanerch Publishers. ISBN: 0947992 76 6 (facsimile reprint of the edition of MDCCCLXXV), published by Trubner & Co. London for the Early English Text Society).

'True Thomas' in *A Children's Treasury of Poetry.* 1975. Collins. ISBN: 0 00 106124 0.

## Other Sources

Branston, Brian. 1993. *The Lost Gods of England.* Constable (arrangement by Thames & Hudson). ISBN 0 09 4727406.

Fitch, Eric L. 1994. *In Search of Herne the Hunter: Cernunnos; The Wild Hunt.* Capall Bann. ISBN: 1-898307-18-0.

Froud, Brian, and Alan Lee (illus.). 1979. *Faeries*. Pan. ISBN: 0 330 257560.

Linsell, Tony. 1992. *Anglo-Saxon Runes*. Anglo-Saxon Books. ISBN: 0-9516209-6-7.

MacKenzie, Andrew. 1982. *Hauntings and Apparitions*. William Heineman Ltd. ISBN: 434 44051 5.

Pollington, Stephen. 1993. *Wordcraft*. Anglo-Saxon Books. ISBN: 1-898281-02-1.

Ryan, Robert E. *The Strong Eye of Shamanism*. Vermont: Inner Traditions International ISBN 0 09 4727406.

# Suggested Websites

*Correct at the time of writing.*
*Publishing Push and the author are neither responsible nor liable for the maintenance or content of these sites.*

**Thomas of Ercildoun:**
Thomas Rymer - Wikipedia
Thomas the Rhymer: Biography on Undiscovered Scotland
The Legend of Thomas the Rhymer–Scottish Highland Trails

Glossary, Notes, Sources & Bibliography

**William de Soulis and Hermitage Castle:**
Hermitage Castle - Wikipedia
Lammermuir Hills - Wikipedia
William II de Soules - Wikipedia
Ninestane Rig - Wikipedia
https://www.ancient-scotland.co.uk/site/nine-stone-rig
A remote Scottish Borders Castle, Hermitage, Roxburghshire, Scotland (aboutscotland.com)

**The Queen of Elfland:**
Queen of Elphame - Wikipedia

**The Norse World Tree:**
https://en.m.wikipedia.org/wiki/Yggdrasil

**Shamanism:**
https://en.m.wikipedia.org/wiki/Shamanism

**Exodus: Old English Poem:** https://en.m.wikipedia.org/wiki/Exodus_(poem)
https://www.academia.edu/82559586/The_Old_English_Exodus_A_Verse_Translation

**Trees: The Rowan and Yew**
Trees for Life | Rewilding the Scottish Highlands
*Note: This website cites a Norse myth I was not aware of when writing but has relevance to the chapter 'Grimsdene'.*
https://treesforlife.org.uk/into-the-forest/trees-plants-animals/trees/yew/

Printed in Great Britain
by Amazon